Adolph's Gold

Donan Berg

DOTDON Books
Moline IL

Donan Berg

DOTDON Books are published by

DOTDON Personalized Services
PO Box 1302
Moline IL 61266-1302

Author e-mail: mystery@abodytobones.com

Library of Congress Control Number: 2014905712

This is a work of fiction. The places, characters, and events exist only in this book and the author's mind. Any resemblance to any person, living or dead, is unintentional and purely coincidental.

Copyright 2014 Donan B. McAuley

ISBN 13: 978-1-941244-01-2

ISBN 10: 1941244017

First U.S. Edition: May 2014
10 9 8 7 6 5 4 3 2 1

Adolph's Gold

To family and friends.

May we all press our hands together,
express our hearts full of love, and pray for
all who have or will sacrifice
to keep this world safe.

Donan Berg

Novels by Donan Berg
Skeleton Mystery Series

A Body To Bones
First Skeleton Series Mystery

The Bones Dance Foxtrot
Second Skeleton Series Mystery

Baby Bones
Third Skeleton Series Mystery

Abbey Burning Love

Short Stories by Donan Berg
Bubbling Conflict and Other Stories

Praise for Donan Berg's
Skeleton Mystery Series

A Body To Bones

"I found myself quickly drawn into this book…Author Donan Berg (creates) interesting mix of mystery, suspense, hidden secrets, sin, deception and intrigue to weave a book that is well worth the price and in fact is a book which I so readily recommend, that I would strongly suggest purchasing it for gifting."

--S.P., national online reviewer

"Donan Berg writes a nice, clear, consistently readable prose, and he manages to create a winning character in Sarah Hamilton."

--Writers' Digest judge

"Excellent. Greatly enjoyable book, well written and filled with intrigue, suspense and drama. Five Stars."

--L.C., national online reviewer

The Bones Dance Foxtrot

"Five Stars. If you enjoy a good mystery with twists, turns, false leads, a little gambling, betrayal, clues left in the unlikeliest of places and a hidden stash of bank loot, then pick up a copy of The Bones Dance Foxtrot."

--Featheredquill Book Review

"Clues eventually fit together in clever and significant ways."

--National reviewer

About the Author

Having landed three times in the winner's circle of the 2013 Eighth Annual Dixie Kane Memorial Contest, Donan Berg earns a claim to accolades of entertaining mystery, heartwarming romance. His writing talents, honed as a journalist, corporate executive, and lawyer, are vibrantly on display in his three Skeleton Series Mystery novels plus *Abbey Burning Love*, a fast-paced, novel-length, small city murder mystery/romance e-book. A native of Ireland transplanted to the United States Heartland, he's also authored a collection of short stories entitled, *Bubbling Conflict and Other Stories*, where the lead story highlights the never-ending sectarian violence in Northern Ireland

Chapter One

Sonja Maria Sanchez's apartment-ceiling fan blades swirled a
gagging, greasy-bacon aroma that settled like a loose noose on
Detective Second Class Adolph Anderson's shirt-covered
collarbones. He'd carried beads of August perspiration inside
with him, leaving his blue blazer on the front seat of his
yellow Monte Carlo. Listening to Sonja Maria's squeaky and
faltering alto, Adolph failed to conjure up how he'd earn the
shiny gold first class shield he craved. Rather than ask her to
repeat her undecipherable English pronunciations, he pressed
his sweaty left elbow into her living room recliner's cracked
vinyl armrest and rotated his cocked left ear toward her in
faked rapt attention. Behind his well-practiced facial facade,
his distracted mind wandered to the yet to be interviewed bar
homicide witness he'd stumbled upon yesterday. Solving
homicides, he knew from eight years of being a detective,
generated accolades and earned gold shields. He couldn't pin
sentiment to his chest.

Sonja Maria hesitated twice without his prompting or
encouraging her to continue. The seething, curdling waste-of-
time anger clawing his innards was intensified by his
remembering that Bridgetown, Iowa, Police Chief Ronald
Howard had dropped this wild goose chase on him. Adolph
damn well suspected that, with Yancey out, The Chief would
try to appease the League of Women Voters by giving the one
gold shield up for grabs to Luann.

His left hand clamped closed his notepad as Sonja Maria
described the explicit deportation threat, her physical damsel-
in-distress cowering, and her feared sexual assault. For

Adolph, her details too vivid for a real-life assault victim, even if her droopy lower eyelids glistened. He chomped-at-the-bit for an exit strategy that wouldn't rile her to file a citizen's complaint. After ten years on the beat before being promoted to detective, Adolph had promised himself he'd never again wear oxfords whose soles had been scraped holey. He'd paid his dues and his numbing brain had heard Ms. Sanchez's fuzzy TV-drama scenario countless times.

He'd already scribbled notes detailing the absence of visible bruises on her forehead, chin, arm, and the below-the-knee skin of her rail-thin frame. "So, you didn't go to the hospital?" Why he delayed his departure with an objectively answered question, Adolph couldn't fathom. He'd called the hospital to learn no admission record existed for Sonja Maria Sanchez, the name she'd given him and, thus, no traceable rape kit evidence. Wouldn't take an armchair genius, he thought, to determine that any effort he spent trying to nail this gossamer suspect wouldn't enhance his jury-verified reputation for jailing criminals. With his chance for a gold shield needing a higher percentage of cases closed, he planned to administratively deep-six this investigation as fast as he could without risking charges of insubordination or dereliction of duty.

Adolph's mounting disgust for this colossal waste of time splashed in his stomach like a limestone brick plunging into the surface of a nearby backwater river pool. If he abandoned logical reality and believed the story behind the streaking tears, choked words, and pregnant pauses, Sonja Maria, a hard-featured woman who'd celebrated her thirty-fifth birthday the previous month, had been overpowered and/or drugged by an unknown attacker and raped at St. Mary's, a local college populated by scores of comely co-eds.

While it was true he strove day and night to keep his town, his high school daughter, and his arthritis-disabled wife safe, he had no qualms to shun fakers or bend a legal rule or two. He dismissed each transgression as a necessity to remove another scumbag from Bridgetown streets and to earn his longed for gold shield.

He finally said to Sonja Maria he needed to go and would call her if additional info were needed. Sonja's eyes, obscured by a new moisture drizzle, stared at him across the diamond-pattern of threadbare carpet and pleaded that he believe her and shelve all doubt.

If, gold shield or not, he forgot the jailing-the-bad-guys end result, did swearing to uphold the law and serve the public justify emotionally trampling a reeling, weakened fellow human being? His eyes scanned the shabby brown-fabric sofa that almost swallowed Sonja Maria whole, the faded emerald green living room wall paint, the hung picture of Jesus, and that face, hers, smiling at him from a family eight-by-ten photo enlargement set on an end table beneath the lampshade's tattered fringe. This apartment in which he sat, like her, without excess adornment and scrubbed clean. Especially prominent were the back of her hands—purplish, popping veins from calloused fingers that dived to be submerged and invisible under wrist skin en route to a heart in a small muscular body. Five-foot-two, he estimated, tipping scales between ninety and one hundred pounds. Straight, neck-length black hair framed unmoving dark eyes, surrounded by a caramel complexion.

"When were you grabbed?" He angled forward. His interrogation tape recorder pointed at them from atop a stack of People magazines on the glass-topped coffee table. He stopped short of asking her not to drink for that would've been heartless. By the observed halting sips, he fathomed that alcohol had never been Sonja Maria's painkiller; especially the straight undiluted 1800 Tequila she poured into a scratched, clear plastic tumbler.

"Don't want to feel bad again. Dishonor beloved husband Philippe."

"Need you to explain everything to have any chance of putting this guy behind bars where he belongs." *If the scumbag exists?* "Tell me again. Yesterday, where were you?"

With a head bowed, her eyes gazed into a vacant lap.

"Third floor janitor closet."

"That's your job. Cleaning, right?" Adolph re-opened his notepad.

"Si."

"You working?" Adolph tried to distill his questions for he lacked strong Spanish skills.

She waggled her head sideways. "On break, spit out tequila when see bottle worm."

He'd misjudged her capacity for alcohol. "Go on."

"Not wanna be sent back to Guatemala."

Adolph envisioned a defense attorney's field day. Assault cases were hard enough to win, even with a stellar witness. Prosecution attorneys ran the opposite direction on learning alcohol clouded a complainant's judgment and memory. "And, then?" At this rate he'd never finish. Bridgetown's St. Mary's College hired mostly Hispanic janitorial/cleaning staff, forged immigration papers common. He always looked the other way if the illegal didn't evidence gang affiliation and Sonja Maria lacked visible tattoos.

"No hear. Lift head from sink; bag cover face. Can't see."

He remained silent. She raised her head to stare, this time above and beyond his right ear.

"Voice say be quiet. Say police outside."

"Man, woman?"

"Man. He say don't try escape. Squeeze my arms. March me into another room. Feel cold on left ankle. Heard noise, what be English word . . . clinking."

"Any other noises?"

"Un poco pop. Man jerks my head; hand press bag to face and my tongue feels hole. Sweet cola drops wet my tongue. He tell me 'drink,' and cola fills my mouth. Something, I don't know, move along my right arm to back of hand."

"How'd you know it was cola you drank?"

"Fizz makes me almost spit it out. Hand, not mine, cover my mouth. He tell me 'swallow, stand still, drink more.'"

Pad full, Adolph quit scribbling notes. When, not if, she jumbled her story, the tape would be more reliable than his notes. "How long you stand there?"

"Think long time. Piano play. Not Latin. Danced salsa before married. Hear students play music late at night, what they call classical. Don't know. Wild thoughts go through my brain. Me have to do work. Not get fired."

"In the room, what else did you hear?"

"Not hear nothing until tap, tap on car window."

Adolph didn't think he'd heard right. "You were in a car?"

"Si. Man with badge tell me I can't park in Music Department faculty lot. Move pronto. My head aches. Clothes torn. Naked below dress." Her veined hand briefly covered her mouth. "Sun makes me close eyes." Sonja Maria bent forward to lower her left ankle's white sock.

Adolph observed the inch and half wide red mark with faint bluish edge tint that circled her ankle. He passed on further documenting any higher injuries. "You make security report?"

"No. Have to get home to make breakfast. Philippe shout at me saying he be late to drive truck at six. Rosano cry when Philippe slam door. She and Joshua still in their beds."

Above the clanging living room window air conditioner, Adolph thought he heard a small boy in the next room. "Are they your children?"

"Si. Rosano's thirteen. She's at school. Joshua, five, is in my bedroom."

"At St. Mary's, how'd you get from your building work area to your car?"

"Not know." Fresh tears slid onto and moistened both cheeks.

Adolph handed her a folded white handkerchief; he shook his head no when, after use, she extended the floppy cloth forward to offer it back to him. "If you remember the trip to the car or anything else, please call me." He handed Sonja Maria his card, pocketed the tape recorder, and offered a quick good-bye.

Stepping into the mid-morning sunlight, he strode to his

11

Monte Carlo. Road dust dulled its bright yellow color but not
the sparkling broken glass sprinkled onto the narrow strip of
boulevard grass outside 409 Tinley Street. The unseasonable
heat and humidity perspired Adolph's wiped forehead. His
investigative experience convinced him that, if distraught
women remembered anything at all, the narrative would be
distorted by memory trauma half-truths and the forced sobs a
ruse to disguise lies. Adolph deplored the thirty-five minutes
wasted with Sonja Maria. He reached for his handkerchief,
only to remember its loan to Sonja Maria.

A bright graffiti gang tag sprayed on the apartment
building's brick wall visually announced that the Dragons
street gang claimed this turf. Eighteen years ago, he, as a
rookie police officer, walked this Bridgetown neighborhood
beat and residents were safe and the building wall brick
crevices, not filled by canned spray paint, collected wind-
blown dust to be displayed as rain-streaked dirt. He wouldn't
apologize one iota for his hardnosed, boot-to-the-throat tactics
that propelled his promotion to sergeant, then detective.

Years ago, Sonja Maria's Tinley apartment building,
framed in his rearview mirror, was known for marijuana
dealers. Judging by the latest reports, cocaine was now the
drug of choice. He suspected she had little economic choice.
And, while she could've just as easily have been attacked in
her small two-bedroom apartment by outsiders or forced to
submit to an angry drunk husband, that would've meant
there'd be no professor, no college, or no trustees to sue.

Chapter Two

Adolph sputtered throat-choking water past his trembling lips; careful not to splatter the non-breathing toddler he hugged to his heaving chest. His splayed right hand fingers, oozing green river slime, gripped his unclothed left forearm. As he sloshed to the riverbank, Adolph's high-stepping knees challenged the river's under-the-surface current trying to sweep him sideways and the ankle-deep gooey riverbed silt that tried to suck his bare feet into immobility. The delta-bound river, nicknamed Old Man River and popularized in song as "lazy," wrapped its increasing weighted resistance around Adolph's weary legs. As he clutched the clammy toddler, his mumbled words tumbled from quivering lips toward the toddler's ear: "You'll be okay. Mommy's here." His right palm stroked the infant's back. "Please . . . please breathe."

By sheer willpower, Adolph forced his aching legs to splash and carry his precious cargo in an angled upstream direction the final ten yards to where a Bridgetown Community Hospital ambulance had screeched to a stop, reversed its gears, and a blue-uniformed driver had scrambled to throw wide its rear doors. Adolph grimaced. The Iraq war-inflicted shrapnel embedded next to his left thighbone concentrated the tepid water's chill to chatter his teeth and radiated his war zone memories across a spider-web of cranial nerve endings. All he could do was clamp his molars together. In the past, the naked fear generated by being submerged sparked debilitating flashbacks of the active duty explosion that catapulted him off a bridge and into a raging monsoon-swollen river, but he'd prevailed to conquer the worst of these mentally generated sensations. He avoided all reference to the PTSD acronym now embedded into tweets and late night guilt-pleas of dubious charities. He reminded himself he'd passed the preliminary psych exam qualifying him for the detective gold shield promotion list.

Adolph halted his advance in ankle deep water to allow the EMT to grab the child. Adolph's muscles tensed as he watched the EMT's trained fingers check the child's mouth and air passage for obstruction, position the infant's chubby cheek on the EMT's forearm, and then, in quick succession, slap the infant's back five times before pressing a portable oxygen mask across the diminutive nose and mouth. On shore, a second square-shouldered EMT intercepted and bear-hugged a sobbing younger woman, dressed in a dark-colored T-shirt with a logo splash of yellow and blue jeans, rushing across concrete to the river's edge.

Adolph spat. With a relaxed throat, he gulped heavily moisture-laden mid-day air to replenish his oxygen-starved lungs. The murky river water hadn't allowed him to see the bottom silt that sucked in untethered objects and oozed into porous cracks and holes. He'd heard a woman's scream while on one of his frequent lunchtime strolls from police headquarters to the river. Her outstretched arms, with jerky finger movements, had pointed into the water. Without hesitation, Adolph had haphazardly piled his unlaced shoes, socks, 9mm, and billfold, covered by his sport coat blue blazer, on the inclined concrete slab city fathers had poured to be a boat launch ramp. On instinct, to account for the river current, he had chosen a spot to dash into the river twenty feet south of where the woman stood screaming, "My boy, save my boy." Her words raced the easterly breeze that propelled Adolph into the water.

The five fortitude-filled minutes Adolph had challenged Fate to bob under the surface carved out an eternity until the cloth he tugged offered weighted resistance. Shallower-than-normal August river depths had allowed him to wiggle and plant his toes into the silty river bottom. Able to stand with his head above the water's surface, wavelets soon lapped his armpits as he began the splash toward shore. After handing the boy to an EMT, he'd forgotten within seconds his personal effort's degree of difficulty.

Adolph, halfway up the boat ramp concrete, paused where a flagstone path branched off to a nearby riverboat casino. Tilting his chin, dripping droplets creating unrecognizable patterns were absorbed by his soaked gray slacks that clung to his thighs. His matted forearm hair refused to release the green slimy fungus it entrapped. Gooey silt, succumbing to gravity, plopped from swaying trouser cuffs onto the sun-warmed concrete, destined to dry and swirl into irritating dust.

Adolph bent down to retrieve his belongings with the thought that a third hot shower beckoned this day. The second he'd crammed between telephone calls and writing a report after that morning's visit to Sonja Maria and 409 Tinley Street. Standing upright, he braced his shoulders against a riverbank tree to slip his bare feet into shoes. The task accomplished, Adolph first heard two police squad cars, then saw their tires leave wisps of white smoke twisting upward from black rubber tread trails. The compressed front shocks of both vehicles sprung fenders skyward. One uniformed officer dashed away from Adolph toward the ambulance.

Cpl. John Reilly jogged to Adolph's side. "Need a lift to the station?" Adolph declined the corporal's offer and suggested Reilly assist the EMT restraining the hysterical woman. After six steps toward police headquarters, Adolph heard a toddler bawl, cheers, and bystander clapping. Gazing skyward, he mouthed the word "thanks" and hastened his pace. The evaporating water and drying slime tightened his bare skin without the sizzle of heated rollers rotating the city's trademarked sausages at his favorite coffee haunt, Patsy's Cafe.

Not until the warm spray of the police station locker room shower did his skin pores relax and breathe. Despite his body's physical release, mental tension gripped his memory like eagle talons squeezed the riverbank's pin oak branches. He'd come to believe that two rivers—one real, one metaphorical—defined his hometown of Bridgetown. Whatever his, or other's, poetic characterization, everyday reality darkened Bridgetown's idyllic river city image as a double half-hitch knot anchored a moored speedboat. Nevertheless, Adolph believed he stood a chance, however small and uncalculated, to defeat the sinister, symbolical undercurrent he could often sense, but couldn't touch or fully witness. While he feared a stalking evil would forever threaten Bridgetown's youth, he was almost certain the toddler's fall today would be ruled accidental, notwithstanding any negligent parental distraction. More and more each day, Adolph envisioned his challenge as one to imprison or otherwise cleanse his city of the adults preying on the town's youth, scarring victims for life, if they lived.

Adolph's officially assigned locker provided him with dry boxers, shirt, socks, and trousers. Shaking his blazer before slipping in his arms, he let it fashionably drape his broad shoulders. Seating himself on a wooden bench, Adolph towel-dried the inside of his spit-shined black oxfords and began tying the laces when a pair of sharply creased khaki pant legs marched into his view. His upward gaze to the arriving face disclosed his supervisor.

"Congratulations, Adolph," said Police Chief Ronald Howard. Adolph stood to acknowledge the verbal salute with a brisk thank you and then wasn't surprised when, closely on the heels of praise, The Chief unleashed one of his frequently expressed ego busters. "While you should feel proud the whole town's buzzing of your deed, guess you'll never eclipse the harrowing midnight river rescue of two kids by your father during an electrical thunderstorm."

Unconsciously, Adolph's throat dammed his stomach's explosion of bile, letting it drip into a decade-long reservoir of resentment. Chief Howard, veteran officers, and even Adolph's two siblings, always compared and judged Adolph not to be equal to the perpetual champion acclaim showered upon his father. Thus, no matter how hard Adolph labored, his ranking in the eyes of others never higher than that of silver or second place, even three years after his decorated and celebrated father had passed away. Time hadn't tarnished the gold-embossed valor plaque the city council posthumously bestowed upon Police Chief Frederic Anderson with the resolution that it would forever be affixed to the Bridgetown Police Headquarters lobby wall first viewed by entering visitors.

Successful in buttoning his shirt collar to hide his tightened throat muscles, Adolph allowed the silence to build until The Chief exposed his visit's likely hidden agenda. "Do me a personal favor. Check out this vandalism complaint from my cousin."

Adolph glanced at The Chief's offered note and shrugged when reading the B&B reference. Folding it once, he slipped the note into his front pants pocket. While he wished to remind The Chief of the colossal waste of resources in requiring personal interviews in cases like that of Sonja Maria, Adolph held his tongue, fully cognizant that any uttered wisp of criticism would eviscerate from The Chief's mind what little glory Adolph's morning river rescue commanded. "I'll go now," Adolph said, acting to nip in the bud any further idolized reference to his father.

The Chief's sharp military pivot and footfalls clicking on grouted tiles preceded Adolph's sigh upon hearing the locker room door bang shut to restore his welcomed silent solitude. Arising slowly, Adolph calculated that the odds of earning a Detective First Class gold shield would evaporate if he didn't follow up on this tiniest complaint from The Chief's cousin. Sonja Maria he could bury in bureaucratic hell with a ready excuse, if questioned. A cousin would have ample opportunity to bend The Chief's ear and grind Adolph's promotion into the dust without him ever finding out. Thus, Adolph, unwilling to agonize too long on what might go wrong, hustled out the police station's rear exit prisoner passageway to the fenced parking lot to avoid the expected gaggle of newspaper and television reporters ringing the front entrance.

When he stopped for gas on the cross-town drive, a 2006/2007 gray Dodge Caravan blocked his Monte Carlo's exit from the pump to the car wash lane. A thirty-something woman in blue jeans, her chest stretching a purple Vikings T-shirt, jumped from the minivan and ran towards him. He remembered her face and the brunette flip curl from the river.

"Thank you, thank you." She flung her arms 'round his neck.

Adolph fought gently to extract himself from the clinging embrace. "You're welcome. Your boy, is he all right?"

"In the hospital. Without you he woulda drowned. Billy's so precious. He's all I have after his older sister went missing."

"Would you tell me your name?" Adolph's right hand fingered the car wash coupon Mary, his wife, had clipped from the daily *Examiner* newspaper.

"Yvonne . . . Yvonne Whitenmire."

"What I did . . . part of the job. Glad he'll be okay. Billy's fortunate the water was low, since I can't really swim." He lifted his gaze past the pumps. "If you'll excuse me, my car needs to be washed . . . and I'm late for an important appointment."

"Of course. I'll pray for you." She backed up her minivan to clear a lane for the car wash.

When Adolph unlatched his Monte Carlo driver's door at the address of The Chief's cousin, an eye-opening tinny metal sound startled him. A woman, Adolph assumed to be Mrs. Hoskins, The Chief's cousin, stood partially obscured behind two front porch hanging petunia baskets. When her exposed left arm banged a watering can against a metal flower container straddling the porch railing, Adolph lowered his guard and stepped out from behind his open driver's door. With his soles stationary on gray driveway pavers, he waited until Mrs. Francine Hoskins's eyes stared at him. Her creased forehead wrinkles signaled a perturbation, caused by what he didn't know.

If he'd learned anything as a police officer, a gracious

18

smile and a deferential demeanor stroked the ego of city council members and a superior's relative. His personal pretense merely a small-potatoes version of the town's public relations struggle to pretend its 50,000 population created a big city. Bridgetown elected officials had promoted this exaggerated image to lure riverboat gambling, but then diverted its legalized gaming tax revenue to council members' self-styled foreign trade junkets and secretly killed in committee all efforts to fill city street potholes.

To disguise his unscripted hesitation, he folded his blue blazer and laid it on the yellow Monte Carlo's gray front seat and gently shut the car door. From a reflected side mirror glance, he mumbled "damn" under his breath realizing no spoken word this day would dry a reoccurring forehead moisture bead. As he gazed forward toward the two-story house, Adolph wiped his brow with a white handkerchief, and then marched stiffly forward following the home's angled concrete sidewalk to the front brick step centered between the white wooden porch spindles.

"Morning." The nickel-plated detective badge clipped to Adolph's waist's belt shot a glinted sunray off the entrance door's curtained glass window.

"You should be perky," Mrs. Hoskins said to the hanging basket between them. Her sideways step fully exposed to him her tanned face, wide nostrils, and deep crow's-feet radiating outward from deep-set eyes. "See these petunias. I water, water, water and they wilt."

"Yes, madam." While he'd never earned any master gardener credentials, no green leaf appeared unhealthy. Agree with her, Adolph repeated to himself, or you'll find The Chief sacrificing you on the pyre of family squabbles.

"I called Chief Howard." Mrs. Hoskins interjected. "Is he coming?"

"No, madam. He requested I stop by. He didn't want you to worry until he could get free." He envisioned The Chief smart enough, if necessary, to finesse Adolph's white lie with no one destined to be hurt by it. In the line of duty, he'd escaped responsibility for countless well-intentioned fibs more serious.

"He's my cousin, you know." The handheld watering can she dropped bounced noisily against the wooden porch floor. "Well, all right, I guess. The vandals struck out back." Adolph stepped aside as she steamrolled toward the porch's top step. "Say, please bring my watering can?" Adolph tensed at her tone, more a command than a request. "We need to go 'round to the side gate."

"Yes, madam." Adolph's right hand reached forward to grab the can's spout. En route to the backyard he almost collided with her as she halted to bend forward to pick up a discarded gum wrapper and pinch a brownish mum stem. At his house, Mary planted and tended to any flowers, but arthritis limited her to pruning tall annuals or climbing perennials, mostly miniature pink roses. Past the side gate, as Mrs. Hoskins charged ahead, his gaze took in an arc-shaped wooden arbor wrapped in green vines with its four pillars circled at ground level by what he perceived to be snapdragons, coneflowers, and a red rose bush. Towering above and to the left of the flowers was an apple tree so burdened with red apple clusters that a half dozen bowed branches kissed the ground.

"See this," Mrs. Hoskins said. "Horrible, simply horrible." Her multi-colored, capped sleeved, knee-length cotton dress exposed her calves and the words she spoke could've described her varicose veins. Her brunette hair, swept back into a bun, had its crown hidden by her straw gardener's hat. A stray hair tendril dropped below the hat's wide brim that had been encircled with red gingham fabric tied in a rear bow.

"What?" Adolph asked. To catch up with Mrs. Hoskins, he tried raised-knee steps to have his flat-landing soles compress the un-mowed backyard grass and prevent the dusty green blades from dragging across his shoes' reflective toes. Adolph set the watering can he carried on a black decorative-scrolled metal bench.

Adolph's Gold

She pointed to a darkened dirt patch in front of a five-foot high cedar fence. His nostrils detected an incongruous faint whiff of motor oil as he saw an electric lawnmower on Mrs. Hoskins's brick paver patio, its twisted orange cord plugged in. Adolph gingerly lower his right foot on a square concrete stepping stone and swung his left foot around two aster clumps. On the ground, multi-shaded black streaks stained thinly scattered wood mulch and darkened exposed earth. He estimated the affected flowerbed area to be three to four feet wide and ten feet long. The vertical irregularly spaced splatter filling the open grain of the fence boards he presumed to be the result of an inaccurate aim by whomever spilled the liquid on the ground. He didn't need to sport a detective badge to determine that the soiled flower garden spot hadn't been designed to collect decomposing garden waste or double as an eco-friendly compost pile.

"I'll have to take a sample." Adolph didn't relish making a roundtrip to his car trunk for ill-suited paper evidence bags. He gazed at Mrs. Hoskins. "Do you have any small plastic bags?"

"I've quart-sized Ziploc bags in the kitchen. Will they do?"

"Perfect." While she marched off to retrieve a Ziploc, he tiptoed to where the reddish-tinted mulch appeared uncontaminated. He peered over the wooden fence into the adjoining yards. No junked car. No scrap metal or gas engine parts. Refusing to stray too far from the compacted mulch, his gazes into two neighbor side yards yielded no contamination source clue. Stymied, Adolph capitulated to the need to wait for lab results to justify search warrants.

"Here you are." Mrs. Hoskins handed him a Ziploc, a brown paper bag sized to carry home 750 ml liquor bottles, and a pointed metal trowel with a painted-flower handle.

He should have complimented Mrs. Hoskins on her expanded foresightedness, but he didn't and silently crouched at two flowerbed locations to scoop small samples. He dropped the first into the quart-sized Ziploc and with the second he rustled the liquor-sized paper bag. Satisfied that for now this should satisfy The Chief, he rose and raised his right hand to display the two closed bags and spoke to Mrs. Hoskins. "I'll make sure Chief Howard knows what the lab says about these samples. By the way, did you see any suspicious characters?"

"You mean other than my neighbor across the fence?"

"Why your neighbor?" Adolph scanned the house Mrs. Hoskins pointed at. Vinyl-sided, white, two-story, nondescript. Likely built thirty years ago in the late '80s housing boom that erected the majority of Bridgetown's newer homes, a full decade after Adolph's neighborhood.

"He's up weeknights at all hours. The lights don't bother, but that piano music. It upsets my guests. They knock on my bedroom door at two a.m. and later."

Adolph purposely shifted gears so as not to encourage Mrs. Hoskins to gratuitously add a nuisance complaint to the reported vandalism. "You have guests often?"

Her quizzical expression jumped the three feet between them as if to smack him squarely across the face. "Of course, I've a bed and breakfast license. Rent three rooms upstairs."

"Didn't notice any sign." He cringed at having spoken without measuring the consequences. Perhaps not displaying a sign was a code violation he shouldn't have hint at.

A silent reproof crawled from Mrs. Hoskins's brows to her uplifted chin. "Hired my son's artist buddy to paint a new one. Yesterday, Matt unscrewed the old one next to the front door to drive it to his friend's as a sample. I can show you the faded paint square."

"No, not necessary." Adolph backed off, longing also to be on his way.

A small smile he didn't know the origin of erased Mrs. Hoskins's dour expression. "Would you like a glass of iced tea? Awful hot today."

"No, madam. Chief would want me to get these samples to the lab as quick as possible before they dry out." He withheld explaining that her garden watering and/or fertilizing had likely altered or diluted the collected samples' purity. A green grass strip along the flower garden's edge, sharply contrasting with the backyard's brown lawn patches elsewhere gave him strong circumstantial evidence there had been frequent garden watering.

"You'll tell my cousin, I offered?"

Adolph closed his feet together, and then separated his left towards the gate. "Yes, madam." *What choice did he have?*

"He'll be here, you know, in two weeks for our family's Labor Day picnic. He grills."

Adolph executed two steps sideways. "Really?" He didn't care. "That's nice."

"Did I tell you he's the son of my dad's oldest brother?"

"Didn't know," Adolph lied. "Suggest you not disturb that garden area."

Her full lips parted and he ignored her disapproving grunt. He pivoted and strode toward the side gate exit. Sunrays striking his Monte Carlo had failed to vaporize the carwash water drops remaining under his car's wiper blades. He would remember to wipe there next time.

His cell phone indicated a missed message. He dialed voice mail and steadied the phone against his left ear. Daughter Kristen in a whimper said he or mom was required to call the principal by tomorrow. Adolph saved the message. His response to Kristen could wait until shift's end and he sat at the family supper table with Mary present.

To commandeer two parking spots, Adolph centered his 2007 Monte Carlo between three white lines painted on gritty, cracking asphalt inside the police headquarters' rear cyclone-fenced parking lot. He, Yancey, and Luann, as second-class detectives, didn't rank high enough on the official pecking order to garner assigned parking spots. He didn't care if Detective Lt. Turner, Chief Howard, or anyone else squawked. He, not the city, owned the Monte Carlo sport coupe he drove and it still stuck in his caw that, two months ago, he had to personally pay the body shop charges to have it sanded fender to fender to obliterate the spray-painted gang signs.

He waved to two uniformed officers. With their belts and holsters slung over their shoulders, odds were they trailed the three p.m. day shift exit parade. That signaled to Adolph the evening patrol officers were gathered inside, assembled for that day's briefing. When he earned his coveted gold shield, he'd be called upon to present alerts and active case updates.

"Detective Anderson," a feminine voice shouted.

As he rotated toward the fence perimeter, the ball of his right foot squeaked against the asphalt. He recognized Yvonne Whitenmire, still in jeans and a heavier-stained white T-shirt. While Adolph's muscles twitched to cover his butt with Chief Howard before the cousin called, he couldn't ignore the woman's repeated shouts of his name with departing patrol officers within hearing distance. He hurried toward her.

In a raspy-tinged voice, she said, "Can't say thank you enough." Her inserted right hand fingertips clawed the metal fence fabric between them.

"You're welcome." To him, her swollen eye sockets appeared to have been rubbed dry. When he heard an engine rev, he glanced at his Monte Carlo. "Sorry. I need to get inside." He fought his exposed intent to be brusque. "How goes it for your little boy? Billy, right?"

"Hospital doctor say Billy stay overnight. His little body fights . . . fights the swallowed nastiness of the river. I pray for him to be strong."

Adolph understood. Before putting on his shoes earlier he'd inspected his skin below the knees, especially his ankles for insect stings or aquatic bites and his soles for puncture wounds that would've required he update his tetanus shot. He'd plucked out a bloodsucker wedged between his second and third left foot toes, fortunately no blood oozed.

"Your little guy will do fine."

"Billy's not my only heartache." Retrieved from her left palm, Yvonne bent the edges of a small photograph together and stuck it between the fence wires. "My daughter, she disappear two weeks ago. Maybe you could find her."

Adolph's Gold

Adolph leaned forward. In a glance he recognized in the photograph a teenage image of the late-twenties woman before him. He left the photo, wedged in the fence, untouched.

"Have you filed a missing person's report?"

"Last week."

Adolph hoped The Chief had delayed his normal workday departure. Sadness in the woman's eyes, not the uncontrolled sobbing of a then hysterical woman on the riverfront, evoked in his soul greater sympathy than he felt while watching television commercials for impoverished foreign country children. He couldn't brush off this Yvonne Whitenmire.

"Tell me something about your daughter." Adolph flipped his notepad to a blank page.

"Nancy was . . . is twelve, brown hair, hazel eyes. Not tall, nor heavy. She never came home after school. We've posted and distributed flyers for days."

He couldn't recall if he'd seen a flyer. Two or three were always posted on the police locker room bulletin board obliterating from memory those of the previous month. From broken home runaways to kids enticed or dragged into the community's corrupting subculture, all quickly became submerged into statistics digitally stored by a national computer data bank.

"Can I keep the photograph? All I can promise is to keep my eyes and ears open."

She trembled until both of her hands clutched the fence. "Thank you, thank you. Nancy's a good girl. Saving Billy, I'll pray for you every day, forever."

"You owe me nothing." He fit a pen and a two-by-three inch page ripped from his notepad through a fence opening. "Please write your telephone number and what Nancy wore."

Mrs. Whitenmire's right hand struggled to support a plastic purse as her left hand scribbled numbers and words on the notepaper. With the photo, notepad page, and pen tucked inside his blue blazer pocket, Adolph waved good-bye. He jogged into headquarters; delayed, but successful in his mission to catch The Chief in the latter's office.

"C'mon in."

Wishing to exude confidence, Adolph stood ramrod straight. The late afternoon sun, streaking through partially drawn vertical blinds, created dark shadowy lines on the opposite room wall that Adolph swore resembled jail cell bars. He'd chuckled when first seeing the bar effect years ago, now he ignored it. The official case folders that monopolized The Chief's desk, one pile stacked a foot high, peaked Adolph's interest. It meant but one thing. A higher authority, either the mayor or state police brass, had threatened to toss blazing logs of criticism beneath the department's cauldron and sacrifice The Chief in its boiling water. Yet, a reactive rage, evident deep in The Chief's eyes, all but lost in his broader pinkish check-to-cheek sunburn.

Chief Howard, a partner to Adolph's deceased father, gazed from his seated position past Adolph's left side to the office door. "How's my daffy cousin?" The question caught Adolph off guard and he hesitated. The Chief's distinctive untrimmed salt and pepper eyebrows fluttered, and then relaxed.

Could Adolph assume The Chief to be in a tolerant mood? "All right . . . I guess."

The Chief's right hand swept back his thinned, gray hair. He reached for wire-rimmed reading eyeglasses atop the nearest folder pile. "What crazy drop-from-the-sky disturbance bothered her fragile mind today?"

"Looks like someone dumped motor oil in her garden. Lab sent two soil samples."

"That's a new one." The Chief's right hand rolled a pen back and forth within the desk's two-foot square paperless oasis. "If Francine calls, I'll forward her to you. Motor oil or whatever . . ." The Chief gazed at the ceiling. "Just keep me in the loop."

Adolph knew The Chief's signal. Meeting topic completed; go about your business. "Thanks," said Adolph. He pivoted and marched straight to the detective squad room. Four desks occupied the room's center, two partners side-by-side with their desks facing the other two partners. To Adolph's right was his partner's desk, unoccupied, but faithfully dusted by the nighttime janitor should Yancey by chance return the next day. Adolph's last visit to Yancey's home, the eleventh month of Yancey's disability, had brought good news. He learned Yancey's grafted leg and stomach blood vessels and muscles, beneath skin scars where he'd been shot twice by a burglary suspect, neared full functionality. Yet, two weeks prior, when he and Yancey enjoyed the occasional morning coffee at Patsy's Café, his partner's skittish reaction to a mug clink convinced Adolph that the effects of post-traumatic shock still lingered in Yancey's brain.

Adolph rifled a top drawer for his dwindling supply of paper report forms. He'd continue to cajole The Chief's clerical assistant into keyboarding his info into the computer for Adolph entertained no desire to learn typing. An on-duty Yancey had inputted his and Adolph's reports while Adolph adopted the two-pecking-forefingers approach as sufficient to display suspect and forensic data on his monitor screen. Reaching for an old-fashioned telephone book, Adolph thumbed through it to verify a Francine Hoskins at 3492 Rose Lane, Bridgetown. He wasn't surprised the included Yellow Pages listed the same address for the Rose Garden B&B.

His personal apprehension mounted, as he knew he'd have to push the computer power button as the quickest way for him to determine who owned the property north of the B&B's backyard fence. His anxiety quieted as he navigated a familiar path to the city property tax list showing ownership by a Spencer Wainright III. Adolph tapped a second database to learn that a Spencer Wainright III taught at Bridgetown's St. Mary's College. He cast his upper body weight to the right to jot the two tidbits into his notepad.

The distinctive squad room door click and nearing footsteps elevated Adolph's gaze to the approach of Lt. Sam Turner, lead detective and the nominal supervisor between Adolph and The Chief. Lt. Turner had been brought in undercover three years ago to infiltrate a Midwest stolen car ring Adolph had identified and the lieutenant never returned to his Chicago precinct after he surfaced to be hailed and glorified at a Bridgetown press conference Adolph found reason to miss. Turner's unwillingness to give a tip of the hat to Adolph's years of toil, or extend an apology for not mentioning him at the press conference, grated upon Adolph's nerves. When Turner plopped his butt into the lead detective position left vacant by the promotion of Detective Lt. Ronald Howard to Chief of Police upon the death of Adolph's father, Adolph secretly gritted his teeth to await his opportunity to grease the skids for the disgrace of an upstart Lt. Turner.

Within hours after his Dad's funeral, Adolph's late night foray into police headquarters rescued his Dad's chair for himself. A tight-lipped Yancey had noticed the switcharoo, but Turner didn't act like he did. Chief Howard a week later had pulled Adolph aside to say privately he objected to Turner's hiring and promotion, but claimed the mayor's clout prevailed. Be patient, The Chief insisted. Adolph calculated his supply of patience had atrophied in one year faster than Yancey's unexercised muscle.

"You want in the football pool?" Lt. Turner asked. Nicknamed "Bulldog" for his square head with a shortened stubby neck perched midway between shoulders worthy of an ox; the lieutenant sidled up to a seated Adolph. Bulldog's fawn-colored hair with its brush-bristle crew cut failed to add verticality to his squashed facial features or enthrall Adolph's respect. He wouldn't wager a dime with any wannabe card shark and further suspected that a top-line roulette wheel confiscated along with a poker table last year in an Oxford Avenue gambling raid hadn't been destroyed as legally required, but relocated to Bulldog's home basement.

"Put my donation in a church envelope."

"Funny." He poked Adolph's shoulder without force. "You still praying for that gold badge? Two-to-one odds Luann's going to parlay her gender to the front of the line and you'll be watching her ass strut to the promotion ceremony podium."

Adolph's Gold

"I do this damn job better than anyone, including you."

"Stuff it." Turner's tight smile irritated, but wouldn't provoke Adolph. "Don't get your hackles up." As he spoke, Bulldog edged his feet sideways. "Even your Black queer partner, if he was here, would agree Luann possesses better odds."

Adolph jerked his chair toward Bulldog. "Don't need to kiss ass, not yours anyway."

The squad room's banging door interrupted Adolph's slide into insubordination.

"Hi, guys."

Even without the feminine hips swaying in his vision field, the wafting Victoria's Secret scent told Adolph he didn't need to stand for Luann's arrival. At the least, Adolph appreciated Luann never failing to douse herself in Victoria's Secret or he'd have to spend another four-hour evening explaining to his wife that what Mary detected permeating his shirt and tie came from having been forced to sit next to Luann for a full-day forensics update.

Lt. Turner stretched his right hand, palm up, toward Luann. "Football pool. Interested?"

"Yeah." She pulled out a wallet from inside the purse hanging from her left shoulder. "Here's my five and the game sheet obtained from Corporal Riley my son filled out last night."

"He's a suck up, too," Adolph muttered under his exhaling breath as he reached for his ringing telephone. "Sgt. Anderson." He listened as Len, his long ago high school tennis partner, now his forensics lab buddy, relayed the preliminary Rose Garden B&B soil analysis. Motor oil. He'd guessed right. Used motor oil, Len said, correcting Adolph's verbal repeat. When Adolph hung up, he rated the information only marginally more significant than Sonja Maria's assault tale. Because of the motor oil's connection to The Chief, he'd watch his backside, but solving last week's gunshot homicide in the Sixth Street Bar's alley would more likely propel him towards the glory he needed to cement him in and foreclose

Luann's challenge to his gold shield promotion. A late afternoon stomach growl alerted him not to forget supper before his scheduled seven p.m. interview with his uncovered biker, a bar patron/witness to the shooting.

Planning to leave his home after Mary's promised meatloaf, he parked the Monte Carlo on the concrete driveway outside his one-car garage. Inside his 1970's-constructed single-level rambler, he rapped lightly on daughter Kristen's closed bedroom door.

"Kristen, it's Dad."

"It's open."

He rotated the knob and stepped into the dark world of a fourteen-year-old Goth devotee sprawled across a double-bed-sized black velour bedspread. His prior objections about the garb and Kristen's short, black-dyed, and crimson-streaked hairstyle well voiced, if ignored. Mary privately calmed him by stating that teenager fads come and go and growing out of it would be natural and expected, and sooner for Kristen if he didn't stoke the fires of rebellion. Adolph today wasn't so sure. Mary's words had been spoken a year ago.

From the vague personal experience of his own teenage years, a parental summons meant discipline. He tried not to sound judgmental. "Tell me why the principal's involved."

"Angelica claimed someone stole her stupid bracelet."

He awaited further elaboration that didn't seem to be forthcoming. "You accused?"

"Sorta."

Adolph leaned his left shoulder against the doorjamb. "Sorta doesn't answer my question. Either you are or you weren't."

Kristen's lips pursed as her gaze shifted to the ceiling. "Well, ten of us were in the classroom where Angelica said she'd last been before missing the bracelet." Kristen shifted her body sideways and then raised herself to sit cross-legged. "And, I didn't take it. Told that to Principal Held. Wouldn't be caught dead wearing the ditzy charms Angelica does."

"Sure it wasn't a prank?" Kristen shook her head.

"Anyone else report jewelry stolen?"

"No. Evelyn thinks a Dragon swiped it and she's afraid she'll get hurt if she squeals."

He decided not to step in and close the door. "She have proof?"

"Dah, no. Overheard hallway whispers." Kristen cocked her head to the right. "Don't hang with square people like Evelyn."

"I believe you didn't take it, and I'll call the principal tomorrow morning."

Chapter Three

We've got a guest." Matt Hoskins's voice boomed into the Rose Garden B&B kitchen. Francine bumped her left hip against the dishwasher door to roll the full upper rack into the inner tub. With her hands clutching and dripping water into her flowered apron, she hurried into the parlor.

Stopping abruptly, Francine struggled for breath. She confronted, not Matt, but a statuesque gentleman with beady eyes stroking an Abraham Lincoln replica beard. His black rumpled frock coat had been folded and draped on a ruby-tan leather suitcase with brass clasps.

"Welcome." Francine strove hard not to smirk or giggle. "How may I help you?"

"You have room?"

"Yes. One room, shared bath." She'd delayed renting the room to give the nice Mr. Russell an extra day to telephone and confirm a reservation made last year. For the prior four Labor Day holidays, he'd stayed at least a full week each year. All she knew today was that she couldn't wait any longer for Mr. Russell's arrival. Her soon-to-be depleted bank account required she fill all three rooms at the holidays and during school graduation weeks to compensate for vacancies in other weeks. "How many nights?"

"You offer discount for week stay?"

Francine couldn't help but stare at his large hands as they dropped below his waist. His discount question tickled Francine's fancy for she recalled Mr. Russell repeating an identical inquiry every year. He'd always stay a full week, sometimes two, when the circus performed at The Civic Auditorium. Fellow guests at breakfast adored Mr. Russell's fascinating travel stories, especially his claim to have been, in his younger days, a Ringling Brothers roustabout.

"Ten per cent, no refund."

"I have Visa?"

"If you'll hand me your card, I'll get approval. That'll be $315.00 plus tax." When he opened his wallet, she noticed but one credit card, which he gave her. "Please have a seat . . . er . . . Mr. Lincoln."

Francine swiped his Visa card at the B&B credit card terminal located next to her kitchen telephone. Lightly tapping her right hand fingers on the machine, she waited per usual as the machine clicked and a white paper slip emerged with its approval of one Mr. Abraham Washington Lincoln. She carried the slip, fastened to a small clipboard, into the parlor for the hastily scrawled authenticating signature of the B&B's newest guest.

"Right this way, Mr. Lincoln. I'll show you to your room. Breakfast is served between six-thirty and eight-thirty. The front parlor door is locked at midnight. After, until six a.m., you'll have to ring the doorbell." She waited as he, with ease, lifted his suitcase and followed her.

Halfway up the stairs, in a loud voice, he asked, "Will there be quiet?"

Noting the ironic contrast between his booming voice and his question, Francine paused as she grabbed the newel at the top of the staircase. "Yes. Except late afternoon Monday. There'll be a family backyard party . Labor Day, you know."

"That's okay. How far to St. Mary's?"

"Twelve, thirteen blocks. On a nice day, it's an easy hike. Otherwise, there's two taxicab numbers in the white guest information binder you'll find in the parlor. Remind me at breakfast to show it to you." Francine extended her right arm. "This here's the bathroom door. Lock it and you won't be disturbed." She unlocked the adjacent door; twisted sideways to hand him a key attached to a rectangular piece of wood, and beckoned him to follow.

Francine clicked the AC control to "on" while Mr. Lincoln laid his suitcase on the thin floral patchwork quilt. Earlier she'd placed a vase of fresh cut asters, Mr. Russell's favorite, on the dresser. Ah well, she thought, they'll wilt with or without company.

Mr. Lincoln's Eastern European accent created in her no exceptional alarm. There'd been the rendering plant manager from Prague who'd stayed all of February and March a year ago until he found a three-bedroom rental apartment across town to accommodate his arriving family. For the last two summers, he'd steered short-term plant visitors her way. Perhaps this was why Mr. Lincoln chose the Rose Garden B&B.

Francine, wiping the AC unit with her apron, thought she heard the muffled voice of her twenty-three-year-old son, Matt, call out her name. Francine scurried to the room's open door and called out: "What?" Francine heard Matt beckon, "Come downstairs." He'd lived with her his entire life and for the last three years had been holed up in a basement storeroom converted into a bedroom equipped with high-speed cable Internet. His high tech computer toys, especially his linked computer screens, completely baffled her.

"Mom, Chief Howard's here."

Francine shouted, "Coming." Her mind raced as to why The Chief would visit today, two days ahead of Monday's Labor Day party, unless he brought news about the oil.

The Chief embraced her in the parlor and his chest stiffly retreated. With his hands still lightly grasping her shoulders, he asked, "Hope I'm not intruding?"

"No, no." Francine stepped back to disengage. "Showing a new guest to his room."

He smiled and let his arms dangle at his sides. "Business is good then?"

"This week yes, but its been a slow summer. You know, the economy and all. Barely scraped together enough for last month's mortgage." She reached to retrieve the signed receipt still on the clipboard she'd left near a parlor lamp. "Forget business. Why you here?"

"Has Adolph, that is, Det. Anderson, been in touch?"

"He stopped by last week to tell me the lab identified used motor oil as the stuff dumped in my garden. Stupid, if you ask me. I've tried to be green since before Al Gore became fashionable. And, if I say so myself, I do it better."

Chief Howard's right forefinger swiped the crease above his full eyebrows.

"Okay. I know" Francine interjected. "Police chiefs can't be political. But it's true."

The Chief's smile re-appeared. "Have any idea where this oil came from?"

"None. Can I get you something to drink? Your dad liked a glass of sherry."

Sensing agreement, Francine preceded the two of them into the kitchen. Two wood chairs flanked a small pecan wood table, half of its top covered by a folded-back red-and-white checkerboard tablecloth. She'd sold a larger Formica-covered table crowded out by the installation of a perpendicular kitchen counter extension used to serve guest breakfasts.

"Water. Glass of water will be fine."

Francine shook her head, but complied. He sat opposite her and sipped. "Fess up. Tell me what really brings you here. In your entire adult life, you've never acted without a purpose."

"Simple . . . making sure my detective doesn't slight my favorite cousin."

Francine could feel the warmth build up in her cheek's

fifty-eight-year-old capillaries. The Chief never failed to say the nicest things, and she loved him for it.

He continued, "Do you still want me to bring burgers to grill Monday?"

"Of course. Even before that scumbag of a husband, Harvey, ran off last year, I've depended on your wonderful grilling talents. You've never let me down."

She anticipated he'd arrive Monday an hour before other family members for the Labor Day party with an extra charcoal bag in his Jeep, just in case she hadn't purchased enough.

* * *

Hey, Fran, you bury Harvey under the garden roses?" Cousin Conrad finished his taunt with a smirk. "Maybe that's why we haven't seen that stupid crooked smile of his lately."

Chief Howard suppressed a smile and exaggerated a shoulder shrug as Francine's squinting eyes connected with his before she javelined a scowling stare toward Cousin Conrad.

"Go to hell, Conrad," Francine snarled. She pivoted to grab a running nephew.

The Chief didn't cotton to unproven accusations, even in jest. Preparing for an escalation, he hung the oversized spatula and his tongs by their rawhide loops on the grill's utensil hook. He couldn't blame the hot, don't-touch-exposed-metal Labor Day weather. Cousin Conrad had acted with ill humor ever since he stumbled an hour late into Francine's backyard filled with two dozen family members milling about munching on chips, grilled hamburgers, and brats, and/or switching between empty lawn chairs shaded by two picnic table umbrellas and an apple tree. He feared half of the adults had drunk enough keg beer to be volatile, especially if provoked.

Cousin Henry tapped Francine's left shoulder. "Where'd you say Harvey took off to? Leavenworth or San Quentin?"

Francine, the scowl frozen onto her face, completed one full rotation toward Cousin Henry, extended all ten of her fingers to expose her palms, and shoved Henry away.

Cousin Conrad, sidling up to a ruddy-faced Henry, faced Francine. "Truth hurts doesn't it?" Ridicule outlined Conrad's mocking smile until the rim of a sixteen-ounce beer mug obscured his upper and lower lips. Chief Howard sighed with relief when Conrad's awkward right shoulder feign failed to entice Francine into a second physical or verbal retort. Believing a full melee had been averted, The Chief's altercation sensors were alerted when, from the garden fence, Conrad shouted, "Harvey's decaying bones, not the oil, probably stunted these flowers."

Chief Howard, stationing himself as a barrier between Conrad and Francine, guided Conrad toward the backyard's side exit gate. With Conrad's wife, Flora, sliding behind the steering wheel, he buckled Conrad into the passenger seat. After the SUV disappeared down the street, The Chief ambled to the backyard grill to stack the last half-dozen sizzling hamburger patties onto buns and wire-brush the burnt food particles from the grate. When Francine arrived to collect a ketchup bottle, he said, "Conrad was out of line. Beer shouldn't excuse rudeness."

"Don't fret. Heard similar gossip at the store. Why should family be any different?"

"Who strung that yellow tape in the garden?"

As her right forearm corralled three ketchup bottles to her chest, she replied, "Adolph."

The Chief lowered the grill hood. "You got a shovel?"

"In the garage, why?"

Chief Howard, not wanting to be deterred, waved Francine away as he ducked into her house and entered her garage through an interior door. He grabbed a short-handled spade and hustled back to the rectangular box outlined by crime scene tape in his cousin's garden. With his feet outside the tape, he jabbed the spade into the dirt inside the marked box and drove the steel into the soft dirt with a vigorous stomp of his right foot. Family members, gathered in a semicircle behind him, edged closer as he forced the spade's handle toward his stomach. Oily dirt sprayed into the air and women scurried to protect clothes, skin, and hairdos from being soiled by the small flying clods. His second shovel thrust bounced the blade sideways. Not knowing what he'd struck, The Chief positioned his spade two inches from his previous attempt and stabbed it halfway into the earth. Peering at the soil's gash, he wiggled the steel blade back and forth.

"Jesus, Mary, and Joseph," The Chief shouted.

Crushing the murmur of expectation, a hush gripped the assembled relatives.

"What?" Francine called out from the rear of the silent throng.

"You bury an animal here?" The Chief asked, staring towards Francine.

"Not me. Why?"

"Shovel struck something like a fossil. Can't be absolutely sure. Could be a tree root?" The Chief scraped loosened dirt into the small hole he'd made, and then, utilizing the spade's backside, smoothed the ground level. "Everybody needs to keep this quiet until we learn what's buried."

Facing Francine's house while he collected family member nods, The Chief watched the curtains in a second story window flutter. A B&B guest had to have been observing. While the return of backyard whispers escalated to rival the thrum of evening locusts, he perceived his unrestrained curiosity to determine the seeped-oil depth had lifted the lid on a Pandora's box without giving him a satisfactory peek. He fantasized that the unearthing of a yellow jacket nest would've created a lesser family commotion.

A streak of shame permeated his consciousness, triggered by the veiled accusatory glances that flitted toward a pale Francine; her normally vibrant body slumped into a patio chair. The Chief longed to question her, but not in front of relatives. A hissing, foaming keg spout drew his attention to a wiry Cousin Roy, one hundred and twenty pounds if soaking wet.

"Whatcha make of Francine's graveyard?" His words floated between beer-aroma exhales.

"Can't say. Not enough information." The Chief twisted a Mike's Hard Lemonade fished from the bottom of a Coca Cola logoed cooler and swigged his day's first drop of alcohol.

Roy's eyes broadcast a know-it-all glint. "Maybe a dog buried a soup bone?"

"Hope that's what it turns out to be." The Chief privately discounted that possibility for a dog wouldn't likely paw contaminated soil. If the oil came first, that is, an investigative point still undetermined. He finished the spiked lemonade with a gulp. The enveloping backyard silence, and his glance that Francine had vacated her chair, verified he and Roy stood alone.

Matt approached. "I've driven Grandma Mayfield back to her nursing home. Only Mom's left in the house."

"Thanks. I'll join her inside." He left Matt to entertain Roy. When The Chief entered the kitchen, Francine sat at the table staring blankly, a half-full glass of sherry in front of her.

"I'm sorry," The Chief began. "Guess I ruined a great party."

"Don't worry." Francine sighed. "The party went fine. I've been praying for strength."

* * *

Adolph marched to and fro to keep onlookers away from a three-man forensics team that had this Tuesday after Labor Day strung corded twine to create foot-square grid blocks preparatory to the excavation of forty square feet of oil-contaminated Rose Garden B&B backyard garden soil. With practiced precision, the team dug, shifted, brushed, sorted, identified, and labeled every object found to a depth of one-foot where the excavated, but saved, soil had no trace of motor-oil. The oil, Adolph read from a supervisor's notes, extended to six inches in three spots, but soaked, at most, the top inch elsewhere. He could fathom no rational explanation for either the why or the location of the deeper penetrations, each twelve to fifteen inches in diameter. Bored with watching the time-consuming operation and unwilling to chitchat about blooms and dying flowers with Mrs. Hoskins, he sought nearby shade to telephone a favored local barber for a haircut appointment. Because he was unable to steal away to close other pending cases, he chafed at babysitting the B&B forensics team until eight p.m. darkness would halt work.

Joe, the forensics crew leader, called out to Adolph, "Check this out."

Adolph, his enthusiasm buoyed that the team would finish early, jogged in his scuffed crime-scene leather loafers, notepad in hand, from the B&B's east side house shadows to the dig site's center. "Whatcha find?" His eyes spied gray specks at the bottom of a one-foot hole.

Joe squatted and leaned forward. He lifted a huge bone. "Pelvis," he announced.

"You sure it's human?" Adolph asked.

"Ninety-plus percent. Male, too."

One question came to Adolph's mind. "Is that the bone The Chief's shovel struck?"

"No. He nicked an ulna."

Hoping to confirm an early finish, Adolph asked, "How long this going to take?"

Joe glanced at his left wrist. "Til midnight if we get lights." Adolph's shoulders sagged. "Rain's forecasted for early tomorrow. Don't want to tarp if it can be avoided."

Adolph recalled a similar dig three years previous. Rain torrents washed debris into the unprotected site and a defense attorney used the contamination to plea bargain probation for a perp who should've rotted in jail. Adolph reached into a pants pocket for his cell phone to call The Chief for permission to rush an order for a bank of six floodlights.

While Adolph waited for the floodlights, Francine surprised him at five-thirty with a heaping plate of ham sandwiches, two bags of chips, and iced tea. Adolph also observed brown hair, a forehead, and two eyes periscope above the backyard fence as the technicians gathered to eat. He tapped Francine's shoulder, and, in a low tone into her right ear, asked, "Who?"

"Mr. Wainright," she whispered. The hair crown and eyes disappeared. "Neighbor."

Luann's appearance, occurring halfway through his second sandwich, disturbed Adolph's serenity. He swallowed hard as she, clad in a wrinkled dark blue pantsuit, strode into the backyard. Adolph, seated in a webbed lawn chair on the rustic brown paver patio, didn't twitch a muscle to rise. "Whatcha doing? Sightseeing?"

Luann frowned. "Lieutenant requested I relieve you."

Adolph glanced sideways at Francine before he flashed a weak smile at Luann. "Step with me to the gate." He trailed after Luann and didn't speak to her until out of Mrs. Hoskins's earshot. "Bulldog has buggers nothing to say. The Chief personally assigned me to this case."

"I'm not, believe me, shoehorning myself into your life."

"Is that so?" He stared at Luann. "Like a couple of weeks ago when my biker witness failed to show up at the Sixth Street Bar for my interview, and later claimed he spoke to you."

"Not my fault he walked into the station."

"After hours? Stuff it, Luann. You knew I was home and adore cold meatloaf."

She glared at him. "Call Bulldog. Give him a load of your prissy whining, not me."

Adolph, ready to blast back, heard truck brakes shriek in front of the B&B. A husky bearded man in denim overalls unlatched the gate. "Where do you want these lights? Gate's too narrow for the base and its weight restricts lifting them over the fence, too likely to damage."

"Set one up outside the gate. We'll see if enough light strikes the fence."

The bearded one, joined by two helpers, swung the jointed light standard into its extended vertical position. A portable generator hummed. Adolph didn't need to worry about backyard visibility for two local television news crews with their own lights had camped out in a neighbor's yard to the west. Electronic flashes from both the news media and

40

gawking citizens' digital cameras and cell phones intensified the growing circus atmosphere.

He recognized Josh Myles, *The Examiner's* police beat reporter. "No comment," Adolph intoned to four successive questions.

"Bet Luann knows more," Myles quipped.

"Ask her. The Chief could use a good reason to order a new beat officer's uniform. I'll read your every word tomorrow."

Adolph gazed Luann's way. Her right foot sneaker vibrated the dig site's outer perimeter cord. Before he could yell, Adolph's ears, detecting faint wafting musical chords, diverted his eyes. A concerto? He shrugged and closed the B&B gate to encounter a gaggle of citizens thronged on the B&B's front driveway.

"Hey, buddy, lift your butt off that yellow fender." Adolph didn't recognize the teen. The ones who'd earlier defaced his Monte Carlo probably sported nose rings, gang symbols, and multi-colored tattoos not now visible on this dude. Adolph debated whether or not to confront Bulldog or take an hour break at home before returning to send Luann packing.

Onlookers parted when he, backing out, honked his car's horn. Two miles up the hill and he'd surprise Mary. Bucking for a gold badge, and having a detective squad two bodies short, required constant availability, deferred vacation, and extra late night stakeouts. If she watched the local evening television news, she undoubtedly expected him to miss supper.

Adolph strolled through his home's kitchen and walked into the nine-by-ten third bedroom redecorated into Mary's sewing room. The love of his life, and forever his high school sweetheart, sat in front of the window, hunched forward. Her enduring spirit constantly fought the early onset arthritis that had crippled her extremities. He reminded himself often how she'd blessed his life. When, after their marriage, he mentioned joining the police force, she'd supported his leaving safer dead-end factory labor.

41

"Don't do that." Her flinch and jarring first response unexpected to his softly enunciated, "Hello, dear." She nudged her chair from the sewing machine, but struggled to twist her torso the one hundred and eighty degrees required to face him.

"Sorry." He angled forward, to her right side.

"I can reheat dinner." Her crooked left hand fingers dropped a bobbin.

"No need. Mrs. Hoskins served sandwiches." He helped his wife of twenty-one years to her feet by gently lifting her shoulders and, supporting her weight with his left arm, slid the metal walker in front of her with his right elbow. It always seemed cruel for him to walk to the living room and leave Mary elsewhere, but her independent pride streak compelled it. The tennis balls he'd cut and stuck on the rear walker feet had eliminated much of its former drag, which allowed the front wheels to rotate easier on the rug-less linoleum and wood floors. The gold shield promotion would enable him to hire the domestic and personal care help his wife would certainly require down the road. He plopped into one living room recliner already creased by his one hundred and eighty pounds. Mary, minutes later, twisted into an adjacent recliner equipped with a built-in heat massager.

She smiled. "Nice to see your face at home."

He arose, leaned forward, and kissed her lips.

"You home longer than to change your shirt?"

"Maybe." His blue blazer hung on its vestibule closet hanger. "Thinking I should go back because it's The Chief's cousin. Luann's there now. Says it's at Lt. Turner's order."

"Can't see how she can work the hours you do with two teenage kids and no husband." Mary pulled a quilt across her spindly legs. Legs that a teenage Adolph admired as graceful, muscular cheerleader springboards.

"She only cares about herself. Expect the kids make do."

"Maybe so, but don't aggravate yourself. This afternoon, I heard strange noises outside the kitchen window. Wasn't the ball Alice's boy next door bounces, either."

Adolph stifled a throat twitch of anxiety as pressed the

TV remote mute button. "How strange?"

"No thud really. More like scratching . . . or pushing something apart. Didn't hear, nor see, anyone outside talking when I got to the sink."

"Excuse me, I'll have a look." Adolph, in the garage, pressed the garage door opener button, wiggled on sneakers, laces already tied, and grabbed a flashlight. He shimmied past his Monte Carlo into the evening's fading light and turned left. The kitchen window faced the street. He failed to see any significant scratches or new dents in the white vinyl siding. Two never-before-seen gouge marks marred green paint and caulk on the outside kitchen windowsill. A jimmy attempt had been made to force the window. He guessed a small pry since the marks were too wide for a flat-blade screwdriver. His flashlight beam onto the grass crowding the house's foundation showed no incriminating footprints.

After closing the garage door and kicking off his sneakers, he stood between the living room recliners, his right hand resting on the back of Mary's. "Nothing to worry about, dear," he said, his voice low. "Just have to keep doors and windows locked per usual."

She tilted her chin up. "You going back on duty?"

"No." He focused his gaze into her eyes. "You're more important."

Mary smiled and tucked her permanently stiff fingers under a flower-patterned quilt.

He kept the TV volume low and relished being his wife's sentinel and refrigerator gofer. When the ten o'clock news started, Adolph heard a tinny ping, like an object hitting the front outside downspout. He lowered his footrest release handle, being careful not to wake a peacefully dozing Mary in the adjacent recliner. Draped in kitchen darkness, he peered through a street-facing window and spotted a dull white ball on his lawn. He grabbed his flashlight and his Walther P.38 9mm Parabellum from the entry-closet shelf. Re-checking he'd left the safety on, he tucked it deep into his waistband at the small of his back.

In quick succession he flipped on the porch light and cracked open his home's rear door.

"Who's there?" he yelled. His sweeping left-to-right flashlight beam failed to dissolve the murky shadows that engulfed the night beyond the yellowish circle of the stoop's light.

His eyes strained to glimpse a hooded figure running along the gutter that separated his driveway from the street. Young male, Adolph guessed, under six-foot, approximately one hundred and sixty pounds, race undetermined, definitely athletic.

"Stop," Adolph shouted, realizing his command would be in vain, even if he added the word "Police." Adolph couldn't risk firing his 9mm. He stepped into the crisp night air and skimmed his flashlight beam across three similar-width gouge marks, one shinier, on the kitchen's exterior windowsill. To his lower left, a non-rusted nick indicated a tool, not the softball, had slipped and hit the powder-coated galvanized rain spout. He strode onto the lawn to pick up the cover-torn roughed-up softball. What a clever ruse to approach the house.

For the remainder of the night he couldn't stop thrashing and dreaming that the intruder would try again. This subconscious fear trailed him to the Gas 'n' More where he was surprised to find a six-thirty a.m. customer logjam and Sonja Maria. He intercepted her walking out the double-glassed door of the convenience mart. "Where'd you get that black eye?"

"Fell." Her swollen left eyelid reacted slowly to the rays of the rising sun before she could cover it with her left hand. "Gotta go, husband must go to work."

He choked off a challenge to her injury lie. "I forget, where does your husband work?"

"Philippe drive truck." She began to shuffle toward her older Nissan sedan.

"Swanson Brothers?" Adolph guessed the biggest trucking firm in Bridgetown.

"Si. Must go." Her uninjured right eye expressed a

mounting panic.

"We'll talk later." Adolph scanned the pump island as Sonja Maria scurried to close her driver's door. Her newly blackened eye supported his prior skepticism of Sonja Maria's college assault complaint he'd classified as unverified before closing it last month. Collecting his gas receipt, he refocused his thoughts on developing a strategy to rip Luann off the Rose Garden B&B investigation. He hurried through the station's parking lot, expecting he'd not be late for The Chief's meeting.

Chief Howard slapped his right hand on the interrogation room table and asked for quiet. Adolph joined the other six attendees in instant compliance.

"We're waiting for the lab to identify that skeleton found at Rose Lane, 3400 block, two days ago. Preliminary crime scene facts indicate a full skeleton, male, good teeth and bones, no unaccounted for visible trauma marks." Adolph refrained from comment on The Chief's deft word choice so as not to highlight his shovel nicks. "Not a recent burial."

"What about this motor oil we keep hearing about?" Sgt. Timothy Buckworth, patrol division, asked. Buckworth gazed across the table at Adolph.

"Still investigating," Chief Howard replied.

Adolph raised his right hand. "Motor oil is a common blend of 10W30, probably Quaker State. Lab says molecules contaminated with engine sludge. That indicates it was used oil."

Lt. Turner's light tapping of his fingers on the metal table didn't distract Adolph.

"Total quantity estimated to have filled an unlocated fifty-five gallon drum. I've canvassed a three-block radius and there's no obvious outdoors barrel storage location, auto repair facility, nor evidence of a neighborhood shade tree mechanic." Adolph recognized The Chief's dissolving chagrin for not having read the latest lab report.

"Steer everything Adolph's way," The Chief interjected. "He's lead detective on both the vandalism and the homicide."

With a raised hand to shield his lower jaw from The Chief, Adolph flashed Luann a childish smirk. She raised her right hand's index, middle, and ring finger. Pleased he'd nettled her, Adolph returned his attention for the next twenty minutes to those around the table as The Chief completed the week's priority-case briefing. With a lowered head, Adolph dodged a staring match with Luann and strode to the parking lot, leaving her in the corridor leading to the detective's squad room. He steered his Monte Carlo to Rose Lane where Francine Hoskins greeted him at the B&B's front door.

"More questions?" Francine asked. "Please wait in the parlor. I'll be back."

Adolph obliged and found a seat on the parlor couch. When his cell phone rang, he let his cell's voice mail pick up Yvonne Whitenmire's call on the eighth ring. Lifting his gaze while stuffing the phone into an outside blazer pocket, he nodded politely to a tall bearded gentleman, who wore a black frock coat, crossing the room's center. When Mrs. Hoskins returned, Adolph inquired with a flourish in his voice: "Your business includes presidents?"

"Yes, sometimes." A coy smile graced her otherwise dour face. Her flowered apron hung loose, moist at the hem. "That's a real Mr. Lincoln. Quiet and reserved. He must have business at St. Mary's for he's asked about how to get there and I've seen him walk in that direction."

"Interesting. But . . . more important. Do you have a guest register covering the past year?"

"Wait a minute." Mrs. Hoskins wheeled left and departed. She returned five minutes later with three bound eight-by-eleven-inch journals. "These are the registration books for the last two years. I'll need to keep the most recent, started August 1." She piled the two older books on the sofa next to him. "Who are you looking for?"

"Don't know exactly." Adolph weighed how candid he should be considering Francine's closeness to the crime scene. A fenced yard upped the odds it wasn't a random burial. "The Chief informed me he'd sworn you to secrecy." She nodded.

Adolph's Gold

"My initial hunch: the garden-remains are of an individual who either lived or stayed in this house."

"Omigawd. Heaven have mercy." Mrs. Hoskins sank into the parlor's blue-patterned winged-back chair. Her right hand lifted her apron hem to shield her face from him.

Adolph heard a chime ring in the basement that Francine didn't react to. "If you would, try to think of any suspicious man who stayed here since the summer of a year ago. Picture someone of average build, average height. I'll be back in touch by Saturday, Monday at the latest."

Mrs. Hoskins arose without speaking, let her apron fall in front of her skirt, and scurried out of the parlor.

Adolph entertained no idea how he'd identify the skeleton from the registration books and mentally crossed his fingers that at the office he could narrow the names into a manageable short list of potential B&B guest victims, plus Harvey Hoskins.

Only the departing office police dispatcher, with a nod, noted Adolph's station entry. At his desk in an otherwise vacant detective squad room, he took for granted The Chief had tossed four new files into his desk's corner inbox. Was he to feel honored because his recon showed Luann received but two new files? As he examined what detectives, under their collective breath, referred to as "The Chief's crap drop," he didn't feel blessed. Two residential burglaries would be no-brainers, one-stop interviews hopefully resulting in a closed case with either telltale evidence pointing to the burglar or a nervous homeowner tripping himself up with an insurance company scam. Adolph didn't have time to rely on a professional thief being caught by an infrequent Fed sting or a screw-up by a greedy and careless fence.

Adolph's nerves tensed when reading the third file—another Sixth Street Bar patron theft. Damn, oughta shove this file, metal clasps spread, right down Luann's throat. He'd been extra close to nabbing the bar theft ring and closing a half dozen cases. Now, thanks to Luann, Adolph's unearthed witness was likely holed up in a Sturgis, North Dakota, biker bar. Adolph's blood had boiled reading Luann's interview report for he knew he didn't have the authority to cross state lines to confront the biker's tattooed girlfriend and her alibi statement that she and her Dennis-Hopper-wannabe-biker were nowhere near Bridgetown. What Luann had swallowed hook, line, and sinker was as cashable as a three-dollar bill.

The fourth file showed the edge of a typed, unsigned post-it note that Adolph recognized as The Chief's way of passing on unofficial investigative intelligence he would, if it later proved expedient to say never existed, he would officially deny. Adolph paused to mouth the words twice: "kiddie porn ring suspected." He dived into the folder. The first on-scene uniformed officer detailed three computers that St. Mary's College reported as stolen. The officer quoted Melody Records, a teaching assistant, as claiming all music department doors had been locked at ten p.m. The officer documented no forced entry. Dean Spencer Wainright III quoted as saying he switched off the overnight door security at six a.m. and called in the thefts at seven.

Spencer Wainright III. The name clicked in Adolph's brain as the neighbor living across the Rose Garden B&B backyard fence. The college employed Sonja Maria. His cell contained an unheard message from a Yvonne Whitten-something or other. He had read a newspaper hospital story her little Billy had been released after two weeks; the boy's patient stay extended ten days by a bacterial infection.

Adolph, startled by an outside hallway commotion, reacted by slipping the file with The Chief's note under the stack. False alarm. He'd displayed the exuberance of a new recruit long ago. They'd lose, like him, their buoyant innocence after the first witnessed murder scene.

The dispatcher's voice blared through his speakerphone. "Adolph, shots heard. 735 W. Mulberry. Uniforms responding. Luann's not answering. You wanna take it?"

"I'm on it." Adolph opened his double-depth desk drawer already half-filled with pending cases. He deposited the four new files on top. He couldn't surmise that responding would be but another fruitless career dash. Perhaps this would be his lucky day to gild a golden luster on the dull alloy of the detective shield at his belt, and to stick it to the case-jumping Luann.

He parked his Monte Carlo a block from where the pitted street concrete reflected the pulsating red and blue flashes emitted from stationary ambulance taillights. Two squad cars, angled at the intersection before him, blocked off civilian vehicle access. Growing up, his parents mentioned they'd lived on West Mulberry before he entered the world. He wouldn't contemplate living anywhere on this street; and, he didn't need to base his conclusion on an analysis of crime statistics. The street began at Main and followed the setting sun past the looming meatpacking plant that in decades past had been a huge magnet for immigrants, who, disembarking from Mississippi River barges traveling north, sought jingling pockets full of gold. He didn't begrudge the immigrants, actually revered their unflagging work ethic. His maternal grandfather had fought off contagious whooping cough, glib employment hucksters who cloaked indentured-slave contracts in fancy highfalutin words, plus a painful physical hunger to believe a below-deck voyage to America held the promise for a better life. Despite the ordeal, Adolph's grandfather, in spirit, if not riches, prospered by breeding draft horses he would sell to later arriving farmers.

Adolph double-checked his locking the Monte Carlo before he advanced a couple dozen steps to call out to one Officer Finnegan. "What's up?"

The fair complexioned, barrel-chested, six-foot cop with dark reddish hair held up the yellow crime scene tape marking the sparsely populated spectator line. Adolph ducked under. "When you get your gold shield, you'll bless me with a good word for a leg up to be first in line for your detective vacancy?"

"Of course," Adolph replied, slapping Finnegan on the shoulder. "We can't promote enough Irish." Adolph understood that today's words, when added to the recommendations he'd promised to two others, meant he'd met the street's bullshiter definition. His mother, who'd drilled into him her cherished value of telling the truth, likely spun in her grave at that moment.

"Ah, c'mon. You're pulling a leprechaun's leg."

Adolph gazed into Finnegan's eyes. "Who you gonna trust? Do I detect that Luann has put her hooks into you? Haven't I been square, treated you more than fair?"

"Well, you let me carry home that Guinness six-pack after that PBA charity event."

"See, you've remembered how a true pal acts."

Finnegan beamed. Adolph skirted around Finnegan and back-pedaled until his hand wave put an end to their conversation. Three months had passed since he'd spent a week's salary buying drinks on the Police Benevolent Association fund-raising cruise aboard a paddlewheel riverboat. As an event organizer, Adolph had allowed influential uniforms to disembark with beer six-packs tucked under their arms. He'd adhered to Yancey's advice that his promotion rested more on popularity and perceived performance than actual accomplishment. Adolph didn't want to believe this advice, nor bet against its validity.

Out of Finnegan's voice range, Adolph followed the cracked sidewalk toward the crime scene. The closer he got to 735 W. Mulberry, the more his mind wandered to try and remember his parents' address. While the address had to be close, he let his taxed memory cells drift away with the question unanswered. A patrol officer posted at No. 735's doorway was recording names. Adolph's right hand unbuttoned his sport coat to flash the detective's badge on his belt. The unfamiliar acne-faced patrolman nodded to Adolph's muttered greeting, and then smartly stepped aside to permit Adolph's entrance into the story and a half clapboard house.

A dingy living room rug separated a sofa, one stuffed chair, and a nineteen-inch television with a digital antenna. Adolph's nostrils sucked in the stench of mayhem. Speech fragments floated to him from what must be the kitchen. Two voices. The louder baritone voice trampled the halting thin whispering words from another, likely a female.

Adolph visualized a cartoon where the character tiptoed to the doorway. Not him. He marched with authority, and then gasped. Two bodies, one a woman, lay on the floor. A female EMT straightened the woman's left arm and thrice poked a needle into the crook of the elbow in search of a vein for the IV bag. Adolph steeled his emotions to estimate that six steps separated the fallen woman from a pair of red Converse sneakers, heels up. Both heels protruding inches from the hemmed edge of a white sheet that covered a still body Adolph presumed to be male based on the sneaker size. Blood streaked the floor and its splatter hung suspended from the laminate counter's edge and metal cabinet pulls. Without rhythm, red drops dripped to ripple the center of a congealing ragged-edged blood pool, its floor circumference oozing outward.

Adolph closed both of his eyes tight. A familiar smell punched his sensitive nostrils, not the sickening foulness of blood recalled from too many dead-of-night radio calls, but burnt toast. His mind trembled with the singular previous unforgettable horror that had wrenched his stomach muscles and branded a memory through his brain's cortex into his myelin.

As a teenager, twenty-five years ago, he'd discovered his mother's blood-encrusted body lying in the family kitchen two days after he'd spoken hurtful words: "I could if you were dead." Foolish, immature anger had fueled his now deeply regretted outbursts. Other teens in those days pocketed a driver's license. He'd deserved one, too.

After eight years of personal witness to his father's agony, Adolph celebrated, with his father, the death of the thug who'd killed his mother. The official police report listed resisting arrest, justified shooting, but a year later Adolph's father, after reaching the bottom of a whiskey bottle, admitted he had tried unsuccessfully to beat the why out of the husky burglar until the thug brandished a switchblade, hidden until then in a sock.

His father then fired twice from point-blank range. Since his mother's diamond engagement ring had been hocked, Adolph assumed she surprised the thug during a burglary. He praised his father for later joining, and adhering to, the Alcoholic Anonymous program until colon cancer obliterated the need to.

Despite a B-minus average, Adolph abandoned St. Mary's College before completing his final practice teaching semester that would've earned him certification as a high school biology teacher. His stint at warehouse work short lived before the police academy accepted his legacy application.

"Adolph."

"Sorry," Adolph replied. "Just trying to burn the crime scene onto my memory. Someone needs to plug out that toaster."

"Let me go," the female voice shrieked behind him.

Adolph wheeled. The front-door officer hugged about the waist a girl of slight build, aged somewhere between thirteen and sixteen. Her pointy-shoe kicks hit nothing but air.

"Whoa," Adolph commanded. "Hold on, miss. You shouldn't be here."

"My mom. My mom needs my help."

From the side, Adolph grabbed the teenager's right wrist, careful to stay angled away from her kicks until both shoe soles touched the floor. Tears moistened the girl's blue tank top. "If you promise to sit with me on the sofa over there, I'll let you give mom a hug after the EMTs stabilize her breathing." He'd seen the woman's rigidity and suspected his words offering hope were completely off base, but a white lie for human comfort overrode gritty crime scene truth. "God can hear our prayers from the sofa."

The frenzy in the girl's eyes subsided. Adolph nodded to the officer, and, using the girl's right arm as a leash, guided the trio toward the sofa. The officer and Adolph blocked the girl's path to the kitchen. The girl's body thump squeaked the sofa springs.

Adolph stood in front of the sofa. "What's your name?

And, how old are you?"

"Marcie . . . Marcie Connor. I'm fourteen."

"You live here?" Adolph glanced at the EMT behind him hoisting a closed kit. The EMT shook his head twice. Adolph didn't acknowledge, but resumed his gaze at the girl. Both of her hands clasped her facial cheeks tight. He continued, "I'll assume you live here. Who else?"

"My mother and brother. Dad's in Iraq."

"Your brother, what's his name?"

"Leroy."

"Does he go to school?"

"Jackson High."

Adolph knew the school, as his daughter was enrolled there.

"Isn't that maybe three blocks from here? Would he be there now?"

"Yeah." Marcie's nervous hands, swiping her skin below hollow-set dark eyes and above make-up streaked cheeks, kept mixing new tears with old.

"Why aren't you in school?"

"Heard sirens in study hall and outraced two friends."

The front door screen slammed.

Marcie shouted, "Leroy, mom's hurt."

The officer pounced to intercept. In a trained reflex action, Adolph unsnapped his shoulder holster weapon's strap and left his 9mm holstered as the officer pressed the male youth against the room's far wall. "He's clean."

The boy darted to kneel in front of the sofa where Marcie squeezed his shoulders in a tight hug and spoke several words muffled by his shirt. Adolph retreated three steps, ready to cut off either the brother or his sister's attempt to storm the kitchen. With eyes glued to the youths, he noticed the boy wore a red gemstone ring on his right pinkie. He'd seen that ring worn by others, teens mostly. Not so with the left forearm tattoo.

"Watch out," Adolph said to the kids. "Stay where you are. Let the gurney pass."

The previously departed EMT backed into the living room, dragging behind him a raised gurney. The gurney trundled into the kitchen. Adolph, aided by the repositioned officer, screened the youngster's kitchen view. Adolph expected the unidentified male, presumed dead on the kitchen floor, would be removed first, but he'd no guarantee.

After three or four minutes, the living-room-stationed officer tapped Adolph on the shoulder. Adolph rotated his head to see the EMT point vertically aligned fingers for a front door exit through the living room. Adolph glanced into the kitchen to see the red sneakers unmoved and sidestepped closer to the front door. When the gurney approached, he shoved his left foot in front of the gurney's rear wheels to arrest its movement. A raised forefinger signal to the EMT allowed Adolph a moment to lift the top sheet. He motioned to Marcie. She peeked under the sheet, and crying, kissed her mother's forehead. Marcie's solemn, taller brother stood behind her and clasped his sister's shoulders. They staggered slightly in following their mother outside to the awaiting ambulance that Adolph realized might as well have been a hearse.

Kneeling on an unsoiled spot of gray kitchen linoleum, Adolph folded back the covering sheet at the end opposite the sneakers. Adolph estimated the Afro-American male couldn't have been older than twenty-two or twenty-three. The left hand protruding out from under the forehead that pinned it to the floor displayed manicured fingernails. The earring on the right earlobe shouted: "Dragons." Street scuttlebutt had them attempting to intimidate or entice white teenagers into being drug runners. Adolph speculated about three visuals. First, Mrs. Connor's blouse buttons had been popped halfway down indicating she'd been attacked. Second, since both victims had been shot in the chest at close range, a struggle had ensued for the gun found nearby. Third, if drug runner intimidation an underlying motive, why wasn't Leroy in the house?

Adolph scribbled a few scene notes and ducked outside to inspect his Monte Carlo for dings while waiting for the crime scene technician to arrive. Thirty minutes later, he tossed his notepad full of questions without answers on his squad room desk.

Reopening the St. Mary's College computer theft file, he dwelled on the snapshot of a boy's nude upper torso, but, with sand and a floating casino appearing in the fuzzy background, the photo's torn off bottom half could've shown bathing trunks. Thus, ambiguous, The Chief's post-it note wasn't. Could the photo have been printed from one of the stolen college computers?

Adolph knew child porn thieves didn't have to escape with the hard drive and monitor. Any saleable pictures could've easily been downloaded onto 3.5 floppy disks. Oh, how he dated himself. A boring white-collar crime technology seminar the previous month had detailed for him how burned DVDs, or external storage devices, efficiently converted digital files into glossy pictures for salivating perverts or became a master for underground Internet distribution.

A contrite Catholic priest the year before, in a moment of personal catharsis, had spilled his guts to Adolph. The priest's firsthand outpouring had elevated Adolph's muddy understanding of the sleaze trade. Despite his personal distaste for the pornographic material, successful detective work required him to discern and parlay theory into provable court fact. In the fast-paced technology race to laptop computers and tablets, clunky desktop computers lost favor as prime theft targets, unless, of course, they harbored saleable content. Profitable portable and reproducible digital files also avoided multiple USPS mailing restrictions and federal criminal penalties. Last year he'd successfully investigated and closed a St. Mary's computer theft because the student in a biology professor's office, without his absent nerdy buddy for tech support, couldn't download the test questions.

What had this Professor Wainright said? Adolph flipped to and read the uniform's interview report. Office staff used the computers for student practice scheduling e-mails and the department granted upper-class students unrestricted access for educational research and finding musical compositions online. Did he, Professor Wainright, ever logon? Adolph's finger found the quoted reply: "Of course." The professor's answer expanded to say he scheduled private piano lessons. Where? The list of in student homes, at the university, and in the professor's personal residence seemed to Adolph to be perfectly logical.

Adolph almost retched when his mind questioned whether the computer information searches involved molested boys, girls, or both. The victim's gender, Adolph had been taught, often narrowed the search for the sick son-of-a-bitch who ruined these children for a lifetime. When he reached the report's end, Adolph hadn't pulled out one solid theft clue. He stood, gulped twice, and strode hurriedly to the bathroom to splash water on a clammy-feeling face. Was this agony worth a gold shield? With a paper towel drying the final water drops clinging to his mouth, his eyes gazed into the mirror and he imagined a soiled and bed-ridden Mary unable to control bodily functions. His clenching right fist crumpled the paper towel. For Mary's sake, any gold shield price paid would be worth it.

It wasn't Mary's fault, but his, that they hadn't been able to have children to nurse them in old age or other frailty. The problem surfaced early when his left testicle didn't descend as would be normal. It finally did, but neither functioned as God intended. Mary had been a saint to accept him regardless. They'd wept together.

A veil of joyful tears surrounded he and Mary when their adoption of Kristen received court approval. He inhaled sharply to permit his emotions to ease softly into the under-control zone. His unclenched left hand pushed the washroom door open before his eyes pronounced the corridor clear and his oxford heels clomped across the oaken squad room floor to his awaiting desk. He logged on to the departmental computer server to keep his uneasy gut quelled. Utilizing a saved search pathway, his left and right forefingers punched up the list of known sex offenders registered within Bridgetown. He scrolled it. None listed on Lilac Lane where the professor lived; however, it wasn't unusual for sophisticated perverts to bury controlling real estate ownership in complicated trusts. Adolph tried to prioritize his Rose Garden B&B questions. Had a relationship exploded into spousal violence? If not, who then? Were the flowerbed bones those of a traveler? He wouldn't dismiss the idea. His brain cells scrambled the entries in the college theft and B&B homicide files. If the bones were of an older male, was it a former molested youth, now grown, who'd muscled up the courage to come back to haunt or threaten a former tormentor who had stayed at the B&B or, perhaps, lived in the neighborhood?

Adolph slumped into his desk chair. His thoughts had a way of always dancing hither and yon to the point of exhausting him. He needed evidence, proof, not wild strategies pregnant with fulfillment that flourished until squashed by unearthed fact. One day these forays into fantasy and the mystical unknown would be his ruin.

The reality of discerned footsteps dissolved his reverie.

"Working hard?" Lt. Turner asked, his lower lip left twitching.

"Always," Adolph replied, unwilling to assume his supervisor ever engaged in idle banter. His forearms, pushing on the chair's arms, elevated Adolph's torso to be stiffly upright.

"Saw The Chief favored you with more files. Me, too." His legs bumped against Luann's desk. "You know, having a title isn't as glamorous as they trumpet on television."

"Wouldn't know." Adolph's projection lacked the polite icing of empathy. "One question does bother me. Why'd you send Luann to relieve me at the B&B dig? I was fully capable of babysitting that bone excavation myself without her."

"Don't put me in the crosshairs." Bulldog squared his stance. "But, between you and me, what you just said is what I told The Chief when he ordered me to dispatch Luann."

"What? Don't con me. The Chief assigned me the case. Confirmed it this morning."

"Shut your pie hole," Lt. Turner barked.

Adolph flinched. "Stupid crap. That's what it is; furthermore, don't care who knows it."

The tenseness at the corners of Lt. Turner's lips ebbed. "You don't have to convince me, but I don't have to be elected like The Chief. You were in the meeting. Our closed case numbers dived south last quarter. The Chief needs a big splash before the upcoming city vote."

Adolph understood the logic. Realizing he'd best be served by cutting short his verbal jousting with Lt. Hunter, Adolph listened to him continue.

"C'mon, it's his cousin's backyard. He's pressed to give it special attention. Would you blame him for backstopping the assigned detective to quiet family criticism? If he messed up, given it's a relative, the challenging sheriff's deputy would have a field day."

"Still, it gnaws my gut. He speak to you about the thefts at St. Mary's?"

"Yeah. Routine, he said. Chief said he pitched it to you to allow more skeleton time."

Bulldog's statements gleamed with the twinkling surface calmness of a lazy river hiding jagged rocks below-the-surface ready to rip a boat's hull to shreds. What about The Chief's note? Adolph decided to keep his mouth shut and watched the lieutenant leaf through folders atop Luann's desk. Adolph recalled rumors at Patsy's of Bulldog's wife having filed divorce papers in Chicago at the time he began his Bridgetown car theft ring undercover assignment. In the three years since, Bulldog and his wife had clamped a tight lid on a secretive personal life. Barely a month ago did the slightest crack materialize when department whispers sprouted that Luann had spun Bulldog's basement roulette wheel a time or two. That he handed Luann the football pool winnings two weeks in a row without a showing of the filled-in slips could've been a favoritism sign. Yet, Adolph's gut lacked any strong inkling that Luann could be seduced so cheaply; but then again, roulette gaming perhaps a cover for a riskier hands-on game.

Adolph's Gold

Mentally, Adolph slapped his face for letting his mind indulge in this wild fantasy. He'd gained a professional stature based on rock-solid results confirmed by courtroom convictions and wouldn't this day act callously and toss away the integrity he'd polished to sparkle like a precious jewel. He gazed straight at Bulldog until their eyeballs connected.

To enhance the credibility of his bravado, Adolph spoke deliberately: "I'll solve that skeleton case here in the next couple of weeks. My developed sources offer substantial leads." The efficiency of today's modern DNA tests wouldn't fail him. Given a victim's identity, he'd unravel all mystery molecule by molecule to expose and bring the killer to justice.

"If that's your prediction, I won't challenge it." Bulldog restacked Luann's case folders.

Adolph's gut felt the drama hanging in the air between he and Bulldog. He refused to let it strangle his expressed confidence. If it took 268 hours times two to fulfill his spoken design, he'd do it. There might be a silent night after the fight, but he'd not sulk into the darkness.

With Lt. Turner closeted behind his closed office door, Adolph calculated he could forget the skeleton for a day while he awaited lab test results. He telephoned St. Mary's music department to schedule a late afternoon visit and filled the time interval with an uneventful drive to the 1400 block of Golden Boulevard, a middle class residential enclave.

The rumble of ungreased garage door rollers interrupted his entering a cell phone number to a third burglarized home. Up the driveway to his right, black work boots and a J.C. Penney dark green work set became visible within the opening created by the rising double-sized garage door. Adolph flipped his cell phone closed, exited his Monte Carlo, and strode toward Roscoe Hippleman, his interview subject.

"Don't get oily by shaking my hand," the burly Roscoe said. "Can we make this quick?"

Adolph suspected Roscoe was more concerned about his auto repair business in the 2100 block of Fourth Street, a gang feuding part of town, close to, but psychologically distant

59

from, his stucco residence with its attached garage, metal awnings, and trimmed lawn that made the statement of a fortyish striver who'd climbed partway up the economic ladder.

Adolph skipped writing extensive notes about the night of the break-in upon hearing the vague husband-and-wife-dining-out alibi Roscoe recounted. "Can I see the window broken for entry?" The report said glass lay inside the garage. The concrete floor below the typical thirty-six inch wide wood paneled frame door had been swept clean. Cardboard, taped at the perimeter, covered the missing windowpane that allowed reach-in-access to the dead bolt and doorknob.

Adolph didn't notice anything unique about the current garage contents. Workbench neater than his, although Roscoe's bench top, lined with assorted nails, screws, and fasteners in baby food jars, had been darkened by excessive spilled motor oil. Above the bench pegboard hung no tools. Underneath, no lawn mower sat parked next to the red gallon-sized gasoline can. Dust particles, higher than a man's reach, hung suspended in wall-corner spider webs.

He asked Roscoe, who stood behind him, "Anything found missing after the officers left?"

"Craftsman brand sockets. Two sets, one a gift. Filed a scratch line near the boxed end on the older purchased set to keep them separate. Both stolen. One of my employees said he saw similar sockets sold at the Sixth Street Bar the day after. But not worth it for me to make a fuss."

"Understand. Any neighbor hit? Not all file reports."

"Yeah, Jeremy Carlson. Told me one of his kids, same night, left the porch door unlocked and a downstairs computer grew legs. Jeremy griped to me that his insurance agent recently convinced him to double his policy's deductible so, even if he reported it, he'd recoup nothing."

Adolph added this development to his notepad. "The Carlson home on this street?"

"Directly behind." Roscoe emphasized the direction with a finger point.

Adolph's Gold

Roscoe's deductible reminder coupled with the stolen tool value indicated to Adolph that Roscoe harbored little incentive to risk jail for insurance fraud. Potheads most likely. Items either pawned, or became cash sales with a beer chaser. If the thief was motivated by a desperate need to feed a starving child or a pent up rage to get even with the victim, Adolph couldn't decipher either from the crime scene visuals. Stymied, he departed Roscoe's presence after invoking the old-fashioned cop mantra of he'll be in touch. Adolph clocked his Monte Carlo's steering wheel and accelerated in the direction of St. Mary's College.

One-hundred-year-old oaks, beginning to drop leaves, branched out as stately sentinels announcing St. Mary's urban campus. Sunlight streamed through leafy canopy holes to dapple acres of manicured lawn crisscrossed by flagstone paths. Adolph's destination, the six-story music building, a modernistic, large expanse of greenish-glass ridged by black horizontal and vertical steel, loomed one block ahead. Its facade in garish contrast to the squatty, two-story red brick administration building and the rectangular double-hung wood-trimmed windows he now passed. He cursed the lack of a vacant visitor parking spot.

Idling his Monte Carlo in front of a fire hydrant, he telephoned the Music Dean's office. With permission and a police placard fished from his glove compartment tossed on the dash in front of his steering wheel, he parked in the posted-as-reserved, non-gated faculty lot. After flicking a dirt speck from his car's front fender, he paused on the right edge of the sidewalk that led to the music-building lobby to let a rush of students stream past.

On the fifth floor, a middle-aged secretary escorted Adolph into Dean Wainright's office. An upright piano with a covered keyboard hugged the left wall. Dark oak paneling filled Adolph with the unintended feeling that if he laid down he'd be in an unlined coffin. An electric motor buzzed, wood panels slid sideways, and western sunrays danced through a glass wall to erase Adolph's image of being buried alive.

61

Dean Wainright sat behind a large wood desk fronted by two visitor chairs. When the dean rose, his upper torso's shadow lengthened to greet Adolph. A slight right rotation of the dean's shoulders exposed muscular chiseled facial features that contrasted sharply with the languid, soft left hand fingers he extended to point at a chair.

"Appreciate your seeing me on short notice," Adolph said.

"Please sit." Adolph honored the dean's request. "Would you like tea, coffee?"

"Neither." Adolph's eyes blinked four times until adjusting to the room's brilliance. "Could you fill me in on the thefts." He tried hard not to stare at the dean's hands with their manicured fingernails graced by long, tapered fingers not calloused by manual labor and perhaps an applied lotion that explained the barely detectable vanilla fragrance his nostrils perceived. As Adolph listened, he scribbled few notes for the dean parroted the incident file as if it had been memorized until he mentioned a discarded student ID found under a utility sink in a second floor janitor's closet. Quizzed by Adolph, the dean explained that college security had matched the ID to a three a.m. card swipe that had been the building's single logged entry between midnight and six a.m., the theft time window.

The found ID's location puzzled Adolph. Since the desktops and monitors had been pilfered from the first floor, why go up a floor to ditch the ID when it could've as easily been slipped into a pocket or discarded off-premises? "You get a name on the ID?"

The dean rifled through desk papers to locate a thin folder. "Jonathan Green. And, I'll anticipate your next question. He's currently not a student. Had been last year."

"Any hand truck or cart missing or found misplaced?"

"No."

Having been lulled by the museum-like serenity of the office, Adolph flinched at the instant, sharp response. He regrouped. "It would be difficult with a one-time recorded entry for one person to carry three desktop computers all at once."

Adolph let slide the dean's disparaging shake of his head. "He could of had help?"

"Right. And with fake-stone floors inside and concrete outside, shoe treads either non-existent or obliterated by hordes of parading students. What about logs for parking lot entries?"

The dean's head stilled, he replied, "Parking gates don't have memory."

"Rats. Would guess that if the thief didn't have help, he could've blocked the door."

Wainright, a yawning emptiness in his eyes, short-circuited Adolph's follow-up question. "Swipe record doesn't show how long the door stayed open. Perhaps I should suggest that upgrade for the next trustee meeting agenda."

Adolph bit his lower lip to stay focused. "You have any info on this Green fellow?"

In accepting the thin folder handed him, Adolph wouldn't wager it contained case-breaking clues. He shuffled four photocopied pages: Student data, academic record, class schedule, and extra-curricular activities. "May I keep this?" he asked to backstop his nonspecific uneasiness.

"Of course." The dean brushed his brown suit jacket's right shoulder. "It may or may not say so in there, but Jonathan Green possessed great music potential. Talk to Professor Silver."

"Anybody know why he left school?"

"Not exactly. With the poor economy, many students struggle. We've split scholarships, but even that hasn't helped all."

Adolph still didn't have a handle on whether or not Dean Wainright maintained a close relationship with this student. "Did this Jonathan have a scholarship?"

"Look on the top sheet, halfway down."

While Adolph grasped the word "partial," the numerical notation of "one/three" left him confused. "A partial means what?" He passed the sheet across the desk to the dean.

"One-third-time scholarship. That's $7,000 if he carried fourteen credits, minimum."

"Thanks." Adolph returned the sheet to the folder unsure of what he was missing. A student talented enough to earn a stipend wouldn't likely be stupid, or carelessly toss his ID. "I'll check him out. Appreciate your time." Adolph's right hand fingers slid along his chair's supple leather arm as he rose. He left his envy unexpressed. Now wasn't the time for him to dwell on the absent material things in his life.

A hurried pace returned him to his car in the faculty lot. Peering beyond a concrete barrier to the adjacent student parking lot, it dawned on him it wouldn't make any difference if the student parking lot control did or didn't have memory. The closer, unguarded faculty lot would've been empty overnight, that is, of faculty. If his memory served him right, the faculty lot was the exact spot where Sonja Maria said she had been parked?

He racked his brain without connecting Sonja Maria to Jonathan Green. At the second light he turned to follow the posted arrow that led visitors through blocks of shabby, paint-peeling buildings en route to downtown. He slowed for an alley and entered it to park next to the Sixth Street Bar owner's 2008 silver Cadillac.

Adolph's right fist struck steel twice to rattle the grate protecting the varnish-streaked wood door. A black leather-gloved hand moved the interior curtain covering the diamond-shaped window. Adolph dropped his fist to watch the brass doorknob rotate before the door swung in and he came face-to-face with hard-to-forget steely eyes and that familiar scowl.

"Man." The scowl deepened into tensed shoulders. "I'm ready to blow this place."

"Always knew bar owners had banker's hours." Adolph, by experience, knew he could jest with Theodore "Ant" Carpenter for the once-convicted beer slinger respected Adolph's badge just enough to foster a standoff. Adolph remained convinced Ant's railroad-tie arms wouldn't toss

Adolph into the alley as they had a dozen unruly customers. He rubbed his nose, safe as it was from scattering alley pebbles at the conclusion of one of Ant's famous jerky underhanded thrusts memorialized in the police reports Adolph had scanned. "Only need a moment."

Ant unlatched the protective gate. "Let's step into the storeroom."

Adolph recognized the code word for the high-roller poker room with its crazy use of empty top-shelf liquor boxes to decorate a wall. The premium liquor bottles removed and locked in a basement steel cage Adolph had only seen once. Adolph's right fingers glazed across one of the room's six chairs, its leather, slightly more creased, but otherwise identical to those in the dean's office he'd just left. He leaned against one of the room's short walls, careful not to bang his head on the gilded wood frame of a Roman gladiator oil painting. "Jonathan Green, he been in lately?"

The black pinstriped silk suit jacket draping the six-foot-four bar owner didn't discourage him from patting his sculptured belly beneath the European tailoring. "Who wants to know?"

"Me." Adolph stared straight at Ant's coal-black eyes. Both of Ant's irises tinted pale red in what Adolph thought should've been white. The stare game lasted fifteen seconds. "And, maybe, a bunch of innocent kids who don't need their life destroyed by perverts."

"Don't mess with unripe fruit. Fine ladies keep me straight."

Adolph could believe that. "So, quit stalling. What about Mr. Green?"

"Dude's been hanging elsewhere. Let me tell you, Dragons bad for business."

Adolph's attention perked up. "Dragons. He one of them?"

Ant tugged on his second glove. "Yup. How 'bout anonymous ring if the dude shows."

The offer surprised Adolph. "You'll do that?" *Green*

65

Donan Berg

musta crossed Ant big time.

"I gotta go, man. Hot date. I'll need new pants if I wait much longer."

Adolph's sidestep blocked Ant's path to the door. "One question." He didn't expect a straight answer. "Who here has been selling hot wrenches in plastic covers?"

"Damn it, man. I'm not here at all hours. How the hell should I know?"

Adolph pinned Ant's hand against the light switch. "Take an employee survey."

Ant slid his fingers free. "If the moon's pink—"

"Cut the crap." Adolph didn't let the rear door close and gazed at Ant. "I've a hot date myself and, oh, by the way, The Chief put a third reported patron theft on my desk. Before a fourth arrives you might consider a little neighborhood watch action to save your liquor license."

Ant's right shoulder leaned heavy on the back door. "Bullshit. Jerks who inhale those free drinks bought by Patsy's owner are the one's who make up those goddamn reports. It's that hothead's payback for losing his shirt and wanting to welch on the chit I hold. You check."

"Just might do that." Adolph stepped aside and Ant clinked the metal gate closed.

While Ant's Cadillac zoomed off, Adolph's Monte Carlo treads rolled slowly on the alley gravel until hitting the street's asphalt. He did have a hot date with Mary later, but first he planned to stop by the Rose Garden B&B.

Deja vu for Adolph was his finding Mrs. Hoskins tipping a watering can on the front porch. If it were he, he'd poke a mixed cluster of plastic blooms from Hobby Lobby into each hanging basket and be done with it. He stepped onto the porch. "Finished paging through your registration books. Didn't find many presidents, but a few names repeated."

Mrs. Hoskins let her watering can slosh on an Adirondack chair seat. "Let me guess, Wilbur Menowirth, Chester Day Lewis, Raymond Kliner, and Arnold Zender."

Adolph, his notepad out, mentally checked off the names

as Mrs. Hoskins spoke. "Think you missed one."

Mrs. Hoskins rubbed her left hand forefinger to her chin. "Don't think so."

"Mr. Antoine Russell."

"Silly me. How could I forget my best late summer guest?"

Her girlish inflection struck Adolph as at odds with her lined brow. She offered no clue as to the honesty of her memory lapse. "Regardless, what can you tell me about the five?"

"Let's talk in the kitchen." After a sigh and three heavy strides, a sluggish Mrs. Hoskins paused at the front door. "You go right ahead. I must say good-bye to Mr. Lincoln."

Mr. Abraham Washington Lincoln, carrying a suitcase, nodded to Adolph as they passed in the parlor. Adolph pulled out a chair at the small kitchen table. Seated, he stroked the emerging veins on the back of his left hand until Mrs. Hoskins entered the kitchen.

"Sorry about that. Mr. Lincoln's been so terribly nice. Stayed longer than originally planned." She shuffled to face the upper cabinet next to the sink and her left hand grabbed a six-ounce un-stemmed glass. "You care for sherry. It settles my nerves." A purple plastic bottle stopper protruded from a 750 ml wine bottle partially hid by a lemonade jug on the counter.

"No, on duty, but thank you. I'm interested in the guests we identified." He hoped to get through all five men before Mrs. Hoskins emptied too many glasses. He now had an inkling of what had likely induced her slow porch movement.

"Oh, yes." The wine glass clinked on the Corian countertop. "Wilbur Menowirth was a disagreeable fellow. Nothing ever right."

"Would you say he was of average build, average weight?"

"Heavens no. Big slob he was." She swiped her right hand across her thin lips, and then raised the glass to sip previously poured sherry. Gazing upward she whispered, "Excuse me,

Lord, I shouldn't be so unkind."

"Maybe I should ask which men, in addition to Mr. Menowirth, weren't of average build." Adolph tapped his ballpoint pen on a notepad page fearful Mrs. Hoskins wouldn't complete his questions before her nerve-calming sherry skewed her long-term memory.

"I'd say all could be called average except Wilbur and the one with three last names, you know, Chester Day Lewis. All skin and bones he was. I'd call him the litter's runt."

"Good. I've crossed those two off." He noted her shoulders sway. "Please, have a seat." Mrs. Hoskins shook her head no. "Tell me about Arnold Zender."

"Let's see. Traveling salesman. Had this little sample kit of stationery. Tried every time to sell me paper with roses. Said would be a good image considering the B&B's name."

"Anything stand out as unusual about him?"

"Not really. Talked a lot, but I figured that was his salesman's personality. Never said anything hurtful. But his van, what a mess! Splattered mud never washed off." Mrs. Hoskins sank into a chair. "Lucky for me he parked on the street and never in the driveway."

A muddy van indicating rural roads and shying away from easy inspection had Adolph scribbling with a flurry. "Did you record the van's license number?"

"No. No reason. He paid cash in advance. Recall he stayed no more than two days at any one time. Stopped in say . . . five, six times a year. Always during the school year."

"Did he mention any kids?"

"Don't think so." Her eyes drifted away. "Once, after he mentioned how busy the college was, I asked if he had child in school. He said traveling didn't leave him time for romance."

"What about Raymond Kliner?"

Her eyes refocused on Adolph as she tipped the sherry glass to her lips. "Courteous Black man. Think he played sports. Every summer he talked baseball, and then football in the fall."

"Know his profession?"

"Come to think of it, no." Her one gulp emptied her glass. He hoped she'd stay seated, but she arose, steadied herself, and weaved with heavy steps to the counter where her right hand lifted the sherry bottle to pour a full glass. "He did have two or three visitors with expensive cameras. Thought it awful nice for him to be able to visit another town and have club friends."

Adolph scribbled a note as he struggled to narrow his thoughts to identifying the skeleton and/or the assailant. Bits and pieces of earlier afternoon conversations intruded. Spilled oil and stolen tools and computers competed in varying degrees with Dragon gang involvement, Ant Carpenter, and The Chief's file of disturbing child porn images. Roscoe's smashed window glass could or could not be related to the fresh gouges on his kitchen windowsill. He had to hurry Mrs. Hoskins along before the sherry-induced haze completely clouded her memory. Or, perhaps he should dilly-dally and let the loosened lips of the cousin The Chief called "crazy" dig her own grave and implicate herself? Adolph mentally wandered in the garden of disbelief that a kindly Mrs. Hoskins could physically bludgeon a man until the ghost of Agatha Christie poured poison into breakfast cereal. Apart from Mrs. Hoskins, he reduced his original count of viable suspects, or victims, to three of the B&B guests. "Mr. Kliner ever show you any his pictures?"

"Faint memory recalls he said he didn't travel with a computer that would download his saved pictures. He had this little plug in thingofamajig. Not a film canister familiar to me."

"That leaves Antoine Russell."

"Kind gentleman, face resembled Colonel Sanders. He always talked about his kids. Grandkids, too. Had a wallet full of pictures he'd display to anybody asking at breakfast. Don't think he could've crammed another school snapshot into that plastic accordion picture holder."

Now Adolph had two child references. "Did he ever bring any kids around?"

"No." Mrs. Hoskins braced her backside against the counter. "Sure you'll not join me. There's very little sherry left."

"Like I said, on duty. And Mary doesn't like me to drink before supper."

"Your wife's a lucky lady to have you listen." Adolph strained his head forward, but that only slightly improved his deciphering of her slurred words. "My young Harvey started out in a same loving way. When he got older, well, bless his soul, that's another story."

"Is this Harvey your son?"

"Husband. R-r-ran off. Lord says one should be kind so I think of him as dead."

Adolph closed his notepad, convinced further questioning would lead nowhere. His subconscious fear, brought to the surface by Mrs. Hoskins's use of the word "dead," accentuated his remembrance of the nighttime runaway visitor discovered after he'd seen the kitchen window gouges. Mary could benefit from his being home.

"I do thank you, Mrs. Hoskins." He rose. "I'll see myself out. The lab tells me they'll have more on that skeleton, maybe its identity, in a day or two."

"Please call me Francine. You've been here more than family, except Matt."

"Well, good night . . . Francine."

After pulling the front door closed, Adolph cried out, "Damn," as the watering can his right foot kicked skidded into the porch railing. Who removed it from the chair? He let his chagrin evaporate as he said "Mary" into his cell phone. "I'll be home shortly. Love you."

"Hi, dear." Mary's broad smile greeted him as she turned from their kitchen sink.

He cherished her every smile. The day's inconsequential worries he left hung up in the vestibule closet along with his blue blazer. The weight of his 9mm no longer tugged on his shoulder as it rested on the shelf above his blazer. "Any great things happen today?" He wanted to inquire about strange house noises, but decided bluntness would needlessly alarm Mary.

"Sarah stopped in from next door. That's all. Woman talk."

Adolph spotted a flyer on the kitchen table. "Who sent this?"

"Sarah dropped it off. She's hosting a Neighborhood Watch meeting next week."

Adolph's stomached tightened. "This says there'll be an update on attempted break-ins."

Mary clicked a stove burner dial. "Yeah. Sarah said there's been two break-ins three blocks down. Told her I'd heard noises this week, but otherwise nothing suspicious."

Adolph trusted Mary hadn't heard his gulp. "Was a burglary on Golden Boulevard, but that's not close." Adolph's eyes spied Mary's two-handed try to lift a pot spewing forth steam and he jumped to his feet. "Hold on, I'll get that. Sarah mention houses or garages?"

"Didn't say."

Adolph dropped the subject of home break-ins and dished onto three plates Mary's prepared supper of pork loin, boiled red potatoes, and kernelled yellow corn. Kristen, responsive to Mary's shout, slouched in and joined them at the kitchen table.

He stifled his disapproval of Kristen's layered smoky mascara. "You know of a Leroy or Marcie Connor at school?"

"Leroy's in my home room. He's weird."

Detective and parental impulses met at Adolph's lips. "How so?"

"Always talks big. Like he's a king, going to have it all."

"What's wrong with dreams?"

Kristen didn't pause to think. "He's a jerk, that's all."

Adolph, unwilling to even try to separate into definable fact the expanse and subjectivity of Kristen's word "jerk," altered his focus. "You know Marcie Connor?"

"Nah."

Adolph didn't relish the double dead end, but then he also tried not to be a police detective when at home. Kristen, after carrying the last plate to the dishwasher, departed to hole up in her bedroom. Mary cast Adolph a wary eye when he filled a tumbler with three ice cubes and a healthy double jigger whiskey splash. After he changed into sweats, the dissolving cubes clinked as Adolph set the drink on an occasional table coaster next to his living room recliner.

Kissing Mary, his tongue-moistened lips lovingly lingered on hers for several seconds. After he sat, Mary, in her matching recliner, hoisted a quilt and stretched it across her clavicles.

"Want me to check the thermostat?"

"Won't be necessary. Your kisses will keep me warm."

He rose and kissed her forehead. At these moments, life treated him better than he deserved. He remembered the glassy-eyed Mrs. Hoskins and let his drink ice cubes melt without a drop of poured whiskey crossing the lips Mary had kissed.

In the silence between the intermittent refrigerator hums, Adolph listened for unusual creaks, thumps, or strange outside sounds that would indicate an attempted home invasion.

Chapter Four

The next morning, within a half hour of his station arrival, Adolph pounded his clenched right hand on his metal desk. Had Len accessed the federal database? The lab report confirmed the skeleton to be human, male, but listed no DNA match. Adolph's aching hand throbbed as a symbol of too quick a reaction to unjustified frustration for an "x" appeared in the "yes" box next to the acronym CODIS.

But twelve days remained for him to satisfy his boast to Lt. Turner. He'd pump lab buddy Len tomorrow for scene details the supervisory bureaucracy omitted from the official report because they considered the minute details unsubstantiated and, thus, unworthy to be stated with the necessary conviction to support a cya mentality. His morning's Internet search located a potential sister to Antoine Russell residing in the St. Louis, Missouri, suburb of Felix. Putting exhilaration into his morning, Adolph's phone call confirmed the sibling relationship. She reluctantly agreed to contact a dentist for records or mail him a used toothbrush or comb.

Unfortunately, by the time Luann sashayed into the squad room, he hadn't dug up a family member or home location for Mr. Kliner.

She twirled her desk chair with a flourish, sat, and eyeballed a folder from a stack on her desk. She gazed at Adolph. "Want me to take control of this West Mulberry shooting?"

"What?" He wasn't giving Luann any active case, least not a closeable homicide.

"Courier left this on my desk." Her left hand hoisted a tan file folder.

Bitch. If a heart beat under that bulging, buttoned pantsuit jacket, he'd never fantasize about trying to massage it if it conked out in his presence. "What's that?"

"Lab's Mulberry report. Two white victims. Dorothy Connor and Jonathan Green."

"Can't be," Adolph replied. "The Mulberry male was Black."

"If you say so." Her lips twisted into a smirk. "That's not what this lab report says."

"Let me see. Your wire-rims probably fogged."

"Go to hell." Luann tossed the report onto his desk and disappeared into the hallway.

Adolph gingerly picked it up as if Luann's touching had been a 400-degree flame. All appeared official, no practical joke. Top page detailed Dorothy Connor's mixed race physical stats plus a marriage to Daniel. A string of Army base addresses detailed their nomadic life.

Adolph's crime scene observation, minus the blood, matched her driver's license photo. A wedding photograph captured a striking young woman with alluring high cheekbones and seductive eyes. The birth dates of a male and female child matched Leroy and Marcie. While nothing Adolph read in the file alluded to, or hinted at, gang involvement, his visual of Leroy's forearm tattoo and the right pinkie gemstone when he hugged his sister cued an unknown gang. The file listed no high school club or after school activity or sport for either Leroy or Marcie. Daniel's latest deployment to Iraq represented his second tour. A scribbled note said her funeral delayed two weeks to allow for his compassionate leave travel time.

The file's second section, devoid of photographs except for crime scene sneakers and the white covering sheet, left Adolph perplexed, not so, Jonathan Green's post-juvenile gang history of three arrests, which resulted in one assault conviction and judge-ordered probation. If he finished Bridgetown High School as the report said, Adolph pondered where the graduation mug shot was. Green's birth date translated into age twenty-four. School activities listed musical recitals and marching band percussion. No military enlistment or college attendance chronology listed, although a GPA slightly above a C+ would've permitted either. An interviewed neighborhood band classmate said Green once applied to be a bartender at the Sixth Street Bar.

Adolph scratched his head. How could the lab present a Caucasian when he'd seen an Afro-American? He had no logical explanation. Nevertheless, Adolph determined his best bet would be to revisit Ant Carpenter and sniff out Jonathan Green's Sixth Street Bar trail.

Adolph's Monte Carlo front bumper stopped short of the brick wall, below the bar's loading and unloading only sign next to Ant's Cadillac. Rather than rattle the metal door, Adolph strode to the bar's neon-signed front, pushed the ajar steel door, and stepped into a din of disembodied conversation. Even at mid-day, barstools and tables were populated by a dozen guzzling males in well-worn jeans and T-shirts, darker in color at the midsection, stretched tight by protruding abdomens. Sweating beer mugs rested on the spotlighted foosball table. A greasy burger aroma wafted from the kitchen.

Adolph's abs butted against the bar. "I'd like to speak with Ant, private like."

"He ain't here," the bartender said, his eyes averted from Adolph.

Adolph reached his right arm across the bar to crush the bartender's apron bib into his right clenched fingers and yank the bartender's face close. Adolph spit out the words. "That may work for any yahoo off the street, but you'll quietly tiptoe through the galley and tell Ant that best friend Adolph would like a word. Kapish? If he says no or later, tell him to grab a fire extinguisher while he listens for the fire department siren to shut this place early."

Straightening four fingers loosened Adolph's grip. A sheepish, sidestepping bartender disappeared into the kitchen. He returned in two minutes and leaned over the bar toward Adolph. Seems Ant had just returned and would be keeping a lookout out back. Adolph snapped a salute.

Two familiar eyeballs gazed out the rear door's diamond-shaped window as Adolph approached. Inside the bar's storeroom, the cheap perfume captured in the tabbed-curtain red velvet fabric's interstitial spaces contrasted with the stale tobacco smoke that rode piggyback in and out of Adolph's bronchial capillaries when at the bar. Ant suggested Adolph sit. He did.

Ant fiddled with a deck of cards on the poker table's green felt. "Why break my chops?"

"Don't yank my chain." Adolph interlaced his fingers and stretched his arms forward. "Saying you'd call me when Jonathan Green came by was a damn lie when you knew he'd met the Grim Reaper."

"Bullshit." Ant idly cut the cards. "Ain't got no time for

fricking games."

"Then where's Green?"

Ant exposed a trey. "Hell if I should know."

Adolph arose, and whirled to the advancing footsteps. The bartender held a plated burger.

"Not now," Ant said. "Grill me a new one in ten."

As the bartender left, Adolph faced Ant. "We gonna circle the bush again."

"You better remember when a favor's due." Ant focused his eyes on reshuffled cards. "Watch the alley later."

Adolph's sidestep put him in Ant's raised sightline. "What's that mean?"

"Hell, I ain't laying it out for you. Leave out the back. Watch the alley. I've got lunch customers up front and you'll scare them off if you're seen visiting too often."

Adolph heard the two locks click behind him as his eyes scanned the alley unable to detect anyone lurking. The window curtain of the closed rear door hung straight. In a roundabout way, Ant had hinted no one likely to stop in the alley if seeing a suspected police vehicle. Adolph hopped into his Monte Carlo and backed toward the street he'd used to enter the alley.

Hungry himself, he'd find his own burger joint. Patsy's would do, now owned by Randall Quimby, a pugnacious man whose trademark red bandana and ten-gallon hat embodied Patsy's hallowed Old West motif. Adolph spied an empty rear booth and slid in. Within moments, Rebecca, a petite blonde in a fringed Annie Oakley outfit with white-handled cap pistols holstered at her shapely hips, stared at him.

He ordered a Longhorn burger and fries combo. "So, where's the ranch king?" Adolph had harbored a vestige teen crush on Rebecca and never understood why she married Randall. Had to have been that opposites-attract theory.

She crossed her right boot with her left. "I'd normally say out with the posse, but then you'd know I'd be lying." Her hazel eyes twinkled. "Never lie to Marshall Dillon, right?"

He wouldn't condemn himself if he encouraged a little

flirting he'd never act on. "You'd never do that." Adolph made sure his gaze didn't dance lower than her chin.

A diner's shout diverted Rebecca's attention. Her buckskin skirt fringe swirled into a prancing-away blurry tease. "Your burger's coming pronto," she hollered from across the room.

A hunger pang didn't disrupt his work thoughts. If he was to give credence to Ant, he should cruise the Sixth Street alley after he'd eaten.

A heightened cafe murmur preceded Officer Finnegan's prodding of a reluctant teenage boy through Patsy's front door. Rebecca scurried to Finnegan and the boy and Adolph couldn't make out what Finnegan's lowered voice said. The boy's dipped head watched his left foot blue sneaker paw at the floor. Finally, Rebecca grabbed the boy's left wrist and led him behind the counter and into the kitchen.

Adolph stood to call attention to himself. Finnegan sauntered to Adolph's booth.

"Take a load off," Adolph suggested. "Why'd you drag that boy in?"

"Spied the youth kneeling next to a yellow Monte Carlo. Figured the boy, just released from juvie, was up to no good." A streak of white enamel separated the uniformed officer's full lips. "Say what, could've been yours."

"Excuse me." Adolph's fingers released his grip of the tabletop and he rose to curl his right fingers into a fist. "Paid a fortune last month to have that entire chassis repainted."

"Jesz, just relax will, ya." Finnegan slid into the booth. "Guess you're amped up about material things. Rebecca's kid cost her a couple grand last month to hire a lawyer. Think she's in hock up to her eyeballs. You don't see that rock on her finger any more."

"What about this place? Full on days I'm here." Adolph confirmed with a glance around.

"Guess you haven't heard the word on the street. Randall tried for a quick score in the Sixth Street back room and his best hand all night wouldn't beat a pair of tens."

Adolph didn't twitch a facial muscle as his descending butt pressed audible air out of the booth seat cushion. So, he thought, on that account Ant could be believed. "Cash or markers?"

"Heard a fistful of markers. And, it's not healthy to welch on Ant."

"You seen Quimby lately?"

"Heard he left town. Some say Vegas. Doubt that. But, I gotta go." Finnegan rose. "You'll keep your promise to put in a good word for detective?"

"Sure, you bet."

Adolph rubbed his tingling right hand fingers. He could've burnt that ordered burger patty three times over. Rebecca, collar fringe darkened, offered no excuse as she delivered his plated lunch. He didn't ask one question, call her back to complain about the cold fries, but left a double tip and waved a spirited right hand adios to Rebecca upon his exit.

Suspicious of even a practical joke, he circled his Monte Carlo twice; first, to ensure that no spray paint streaked the exterior luster; and second, to vary his viewing angles in his attempt to pinpoint any new scratch. Satisfied no finish damage existed, he stretched his right hand fingers behind the tire treads to make sure no one left any shingle nails, points up.

Worried about too visible a presence behind the Sixth Street Bar, he interspersed his second and fourth alley patrols with a stop at the Carlson home, where no one answered his doorbell ring, and an odometer check to confirm the flat one mile walk from the Rose Garden B&B to St. Mary's College. The simple tasks allowed him to wonder why street youths interested Officer Finnegan. When he'd been on a beat, he'd shoo kids home, never give them a personal escort, except to scare them with a jail cell visit. Blabbing an accusation to a kid's parent earned a patrol officer little community goodwill, and no promotion points.

Low sky sun streaks splintered in reflection off Adolph's windshield on his eighth five-mph cruise through the Sixth

Street Bar alley. At this pace he'd have to phone Mary to apologize for being late for supper. To prime his recon for results, Adolph abandoned standard procedure, parked three blocks away, and reactivated his beat officer's persona. If he scuffed his black oxfords, spit-shined that morning, he'd be doubly peeved. At least donning a crumpled brown tweed sport coat, stored in the trunk for undercover drug busts, would protect his blazer and help him blend in, that is, if any denizen gazed up. Peering into a pawnshop window two blocks from the bar, Adolph followed the reflective slow crawl of a Salvadore Pizza van as it passed him a second time within the hour. He didn't recall the town had one. When it turned right at the intersection, Adolph jogged half a block to follow, and then slowed to an accelerated stride as the van braked and entered the Sixth Street Bar alley.

The van, with its reversed wheels generating a spray of dust and gravel, bypassed the loading spot where Adolph had parked earlier and soundlessly backed up to the Sixth Street Bar door. Stepping forward twenty feet, Adolph's sidestep shielded his presence behind an electrical utility pole. His second peek observed a desktop computer, not pizza boxes, placed on the ground beside the van. From his viewing angle he couldn't count the van population or if a bartender helped. He flipped his cell phone cover upright and punched in dispatcher numbers for backup.

Worried that the van and any suspect would evaporate before help arrived, Adolph un-holstered his Walther P.38 and jogged forward toward a muscular figure hopping out of, and then into, the van. The male's right side, his hip and a bare elbow, exposed beyond the extended rear door offered Adolph no realistic shot; yet, Adolph had his trigger finger feeling metal.

"Police. Don't move." A motionless six-foot Caucasian in a purple tee and khakis, flat-screen computer monitor clutched to his chest, gaped at Adolph. "Stay still," Adolph commanded as he pointed his weapon at the suspect's rotated head. As Adolph circled, two desktop towers, resting on the van's cargo floor, became visible. "What's your name?"

"Jonathan." The suspect's forehead pinched by a pulled down baseball cap.

"You got a last name?" Adolph fixed his gaze on the suspect's eyes, four feet distant.

"Green."

A sharp pain at the nape of his neck terrorized Adolph's entire body. Staggering, the pain twisted within his head as if uncoiling barbed wire was being yanked by blood gushing through too-small capillaries. He reached for and failed to grasp the center pulsating image of three fuzzy van doors flickering on his retinas. His knees buckled and his right shoulder thudded against the van's side as he collapsed, firing one shot into the ground. Shoots of stinging pain radiated from his right knee, lost among the intensified throbs from the base of his skull that overpowered his brain's pain center. His vision danced from swirling pizza images into a dark cloudiness; his entire sense of balance tilted leftward and he crumpled sideways to the gravel.

His entire world faded . . . brilliant white light and hazy dots consumed by blackness.

* * *

Adolph, speak to me."

Adolph faintly heard his name. His mind, in a Rubik's Cube solution frenzy, spin-cycled the scrambled syllables into words, and then into a command, yet, his mouth and limbs didn't react. Through the slit of one eye, shards of orange sky pierced his cranial cavity. What happened? He craved more details than repeated bland encouragement he would make it.

"Adolph, this is Finnegan. Can you hear me or do I have to slap you around again?"

"Oh, my head," Adolph muttered. His tensed shoulders stayed rigid as Finnegan elevated them inches off the ground. "Tell me you're not guarding the pearly gates?"

"Considering that welt on your neck, you're lucky to be seeing any gates."

"Where's Green? The van?"

"Dispatcher mentioned no van. Found only you laying here."

Adolph moaned and didn't fight the EMT's pressing an oxygen mask to his mouth and nose. On the gurney before the straps were tightened, he touched the nape of his neck and winced. Mary's comforting smile flashed into his consciousness. She had to be frantic.

At Bridgetown Community General, the white-coated woman flashed a light beam across both of his eyes. He tried to scrunch his shoulders and a uniformed male's hand restrained him.

"Lie still," the woman said. "You've suffered a serious trauma. We need you to rest quietly for two to three hours to see if you should stay overnight. Do you understand?"

A stab of pain halted his head nod. Adolph mumbled, "Yeah."

The wall clock hands indicated nine o'clock. He last remembered six. At least his eyes had regained focus. This wasn't the draped curtain emergency room enclosure. He must've been admitted. A note pinned to his pillowcase said his family had been notified. He heard voices in the hallway. A candy striper pushed a wheelchair with Mary aboard into the dimly lit room, and, the striper, on her departure, toggled a switch to bathe Adolph in fluorescent light.

"Dear, good to see you awake." Mary stretched her right hand toward his.

He extended his left arm through the bed rail and lightly squeezed her bent-knuckled right hand fingers. "You didn't have to come. I planned to call." He let her hand go.

"Nonsense." Mary's left hand set the wheelchair brake. She grunted slightly as she pushed herself upright into a standing position and her right hand grabbed the raised bed rail. "Chief Howard's in the waiting room with Kristen. He'll be in shortly."

"I'll go meet him."

"You'll stay in bed." Her words impacted him like an iron

81

fist inside a velvet glove. "The doctor told me it was a strong blow." She hesitated, her face lambent. "Don't worry. Didn't mention how hardheaded you can be, but she told me you need to worry about complications."

"Hardheaded? . . . Hardheaded, you say?" He winked his left eye.

"If you were at home, I couldn't lift you if you fell?"

"Always the worrier you are. What's that Cubs baseball announcer say on TV? Yeah. 'Yes dear, you're right, I'm sorry.'" He squeezed Mary's hand. "You have a way home?"

"Sarah's waiting. She brought me and Kristen. Now, you rest."

He didn't protest nor wish to cause her needless worry. Her showering unconditional love always solidified his resolve to protect Mary and Kristen at all costs. After a companionable silence, a nurse responded to Adolph's call button push and, at the doorway, a uniformed Chief Howard stepped aside to permit Mary's wheelchair exit.

"I'll second that hardheaded comment I overheard," The Chief said.

"Lay off." Adolph couldn't instill force behind the bluster. "It's a term of endearment."

The Chief laughed. "So what's with not following procedure? Not waiting for backup?"

"Simple." Adolph's hands struggled to tug the bed's white top sheet to his chin and stretch it wide across his shoulders as he sought an answer. "Sometimes one has to act."

Chief Howard edged closer. "Granted."

Adolph buried within himself the sigh of relief he wished to let fade into the galaxy.

The Chief rested his right hand on the bed rail. "Consider yourself fortunate your dad saved my butt at least twice. Therefore, I've decided that, with a vacancy and Yancey still out, I'll skip the present and, for the future, you and Luann will buddy up."

"Hell no." Adolph's neck muscles spasmed; the prescribed Vicodin dulled without eliminating the heart-pulsed rush of blood into a constricted-brain-capillaries headache.

"Knew you'd likely object; thus, you can consider it an order, effective tomorrow."

"Chief, no disrespect." Adolph stared into The Chief's somber face. "But you'd kick a man when he's down, flat on his back?"

"Need my best detective on the job. Safe. Not taking up bed space." The Chief added authority with a square of his shoulders. "I've already noted your objection and, considering you might honestly not remember my words when you're released, the official written order I'm placing on your desk tomorrow won't mention this conversation." The Chief's right eyewink softened his serious mien. "Wouldn't want a paper trail that you're insubordinate."

Adolph, squelching a self-reliant pride that wanted to argue, rotated his stare to the ceiling. What had walking a beat taught him? Know when to duck, when to charge, and when to retreat. His father's ingraining of this mantra of duck, charge, and/or retreat by repetition had kept Adolph's personnel jacket clean of negative evaluations and no labeling of him as a departmental rebel. The promotion board hated rebels.

"You rest; sleep well. I'll be going now." The Chief paused before he exited. "If it's any consolation, Luann has taken to being your partner as well as you."

Adolph still gawked at the door when Kristen's boot-heel clicks advanced across the floor's linoleum to his bed, drowning out The Chief's fading corridor footfalls. Kristen's extra somber Goth-like expression caused him to tense. Her terse words, from darkly painted lips, of good night and a promise she'd help her mother get home left him relaxed.

Fighting heavy eyelids, Adolph, wary of the next nurse interruption, welcomed the engulfing solitude to plot how he'd derail being partnered with Luann. He dismissed the easiest solution—convincing Yancey to sign off disability—as the most unlikely. Nonplussed by a nurse inserting a thermometer bulb under his tongue and pressing pulse-measuring fingertips to his right wrist, he temporarily shelved the idea to volunteer for the SWAT team. He uttered a short thanks when the nurse announced he registered no fever, she'd close the room's window blinds, toggle off the lights, and slip the mini no-visitor-placard into the exterior door holder. The resulting closed-door darkness eased Adolph into a doze.

A jolting fear that riding with Luann would give her surreptitious gold badge campaign a credibility boost roused Adolph awake. Behind his blinking eyelids, a grotesque floating female image combined Kristen's Goth outfit with Luann's teasing grin. His head tilt left to the illuminated digital clock on the nightstand alerted Adolph that the glowing "10:30" meant his nap consumed almost an hour. He flexed both feet and hands to circulate blood to his extremities and ground the blunt edges of his upper front teeth into his lower lip's flesh to summon the one bold stroke needed to outflank The Chief's partnership order. In his mind's pool of repressed anxiety, only one course of action bobbed to the surface. If The Chief's report of Luann's lack of enthusiasm proved accurate, he had to convince Luann to voice stronger objection to their partner assignment, and the sooner the better. His body's adrenaline surged.

Swinging his feet left and sliding his butt to the bed's edge, he let the loosened top sheet fall behind him while he gingerly pulled the IV needle from beneath the adhesive strip that had secured the needle into his left forearm. His right thumb press, to a fast ten count, stemmed any possible blood leak. Free from the IV's tether and confident he could find Luann at home, he stood to strip off his hospital gown and dress for the street.

On tiptoes at his room's door, his ears sensed; and his eyes, with a peek in both directions, confirmed the vigilant silence pervading the hallway's length. To his far left, four illuminated red letters spelling "exit" dripped eerie light streaks on a push-bar equipped door. This he abandoned as an escape route, since the inviting door would likely activate an undesired security alarm. As he rotated his eyes right, a female nurse emerged from the room three doors distant. He jerked his head and shoulders rearward and clamped his lips tight. When no footsteps advanced his way, he sighed, squashing his held breath's audible exhale. With his fingers crossed that his IV disconnect had triggered no floor-station nurse alert and that no security video camera would monitor his movements, he quickstepped across the vacated corridor to edge along the left wall toward the floor's elevator. At his destination's halfway point, he adjusted his footfalls to the rhythm of evenly spaced bleeps emitted from a room's respiration monitor.

Circular bubbles of light flashed in a left-to-right semicircle above the closed double doors indicating an upward passenger journey. He tapped the arrow-pointed-down button and lifted his left hand to gently touch the bandage at the nape of his neck. He'd had no scarf to disguise what announced his status as a patient. Ready to lie profusely or admit defeat, he froze as the elevator doors opened. He gagged in response to the pungent bleach smell spewing at him from a car empty of people. This good fortune, he believed, portended his eventual success.

After a clunky bump signaled the end of a plunging three-floor express, Adolph exited the elevator flashing furtive glances in all directions. He raised his brown sport coat collar to partially hide the neck bandage and slid his plastic hospital ID bracelet high and tight against his forearm hair to be beneath his sport coat sleeve. Obscuring his facial features behind an upraised left arm as if checking his wristwatch, Adolph hurriedly shuffled past a pudgy white-bearded uniformed security guard seated behind the reception desk and distracted by a woman entering. Automatic rotating doors ushered Adolph out onto a sidewalk where a posted sign, with a diagonal arrow, directed pedestrians to the visitor parking lot that began at the end of a yellow-striped crosswalk. His right hand fished out his Monte Carlo key fob, but his end-of-the-car-aisle left and right glances found no ignition slot to insert his key into. Lengthening his strides, he retraced his path wary of any wandering security guard.

The cabbie at the hospital stand flashed inlaid gold teeth

and scurried to open his cab's rear door when Adolph
requested a Sixth Street Bar drop off. At the bar's street-side
curb, Adolph, awash in streaks of neon beer-sign yellow and
blue, feigned tying his shoe until the cab departed. Lifting his
torso, he kept his head bent toward the concrete, let the dark
storefront's drape his shoulders in shadows, and meandered
away, Ant's noise-emitting bar in his wake.

Angling into the street, Adolph stopped dead in his tracks.
"Crap," he shouted. Slow in realizing his shout could draw
unwanted attention, he pressed his parched lips together. An
unworthy son-of-a-bitch with jet-black spray paint had
scrawled the letters "PIG" across his Monte Carlo driver's
door. That the in-your-face insult didn't require a complete car
repainting, didn't suppress his bubbling anger that tightened
both facial and neck muscles. He winced in agony. Adolph's
deep oxygen inhale before a stab of his seatbelt's metal tongue
into its latch, and his exhale against the windshield after,
didn't repress his roiling anger. He fought off his swirling urge
to cruise city streets until he found assembled Dragons and
concentrated his resolve on obtaining Luann's unholy alliance
to defeat their forced partner assignment. For him, undoing
The Chief's order ranked notches higher than lying in a
hospital bed, doped on Vicodin after being cold-cocked.

The street where Luann lived captured the poetic
tranquility of a quintessential residential neighborhood with its
peacefulness highlighted by the idyllic quaintness of the half
moon above his head that he drove toward, but never reached.
He didn't see her car in the driveway. Had her detective room
chirping about having to park on the driveway because of her
son's newer car been merely a ploy to create sympathy? He
wouldn't put anything past her in her campaign to best him for
the one gold shield. He parked across the street, a diagonal
forty yards to her front door. He felt his forehead, no fever or
chill. He assumed his brain's lightheadedness would pass; the
in-hospital episodes had lasted but a few minutes each.

He slid his hips toward the foot well and scrunched his
chin's fresh stubble to his chest as car headlight beams

approached. He peeked. Appeared to be Luann. But while the Chrysler sedan stopped on the driveway, its headlights didn't dim. A figure dashed onto her porch and entered Luann's home. Adolph backed his Monte Carlo to, and around, the corner to camouflage his surveillance. His left forefinger pressed the armrest button to lower the front passenger window. He listened to the Chrysler's offbeat lumping idle, an oasis of sound. No other person's shadow or image showed as he strained to see if anyone lingered behind the car's window glass, and then, he heard a screen door bang. On the porch, a figure reappeared. He guessed Luann from the gait, but the ankle-length skirt passing through the headlight beams confused him.

He relaxed and compressed his torso, bowed his head, and waited. Adolph's ears heard car tires cross the intersection in front of him; his raised eyes observed a Chrysler's taillights turn right at the end of the block. He began pursuit, careful to keep a safe distance. While the absence of vehicles made tailing easier, it also ratcheted up the probabilities of his detection.

Adolph reweighed his guess of a river entertainment destination. He'd often over-thought clues. When the car bypassed normal business district street routes, he turned off his brain and trailed the Chrysler to a northwest residential area. After two uncharacteristic left turns, Adolph cursed. He slammed the steering wheel with his exposed right palm: the car had begun to circle a block. *Damn, he'd been made.* Adolph parallel parked to confuse his target and gather his thoughts. To continue his ruse, he circled his Monte Carlo's rear bumper and shrouded himself in the oak and maple tree shadows engulfing the sidewalk.

Adolph's bemoaned his luck; ready to dropkick his arrogance that he'd earn the gold shield in a rush without opposition. The bubble of expectation that he'd lost the Chrysler punctured when, moments later, Adolph, uncrossed his fingers and let out a sigh of relief. The Chrysler crossed the intersection to his left. He eased his Monte Carlo into the street, executed a one hundred and eighty degree turn, and straightened the wheel to resume his tail.

Six blocks later, the Chrysler slowed and parked behind a dark SUV. Adolph wheeled into a residential driveway, shifted into reverse, and executed a swift arc that ended when his rear tires jumped a street curb. He jockeyed off the curb to park beneath a silver maple whose leafed-out branches dulled the nearby streetlight's brilliance. Ahead and across the street, the skirted woman dashed from the Chrysler to a lighted screened porch. The brief flash of the sedan's interior dome light indicated a second car occupant and disproved Adolph's prior no passenger observation. When the skirted woman, whom he believed to be Luann, reached the porch, its light went out. Two minutes later, the car's second occupant, a male of impressive size, his face never turned to Adolph, strode to and across the house's darkened porch to enter where the woman had.

Adolph, cooling his heels, repeatedly inhaled, hardly exhaling for five minutes.

No other street or residential home activity diverted Adolph's attention from a deepening anxiety. After closing his car's graffiti-painted door so soft he failed to hear the latch click, he forced his street stride to half its normal speed to amble toward the Chrysler. His furtive glances to backlit shaded and blinded windows and into murky side yards detected neither human nor animal movement. When a bird chirped from an overhead branch, Adolph appreciated the shrill would unlikely bring a rush of humanity into the street. In front of his oxford toe, a black street number stenciled onto a white curb rectangle warned him he neared Lt. Turner's residence.

Adolph hadn't picked up any squad room banter of a gambling night for this evening. Bulldog hadn't lately invited him to play roulette or poker, but considering Adolph had, more than a year earlier, turned down his first six invitations made the lack of an current invitation unsurprising. The unfilled driveway and only one street parked pickup bespoke of no late night gambling extravaganza. Adolph didn't wish to waste a chit calling in a vehicle check. He considered a hospital return, but wasn't he already here and undetected? The question enough of a mental shove, coupled with a low grass-skimming light across the side lawn, to convince Adolph that a little friendly snooping into a basement window wouldn't hurt him or anyone.

Adolph returned to his Monte Carlo to fold his sport coat and drop it on the driver seat before he lowered the driver window. If a let-out neighborhood dog barked or attacked, he fantasized he'd be able to dive into his car duplicating the getaway of TV's Hazard County Duke Brothers. While Adolph at the moment didn't feel lightheaded, he braced for being exposed and readied the explanation he'd snuck out of the hospital for fresh air and, seeing a suspicious dark sedan filled with multiple heads cruising the hospital parking lot, he'd followed the suspect car, which zoomed into the night. Twice he'd lost the tail, but refused to give up until given the slip a third time. Calculating his lie sufficient to cover all bases, Adolph paused on the sidewalk to glance toward Bulldog's home.

Upon sensing it was now or never, he dashed for the home's corner foundation bushes and launched himself to land face down on the lawn. Lifting his head, he crawled military-style toward the basement casement window emitting light.

Fabric halves of the basement's inside window curtain left a two-inch center gap. *Damn.* He couldn't believe his eyes. Adolph thought he recognized the side-growth of a beard on the man sitting in a burnish-brown leather club chair. A video camera, perched atop spread tripod legs, visible to the man's right, seemed to be aimed at an empty platform raised three-to-four inches above the dark green linoleum-tiled floor. Two mounted high intensity floodlights, fifteen feet apart, faced each other and cast crisscrossing beams illuminating nothing but floating dust particles. A dark blue backdrop, nailed to a ceiling joist, hung with its billowy bottom piled at the rear of the improvised stage. In front of it, perpendicular to the man, an empty futon or twin bed with untucked frilly pale sheets, which Adolph guessed had once been hot pink.

A shadow from the right preceded a female in an Annie Oakley outfit—Rebecca.

She gazed toward the male and beyond. Adolph retracted his head should his peeping tom presence be discernable in the curtain's crack. When he summoned enough courage to resume viewing, Rebecca lay topless on the futon aside a second woman—Luann, fully clothed.

Adolph gasped. It had been Luann in a flowing laced-trimmed pioneer skirt.

What happened to the male? Adolph's question answered when the male, dressed in a black T-shirt and boxers, no pants, strutted into Adolph's view, holding a brown bottle. Adolph thought beer. Until the male plopped into the club chair, a pointed-brim black cowboy hat kept the male's eyes and nose in shadow, but not his trimmed dark facial hair.

If Luann had been undercover, he'd have been advised. No, can't be undercover. When the male rose, he extended his right arm to pull the camera closer to the bed and point the lens lower. Consenting adults? The incredulous and unbelievable scene more than Adolph wanted to know. Yet, his eyeballs remained glued to the drama playing out through an elongated two-inch portal. Again becoming lightheaded, he rubbed his strained eyes hard.

The women bumped shoulders in arising and vanished from his view.

Adolph heard the house's front door creak. He rolled onto his side and tucked his knees to his chest, hoping the foundation juniper hid both oxfords. Pressed together, his lips sealed all air in and his abdomen muscles tightened his lower abs to his spine. The door finally slammed. He flattened his chest and thighs to the grass to resume his peeping tom act. Rebecca and Luann filed back into view and each carried a colorful, full-face mask. Trailing them was a masked, breasts exposed, third woman. Blond hair wig curls surrounded the three faces; individual features obscured by each woman's

Adolph's Gold

feathery Mardi Gras mask.

After Rebecca led the semi-nude woman to stand at the far edge of the bed, she returned to Luann's side. The third female stretched her mask free to adjust the rubber-band-ear loops. The dropped-mask opportunity sufficient for Adolph to recognize the mother whose son he'd saved from the river. His mind refused to grasp the totality of what continued to unfold. He assumed he wasn't dreaming. He couldn't discount a hallucination induced by an IV infused Vicodin meant to stop his head throbs? His left hand's rub across the damp grass he laid on proved he'd left the hospital bed.

Yvonne Whitenmire, who stood behind the bed, mask in place, and naked above her faded blue jeans, appeared to shiver, but Adolph expected the lights to be warm, not cold. In front of the bed, Rebecca, fully dressed in her Annie Oakley server outfit, extended splayed fingers to first lightly stroke Luann's clothed chest, and then, in turn, Luann's outer and inner thighs. The male's raised hands clapped and Rebecca began a methodical blouse-to-bra and pants-to-panties disrobing that left a masked Luann wearing no stitch of clothing except her nude-colored nylon shoe liners.

Rebecca's painstakingly slow disrobing of Luann and Yvonne's swaying breasts aroused Adolph's maleness. Transfixed into a high state of sexual tension, Adolph's rigid body didn't soften when Luann wiggled her naked buttocks on the futon as Rebecca caressed Luann's now exposed breasts before splitting Luann's knees to expose a junction's delicate treat. The basement male arose from the club chair, removed his T-shirt, and, when he turned his head, Adolph could now positively identify Abraham Lincoln maneuver an upright Rebecca to face Luann. Mr. Lincoln bent Rebecca forward and flipped the fringed skirt she wore toward her shoulders to reveal that no panties of any description protected her feminine modesty. Adolph could only image the full extent of what happened next as the Lincoln impersonator's sidestep and shimmy slid his boxers to the floor and his muscular hips pulsated and swayed behind Rebecca.

91

Donan Berg

After an agonizing time lapse, including a minute when Adolph averted his gaze from the basement, Adolph grappled with what action he should take. Before Adolph could decide, the Lincoln look-a-like stepped backward and, with his right hand, shifted the tripod forward to aim the camera lens in a lowered forty-five degree angle to his pubic area. Mr. Lincoln's wiggling buttocks again completely hid Rebecca's hips.

Adolph eyeballs strained to see Luann, but Mr. Lincoln blocked Luann completely and Yvonne was only visible from the waist up. When he realized he couldn't see Yvonne's hands, he shut his mind to all imagination of what body manipulation either she or Luann attempted. Finally, seeing Yvonne elevate her arms to lift and cup her breasts, Adolph gazed at her sway gently until, obviously spurred by Mr. Lincoln's disengagement from Rebecca, she froze in place. When, without turning, Mr. Lincoln jackknifed his glistening torso into the club chair, Rebecca straightened up and pointed at Yvonne. With hesitant steps, Yvonne advanced to stand in front of the seated Mr. Lincoln. Adolph could see her swaying had been replaced by stronger shivers as Mr. Lincoln's right hand stroked her conical left breast. She lowered her torso, lifted her frozen-in-time mask, and with parted red lips, dropped out of Adolph's view.

Rebecca stripped off her frilled brown cowboy skirt and white top embroidered with blue and brown swirls before she tilted the camera lens at the futon and a reclining Luann. Adolph glanced away from the two women and contemplated a move to the basement window on the far opposite side. His conscience immobilized all of his leg muscles, a strong omen to say he wasn't a pervert. He'd seen enough. But, whom could he tell? His first realization closed all options—nobody would believe him.

His digital watch displayed two a.m. as he scampered to his Monte Carlo, now joined at the curb by a Salvadore Pizza van. He couldn't be positive that this recently washed van had cruised near, and behind, the Sixth Street Bar. Adolph jotted

92

down the van's plate number. Harboring the hope he hadn't been reported missing, he hustled to return to his hospital room.

* * *

A perky nurse entered at five to wake him. She didn't ask why he laid across the bed's top sheet dressed in street clothes, and he didn't volunteer anything but his arm to have the IV reconnected. When a doctor visited two hours later, Adolph, his hair damp from a permitted shower ten minutes previous, sat freshly shaved in the room's speckled-red molded-plastic visitor chair. Given his discharge paper, he strolled to the only yellow Monte Carlo waiting in the hospital parking lot. After a cell phone call to alert Mary of his release and a trip home for clean clothes, he nibbled on peppered scrambled eggs and buttered toast at his kitchen table. He dreaded reporting for duty with new partner Luann, expecting it to be jarring and uncomfortable. He hoped she'd had as much sleep as he.

Chapter Five

Adolph lifted his droopy eyelids and elevated his retina focus. To him, Luann, entering the squad room this morning in her everyday pantsuit, appeared bustier than what he remembered from seven hours ago, but then, on the basement futon, the naked mounds were far more distant, horizontal, and fighting gravity without wired support.

Luann's heels clicked louder the nearer she got. "Was hoping . . ." She froze in place. "Er . . . What I mean is . . . Word was you'd be in the hospital a couple of days."

"Convinced the doc that work needed me, and besides, The Chief says you've been assigned to baby-sit me."

"I'd say not." Her full eyebrows squeezed closer together.

Across the paired desks, Adolph's gaze, now level with a seated Luann, delved deep into her hazel eyes. He didn't search for lingering contempt, merely confirmation she fought a sleep deprivation that he himself felt in his bones. Outwardly, beneath her mascara-laden eyelashes and applied heavy blue eyeliner and above the feathered foundation with its rouge highlight, he glimpsed no lurking haggardness. She must've taken an afternoon nap yesterday. Yes, that would explain it. Maybe not? In the last five years, his Mary had replaced store-bought bottled cosmetic applications with a hot, soapy washcloth swipe. He'd come to appreciate the fresh natural look.

"We need to recon the Sixth Street Bar alley," he said. "You drive."

"Why? Patrol did the crime scene." She reached into her in-basket for a file jacket.

"Is that it?"

"No. Was planning to close out an accidental shooting—"

"Let's go." Adolph bolted upright. He glanced at Lt. Turner's empty office, soothed that he need not delay or seek approval for his search to uncover the tiniest clue that would lead him to the coward who'd whacked him. "You drive."

He heard Luann's heel clomps behind him and held the station's employee entrance/exit door open. He missed the warmth of sunshine. While buckling the passenger's seatbelt, he asked, "Have you seen Rebecca lately?"

"Don't recall." Luann, staring straight ahead, keyed her Chrysler's ignition and shifted into reverse, and then, when clear of the adjacent parked vehicles, jerked it's gearshift into drive.

"Stopped by Patsy's yesterday. That place would go to hell without her."

"Guess so. Really don't know . . ." Luann, while cruising through several intersections, avoided all eye contact with Adolph. "I'll stop here at the end of the alley."

"Great idea." Adolph strode into the alley, toward the

Sixth Street Bar's rear entrance. He didn't know exactly what he should be looking for—lead pipe with his type-O blood? No. His neck/head wound hadn't bled, merely throbbed like hell. The passage of eighteen hours, including heavily trafficked dark night alley hours, didn't help his cause.

Luann, behind him, tapped his right shoulder. "Anything?"

"Nothing jumps out." He didn't face her. "Except I remember a pizza truck."

"That's not unusual. Pizza deliverers crisscross city streets every night."

Adolph pivoted toward her. "Not pizza home delivery, a van."

She shrugged. "Vans, trucks. They come and go from Bridgetown every week."

"You're right." Adolph, convinced Ant would be inside, skirted the Cadillac's fender and pounded his right fist twice on the Sixth Street Bar's back door. The window curtains parted.

"Pretty company." Ant's burly right arm retarded the door's piston closer.

"She'll click the cuffs while I sit on your head."

"Whoa." Adolph's hand on the door replaced Ant's arm.

"He's kidding," Luann interjected, slowing Ant's subtle backpedal.

Adolph's step to the side allowed Luann to trail Ant into the poker room. Without a word, Ant slumped into a high-backed leather chair already pulled away from the room's table. Small, uneven chip piles indicated to Adolph that three persons had skidaddled.

"Simple recreation you have here," Luann said. Her fingers clicked two green chips.

"Guy's work earns some fun, don't you think?" Ant's extended arms swept the center table pot towards his chest. He left the striped chips unstacked.

Adolph, still standing, ran his left hand across the cardboard boxes stacked against the wall. He'd never really examined them. Merely recognized the expensive, advertised liquor names that never graced his home. Ant stared at him. When Adolph compressed a box's top edge parallel to and six inches above his waist, the box above it didn't move. He slid two fingers into the gap he'd created between the boxes. The depth didn't exceed three inches. Yanking his left hand downward and toward his stomach, the cardboard ripped in a jagged line with the box side hanging loose from the wall and exposing a brass doorknob.

"Gracious, Hogwarts," Adolph exclaimed. "Pray tell, what do we have here?"

Ant scrambled to his feet and sputtered, "Broom . . . broom closet."

Luann, dragging her right hand atop chair backs, circled the table to face Ant's back.

Ignoring Ant's glare, Adolph rotated the brass doorknob. "Must be expensive brooms, right?" He easily pulled the unlocked door outward, not expecting Ant to answer or physically intercede. With jagged edges left behind, the interlaced box fronts separated to allow the door a full extension. Adolph repressed a smile. One brown-handled broom, its synthetic bristles six inches from touching the floor, hung from a bracket screwed to the door's interior side.

Ant threw back his shoulders. "You satisfied?"

"C'mon," Luann said. "Guess we're supposed to believe some artsy janitor built this illusionary box wall to hide a gold-plated mop bucket?"

Adolph wondered where Luann came up with that. Sarcastic, wonderfully sarcastic. The tone fit her to a T. Four paces in, he pulled a light cord to illuminate his environs and executed an about-face. Adolph tightened his lips into a coy smile, casting a momentary gaze at Ant standing between the doorjambs. "A broom closet? Right-o, 'tis that, but, oh, oh, so much more." On the shelves to Adolph's right rested three computer CPU towers and two flat-screen monitors.

"Whatcha see?" Luann asked. She elbowed Ant aside, entered the closet, and reached out her two bare hands to lift one computer tower off the middle shelf.

"Hold on. Don't do that," Adolph admonished. "St. Mary's is missing three computers. These might be them."

"Sorry." She thrust the computer forward, sliding it back onto a dustless shelf.

"I'll stay here. You call this in."

Luann departed and Adolph heard the outside bar door close. He stepped from the closet to find Ant slouched in a poker table chair next to his previously corralled poker chips.

"You gotta believe me," Ant began. "Didn't have one blasted thing to do with putting them computers in there."

"How'd you know those computers were there?" Adolph marveled at the ingenious idea and the craftsmanship that had disguised the door. "You couldn't have seen them just now."

"Heard you mumble about the college missing computers. Just figured, that's all."

Standing, Adolph thought about sitting for he didn't fear an attack from Ant, but he didn't know who else lingered nearby. To protect his blindside, he squared his shoulder blades to the closet door. *Where's Luann?* It shouldn't take ten minutes to radio in for technicians.

Adolph's voice broke through the stilted silence. "Who has access to this closet?"

Ant stared at him. "You mean besides me?"

"Don't be a jackass. Yes, besides you."

Ant's multiple glances all but twirled his head before he fixed his gaze on Adolph. "You've been square with me and I'll not be a fall guy for anyone. You need to do me a favor?"

"What kinda favor?" Adolph feared Ant would grease a slippery slope.

Ant lowered his voice. "I'm on the scaffold no matter what."

"Come again. I'm not following." Adolph's neck throbbed. He shrugged and straightened his shoulders without obtaining any measurable relief. "You fear going to hell?"

"Fear hell?" Ant's chest caved in like a bellows expelling air. "No way. Soldiers don't go to hell." His distended neck veins shrunk as his normal volume returned. "There's a folder, pictures, will blow the lid off this town. You take it. They'll kill me."

"Who's they?"

Ant's gaze flitted to the door. "Bigshots." His right eyelid twitched. "Don't ask."

"Don't know." Adolph sighed. He reckoned Ant's fear could be real, or not. Whether a bluff or not, Adolph climbed onto a high, narrow ledge either way. He'd be obstructing justice if he went along with knowledge of a crime and didn't turn Ant in. But, if Ant copped to a stolen property possession charge, within months he'd be swaggering on the streets and he, or his boss, possibly gunning for him, gold shield or not. Yet, if these unnamed bigshots made Ant as jittery as he appeared, then Ant wasn't shaking in his boots about jail time.

"C'mon, your partner's back any moment. Ain't friendship worth something?"

"Tell you what. Until I can check it out, I'll protect this so-called folder. Let me put on vinyl gloves. Don't need my handling to smear existing prints, you know."

Ant's left hand reached under the poker table, reappeared with a clear plastic bag, and dumped a dozen boxed card decks out of it onto the table. "I'll use this." Ant rose, waved Adolph aside, and barged into the closet. Adolph pivoted to watch. From a wall safe behind two cardboard boxes on a shelf opposite the computers, Ant extracted a dark brown nine-by-twelve inch folder and slid it into the former card bag. Ant thrust it forward. "Here."

Adolph, puzzled by what to do with the bag, finally untucked his dress-shirt front, sucked in his stomach, and shoved the encased folder three inches below his trouser belt. This strategy, he recognized immediately, didn't hide anything. He laid his blue blazer on the poker table felt, unfastened his belt, and snuggled the bag between his shirt and T-shirt at the small of his back before tucking his shirttail in and cinching his belt one hole past comfortable. Ramrod straight, he donned his blazer, daring not to bend too far in any direction as Ant squeezed past to his seat.

He buttoned his blazer a second before Luann stepped inside the poker room. "CS techs promise ETA in ten." When she ratcheted her gaze to the exit door, Ant winked at Adolph.

Adolph tapped Luann on her right shoulder. "Check to see who's in the bar?"

She exerted no effort to move. "Why?" Her one word sliced through the air.

"I would, but then we'd both have to testify about watching Ant. Simpler if you do it."

Exaggerating a slight sashay exit with a flourish, she said, "Won't be long."

Adolph glared at Ant. "You'd better keep your trap shut." He stretched his right arm backward to confirm his blazer hung straight from his shoulder. "That's all I'll say."

Ant's lips stretched into a smirk. "When have you known me to gab?"

After hearing a boisterous exterior door knock, Adolph admitted two crime scene technicians and explained his computer hunch. When Luann returned to report she'd struck out with the bar patron interviews, Adolph requested Ant to stand facing the wall before informing him he was under arrest. He motioned for Luann to handcuff Ant.

Letting the technicians work inside, Adolph poked at detritus with a stick he'd found propped against a wall and scanned the length of the alley in the lingering hope he'd find a previously missed assault clue. When Adolph saw a technician emerge into the alley, he retraced his three paces to be informed that two of the computer serials linked them to St. Mary's. In answer to Adolph's questions, the technician explained he'd etch the filed off third serial number's metal plate with acid at the lab to try to recreate and decipher the manufacturer's original letters and/or numbers.

With Ant safely ensconced in the backseat of a summoned squad car, Adolph stiffly climbed into Luann's car.

"You feeling all right?" she asked. Her glance struck Adolph as unsympathetic.

"Muscles tightened. That's all. Could you drop me off at home? I'll give you a call later."

Her fingers twisted the ignition key. "What about your car at the station?"

He formed his words with a snarl. "That's why I'll give you a call later." If Luann didn't respect his simple requests, that piled another reason on to the stack of why she didn't deserve to be his partner. Plus, he wasn't a pervert or a pimp. "Tell The Chief, if he asks, which I doubt he will, you dropped me off for lunch."

He figured it probably appeared doubly strange to Luann for him to pull out his cell phone with his garage's exterior keypad so close after walking backward up his home driveway. However, he didn't dare trust his blue blazer to hide the folder outline. The tension in his jaw muscles dissolved into a sigh of relief when Luann gunned her engine around the intersection corner. To prevent giving Mary a panic attack, he left a message on his home phone, counted to ten, and punched in the forever unchanged four number garage-door-opening code.

"Mary," he shouted. "I'm home." Hearing her acknowledgment from the living room, he detoured from his usual kitchen entrance and bounded down the basement stairs. At the bottom, he glanced left and right. Where could he put it? The sparse basement furnishings lined against gray concrete block walls provided few options. Under the sagging sofa cushions would be too commonplace and risky. Removing the folder from his belt, he squashed a budding urge to peek. An old dresser, with missing drawer knobs and relegated to storing sentimental items no longer useful, had been crammed under the stairs. Unable to budge a knob-less middle drawer, he yanked at the bottom drawer until it creaked and slid ten inches toward him. This would have to do. He slid the folder, still in Ant's plastic bag, under a Space Bag containing compressed pink infant blankets that should've been donated to Goodwill or a church clothing appeal years ago.

Adolph's Gold

Slipping off his blazer on the trip upstairs, he completed his arrival-home closet routine and entered the kitchen. Mary stood at the sink. His affectionate kiss landed on her turned cheek.

"This is an unexpected surprise. You okay?"

"Little stiff, that's all." He noticed two frozen TV dinners on the counter. "I'm going to lie down for thirty minutes. Luann will be back to pick me up."

"Don't you want to eat?"

He fought off capitulating to her dismayed expression. "Not hungry. You'll have to excuse me." In the bedroom, Adolph kicked off his shoes, lay supine on the comforter, and lowered both eyelids. When his cell phone on the nightstand rang, he didn't immediately realize how long he'd slept but recognized the crime lab number. He listened to buddy Len's question.

"Did Luann touch the Sixth Street Bar computers?"

Adolph hesitated, perplexed. He hadn't communicated a rush priority. "One."

"Then I need to talk to you at the lab."

"Will take an hour; must call Luann first." Dead air engulfed Adolph's expected confirmation and he struggled to explain. "We split for lunch, and I've no car."

Len's words mimicked a command cadence. "You best come alone." And his disconnect prevented Adolph from seeking clarification.

His bent right knee, lowered to the sidewalk concrete in front of his home, permitted Adolph's hands to tie a loose shoelace. While he awaited Luann's pick up, he failed to concoct a satisfying ruse to ditch Luann and justify a solo one block walk from the station to the crime lab. After he'd latched his seatbelt and before his short snort acknowledged Luann's comment he moved better, he quickly volunteered that he required the squad room computer to run the Rose Garden B&B guest background checks. Sorta true. She made his day by replying she didn't think The Chief required they both roost at the station. And, for the second glorious time that day, Adolph's brain registered the sight of her Chrysler taillights vanishing around a distant corner.

With two aspirins dissolving in his stomach, Adolph stood next to a white-coated Len, the pair of them an atoll in the center of horizontal lab office space cluttered by brown evidence bags, fabric scraps, and reports. Adolph's left hand steadied a leaning book stack that resembled a famous tower in Pisa, Italy. "What's the big secrecy about those computers recovered today?"

"A simple fingerprint twirling discovered Luann's prints on two towers. Needed to confirm that you said she touched one, not two."

"She picked one up by the sides. Until you called, thought it amounted to a common mistake of not putting on gloves first. Has happened to me. But then I was a rookie."

Len raked his separated left hand fingers through his short blond hair and then, before reaching forward to grab a sheet of paper atop a manila folder, rubbed his fingers and palm twice on his left thigh. "Let me show you this sketch." Adolph gazed at three rectangular boxes with red Xs on two and listened to Len explain. "Each X marks where I found Luann's fingerprints."

Adolph lifted his left hand and the books didn't fall. "Six or seven. That's a lot."

"That's what I thought." Len set the paper on the desk corner. "Eight, actually."

"What about the filed serial? That one from St. Mary's?"

"Maybe, but experience tells me to doubt it. Same manufacturer, different model."

Adolph recorded this latest development in his notepad. Then he had to ask: "What can you tell me about the data on the hard drives?"

"The two identified with St. Mary's had been erased. The third had deletions mixed with stored document writings. Most common file-saved name turned out to be Carlson."

"I've a good idea where that computer came from." Len's eyebrows rose. "Unreported theft I stumbled upon. Will send you details." Len nodded. "What about resurrecting that deleted hard drive information?"

"Professional job. Both hard drives are tell-no-tales clean slates."

"Try anyway. You guys are wizards at all this Star Wars CSI stuff."

Adolph excused himself after Len promised to delay for a few days his report of finding Luann's fingerprints on the stolen computers. Ambling along a city sidewalk toward the station, Adolph tried unsuccessfully to connect the dots of Luann, Rebecca, Mr. Lincoln, and the Whitenmire woman in Bulldog's basement taping sex videos with the stolen Carlson and St. Mary's computers stored in Ant's closet. While Adolph wouldn't discount that Bulldog and Luann were possibly on the take, he dared not be perceived as a departmental rat, even if he forfeited his well-deserved gold shield. Did Dragons and drugs interlace the pervert circle? He couldn't trust anyone. So what else was new?

He passed the now empty parking lot spot Luann used. Five steps before he reached the rear entry door, his bellowed name stopped Adolph dead in his tracks.

"Adolph, what in the hell's going on?" Chief Howard called out.

Adolph's eyes hadn't separated The Chief's bulk from the cloak of the building's shadows. "Been at the lab. Decided walking met the doctor's goal of light exercise."

"Where's Luann?" The brass buttons on The Chief's ceremonial dress uniform sparkled when he stepped into the sunlight.

"Left to close one of her cases. I untied the apron strings."

"Don't push. I was serious when I paired you two. Don't ever forget that."

Adolph gulped. Be it the tightness of his neck veins occasioned by the worse-than-Satan snarl of The Chief or the healing grip of Heaven, Adolph, without hesitation, bit his tongue so as not to further rile his superior. A plaintive "Yes, sir." dropped from Adolph's lips.

"Good. I'm scheduled for a community panel at the Elks." The Chief strode away.

Adolph sneezed, shrugging off the fear of a late fall frost. Inside, he plopped into his desk chair, his cranium dome full of exhausting reverberations. He exhaled, revitalized by a lessened anxiety when he spotted no new case files on his desk. When Lt. Turner uttered a nondescript hello in passing, Adolph grunted without lifting his gaze from the Rose Garden B&B file. The forensics section reported scant information except to identify the skeleton as male. A footnote described the winter's historical freeze-and-thaw cycles. Adolph deduced the inclusion indicated the victim had been buried before last winter. His brain ached. Trying to conjure up how to proceed confounded him to a greater extent than connecting existing knowledge. He'd never dismissed the conundrum that verified facts solved cases, but that justice challenged him to acquire an artful understanding of subjective human nature to decipher the truth.

A state trooper e-mail confirmed one Harvey Hoskins had been located, through a car purchase, living in a New Jersey south shore beach community. Adolph replied with thanks and printed a copy of the message for the skeleton case folder. Unless pressed, he'd not volunteer Harvey's location to Francine. Adolph hated domestic cases with a passion for he found it difficult to determine who'd been wronged. In his experience, probably both equally guilty, and he reckoned the enmity evoked by divorce rituals choked compassionate marital reconciliation.

Luann's voice broke into what little concentration Adolph's brain mustered.

"Add another case to the closed stats." Her stuck desk chair roller scraped the floor.

He gazed directly at her. "Rub it in." There was no jest in his words.

"Maybe that's why The Chief chose me to lead you around town. You might learn something." Her smirk rose and fell, leaving a painful imprint on Adolph's psyche.

"Yeah, sure. Be careful. Fanciful boasts can sneak up and bite you in the butt."

"If you want to stay here, I'm taking comp time. My daughter's starring in a school play tonight and I've got two front row tickets for me and my son."

Adolph briefly averted his gaze. "Acting must run in the family."

"My mother had early television extra roles. You know, like the lady walking the dog on 'Father Knows Best.'" Luann crammed a folder into her black shoulder bag.

"You amaze me every day." *Boy, Luann's nonchalance terrific.* No hint in her mien to confirm she grasped the dark undercurrent of his comment. "Well, break a leg."

"That's for the actor." Luann shook her head. "Not for the proud parent watching."

"If you say so." Adolph held back on informing Luann The Chief roamed the streets. "I'll meet up with you here tomorrow morning, regular time."

"Chow." Luann flashed a thumbs-up to an entering Lt. Hunter crossing to his office.

Bored with the skeleton file after a fruitless fourth rereading. Adolph decided he could use a fresh cup of coffee. Convinced the detective's pot in late afternoon would resemble Texas crude, he hoped walking plus coffee would invigorate his brain.

On the way to Patsy's, Adolph encountered a fellow Lutheran churchgoer. To divert the conversation from Adolph's recent lack of attendance, Adolph promised he'd be there Sunday.

Swinging open Patsy's front door, Adolph shouted at the top of his lungs: "Put that knife down." His adrenaline spiked. In Randall Quimby's right palm a straight blade butcher knife threatened Rebecca's throat. Adolph's left hand fingers unbuttoned his blazer. He doubted Randall would drop the knife with his one shout and Adolph possessed no Superman ability to reach Rebecca before the knife plunged into her soft skin, or sliced through her jugular.

With his Police Academy training kicked in, Adolph's scan noted four cafe patrons, one man and three women, braced against the wall in the room's far corner. Horrified expressions, all reflecting fear's advancing rigor mortis, outnumbered a feminine blank stare three to one.

Adolph weighed his options. If the knife was Randall's only weapon, controlling logic meant it presented little present danger to the cowering patrons. Not so Rebecca. A blade slash across her jugular would drench her in blood, more so than the drips pooling in the crook of her right arm from the higher inch-long laceration on her shoulder.

"Hold on now, Randall." Adolph's desire for fresh coffee had vanished. He spoke evenly while gazing into Randall's glazed eyes. "You don't want to make this worse."

"Back off . . . or . . . or I'll kill the bitch right now."

Adolph had to stall, think of the broad picture. "Hold on. Let me close the door." When he turned, his left forearm and elbow pressed his blue blazer to his side to keep his holster leather concealed. "There's innocent people here. Let's do what's right." Had Adolph tripped up? What was "right" in a twisted mind? Had he encouraged Randall to harm Rebecca with his own ill-chosen words? Randall's fingers on the handle twitched. *Think, Adolph, think.*

Sobs from a woman hostage alerted Adolph his focus had deserted them. "Let these people leave." He watched Randall glance at them without a change in either his expression or a lowering of the knife pressing Rebecca's throat. "They aren't part of your turmoil and you certainly don't want them to spread gossip, now do you?" Adolph, not knowing what to do with his hands, let both dangle at his sides, his right hand fingers curling, and then stretching.

Randall's eyes, unmitigated by his tight lips, flashed hateful glances in uneven pulses. Adolph had only witnessed a similar rage one previous time. A lanky seventeen-year-old, with three hogtied hostages in a barn, fired warning shots at the sheriff's posse interrupting his planned revenge against three classmates who'd gang raped his girlfriend. Adolph, in a perspiration-soaked rookie uniform, shivered throughout the entire nightlong confrontation. His memory's prickly horror remnants began to resurface. Today had to be different. Adolph wouldn't repeat the sheriff's hoarse-voiced command. The sheriff's words, amplified by a bullhorn when the youth slid the barn door open at sunrise, echoed deep in the chambers of Adolph's memory. Before a ring of police and restrained curious neighbors, the sheriff shouted that the youth was gutless, didn't have the balls to pull any trigger. The Remington rifle in the youth's hands swirled with his pivot. Adolph's knees, upon hearing the rifle's magazine empty, had locked his torso upright while his chest quaked. He'd never forget counting the lined up ambulances. Three shot hostages, transported one by one, reached the hospital where one with his chest wound blood dripping from pressed bandages survived long enough to be admitted. The two other youths were pronounced DOA. In a last act, the youthful avenger dropped his bullet-less rifle, yanked a .22 pistol from his belt and fired. The last ambulance shuttled the seventeen-year-old straight to the morgue. He'd eaten his gun.

"Whatcha say, Randall." Adolph felt his knees stiffen. His gaze couldn't decipher whether or not Randall would be a coward or an avenger. "Let your customers go. If they owe you any money, I'm good for it. They're expected home. Let's not—" He abruptly shut up when Randall flicked his head in what Adolph interpreted as a yes. "That's good, very good. You're a good man." Adolph gazed at the spellbound customers. He needed to keep talking before Randall changed his mind. "What I suggest isn't a trick. I'll walk halfway to them, and then, one at a time, they'll step behind me, taking a straight line to and out the door."

Adolph waited while his knees relaxed and again stiffened as an uneasy silence ruled.

Randall's eyes glared at him.

What could Adolph say and do? "I'll put my hands up and you can watch me slowly step toward Bernice." He lifted his right sole, put it down six inches forward. Randall, stiff as a wooden cigar store Indian, watched Adolph repeat the initial baby step. "Good." With his head still, Adolph met Bernice's petrified gaze. "Bernice, easy short steps . . . that's great . . . now walk behind me." Adolph, his eyes glued to Rebecca's twitching torso and her reddening eyes, angled sideways to allow Bernice a path to the front door unobstructed by a table. "That's good, Randall. We all know you didn't wish to harm Bernice. Bet she's your best customer. She'll remember your kindness and be back soon to patronize Patsy's."

Adolph consciously steadied his voice, trying not to shrill its inflection. He heard Bernice rotate the front door's doorknob and, with his babble and polite inane conversation, fought to keep Randall's focus off the butcher knife and on him. He'd rescued one. The three remaining hostages nervously eyed each other, each leaning toward the door. Adolph, anticipating their desire to scamper, foreclosed their mad dash with a slight shake of his head and pointed his right index finger at the middle-aged woman in a print dress to be the next to go. She abided by Adolph's subtle cupped hand finger waves to start towards him.

Shudders by the two hostages remaining erupted when, a time or two, Randall brandished the knife's hilt above Rebecca's head and jabbed its tip at them. Adolph squared his shoulders and feared the worse when Randall again touched the honed blade to his wife's throat. The second-to-last hostage's hip bumped a table and Adolph imprisoned a breath behind his compressed lips. Glancing to observe the third patron's foot cross the front door threshold, Adolph saw Chief Howard and Lt. Hunter standing outside with three uniformed officers outfitted in helmets, shotguns, and bulletproof vests. Inwardly terrorized that Randall had seen what Adolph had, Adolph snapped his face toward Randall.

"You're doing the right thing, Randall," Adolph sputtered. The last hostage's head-down dash to safety ended with the entrance door's slam painfully chilling the nape of Adolph's neck with a rush of damp air. "You've showed what I've always known, Randall." He hoped repeating Randall's name created the de-escalating empathy he was trained to believe it did. "Everyone knows, Randall, you're a decent man."

"Don't come closer." Randall threw back his shoulders; his left hand clutching Rebecca tighter to his chest. "Now it's time for you to leave. This is between Rebecca and me."

Adolph witnessed teeny tears trickle from Rebecca's reddened eyes. Had Rebecca slipped up for Randall to discover her extra-curricular nighttime activities? Adolph didn't wish to moralize, but proving infidelity in modern times didn't require the medieval practice of squeezing a red-hot poker yanked from a blazing fire.

"Randall, you must understand, I can't leave without Rebecca." His voice commanded the silence. "She needs medical attention."

Adolph heard the door latch jiggle behind him. *What the hell!* With his right hand raised under his blazer, with only Rebecca left to save, he abandoned the prior necessary caution to now grasp his Walther's molded grip. He whipped a glance past his right shoulder. *Luann!*

"Get that whore out of here," Randall screamed. The heightened agitation in Randall's voice punched Adolph square in his face. Randall brandished his knife. "I'll kill her, too."

Adolph's vigorous panicky exhale capsized his chest. How'd Luann get past The Chief? The last thing Adolph needed was for Luann's stupid hero grandstanding to risk Rebecca's life—or his. Before Adolph's gaze swiveled to Randall to devise a desperate rush route or to execute a dive and roll to pop up firing, Patsy's front door closed with Luann on the outside.

Randall, Adolph gauged, had shuffled backward a step or two, dragging Rebecca with him. Worried that Randall's retreat put him closer to a firearm stashed beneath the restaurant's counter, Adolph's hand squeezed his Walther P38. His thumb pulsed rapid heartbeats onto its grip. Since he'd exploited his experience-honed survival instincts and followed the book to save others first, he prayed for Fate's personal saving grace. Until Luann's interruption, his prattle had eased the tension of an emotionally-charged confrontation. Did she want Rebecca dead? What about The Chief? Adolph could've expected command laxity by Lt. Hunter, but The Chief? How much explosive fuel had the prior night's activities doused on today's event?

Adolph cast aside his psychological musings to reassess the restaurant's layout. As a former bar with high street-side casement windows, no outside sniper would have a shot at Randall. With booths and tables empty and the safety of the patrons achieved, his mind succumbed to the pulsating throb of his engorged neck veins. By force of will, Adolph shrugged off the pain, kept his 9mm holstered, and raised his palms in obvious surrender while his right foot hooked a chair closer. He sat down, his eyes remaining locked in on Randall.

"Let's take a breather, Randall." Adolph raised his left leg to rest its ankle on his right knee. "If you didn't know, there's a posse milling around outside. There's no escape." Randall's brows narrowed and his eyes became darker. "You've been a friend." Adolph couldn't think of specifics. "We can forget this. Remember the good days. We can make this a good day too."

"Bullshit." Randall jerked Rebecca behind the restaurant's waist-high counter.

Adolph repressed his urge to jump up. When Randall repositioned his grasp on Rebecca, his finger shift highlighted the black and blue depressed skin marks on her left wrist. "Why hurt Rebecca?" Adolph sensed he needed to unearth Randall's motivation, and there wasn't time to beat around the bush. "What about Bradford? A son, wow, that's every man's dream."

"That's yesterday's damn history. She's played me for a fool. A fool to believe she wore that Annie Oakley costume to bring business in. She only shook those leather frills to satisfy a woman's lowest goddamn desire, to tease every male past puberty."

"Never saw that." *Well, not in Patsy's.* "And, you know, I've stopped in often."

"Expect you to lie." Randall's sweeping left arm motion scattered half-a-dozen condiment bottles off the counter. Adolph listened to them bounce willy-nilly on the floor.

"What's the word you used, Randall?" Adolph asked. "Yeah, bullshit. I'm not sitting here because I'm tired. I'm sincerely concerned about your future . . . and Rebecca's . . . and the legacy you'll leave for Bradford. He's important, now isn't he?" Randall stayed silent. "Neither of us wants to do anything stupid, right? There's a whole lot to live for. Think about it."

Randall slanted the knife to his own jugular. "I've nothing to live for."

"Bullshit," Adolph called out, immediately clamping his right hand to his mouth to quell a further emotional outburst. "I swear, Randall, you'll burn that word into my mind. Whatever you might think Rebecca did, it's not permanent. People change. Love forgives mistakes, and Rebecca loves you. Didn't she give up a fortune?" Adolph didn't wish to elaborate that Rebecca had hocked his engagement diamond. "Yes, a fortune to offer your son a second chance, a new life opportunity? She didn't have to do that. She could've spent the money on spa treatments or slid coins into one-armed bandits, but she didn't." Adolph caught himself. He didn't want to pontificate too much lest he dilute his main point. "You can't twist that."

"Well, maybe."

Rebecca's shoulders had slumped and Adolph failed to catch her eyelids blinking.

Adolph stood, shaking the prickling sensation from his left leg. "Let's end this and save me a caffeine headache. May not be important in the long term, but I just came in for a cup of coffee." He kept his left arm pinned to his side and extended his right hand waist high, palm up. "Give me the knife." *What are you doing, Adolph?* Cool it, sit down. His thoughts whirled. Impulse blurred the outlines of calculated risk. How'd Randall react? Be emboldened? What did Adolph want to happen? Adolph inhaled to calm his inner and outer voice. "You really don't want to harm Rebecca. She'll cherish your love and keep Patsy's prosperous until you can get everything straightened out. What'll you say? Let's both protect your future."

"Don't know." Randall, without exposing his knife-wielding arm, shuffled Rebecca and himself to the counter's open end.

"Look at Rebecca." Adolph's horizontal right hand trembled, even with his right elbow pressing his side. Yet, he dared not retract it. "I'll bet she'll not press charges." Rebecca's head bobbed twice. He couldn't have choreographed her actions any better. "Don't throw away Rebecca's love, and she with a love that'll always be there." Adolph alternated his legs, left then right. Each completed rock forward onto the balls of his feet narrowed the distance between himself and Randall. Adolph tried to refocus his mind, dimming the images gleaned from peeking at Rebecca's naked flesh under klieg lights. Procedure told him to unholster his revolver. Instinct told him to continue to offer his right hand as a non-aggression signal. He heard—and Randall had to as well—the raised voices, jogging footfalls, and metal clicks occurring outside the cafe's entrance. He stared deep into Randall's eyes. "Slide that knife, hilt first, down the counter. Let it hurl itself off the end." What more encouragement could Adolph offer? "We can shake on our friendship."

Randall's facial muscles tightened, frozen into a grotesque Halloween monster mask. Adolph gulped; his gaze froze on the glint of the butcher knife. Not until Randall's left hand middle finger lifted was Adolph aware of Randall's loosening grip on Rebecca's left forearm.

Rebecca collapsed out of sight behind the counter.

Adolph balled his right hand fingers. When Randall's gaze dropped to where Rebecca fell, Adolph charged the counter's open end, cocked his readied fist, and let it fly.

Randall's head lurched sideways. Adolph's punch forceful enough to propel Randall's entire body into a reel. Randall's knife ricocheted off the counter, bounced twice, and clattered on the floor.

His fury unleashed, Adolph shuffled his feet to follow the right haymaker with a solid left jab to Randall's chin. A second jab blocked Randall's flailing right fist arcing toward Adolph's head. Adolph's second right landed squarely on Randall's solar plexus. Adolph shouted to the ceiling for help. A ramming bar crashed and splintered the front door. Two officers clamored into the restaurant. A third, obviously creeping forward for a planned surprise assault, bolted from the kitchen, hopped a crawling Rebecca, grabbed Randall, and, with a bear hug, wrestled him into a face-to-the-wall handcuff position.

Adolph bent down to lift up Rebecca by her shoulders and surround her with his arms. Two large blood drops dripped onto, and soaked into his left blazer sleeve.

"Thank you," she murmured.

"Sssh," Adolph said. "Save your energy. Let's get you to the hospital. A doc needs to check you. I'm sure Randall will eventually come to his senses."

When the arriving EMTs signaled, Adolph eased his grip of Rebecca. He trailed after her gurney and stopped in the cordoned off street to survey the gathered officers and curious onlookers for any sign of Luann. He couldn't locate her to unleash his inner rage. The Chief strode to Adolph from the far side of the departing ambulance.

"Great job. Don't know what went on inside, but the hostages tell me of your bravery, putting safety of others before yourself. For a precaution we've transported them to the hospital. You should follow suit."

"I'm okay. Cup of black coffee is what I need." He felt mentally exhausted.

"Your choice, but I've assigned a uniform to drive you and your car home." Adolph hid a wince when his right hand fingers touched his neck's nape. Strange how the mind could block out throbs until danger passed. "Complete your report in the morning. Here's Officer Finnegan."

Adolph accepted the crowd's applause with a hand wave and tried to maintain a stoic facade as he continued his quest to isolate Luann from amongst the gapers. On the stroll with Finnegan, he rubbed the pads of his left fingers across his bruised right knuckles. When reaching the station parking lot, a motionless Adolph tossed Finnegan his Monte Carlo keys. The sputtering fuse ignited by his anger toward Luann enflamed his passionate urge to confront her in the detective squad room since her car filled Lt. Hunter's reserved parking spot.

Adolph hesitated, lightheaded. He needed to jerk the mental fuse free before his racing heart exploded his bulging carotid artery and did more damage to him than Luann.

"You coming?" Finnegan asked.

Adolph muttered. "Right there."

"Would be best if I drop you off at the hospital."

"No, no. Home's great." Adolph reached into an inside blazer pocket for his cell and speed dialed Mary. No answer raised little immediate concern for, unless she sat next to an extension, she'd struggle to reach a receiver before the answering machine kicked in. He left a message he'd be home in five. Office voice mail said he had no new messages. Although saving Rebecca would bolster his gold shield pursuit, the ticked by hours robbed him of time to fulfill his skeleton case bravado and thereby flatter The Chief.

With Finnegan behind the wheel, Adolph buckled himself into the passenger seat. To be sociable, he asked, "How long you been on the force now?"

"Got my twenty-year pin last year." Finnegan revved the engine to test the accelerator.

Adolph frowned. "I'm a couple years behind you. Why you keen on being a detective?"

The Monte Carlo idled with two others at the second intersection's red light.

"It's economic. Got kids talking college."

"Wouldn't it be easier to take the sergeant's exam?" A right side pothole jolted Adolph.

"Been a sergeant." Finnegan kept his eyes riveted straight ahead.

"Didn't know that." A pang of embarrassment erupted in Adolph. "Sorry, not trying to pry." He didn't track the career advancement of others beneath him. He gazed out the side window to the maple tree trunks beginning to be encircled by the red carpet of dropping leaves. As much as he enjoyed autumn's barrier to the snow of winter, the decaying leaves would require his obtaining an allergy prescription refill.

"You're not. Learned an expensive lesson when a crook claimed I squirreled away evidence. Although innocent, I couldn't prove it. The higher-ups cocked a knowing eye when a snitch quipped I'd gambled away the bribe money. The crook shaved years off his prison time and, when the furor quieted, the former chief busted me."

Adolph gulped. Was the quicksand that close? Had his father, Chief Howard, or the present promotion board been that willing to side with a perp?

"Doesn't that taint your jacket?"

"Chief Howard, three years ago, reviewed the lack of proof, believed my partner that I'd been framed, and conditionally expunged the black mark. It's now gone."

"That's good." Finnegan's words of a partner reminded Adolph he'd worked solo since Yancey began his disability leave, that is, until Luann. "Appreciate the lift."

Finnegan, as requested, centered and parked the Monte Carlo on Adolph's driveway. From beneath the uplifted garage door, Adolph waved good-bye to both Finnegan and the trailing squad car. Ready to hang up his blazer, he noticed the blood splotches, and tossed it on the entry closet floor for the next dry cleaner trip. He shelved his Walther. "Mary, I'm home."

"In the living room," she responded.

Adolph, navigating through the kitchen, didn't smell any food aromas. Stopping alongside Mary's recliner, he bent forward to plant a kiss on her forehead.

"I'm glad the TV reporter didn't tell me you were inside Patsy's until the news showed your face outside. Kristen begged off supper and left."

"We know what friend she's with tonight?"

"Katie. And how's your head? Let me make you a sandwich?"

"It's fine. I'll microwave instant coffee." Mary, he realized, more often than not, shifted the conversation away from Kristen. "On second thought, I'll order pizza."

"Thirty minutes," he called out to Mary from the kitchen. After two coffee sips, he laid his folded arms on the kitchen table, lowered his forehead, and closed his drooping eyelids. The doorbell startled him awake to collect and pay for a pizza. He assisted seating Mary by shifting her walker away from her kitchen chair. Between pizza slices eaten off white napkins to avoid dishes, Adolph encouraged her recitation of the day's events, slipping in a question about strange noises. When she said she hadn't heard a new noise, Adolph exhaled a quiet sigh of relief. He gulped down his third pizza slice and excused himself to park his Monte Carlo in the garage. Pleased his quick visual inspection of his home's front windows found no new marks, Adolph joined Mary in front of the living room TV, each in their respective recliners.

The warm in-house temperature hastened his return to slumber. When he awoke and massaged the sleep out of his eyes, Mary's empty recliner and a turned off television signaled she'd gone to bed without him, reminiscent of times before when she claimed he snored. He always claimed he didn't, but Mary could never be convinced. Kristen's closed bedroom door offered proof she'd snuck in. His warm, pulsating neck caused him to forage in the kitchen freezer for blue ice. Recalling Finnegan's demotion story, Adolph, with a chilling pang of foreboding in his gut, retrieved Ant's folder from the basement and laid it on the kitchen table, confident he'd have time to hide its contents should either household female awaken.

Adolph's Gold

With the top cover flipped by a fork prong, Adolph viewed the top color photograph and swallowed hard. Skin craters, scales, and multiple miniscule skin cracks depicted the after effects of a scalding liquid having been poured on a young boy's genital region. Using Ant's bag as a glove, he carried the folder to his garaged Monte Carlo where, from a rectangular dispensing box in the trunk, he extracted a pair of vinyl gloves. With his hands properly gloved and the folder tucked secure under his right arm, he retraced his route to the kitchen.

Pouring from a 750ml bottle taken from a lower cabinet shelf, Adolph layered a glass tumbler with three ice cubes and two fingers of splashing Jack Daniels and set it on the table in close proximity to the reopened folder. Again seated, he quickly flipped over the revolting first photograph. The second black and white picture didn't incite his percolating anger until counting six, perhaps seven, flogging scars stretching across a boy's back and buttocks. The youth, maybe ten or twelve years of age, hugged a tree. An adult-sized gloved hand with a horsewhip at the photo's right edge re-fired Adolph's rage. He subdued his perturbation to focus on a backyard locale that struck Adolph as one he'd visited. The indistinct, fuzzy gables on the grainy house in the background, Victorian scrolls on the porch façade, and a tree rope swing floated through his mind's opening and closing aperture as bits and flashes of an eerie faulty recollection. Think harder, he coaxed his brain. He leaned back in his chair, closed his eyes, and still couldn't register identifiable concrete details. *Damn.* Flipping the photo failed to disclose any written notations or a photographer's logo to surmount his mind's failure.

Four of the next five color snapshots struck Adolph as garden-variety pornography. Underage boys and girls posed with feature-obscured or camouflaged adults in sexually suggestive and carnal positions. He parted his dry, compressed lips to drown his disgust with a gulp of whiskey. Bridgetown had no vice squad he could shuffle Ant's filth to and, after his up and close peeper episode, he didn't wish to trust either

Bulldog or Luann. Moreover, The Chief's file note on an assigned case hamstrung his backing out.

The next photograph presented Adolph with an incongruity. He saw it as either a commercial photograph of the Sixteenth U.S. President or the Mr. Lincoln he'd first crossed paths with at the Rose Garden B&B. The bearded, clothed image wouldn't stimulate any prurient desires or encourage blackmail payments. Its inclusion in Ant's folder stumped him.

The last, and ninth, color enlargement depicted a female laid across a table, left leg lifted with a copulating male fully engaged. The only identifying mark visible to Adolph appeared on the upper portion of the woman's shoulder, possibly a birthmark or a tattoo. Only an illogical stretch of his imagination would identify the woman as Rebecca. Adolph exhaled a deep breath. Luann? Physically close. He peered closer, but couldn't be positive, or even confident enough to sling the slightest accusation. His whole scramble for a gold shield had descended into a hell engulfed by viewing sexual depravity, ensnared by glossy pictures anachronistic in a new digital age. Had Finnegan foreshadowed Adolph's demise? Ant luring him in. Planted computers he could discover in Ant's closet ready to push him into a bottomless abyss? What difference would a gold shield make? The longer Adolph pondered, the stronger became his yearning to have Yancey protecting his butt. He swirled the half-melted ice cubes and swallowed a mouthful in one gulp. He stared at the tumbler— the whiskey half gone to no effect.

Adolph required a positive perspective. Why did Ant have these photos? Adolph remembered the childhood secret message writing technique using milk or lemon juice. Mary, he hoped, must have an emergency candle in a kitchen drawer. After three unsuccessful drawer searches, careful not to violate the silence by slamming them shut, he found loose birthday candles in an upper corner cabinet. Seated at the table, he passed the candle flame underneath a snapshot. Nothing. He retried with the "tattooed lover" enlargement. Careful not to scorch the photograph's backing, he passed the flickering flame across darkening paper. Faint images began to darken. Laying the warm photograph face down on the folder, Adolph blew softly until he believed room temperature had been re-established. Two visible letter groupings didn't make sense to him. The first read "wuqsvnw;" the second tripped his tongue with "tjfrphlpwh."

The bedsprings in his bedroom creaked. Was Mary getting out of bed?

He frantically closed the folder, rewrapped it, and hustled to stash it into its original hiding place under the basement stairs. Wiping the stain of exertion from his face, Adolph's bruised right hand knuckles flared in pain when they grazed the kitchen table as he stuffed his vinyl gloves, the matches and candles into his pants pocket, careful to first check the blackened candlewick with a roll between his right hand thumb and forefinger.

Adolph hugged Mary. "I'm sorry. Didn't mean to wake you."

"Not wise to drink late at night."

Adolph dropped his gaze to the floor. "Neck hurt." *Sorta true.*

"Medication another reason." Her walker bumped a table chair.

"Only had this one." With his back to Mary, he walked to the sink tipping the glass to his lips to savor the last two whiskey drops clinging to an ice chip. He set his tumbler into the basin before returning to grasp Mary's elbow, a gesture more in affection than to help her navigate her walker to their bedroom. In the adjoining master bath, he trashed his gloves and the pocket's candle contents deep into the wastebasket. Dressed in pajamas, Adolph closed his eyelids to fake sleep until he believed Mary, lying next to him, dozed in the arms of the Sandman. He twisted onto his back. His squinting eyelids let his eyeballs trace the ceiling's interwoven ambient light variants. Disregarding the disgusting vulgarity and the scrambled-letters mystery of Ant's collection, the photographic memorial of a youth's cruel punishment haunted Adolph.

* * *

Sitting at his cluttered office desk with the room's dust particles dancing in the Eastern sunlight, Adolph mumbled two words of a good morning to a late arriving Luann. When her pantsuit permitted no opportunity to view a bare shoulder, he stuffed his disappointment deep behind his lowered brows. Speaking into an uplifted telephone handset, he left a voice message at St. Mary's School of Music requesting an appointment with Dean Wainright, preferably after a student lesson at the dean's home.

Nonplussed by the dead end, his finger pressed the phone's flash button, and then he punched in Len's crime lab number. Len answered and Adolph detailed his Mulberry Street on-scene visual observation of a Black male and asked, as delicately as he could, why the lab report listed victim Jonathan Green as Caucasian. Len apologized profusely. He explained it started with a typo; the dead adult male's surname should've added an "e" for "Greene," not written as "Green." Adolph asked about the given name "Jonathan" and received Len's assurance it wasn't a mistake. A relieved Adolph banked an extra IOU with Len by promising to keep the Caucasian/Afro-American identification mix-up close to his vest. At the right moment, Adolph would spring the corrected information on Luann to wipe, no rub with sandpaper, her prior sneer from her lips. If his festering, growing animosity towards Luann radiated across the squad room desks, she didn't reveal any impact, as she stood near his desk.

"Where we driving to today?" Luann asked.

Grateful she didn't embellish with the word "partner," he replied, "Sixth Street Bar."

"Why?" The word an earthquake followed by three aftershocks. "Ant's in jail."

"Remember that open bar homicide where you tipped the best witness?"

"Bull!" Her vocal tremors remained unabated. "I followed procedure and you know it."

Adolph softened his timbre. "Got another hunch. The day-shift bartender knows more than he's admitted. If you'll chill, I'll explain how Yancey and I would double-team the witness."

"What? Now you're gonna give me Detective 101?"

Adolph's patience, gnawed to extinction by Luann constant reversion to sarcasm, had no compassion left. "You might be familiar with floodlights, but we don't use the third degree. Nor does one partner bust into a volatile hostage situation with the other at risk."

Luann squared her frame. "I have no idea what you're implying, but, scolding me for Patsy's, you can gloat with the guys in the john. The Chief's already dressed me down for that."

Adolph ignored Luann's implicit apology and bulldozed ahead to detail how he and Yancey improved on TV's portrayal of the good cop/bad cop interrogation method. He gazed into Luann's receding pupils and insisted all she need do is repeatedly state to the suspect that she believed Adolph's spiel, and, no matter how implausible Adolph sounded, the suspect didn't need to get into trouble and would be well advised to do what Adolph suggested. When three repetitions convinced him that Luann could be credible, if she wanted to be, they rode in companionable silence in her Chrysler to the Sixth Street Bar and parked in Ant's alley spot.

Striding to the bar's front entrance, Adolph slapped the door inward and stepped in, allowing Luann to protect his rear. To his right, the head-down bartender, who he'd come to see, swabbed the historic oaken bar with a gray-streaked white rag.

"Yo there, Rawley," Adolph called out. The bartender's head jerked up. "Working hard?" Adolph winked towards the bar's two patrons bellied up to, and hunched over, the foosball game handles, seemingly more engrossed in shooting goals then worried about invading detectives.

Luann undid her two-button pantsuit jacket to expose

blouse ruffles frilly and blue.

Adolph's stare refused to acknowledge that Rawley's eyes darted past him to feast on Luann. She had lit a slow fuse, not of passion, but of anger, within Adolph's gut. In the circumstances Adolph couldn't publicly explain to Luann that siding with him against the bartender had been a simple concept that didn't translate into "strip" or "tease."

He boldly angled in front of Luann to break the gaping bartender's visual contact with Luann's hip sway. "Rawley, ol' buddy, we need to have a simple discussion where we each tell the truth. Remember, we spoke a couple of days ago. It upsets me to learn you lied when you said you didn't see nothing the day that patron got wasted in the alley."

"Man," Rawley began. "Told you truth, bro. Why you hassle us working stiffs?"

"You want me to jump this bar and cool your tonsils with the business end of my piece? Or, do you want me to whisper into Ant's ear you're a stool pigeon so, at the least, he'll fire your ass . . . cancel whatever health insurance you've got for your pregnant wife."

"You'll not?" The bartender's hands clutched and twisted the bar rag tight.

"What? You're daring me? Why do you think I brought my partner with this time? She'll swear you resisted arrest and I had to shoot. And your wife's medical coverage disappears."

Adolph leaned his shoulders forward, listened, and heard nothing. *C'mon, Luann, open your frigging mouth.* Without waiting for Luann to speak, Adolph jumped, let his buttocks hit the bar counter and twisted his legs across the bar. His lowered oxford soles crunched ice bin cubes. He lifted both wet shoes from the ice bin and propelled his torso forward to have his feet land, with flexed knees, on the floor behind the bar. The bartender bolted left, running through the galley kitchen toward the rear door. Adolph pursued and launched his right shoulder into the fleeing bartender's hamstrings, the execution of a textbook open-field football tackle. Two body masses, Adolph cushioned by the bartender's, thudded to the linoleum near the exit door.

"Now you did it," Adolph shouted. "Resisting arrest, assault on a police officer. Ant better advertise for a new bartender in tomorrow's newspaper."

"No man. Give me a break. I need this job. Squeaky threatened to kill me."

Adolph, forcing Rawley's right arm into a hammerlock, yanked Rawley erect. He twisted the bartender against the nearest wall and got into his face. "Who's Squeaky?"

"A Dragon enforcer. Ant said the big boss warned we were to treat all Dragons with respect and that specifically meant you didn't piss off Squeaky."

Rawley's reference to Ant having a boss surprised Adolph. That bolstered why Ant, squirreling away blackmail ammunition to protect his own hide, gave him the photo folder. If Adolph didn't understand the specifics, the logic made sense. Nonetheless, the photos showed no recognizable city official or other local celebrity. "Ant's boss? Give me a name."

Luann, nearby with her gun drawn, had shied away when the bartender uttered the "dragon" word as if avoiding the all-consuming fire belched by a mythical Medieval dragon more powerful than St. George. To Adolph, the local Dragons represented more of a Peter, Paul, and Mary version of "Puff, the Magic Dragon."

"Jesus. Don't know," Rawley whispered. "Swear on my mother's grave."

"That's not convincing. Hate to break your arm putting on these cuffs."

Luann edged closer to stand six feet away, her weapon holstered beneath a right hand that seemed to visually thrust out the opposite hip. "Think you should believe him."

Now she spoke. Why the hell wait? Adolph cuffed Rawley's right wrist without breaking it, but couldn't resist a twist. What else could he do? He sure as hell couldn't count on Luann after he'd bullied and assaulted a potential witness/accomplice who'd also not been given a proper

Miranda. And, since both foosball players had scrammed when Adolph leaped onto the bar, he should rip that blue fake silk off Luann's shoulder to reveal the birthmark he suspected.

At the blare of sirens, he crammed the urge to learn the truth about Luann into his mind's darkest cavity. *Who'd called for reinforcements? He hadn't.* Luann? Her contradictions in the last two days confused him. Why should she now superficially follow procedure when she hadn't at Patsy's? A reaction to The Chief's strong words? Adolph wouldn't clutter his mind by asking.

Adolph clicked the second handcuff tighter and, grabbing the connecting metal links, escorted Rawley, via the front door, into the custody of two uniforms outside who ducked Rawley's crown into a waiting black and white squad car.

Luann, her pantsuit jacket rebuttoned, slouched, her butt polishing her Chrysler's front fender. "We gonna hunt up a dragon or two?" she asked, no anticipation in her voice.

"No." Luann smiled until he said, "But let's take a little ride anyway."

On Adolph's exposed skin, the interior warmth of Luann's car approximated the temperature of an 18-wheeler trailer with the reefer dialed to safeguard frozen beef slabs. Rolling past Bridgetown storefronts to reach the river, Luann interrupted the silence to whine: "Don't see what driving along the river gets us other than an empty tank of gas."

An unperturbed Adolph gazed up at the turn-of-the-century old homes that must have showcased the opulent wealth of lumber kings, shipping magnates, and railroad barons. The homes' quarried limestone and kilned brick, although weathered, retained its structural integrity mortared into solid walls, wall veneers, or fieldstone fences. The original wood had capitulated. Refashioned windows encased by aluminum or vinyl tricked Adolph's eye to remember yesteryear. Of course, new roofs and artistically coordinated vivid pastel paint colors pleased the passersby. Sooty brick chimneys had willed their chore to the metal-capped vent pipes of high efficiency furnaces that tried, but often failed, to conquer cold seasonal drafts.

Adolph in years past for fund-raising sorties had visited several of the houses, especially at Christmas. The host's invite served as a charity's polite cover for an assault on his wallet. He couldn't be entirely cynical for he rubbed elbows with the town's elite and the charities performed valuable work left undone by taxpayer-funded social service agencies. One gala, two years ago, funded the police benevolent fund's sending youth to Ohio on a boxing trip. Today, his penetrating gaze searched for a specific house with detail that matched the black and white photo now front 'n' center in his brain's cellular photo album.

Adolph stretched his shoulder harness. "Turn at the next corner, wind up the hill."

"If you say so." Luann one-handedly answered her ringing cell phone. "Sweetie, we need to talk about that later . . . That's a lot of money." Her overdrawn expression lasted but a second.

Adolph shifted his gaze to straight ahead. "Could you park halfway down this street?"

Luann pulled close to the curb. Her slowing front tires crunched crisp, recently fallen, leaves until she halted her car's momentum near a yellow school-crossing sign. "What's the secret?"

"Whatcha mean?"

Luann's raised lower lip faced Adolph. "C'mon. We're not headed to lover's lane."

"You're a sarcastic bitch." Adolph regretted letting his deep true feelings show. "Sorry."

"Better you're honest than not. Learned that lesson long ago when my first husband dipped his stick in the company ink and then lied to me."

Adolph gazed at his black oxford shoe tops. "Don't know that I wanted to know that."

"The Chief, for some unknown, goddamn reason, shoved us together. You scared you might divulge something that'll give me the gold shield?" She rammed the gearshift into park.

Luann's jab bounced against the professional veneer he'd tried to foster of him just doing his job unconcerned about personal rewards. "Not scared. Unlike . . ." He fought against the urge to say not scared by her. "Unlike . . . some people, I'm not uncomfortable about all that I do and how I do it." He reached to unlatch her car's door. "Gotta stretch my muscles." He alighted to stand on the sidewalk with his left hand fingertips tapping his neck's nape. The alley-assault welt had shrunk, although he winced when his fingertips pressed too close to the welt's center.

His extended glance suggested this brick-paved street had to be the one. At the corner, his right-angled gaze verified that Luann lingered in her Chrysler. He guessed her reticence to trail after him a good thing since it protected against missing a dispatcher's call. He didn't fear an unanswered call because, while a promotional black mark, it marred Luann's jacket as well.

After four blocks, Adolph's second right put him into an alley. Choosing to stride forward along the shallower of two ruts, his soles and heels crunched gravel. He paused at the third house on his left and chided himself for not bringing a copy of the actual picture. The vinyl fence enclosing the backyard wasn't in the photo, but it appeared to replicate the wooden pickets captured by the long-ago lens. The rear porch appeared similar, especially the corner scrolls. Two one-foot-high tree stumps, substituting for overturned clay pots, could've lived as saplings in the picture. He wished he could interview the bark of the mature oak before him to determine if it had once allowed a naked boy to hug it. He memorized as many present details as he could. The house faced Oxford. For the exact address, he'd have to visit the front.

He half-jogged toward Luann to compensate for the time spent gawking. She'd rolled down a window to let her left arm rest on the driver door's frame. Adolph buckled himself in. His gaze lingered on Luann, but he wasn't going to ask why she applied fresh makeup.

"Ready, Sherlock?"

Adolph's Gold

Adolph tightened his throat muscles to bottle up a first response of "Yes, Watson." He determined she'd probably interpret the comment as a slight that Watson was the dumber of the two, so he uttered a simple: "Yes." When he and Yancey had had a blowout, Adolph recalled that the eruption wouldn't last longer than a minute and, once expressed, consumed all lingering fallout. Perhaps he glamorized their developed relationship with a submersion of their testy early months. Yancey's never lost rock-solid idealism had rounded the edges of Adolph's cynicism. Yet, Adolph had never adopted Yancey's exterior cool demeanor exemplified best when a suspect hurtled taunts labeling Yancey a Black fag. Adolph would've planted a boot in the suspect's groin, intent on inflicting serious injury, if not with the first kick, then with the three follow-up stomach punches necessary to bring about present and future respect for the badge.

"I've called in for personal time. I'll drop you at the station."

"Fine." The word became the last Adolph spoke until he was seated in the squad room and responding with a "yes" to The Chief's intercom summons to the latter's office.

"Close the door; take a seat," Chief Howard solemnly intoned.

Adolph sat stiffly upright in the Chief's visitor chair. Reading The Chief's facial expression as ominous, Adolph grabbed the offensive. "Your cousin's been helpful in narrowing the potential identities of the skeleton your spade found buried in her backyard." This positive stroking of The Chief's cousin didn't loosen The Chief's jaw line.

"That's nice, but there's another matter." Since The Chief didn't rifle or grab a case folder, Adolph perceived that he wasn't summoned for chitchat. The Chief's chair squeaked as he leaned back. "When's the last time you were at the Sixth Street Bar?"

"Earlier today. If you need my report, it's on my desk partially done."

"More serious than a late report. When did you last

browbeat Ant?"

If a rookie, Adolph would've cringed at the accusation. Years on the job told him best not to quibble. He needed The Chief to spill the beans, stop the agonizing slow drips of water. "The day I arrested him for concealing St. Mary's pilfered computers. Why?"

The Chief clicked a pen. "His lawyer claims he had a folder that hasn't shown up in your report or the evidence inventory." Adolph gulped. "Now I know you and Ant have a history."

Adolph fought the urge to squirm or wipe the moisture he felt wetting his healing neck bruise. "We aren't bosom buddies, if that's what you think."

"Hell, I know that." The Chief pitched forward. "It's just that I can't have Ant, or any other criminal, cry we're dirty if there's a smidgen of truth behind the squawking."

Finnegan's story flashed across Adolph's mind. He raised his left hand to his neck's nape to buy time. "Sorry, still hurts if I twist my head a certain way." He swiped his moist hand along the pant cloth of his left outside thigh. Best he could do was to rely on his pet peeve by answering what was definitely The Chief's question with a question. "What kind of folder?"

"Didn't ask since I didn't want to lend any credence to the shyster."

That didn't turn off the torture spigot. Adolph pressed both of his palms to his thighs and tried to look serene while waiting for The Chief to fill the conversational vacuum.

"Not out of the question that an accomplice of Ant's would try and plant whatever . . . And, you're a prime candidate. On the short list for promotion and all."

Adolph's ears caught the promotion reference and didn't wish to dispel from The Chief's mind that the assumed folder had yet to be delivered. "I'll finish and get you my report on the Sixth Street bartender arrest. While legit, I don't care if he gets off with a slap on the wrist. It won't be in my report, and the bartender might be blowing smoke, but he let slip that Ant might be scared of a bigger fish that has a tight connection with the local Dragons."

"That's all I or we need." The Chief's body rocked. "Another gang war erupting. Francine pesters me enough and a male cousin's upset. Just keep me in the loop. That's all."

Outside The Chief's office, Adolph released a sigh of relief that The Chief hadn't pressed him about Ant's porno folder. However, if Ant's lawyer pressured The Chief with intimate folder details, the crosshairs would swing to Adolph as having been the detective writing the stolen property report. On his slow stroll to his squad room desk, Adolph mulled the potentially painful truth that he and Ant weren't the only persons with firsthand knowledge of the folder's contents. Adolph sat, clearing his thoughts to complete the bartender arrest report.

"You ready to stick it to Luann?" Lt. Turner asked, holding up a piece of paper.

"What?" Adolph gazed up from his desk. "Hell no."

"Your loss. Her football pool luck can't last forever."

"Oh. Oh, yeah." Adolph belatedly recognized the weekly pool form in Bulldog's hands. He wanted to send Bulldog packing along with shutting down his basement porno movie operation, but couldn't summon the courage. If challenged, as he would surely be, he'd no physical proof. Even if Luann's shoulder sported the tattoo design or mark, who's to say the sex act wasn't consensual and the photo of consenting adults merely stolen. He himself hadn't acquired it through public distribution channels or checked it out of the library's DVD collection.

"If you change your mind, give me a holler and five bucks. No risk, no gain."

Adolph fit his knees into his desk's kneehole after Bulldog departed and concentrated on unraveling at least the B/W photo mystery in Ant's folder. Real estate records confirmed 415 Oxford Drive had been sold six months ago to a relocation company. Transferred owners posed a roadblock to Adolph's quest to forge a link with the past. While this tangent inquiry interfered with Adolph's self-imposed skeleton investigation deadline, The Chief's heads-up required action. Either a skeleton cold case or an internal ethics investigation could torpedo his gold shield promotion.

With a portable radio clipped onto his belt next to his silver shield, he marched the three blocks to Bridgetown's public library expecting to find Henrietta Grayson, reference librarian. He did, and, to the rhythm of her springy bounce, he followed her bright floral peasant dress into a high-ceilinged room with sliding shelf ladders that towered above their heads. With her wire-rimmed glasses and gray/white hair fashioned into a bun, he fantasized she could successfully audition for an Agatha Christie Miss Marple sleuth role.

She halted next to a pub-styled wooden stool and pushed her eyeglasses higher on her thin nose. "You been sick, Adolph? Haven't seen you in church these last four Sundays."

Why's Henrietta so nosey? Not like her. Adolph kept his mind on track. "Reason I'm here is that I need your help. Oxford Drive, any old photographs?"

"A few, but the original owners, it seems, feared burglaries."

While watching Henrietta pull out a map drawer, Adolph enjoyed the silence of no church follow-up question. She pointed to, and Adolph sat on, a high barstool at a square pub table. Henrietta set a photo album to his left and laid a street map before him.

"What was the address you looked for?"

"415 Oxford." His fingertips lingered on the map. A three-block rectangular strip that included Oxford Avenue started at the river and moved up the bluff for ten or twelve blocks.

"Very few early Oxford photos. Every parcel initially purchased by Wainright Barge Co. Is Mary ill? That why you've missed coming to church?"

He shook his head, not wanting to waste time discussing church attendance. Why hadn't he remembered Wainright Barge? "Did a Wainright relative live in all those houses?"

"No. The center block had three Wainright families,

father and two sons, originally surrounded by small bungalows rented cheap to company workers. 'Member I said there existed a burglary concern." Adolph nodded. "The outer homes served double duty as guard shacks. The father, Johan, was said to have exhibited the most paranoia. He enrolled and paid for a private security force that rivaled the police in training and equipment. There's an old newspaper clipping with recorded rumors he'd hosted Mr. Pinkerton one weekend."

Adolph hated to act anxious, but he didn't need gossip. "You have a house picture?"

Henrietta gazed momentarily at a library ladder. "Unfortunately not. The original house at 415 and that of one son . . . don't remember which . . . burned to the ground in the late 1890s. There's a photo here somewhere of the second son's original home." Henrietta rotated the album and began lifting page after page. "Here it is."

Adolph tilted left. "This photograph shows the front of the house. Any of the rear?"

Henrietta extracted the photo from a plastic sleeve. Two more photographs slipped out. She handed them to Adolph. Careful to touch only the edges, he laid all three on the table. Now he was getting somewhere as one showed a rear porch close-up. Or, at least, that's what Adolph thought. To his question Henrietta explained that later historians believed the photograph to have been the son's original backyard porch at #421. However, since the father built identical houses, the porch photo could visually represent the original appearance of the 415 Oxford porch.

Adolph narrowed his focus to the center black-and-white photograph. Within it, on the right, stood a fence similar to the style he'd observed earlier that day. While the camera viewpoint was reversed, the two mature linden trees matched his morning's observed stump locations. To the left, guide wires anchored by ground stakes met high on a sapling's trunk to form three triangles. If the identical houses had identical landscaping, Adolph had no doubt the young tree in the picture before him could be the nursery-version of today's mature oak.

The soft taps of Henrietta's fingers on the table's wood ceased when Adolph asked, "How long did the Wainrights live on Oxford?"

"From memory, the barge founder lived there until his death. One son moved east, and the second son lived on Oxford until he died. Two more generations followed until the sheriff auctioned the house during the barge company's bankruptcy proceedings in the late 1960s."

"Would the library have any company history books that would have photos?"

"One, but not of the houses. Merely family group shots and company facilities."

"I know there's a Dean or Professor Wainright at St. Mary's. Is he related?"

"Barge founder was his great-great-grandfather. Believe he's talked about living in 415 as a young boy. See this Christmas open house notice?" Adolph squared his body on the stool. "That address definitely had been the dean's dad's residence."

"Big family?"

"Don't recall." The corners of her lips dipped. "I'm sorry."

"You needn't be. You've been a great help. Assume these photos don't circulate." Adolph didn't hear Henrietta's spoken response, if any, as she inserted all photos into the album. During his three-block march to the station, he mulled the major relational/historical gaps between the Wainright personages and the Oxford houses. He'd uncovered the tip of an iceberg.

On Adolph's desk laid a telephone message from Dean Wainright saying he'd be free at seven that evening. A second message, this one from the crime lab on office voicemail, raised Adolph's spirits until he listened. A heads-up from Len said the powder burns on Jonathan Greene's shirt indicated the fatal shot traveled farther than the five feet that separated he

and Mrs. Connor and that the only printable kitchen
fingerprints nearby were those of Mrs. Connor.

Damn. Another mess. Adolph slumped forward to rest his
forehead on his folded arms. Yes, but also, his inner voice
said, the opportunity to demonstrate superlative, gold-shield
worthy, detective prowess. He'd need help. Adolph held off
contacting Officer Finnegan, his most logical choice until his
meeting with The Chief. However, priorities placed Mary first.
Lifting his head, he dialed his home from his cell and left
Mary a message to expect him within minutes.

* * *

Adolph rushed to set out the supper dishes, assisted by Kristen
who centered a kitchen table trivet for a skillet full of chicken
he carried from the stove. Mary sniffled. Knowing that his yet-
to-be made evening departure announcement would heighten
already existing angst, Adolph stifled his month-long nagging
that Mary reconsider her choice not to take allergy medication.

When he finished eating, Adolph rose and mentioned his
appointment with Dean Wainright. Mary cringed slightly, and
then covered a sneeze with her sleeve. "How long?"

"Expect an hour, no more," Adolph replied. His kiss of
Mary's forehead lingered until a smiling, gracious Spenser
Wainright III greeted him at his Lilac Lane home's front door.
Led inside, Adolph marveled at the glistening black baby
grand piano that over-filled the family room. Snug to the right
wall with its bench touching a pressed-back oak chair, the
piano dwarfed two scaled-down winged-back chairs and a
rectangular oaken coffee table along the left wall. A bay
window, straight ahead, allowed Adolph to see the second
floor of the Rose Garden B&B. All windows lighted meant
that Mrs. Hoskins labored with a house full of guests.

"Lovely home . . . very cozy," Adolph said. He accepted
his host's invitation to sit.

"Thank you. Could I offer you something to drink?"

Adolph declined. His initial impression indicated a
dweller valuing order and precision. He'd half-expected to see

Mark Twainesque turn-of-the-century antiques rather than space-expanding pale beige walls in sharp contrast to the dean's dark claustrophobic office. Frameless, vibrant-pastel abstract paintings graced the walls in two locations and could've been featured in Adolph's friend's "New York Magazine." The room's only whimsy consisted of a shaded musical-clef lamp base.

The dean, his back arched, perched himself on the adjacent chair's front edge. Adolph calculated that, if he received the answer to only one question, he should ask it first. "Was curious, after I called upon you at the university, that you might be related to the Wainright legacy, one of Bridgetown's founding families."

His host's facial muscles tightened. "Simple answer is yes, but I prefer not to be moored to the past. Any ancestral glories have faded. Music fills my days."

"But it must give you pleasure to occasionally pull out the family album, so to speak."

"There's only one photograph I have and that's of my mother, God rest her soul." His brow furrows relaxed. "She did everything to protect . . . no, nurture me, but then you can realize that years ago a woman's powers were very, very limited."

With the dean's clenched right fist a nonverbal sign, Adolph decided to drop family history to see if his host could be tripped up on the computer theft. "It hasn't been released to the press yet, but we're recovered two of the three stolen music department computers. However, there's ownership confusion on a found third tower."

"That's commendable. Were the files intact? I'd hate to have those disgusting photos publicly distributed."

"What photos?" Adolph couldn't acknowledge he knew critical facts.

"The nude ones, of course." The stark admission knifed through Adolph's consciousness. "Certainly not like the co-ed pictures the college publishes on its website, that's for sure."

Adolph hadn't devised a line of questions premised on the

supposition that the dean knew of, and would willing disclose, the existence of erased hard drive content. His crime lab had yet to isolate, or crack, the coded URL digital trail to the porn's server. Adolph improvised. "Who told you about the nudes?"

"I'd rather not say. If you're like my journalism colleague, I'm sure you want answers to the other "w" questions. Let's say I received an anonymous tip about four days before and went in late the next night. You can verify that with the department's security logs. Checked the files of all six first floor computers. Only one contaminated with those ugly pictures. I assumed a male student, definitely not one of the all-female staff, and sat outside the music building for parts of the next two nights determined to catch the pervert red-handed. No one showed."

Adolph was skeptical. "You could have notified the police."

"Of course, you're right." Wainright scooted back in his chair. "No disrespect, but the police have a dismal record dealing with sexual issues. Look at prostitution. It's illegal and, other than an occasional bust during mayoral election campaigns, hookers, and the men who skim greenbacks off their bodies, flourish. And then, there's the associated illegal drugs."

Adolph couldn't readily deny the verbal punch. Visible street crime like robberies and shootings plus reported burglaries drained his energy in an era when the mayor's budget cuts handcuffed Bridgetown's understaffed police department. He gazed at the dean. "The other side of the coin is that citizens needlessly suffer because we police aren't notified."

"I'll admit there's a standoff in opinion. However, in the music department, who better than me to investigate without causing unnecessary suspicion. A police presence would panic innocent staff and falsely tarnish the university's public image."

Adolph could concede an undisputable logic pervaded the

dean's slick self-serving argument. "Not that I'm in anyway agreeing what you say is laudatory," Adolph cleared his throat, "but did you uncover any clue to the person responsible?"

Wainright exhaled deeply. "Sad to say, not enough time."

"What about this Jonathan Green?" Adolph didn't get the quick reply he expected.

The dean unclenched his right hand. "Sorry, is that who's ID was discovered?"

Adolph nodded. "Any new information about him since we last met?"

Wainright didn't blink. "All the information I have was in that folder I gave you."

Adolph couldn't dispute the plausibility of the dean's answer. Yet, the reality remained that, except for admitting knowledge of the porn, the dean added nothing new. Even though Dean Wainright exhibited a maternal focus that excluded the male lineage of a Bridgetown founding family, Adolph guessed psychologists could explain this as normal. While Adolph assumed that the flogged boy in the photo he had been given had been tied to a tree in a Wainright backyard, he faced a Herculean task to prove it had been the man now sitting across from him. While understanding the grown youth would want to forever lock those memories away, Adolph wouldn't surrender his most adventurous theory that the boy sat before him, nor dismiss any psychologist documented theory that a history of abuse could later fuel the adult's abuse of other youths. Adolph, without solid proof, encountered a brick wall. The sexual videotaping he'd peeped at had been all adults. Sonja Marie, if attacked, was an adult. The only child, the missing Whitenmire girl, had no relationship with the college or Wainright Barge. He'd have to find the connecting threads and, if the dean was guilty, the chink in his armor.

Adolph filled the conversational void. "How many computer pictures were there?"

"Detective, please." The dean averted Adolph's gaze. "I

136

didn't count; and if I didn't see them all, then thank goodness."

Adolph flipped his notepad closed.

"We're through then?" The dean's gaze stayed with Adolph.

"Well, while I'm here, do you recall observing anyone with a large quantity of motor oil or abandoned machinery in this neighborhood, say within this past year?" Adolph realized he hadn't jotted a single note. Well, nothing lost.

"In the summer, residents . . . or their guests . . . park motor homes on the street. They might leave an oil spot. Other than that I can't answer."

Adolph suppressed his chagrin at the evasive answer. He discarded a popped up thought he could scare the dean into an admission by bullying and switched gears. "Ever have a visitor at the college, or here, that would be a dead ringer for Abraham Lincoln?" Adolph perceived he spied a renewed facial tension in Dean Wainright's gaze.

"At school, saw a gentleman like that outside at a distance. Thought a pageant actor."

Adolph opened his notepad. "Has Sonja Sanchez returned to the music building?"

"Don't know if I know who you mean." The dean slid forward. "Is she a student?"

"Custodial worker." Adolph held off giving Sonja's physical description.

"Name obviously Hispanic and the college, like a revolving door, employs so many. With only a name, don't think I can be of much help."

Expecting a dead end, Adolph, nevertheless, asked a final question. "Notice anyone suspicious these past few months, say, across your backyard fence?"

"Can't say that I have. But . . . not that I wish to make a complaint . . . there's always commotion there, if you know what I mean? A neighbor approached me with a petition last spring. Wanted to present it at a public hearing in opposition to the B&B's license renewal."

"Did you sign?"

Wainright shook his head. "Didn't want to cause St. Mary's any trouble."

"Thank you for your time." Adolph stood.

After Wainright escorted him out the front door, Adolph heard faint sounds of the piano scale repeated twice and the beginnings of highbrow music. A narrow wooden fence gate and the absence of lawn ruts confirmed it unlikely that any vehicle drove into the dean's backyard.

Adolph proceeded home. It gladdened his heart that he'd not mislead Mary on his absence's length. All seemed calm. As he rose often from his living room recliner to wait on Mary during TV commercials, Adolph happily banished all work thoughts. His and Mary's bland daily living conversation wouldn't have electrified the world, but, for him, the diversion re-energized his spirit. Early the next day he'd drop his Monte Carlo at the body shop to have them sand off the driver's door graffiti and repaint. Where Luann would drive him, Adolph didn't have a clue, and, with Mary content, he didn't care.

Chapter Six

Adolph covered the telephone's mouthpiece with his right hand to muffle his exasperation when Luann ticked off two dubious reasons why she couldn't detour to the body shop to give him a lift to the station. He shrugged off Luann's selfishness as an omen of good fortune and telephoned an enthusiastic Officer Finnegan.

Adolph paced the body shop's sidewalk. Good manners really required he remember Finnegan's first name. A Bridgetown patrol car swerved and bumped the curb before stopping. Without waiting for an invite, Adolph grabbed the door handle, squeezed, and began to buckle his seatbelt. "Many thanks for your courtesy."

"Ain't no big deal. City gas." Finnegan laughed.

Adolph chuckled. He surmised Finnegan would help, even if not at city expense.

Finnegan signaled to enter traffic. "Have an idea which gang this time?"

"No clue." And, that was the truth, although Adolph suspected the Dragons. "Off the record, could I ask for a bigger favor than today?"

"If it doesn't land me behind bars." Finnegan repeated his earlier laugh, only louder.

"Could be thin ice, but I'll not scapegoat. Pull over, call in for a personal break."

"We're almost at the station. The dispatcher might question, asking to log the address."

"Right. I'll meet you in the john in five." Adolph appreciated Finnegan's street smarts. He would leverage Finnegan's detective-recommendation solicitation and create the perfect ally, each having something to gain. Adolph's bathroom recon a minute later found the two stalls empty and he rested his butt against a sink until Finnegan entered.

"What's up?" Finnegan asked.

Adolph waited until Finnegan closed the hallway door. "I'm in a delicate situation. Have an evidence bag I shouldn't have." It wasn't a complete lie. "If I gave it to you, could you toss it or drop it off at incineration? And, if asked, say you found it in an alley or in a street gutter."

"How risky?" Finnegan interlaced his fingers. "What's in it?"

"Pictures. Adult and kid porn."

"Damn." The officer shook his head. "Vice isn't my beat."

Adolph felt his skin prickle as Finnegan's glazed-over eyes triggered an episode of never-envisioned global amnesia. "If you don't want your name connected . . ." Adolph's warm blood circulation eliminated the transient chill of Finnegan's eyes, until, within seconds, the officer's eyes refocused normally. "How 'bout dumping it in the crime lab parking lot. In the hustle and bustle it coulda fell out of almost any vehicle or transfer box."

"Wouldn't that get someone in trouble?"

"Whole thing's going to create trouble sooner or later." Hopefully, Adolph's growing frustration didn't show. "Just thought I'd ask a buddy, that's all."

"Don't get all hyper." Finnegan glanced at his wristwatch. "Where's these pictures now?"

"At home. I'll get it when you drop me off. Everyone will figure you're doing me a simple favor with my car in the shop."

"If this goes haywire, you'd better cover me."

"Count on it. Now leave. I'll wait."

Adolph racked his brain: where'd he get an evidence bag? Procedure required closed case evidence bags to be disposed of as an old bag could cross-contaminate new evidence.

While still trying to develop a plan on where to look for the desired evidence bag, Luann intercepted him a half dozen paces from reaching his squad room desk. "About time. I've cases to process and close." Her beige clutch purse hit her desk with a splat.

"Drop me off on Oxford Drive and then you can hightail it to wherever you want."

Her upper lip rose. "That's not The Chief's assignment."

Adolph bowed close to Luann's ear. "You going to rat? Don't threaten."

When Adolph, in Luann's Chrysler, neared 415 Oxford, he pointed to the curb. She hadn't uttered a word since he'd buckled up. As far as he was concerned, she didn't have to. Yancey and he would've buried the hatchet. He doubted that with Luann. He expected her retaliation plus the continuing silent treatment.

"I'm connected with a portable radio." He patted his side at the waist. "I'll call."

Luann, stiffly gazing straight ahead, braked her car

against the curb.

Adolph exited. A maple tree or two had dropped red leaves. He crunched one under his left foot as he crossed the street from #415 after Luann had hi-tailed it. He knocked on three unanswered front doors until he faced a heavyset Slavic woman, severely deficient in English, dressed in black, sporting a white apron. Adolph left his card. Without bothering to knock on any door, he continued a two-block stroll, eyeing cookie-cutter brick bungalows he wouldn't wish to live in. Up ahead, he spotted a small two-lot pocket park. A lone gentleman sat on the park's only bench. Its bolted wood-planked seat and backrest fronted the street. The man didn't.

"Howdy," Adolph yelled. Walking closer, he tried to encourage a response with an added, "Nice day." The heavy dark-blue wool coat, more appropriate for the winter cold yet to arrive, perplexed Adolph. A yellowed, once white, yachting cap rode high above gray-streaked brown hair. From the rear, Adolph expected its visor had been tugged to disguise facial features.

"Howdy," Adolph repeated. Without a reaction to this second greeting, Adolph executed three full-circle strides to gaze down at the slumped-shouldered elderly man sitting on the bench.

The gent gazed up and reached his right hand to his right ear. "You say something?"

Adolph heard the click of a hearing aid switch. "Howdy."

"Sorry 'bout that. Noisy cars disturb nature's beauty." He gazed skyward. "I've watched these here trees change color for decades."

"Mind if I join you?" Adolph interpreted the grunt as permission. "Name's Adolph."

"Suit yourself."

"Your name?" asked a seated Adolph.

The gent lifted the right side of his mouth. "Who's asking?"

"Like I said, my name's Adolph. I'm with the police."

"Them young thugs with the loud muffler get another

141

complaint filed. Wasn't me."

"Nah, I've been trying to locate someone at home. Your name was what?"

"Silas . . . Silas Maurer. Don't bother nobody."

Adolph watched the loose end of a handkerchief Silas retrieved from his outer coat pocket flutter in Silas's shaking hand. "Ever know the Wainright family who lived here?"

A disdainful expression etched itself into Silas's features. "Worked hard for them. A pilot I was. The family made big promises and the judge gave our pensions to greedy banks."

"I'm sorry. You know Spenser Wainright from the college?" Adolph sneezed into his sleeve.

"Little bit. He'd play on the docks. I'd see him pick on other boys."

"How'd you mean?" Adolph reached into his blazer inside pocket for a notepad. He stood upon hearing a loud muffler in the next block. Silas cupped a hand on his right ear. The car didn't pass their way. A woman pushing a stroller crossed the intersection without stopping.

"He'd push and shove those smaller. Saw him take a kid's apple one day. Big bully that's what he was. Most despicable, he'd run backwards and taunt a boy with a metal leg brace."

"Wouldn't he get punished? Where were his folks?"

"Why all the questions?" He stared at Adolph. "This here stuff's old news."

"Humor me a little." Adolph sat. "Most likely I've not have heard it."

"Ain't going to testify for no children's welfare. I'll tell you that upfront."

Adolph rubbed the back of his left hand with his right. Maybe this stuff about the dean's young years wouldn't amount to a hill of beans, that is, if he could believe he was being fed the truth. Well, he could suspend his fruitless house canvass and waste a few minutes with this old codger. "Not asking you too."

"What again were you asking?"

"Didn't the boy get punished?"

"Months went by and little Spence, as he was called, never showed. Word spread that he'd been whooped and lit out." Silas gazed skyward. "My son, not by me, mind you, got scarred by a lash once. Never could prove who done it."

"Could Spence have been back when you were off on the river?"

"Not that year. A winch let a steel cable fly. Knocked me down. Broke an ankle it did. Old man Spenser had me doing warehouse paper stuff. Better than staying home, he said."

"Okay." Adolph tracked the old man's upward gaze. "Ever see little Spence again?"

"Sure. Months, maybe six, seven, he ran the dock again. Skipper friend said he hauled the boy from the dock next to that St. Louis Gateway Arch. That, you know, was his mother's hometown. We all figured the boy hitched to Missouri or his mother snatched him."

Adolph tried to get a read of the man's face. "Were the parent's divorced?"

"Guess so." Silas's volume dropped. "Don't rightly know for sure."

Adolph leaned forward. "How old did you say the boy was?"

"Guess twelve, or thereabouts. My two sons older so he didn't mess with them."

A shiny, jacked-up, red pickup roared past. Silas tugged his cap lower. Adolph stood. He assumed the three youths crammed into the pickup's front seat were Dragons. Smeared mud obscured a license plate ID. If they were searching for his Monte Carlo, he'd outsmarted them this time. He held his gaze on Silas. "Appreciate your help. You live around here?"

Silas listed to his right before his right arm, its palm resting on the bench seat, straightened to boost himself erect. "Next block on Devon. Raised my kids there. Most days I'm here."

Adolph handed him his card. "Thanks again. Call me if you remember anything or if you have any picture that includes a Wainright, especially a young or old Spenser."

Silas grunted twice and, rather than lift his feet to walk, slid his soles across the sidewalk. Adolph radioed for Luann. The rust-covered steel-linked chains on three park swings behind him, in response to a breeze, filled his wait with uneven creaks. He thought he heard a mewl, but dispatched the crazy idea when the stroller he'd seen earlier appeared nowhere in sight. After he settled into Luann's Chrysler, she resumed her silent treatment. A brown paper bag perched on Luann's desk easily convinced him he'd been right not to suggest they find a cafe for lunch.

With a curt "I'll be back in thirty" statement, Adolph exited the squad room. If he missed eating, that'd be fine. He strode towards the crime lab. At the back of the building, two bales of scrap cardboard kissed a dumpster. On the ground laid an evidence bag with its red sealing tape peeled back. He squatted down. Careful to touch only the tape and not the bag, he found it empty. He heard footsteps and then a voice.

"Dumpster diving to see if we threw out an extra lunch?"

Adolph arose and pivoted to find Len with two hands grasping a fast food bag and a lidded pop. "Of course not." The evidence bag hung from Adolph's right hand; its tape stuck between his thumb and forefinger. "Didn't know if this bag had been lost or badly tossed."

"Show me the bag's front." Len stepped closer.

Adolph twisted his wrist to allow Len to read the bag's outside label.

"Old Riverfront Motel case," Len said. "Know because the appeals court upheld last year's drug conviction and we repackaged evidence for storage three days ago."

That information exceeded all that Adolph cared to know. "I'll shred it at the station. No need to interrupt your lunch." Still holding the bag by its tape, Adolph dropped his right hand.

"Fine. Give me call later or tomorrow morning. We've hopefully come up with a stronger ID based on the clothing fibers found with your skeleton."

"Laundry mark with the victim's name?"

Adolph's Gold

"You watch too much TV." Len disappeared through the crime lab's rear door.

Perhaps other cops wouldn't be, but Adolph felt extremely self-conscious on a public street dangling an old evidence bag six inches from his lowered right hand. The most curious passerby, a sniffing dog on a leash, had been yanked away by a nervous owner. Adolph appreciated Luann's squad room absence. When he glanced up after stashing the bag into his bottom desk drawer, Adolph pressed his lips together without uttering a word as Bulldog stared at him. It wasn't Bulldog's lined face or the sagging eyelids and blood-shot eyeballs that startled Adolph, but that Bulldog stared at him expecting an explanation.

Finally, Bulldog capitulated. "FYI. Luann's taken off for the rest of the afternoon."

Probably had another late night. "Thanks," Adolph mumbled.

At once intrigued why Bulldog jogged half-a-dozen steps to answer his ringing desk telephone, Adolph passed off his interest as worthless clutter. He'd capitalize on Luann not bugging him and initiate a computer search into Dean Wainright's background. Utilizing hunt-and-peck, he clicked on links to online playbills and performance critiques that listed Spenser Wainright III as a University of Iowa music graduate who toured for three years with an acclaimed 1940s-era big band before returning to Iowa State University for a M.F.A. and Ph. D.

He slogged through multiple dead ends, irritated often by advertising pop-ups, and squinted at the monitor screen when the Wainright name surfaced in a St. Louis Post-Dispatch society page article highlighting clubs and bands. His mother was mentioned as a St. Louis nursing home resident entertained by Spenser at monthly Sunday afternoon recitals. While Adolph didn't like it, he shrugged off the year gap between Iowa State and St. Louis.

Carefully, Adolph typed in Mrs. Wainright's name. He clicked on an obituary, and then a court probate dispute. His eyes widened. A trust, in an amount unreported on, had been awarded to her son, Spenser. Now, this adds possible sense. To Adolph, this family dispute could explain Wainright's at home comment last night that he kept only his mother's photograph. No court records linked to Wainright's father's estate. But, of course, there'd been the barge company bankruptcy and an exhausted Adolph reckoned legions of attorneys created straw men and dummy interlocking legal entities to obfuscate and obscure any actual money trail.

Rubbing the twinge at his neck convinced Adolph he didn't have weeks to sift through 100,000 Wainright Barge entries. He narrowed his search after finding one Spencer Wainright who had obtained a music instructor's position at an Illinois college in Carbondale. A stagnant academic trail pricked at Adolph's concentration until a Wainright filled the Wainright-endowed St. Mary's music department faculty position six years ago. Ya sure, why didn't I remember? Adolph mused the recent head knock must have also jarred his memory sufficiently to delay his juxtaposition of the suspicious drowning of the Music Department Chairman in nearby West Lake two years ago and the subsequent promotion of Professor Wainright to be dean.

By prearrangement, Adolph telephoned an ex-music department secretary who'd transferred to the St. Mary's Art Department. He'd met Joy Higgins at various charity fund-raisers. Ms. Higgins, shy at first, began to speak freely after Adolph explained she wasn't under suspicion for the computer thefts and he merely sought to learn as much as he could about music department computer use without alerting current employees. She confirmed student scheduling.

When he asked if Dean Wainright enjoyed administrator computer access, she replied, of course. When Adolph paused, Ms. Higgins blurted out that perhaps she shouldn't discuss Spenser Wainright since she'd dated him for four months. Who ended it? Adolph asked. Ms. Higgins replied she did, and then hastily requested the matter be considered closed. When he asked her how Wainright interacted with staff, Adolph listened intently as Ms. Higgins said that Wainright would most often be cold and self-centered, showing little empathy for anyone. She twice paused to interject she wasn't trying to single him out for criticism explaining that the department employed many contending egos.

Ms. Higgins, in her final remark, expressed regret in having no Jonathan Green remembrance. Adolph tried to ease her conscience by reminding her she'd transferred departments. Offering thanks, he concluded their conversation by saying he might need to contact her again. She said she hoped not.

Adolph scratched a reminder on a post-it to set up an appointment with a Dean Wainright colleague. The intercom buzzed. The Chief requested a word and Adolph, upon entering The Chief's office, couldn't remember when he'd last seen Chief Howard's desktop wood.

"You don't need to sit," The Chief said. "Cousin Francine telephoned. She said she was worried you'd forgotten her dug up garden. My mention of your hospitalization calmed her."

"I'm awaiting lab results." The Chief would know that if he'd read Adolph's last report. Why'd he do paperwork at all? He needed Len's promised information update to emphasize the head conk and not having a partner wouldn't hinder his efforts. "Talked to Len earlier today."

"I know, I know. Stop by and charm her. Family peace, you know." The Chief's body bent sideways. "Here, take this bottle of sherry. It'll dull her tongue's sharpness."

Adolph didn't completely comprehend as he tucked the bottle, wrapped in brown kraft paper, under his right arm. "Consider it done when my car's finished having graffiti repainted."

"Again?" The Chief didn't wait for a reply. "Do it quick. Say, how's riding with Luann?"

"She ain't no Yancey. Been MIA last two afternoons." Adolph gulped. "That's not bitching. It wasn't intended that way."

"You know I don't reward detective sniping. Since I'd

have seen the non-duty hours log at week's end, consider it's no harm done. Say hello to Francine for me."

Adolph mentally chastised himself for speaking out of turn against Luann. An unwritten code, personal likes and dislikes aside, required a detective to protect all, unless The Chief asked a direct question. Adolph realized The Chief would likely never explain his reasons for pairing him with Luann. Running superior errands also represented an unwritten rule. An idea dawned. At his desk, he lifted the used evidence bag from the bottom drawer, touching only its tape, and inserted the sherry and The Chief's bag. The impromptu action filled his desired need to have a defendable reason to exit the station with the misappropriated evidence bag.

He telephoned the Rose Garden B&B and reached voice mail. For his effort, he wrote a formal ass-covering note into the case file. Next, from his cell phone, he dialed Officer Finnegan. They agreed Adolph would meet him at Patsy's. He left a message for Mary he might be a few minutes late, explaining he had to depend on another officer to give him a ride home.

Careful to avoid fingertip touches to the evidence bag, Adolph carried it tucked under his left arm when Lt. Turner intercepted him near the squad room's exit door.

"What'd you tattle to The Chief about Luann?" Bulldog's eyebrows twitched with anger.

"Nothing."

"Had to be something. He'd not call me about her detective duty hours unless he had a reason. And, you're the only other detective."

"Hell, I've more important things to do. Ever think The Chief has two eyes."

"Don't be a smart-ass." Bulldog's legs spread to a shoulder-width defensive stance.

"Ride somebody else. I'm on a mission for The Chief."

Bulldog's lower lip curled. "Bullshit. Just because The Chief assigns you the goofy cousin's case doesn't mean you have a special Harry Potter invisible cloak. It takes more than that to wear the gold shield that shines from this chest."

"Back off. You'd lose that fricking gold shield if The Chief had someone tell him you're sexually harassing Luann."

"You've gone mad . . . effing mad."

Adolph's shoulder and bicep muscles tightened. An inner voice broke into his consciousness. *Get yourself under control. Don't break the sherry bottle.* "Forget I said anything. Let's drop it all. I need to catch a ride home."

"Run scared," Bulldog sneered. "Keep that tail between your legs."

Adolph ignored the explicit manhood threat. He didn't have the fail-safe proof necessary to prove his harassment allegations if Luann denied everything. The next time he laid on clammy grass as a peeper he'd verify Bulldog's address and document his mental images with a digital camera. Too bad he hadn't bought a smartphone with picture capability. He refused to glance back at Bulldog. When the humid air of the outdoors struck his face, he lengthened his strides toward Patsy's. Each step diffused his anxiety that his outspokenness would be fatal.

"Saved you a spot," Officer Finnegan said. "Have time for coffee?"

"Yeah. Thanks for sticking around. Saves me a walk home." Adolph completed a gaze of the small too-early-for-supper crowd and slid onto a booth seat opposite Officer Finnegan. "Apologize, but I've forgotten your first name. Job has so conditioned me to using badge names that I forget that the wearers have first names, too."

"My mother wasn't too original. Named me Sean."

"Sean. I'll try to remember that. Of all the Bridgetown patrol officers, you've impressed me as being one of the best."

"Flatter me more and I'll bestow upon you the title of honorary Irishman." He laughed.

"Any reason we had to meet here?" He tilted the evidence bag against the seat's corner.

Finnegan bowed his head and spoke in a lowered voice. "Rebecca wanted to speak to me and I said I'd only do that if I had a witness."

Adolph understood. When walking a beat, he'd often encountered a citizen who wanted to provide hush-hush top-secret information. If he knew the snitch, no problem with talking one-on-one. If not, the likelihood of being set up loomed too great. Finnegan was demonstrating supreme street smarts. Across the way, Rebecca's fringed-skirt bounced against nude-colored nylons disappearing into white running shoes. After distributing a tray of drinks to a nearby table, she headed in their direction. As she got closer, Adolph's mind corralled the impression that today's skirt hung twenty inches longer than her basement acting costume.

"How 'bout you two find a table in the party room," she said, and then pointed to two curtained French doors at the cafe's seating area's far end.

Adolph grabbed the evidence bag's red tape and followed Finnegan into the party room. With an expanse of tables, they decided on mid-room. Adolph hid the sherry by placing it on the floor. Rebecca entered with cups and a coffee carafe. He could detect the typical skittish witness symptoms in Rebecca—the constant glances, tentative steps, and always maintaining a clear exit escape route. He stretched out both arms to invite her to join them. He would've kept an eye on Finnegan, but Rebecca seemed to require his full attention. He cast aside all doubt to believe she wouldn't have asked to meet with Finnegan for no reason.

She stared at Finnegan. "Didn't think you'd bring him." Rebecca poured, and her shaky right hand caused coffee to slosh from the cup into the saucer sitting in front of Adolph.

He plucked a napkin from its metal dispenser. "What's the problem?" Adolph would've appreciated an answer, but the fact he didn't get one wasn't disturbing. He refrained from repeating his question as Rebecca steadied the carafe, set it down, and seated herself, her arms folded.

"I'm confused," Finnegan began. "Said I'd bring someone. If you don't want to talk in front of him, that's okay with me. We can leave."

Adolph's Gold

Finnegan, you'll never be a detective with that brash technique and attitude.

"It's okay, I guess." Rebecca hid her hands beneath the tabletop.

"Adolph's only here to listen. I've been upfront. What's troubling today?"

Rebecca lifted her gaze to Finnegan. "You know I can't thank you enough for what you've done for my son." Her eyes glistened. "Try to be a good mother to him."

"What's happened to Bradford now?" Finnegan asked.

"Had to make a decision. Lawyers are expensive and I can't lose Patsy's."

Adolph didn't understand the dynamics beneath this conversation. His unmoving gaze noticed a tear emerge at the corner of Rebecca's left eye. He waited with baited breath.

Finnegan's left hand fingers tapped his cup's rim. "And—"

"I agreed to do things for money."

Adolph fought hard not to stare. He interlaced his fingers to prevent them from drumming the table. If Finnegan hadn't an inkling, Adolph did. He couldn't interrupt.

"Rebecca," Finnegan murmured, "your words float past my ears. Gambling, is that what this is about? Sold your son to the gangs? You have to tell me if I'm to help."

"I fear arrest." She bowed her head. "I don't want to be arrested."

Adolph waited for Finnegan's response. The police couldn't grant amnesty, although that's what they often explicitly or implicitly promised to obtain a suspect's confession.

"I'm here as a friend," Finnegan replied. "That's all, nothing more."

Adolph coughed, not by design, but of necessity. Finnegan's response the classic dodge taught at the police academy. He wouldn't tell Rebecca one could still be a friend if speaking into a handset mouthpiece from the visitor side of the state prison's glass partition.

"I'm sorry. Made a bad decision. The coffee's on me."
Rebecca stood, pivoted, and, with her head tilted forward,
quickstepped from the party room.

Adolph gazed at Finnegan's perplexed expression. "I
didn't do anything."

The officer twisted his shoulders left. "Seems to me
somebody's scared her good."

"Would say you're right." Adolph believed he probably
spoke too quickly. Rebecca hadn't shivered like that
Whitenmire woman. "Any idea of who it might be?"

"Don't know . . . could be her husband, but I doubt it."

Adolph could speculate, but it wouldn't help Rebecca nor
hurry him home. The evidence bag on the floor required a
contents switch. Finnegan didn't need to understand the
particulars. "We ready?" Adolph stood.

"Guess so." Finnegan's chair scraped the floor as he
pushed it backwards. "I guess you need me to give you a lift
home?"

"Right. And, on the trip I'll expand on my favor request."
On his walk through Patsy's, Adolph's rotating gaze didn't
locate Rebecca. Past the entrance, the sun's rays blazed weak
across his oxfords and Adolph let Finnegan lope ahead to get
the squad car. Arriving at his house, Adolph asked Finnegan,
or as he belatedly recalled, Sean, to wait a moment.

Adolph pressed the outside garage door remote entry
combination to lift the panels giving him access to the
garage's interior house door. He shouted, "Mary, I'm home."
Without hesitating for a response, Adolph bounded down the
basement stairs with The Chief's sherry to retrieve Ant's
folder. Donning vinyl gloves, he set aside the black and white
shot of the boy tied to a tree and the one with the secret
inscription. He slid all other photographs and Ant's original
folder inside the used evidence bag to replace the removed
sherry.

At the top of the basement stairs, he met Mary. "Saw a
police car in the driveway."

Adolph kissed her. "That's Officer Finnegan. He's

waiting for this evidence bag. Kept it in the basement for a day figuring it wouldn't be safe in my car headed for the shop."

"If you say so."

Adolph dashed outside. Still wearing gloves, he tossed the haphazardly resealed evidence bag through the lowered passenger door window into the squad car's front foot well. Stepping back, he waved an ungloved right hand to a departing Finnegan. Behind his butt, he crossed a left hand second finger over the neighboring index finger, hoping that Finnegan would execute the bag's delivery without a snafu, or opening it.

He ambled to his home's front window. Weathered bar marks calmed his anxiety that a new jimmy attempt hadn't been tried. Nevertheless, deepened lines radiating from Mary's eyes told him she fretted about him more than she let on, especially since his head knock.

Chapter Seven

Luann's cheerfulness on the telephone, interrupting Adolph's breakfast, sounded forced, but he caved in to accept her offer to pick him up in fifteen minutes. During the ride to the station, her rouged face radiated the smile he remembered from her first detective days. Conscious of her recent dour silence, Adolph limited his conversation to the TV news and the weather lest she reinstate the lengthy episode of sour expressions he'd witnessed this last week. While he didn't fear her, Luann's sunnier disposition shortened his perception of the ride's length.

When their footfalls echoed in the squad room, Bulldog's hurried about-face struck Adolph as feigned busyness. Adolph, burdened by the specter that he hadn't yet received

Finnegan's message of an accomplished evidence bag dump, pooh-poohed his insight.

Bulldog slammed the telephone receiver into its cradle. The sharp cachunk echoed in Adolph's ear until chased by Bulldog's bellow: "Lilly-livered prosecutors."

Adolph braced for Bulldog's erupting diatribe.

"Attention." Bulldog paced outside his office door. "Everyone listen up."

Adolph lifted his head and Luann did likewise. Adolph waited for the lava to flow.

"County Attorney released Theodore "Ant" Carpenter. On bail, I guess, but don't know for sure. No matter. He's free on the streets. Expect fireworks at the Sixth Street Bar."

Nervous anxiety sparks arcing from one vertebra to another leaped into Adolph's mind. A panic call to Finnegan would serve no purpose if Ant had squealed or copped to a deal exposing Adolph's possession of Ant's folder. Negativity encircled Adolph's promotion like he was adrift on a raft being swallowed by a river whirlpool. He halted the wild cranial flashes of forthcoming humiliation when he saw Luann stare at him.

"Your friend Ant won't let anyone clobber you now," Luann teased.

Adolph feigned undivided attention to Bulldog's pacing and continued rant. When Lt. Hunter sputtered, Adolph searched Luann's expression for a lingering smirk. "Whatcha saying?"

"Saw the way he interacted with you in the bar's poker room. He's your snitch, right?"

"Give me a break." Adolph screwed up his face. "Hell no."

When Bulldog's office door slammed, Luann completed her swivel right to face Adolph full front. "Well then, what's up?"

"Nothing more than professional respect. He knows I can cause him problems he doesn't want. He's adept at reading the tea leaves that spell out 'live and let live.'"

"Bull. I've been out of the academy too long, and in this room three years, not to detect when I'm being spoon fed buffalo chips."

"Think what you like. I've scheduled an interview with a female teenager. It'd help if you came along." Luann's lowered eyebrows broadcast to Adolph he could've probably phrased the need for her help better, or asked on bended knee.

"Whatever." Luann arose from her desk, keys in hand. "What case? Not Ant?"

"No. Mulberry Street murder. The initial murder/suicide conclusion doesn't jibe with the crime lab's powder burns analysis. That is, not unless the mother held the gun with one of those grippy extenders used to grab cans from an upper shelf."

"That's fantasy television stuff. Will you car be ready this afternoon?"

"Tomorrow. I've requested extra sanding between the two finish coats."

"Why would I not have guessed that?" Her displayed smile indistinguishable from a grimace. "Tonto ready, Kemo Sabe."

Adolph shrugged and followed Luann to her Chrysler. He'd fashioned himself as the Lone Ranger ever since Yancey went on the shelf. Highly coincidental that Luann would use a cowboy reference. He'd not probe the remark's Freudian fringe, but focus on today's goal to close the Mulberry murder case. Mary had pointed out to him a Bridgetown Times editorial the prior week that highlighted the greater statistical likelihood that murders of the poor would remain unsolved. Wish as he might, he couldn't solve all of the town's murders. Ant's porn had generated a lead. Mrs. Connor, in an autopsy photograph, had displayed a shoulder mark similar to Ant's copulating woman's photo. He'd confront Ant later.

"Where we going?" Luann asked, waiting for the light at the first intersection.

"Jackson High School. Ten hundred block on Chestnut."

The expansive, behind the high school, parking lot always

amazed Adolph with its rows of student vehicles. He'd walked, even in his senior year. Luann parked in a front row visitor spot within yards of the principal's office. Adolph, his confidence gaining, asked to speak with Marcie Connor. The principal's secretary said she'd have Marcie excused from study hall to report to the guidance office. Luann replied she knew where that was, and then whispered to Adolph that it had a private room to facilitate interviews.

Adolph didn't need the unsolicited information. His daughter went to this high school. He stifled his annoyance, even after he and Luann were seated side-by-side on un-cushioned metal chairs where the widest part of his tie touched the laminated table with his chair back jammed against a wall. They declined the guidance counselor's offered coffee. She then brought a filled water pitcher, small plastic cups, and, on departure, left the room's door ajar.

A slender hand, fingernails painted red, grasped the door's edge without moving it.

"Come in, Marcie," Adolph said. "Please sit down. This here is Detective Nettleton."

"Marcie, I'm Luann." She reached for the pitcher. "Would you care for water?"

Marcie eased into the room. "No." The door's closing caused her to flinch.

Adolph attempted to establish rapport. "You've got nothing to be afraid of." In her living room, he hadn't recognized the grace and dignity of the young woman now before him in a light red blouse, blue jeans, and sneakers. Gone were her cheeks' purple blotches inspired by grief and deepened by recurring sobs. Fresh, copper-toned face powder added a silky glimmer to her high cheekbones and, to Adolph's amazement, hid the former creases, except he remembered her dark deep-set eyes. He didn't repeat his request that Marcie sit. "How you doing, Marcie?" He waved a hand at Luann for her to put away the displayed notepad.

"Okay." Her pupils, centered in eyes without gaiety, surfaced like periscopes and then sank back into the depths below bangs that obscured her eyebrows.

"That's good. Maybe the Army can ship your dad home early?"

Marcie sat across from Adolph and hid her hands under the table's green top.

Adolph straddled a fear that starting with Marcie's murdered mother would likely renew Marcie's sobs and defeat further inquiry. He tried to blend in empathy with his news. "We're all so sorry for the loss of your mother, but she didn't shoot the other person."

Marcie's forehead dipped forward. Her right hand brushed her bangs to the side and exposed long shallow wrinkles spread across Marcie's brow. "Don't know what you're saying."

"I'm saying there had to be another person in the house."

From the corner of his eye, Adolph caught Luann shift her gaze to the ceiling. Good, she'll not interfere. Adolph laterally spread his hands, palms down, and rested them on the table.

"Who?" Marcie asked. Adolph allowed the silence to snake whatever fear it could into her psyche. Marcie pursed her lips before whispering. "Not me it wasn't."

He rubbed the back of his left hand with his right palm. "I've a suspicion . . ." Marcie averted his gaze. He twice tapped his right forefinger on the table. "A suspicion your exaggerated kicking act was meant to distract others from questioning you about your earlier visit home that morning."

"No, no way." Marcie jumped up without shifting her blue sneakers toward the door.

"It's okay," Luann said. Her voice as soothing as moisture cream gently rubbed into the skin. "If you'd sit down, perhaps you can give us, especially me, a clearer picture of what you did that day, beginning from when you woke up."

Adolph ceased his finger tapping. Marcie slumped into her vacated chair.

"I went to school."

"And," Adolph asked, "your bedroom is at the top of the stairs on the right, correct?"

"Yeah." Marcie unwrapped a stick of gum and folded it between her front teeth.

Adolph coaxed himself to keep his question rhythm measured. Marcie wasn't street tough, not yet anyway. "That morning you made your bed without changing the sheets."

She spit out the words, "Yeah, so what."

"Suspect you didn't want to get grounded."

Marcie failed to protect her mouth corners from the indentations of a smile. "Yeah."

"Even so, you loved your mother and you'd do anything to protect her."

Marcie hung her head. Adolph pressed a finger to his lips to forestall Luann.

"That was your fresh blood on the sheets that morning wasn't it?"

"So what if it was?" Marcie glared at Adolph. "I ain't saying nothing more."

When Luann tapped his shoulder, Adolph flicked his gaze at her, frowned, and snapped it back to Marcie. "Okay. I'll need to get in contact with your grandmother. Wait here."

Adolph motioned Luann to step out of the room. He approached the guidance counselor to both thank her and to mention that Marcie could go back to study hall.

"Dead end I'd say." Luann's first words since exiting the school bounced across her Chrysler's hood. Adolph reached for the Chrysler's passenger door handle. Luann swiveled her head and easily bested him in clicking their seatbelts, as if an Olympic event. With the ignition key between her fingers, Luann shoveled more gloom on solving his Mulberry case. "A young girl past puberty staining bed sheets doesn't count for much."

Her comments stuck in his craw. He'd never spout off without having read the case file. "It does if the blood contained semen, which may match the dead Dragon."

"What?" The Chrysler lurched backward. "Where's this going?"

"Hell if I know, except the lab not supporting my personal

theory of the mother's self-defense shoved me off a cliff. Need to confirm the brother's whereabouts that morning and pressure Marcie, with her grandmother present, so we can use what she says or arrest."

"The brother likely wouldn't shoot his mother. You think he shot the Dragon?"

"Entirely possible." While he'd give Luann the benefit of parental intuition, he preferred provable facts. "Lab report says powder residue doesn't support Mrs. Connor as a shooter."

"What evidence he did it?" Luann maneuvered her Chrysler out of the parking lot.

Adolph assumed she meant the brother. "None, or better put, none yet found."

"And the girl?"

"Motive could be revenge for either the mother's murder . . . or the rape."

"Mother raped?" Luann pumped her car brakes at a red light, a block from the station.

"Don't believe so. Mother's body, lab said, had no semen traces or physical trauma in . . . you know where. The popped blouse buttons hinted it may have come to that, but the shooting intervened. I'd originally thought this Jonathan Greene came to the house to recruit the brother into the Dragons. He could've, and then Marcie showed. Wouldn't be out of character for a reluctant parent to be either threatened with or persuaded by a child's deflowering."

"That's cruel, if not inhuman."

"Agree." Adolph left unsaid that the mother's shoulder mark linked her to the porn trade. He glanced at the side of Luann's exposed and unmarred neck and followed her into the station.

After putting her purse into her desk drawer, she asked, "You calling the grandmother?"

"Prefer to let the girl sweat." Adolph grabbed the Mulberry file and motioned to Luann to join him in the interrogation room. He pushed three chairs away from the room's centered table to leave space for his unimpeded pacing to and from the file contents he spread out on the table and the dry-erase whiteboard he dragged into the room.

Adolph leaned both palms onto the table and gazed at Luann, who'd pulled up a chair across from him. "You got the tech's report on Marcie's bedroom? What stands out?"

Luann parted two upper page clasps and flipped through several eight-by-eleven paper sheets. "Pictures show a tidy room by teenager standards. First photos show the bed made. This photo of the sheet's darkened stain indicates the technician pulled back the coverlet. If the girl was raped in this bed, doesn't make sense for the perp to flip the bedspread over the pillows."

"Right. Whether unprotected consensual sex or rape, Marcie had to have been the last in her bedroom as indicated by the made bed. If the mother had been an unwilling witness to her daughter's rape, say roped to a chair, or, perhaps, she surprised Jonathan and Marcie. Who knows? If either happened, my assumption is the bed would've been left a mess."

"But there's no report finding the mother or Marcie had ligature marks."

Adolph, using black marker, drew a crude cross-section of 735 E. Mulberry. "That no one checked could be one reason. But in my event memory, Marcie could've had marks or scratches from the patrol officer's restraint when she tried to run to her mother in kitchen. Don't recall seeing rope burns or anything similar when she hugged and kissed her mother on the gurney." He watched Luann peer through a magnifying glass at one of the kitchen photographs.

"What are these white floor specks?" Luann asked.

"Think you'll find they're listed as sea salt crystals. Pretty common kitchen item."

"And one to throw in another's eyes."

"Hadn't given much thought to that. Did the male victim have salt on his skin?"

"Not that it says here. Supposition is that they'd be foreign objects his eye fluid would've washed out or this Jonathan, given time, wiped the salt away."

Adolph craned his neck toward Luann. "Check the vic's sleeve."

"Can't. He wore a tank top."

Did he have to do all the thinking? "Then check the front's bottom hem. See if he followed today's untucked style."

"Report says top had traces of NaCl." Luann the lifted page and pointed.

"That's salt. Gives us a scenario of the male vic holding a gun on the mother. Marcie or her brother sneaks in, tosses salt into the male's eyes. The gun discharge kills the mother and the male then loses the gun in a shuffle, or it's twisted against him, to be shot dead at close range."

"Then, after watching a zillion cops on TV, the real killer wipes his or her prints from the gun, places it in the dead male's hands, and scrams."

Now that's the sarcastic Luann he'd come to know. "Who called 9-1-1?"

"West side neighbor said she heard two shots. To answer your next question, the neighbor's visibility of the direct route from the Connor's house to the high school is blocked by a rear garage and a tall line of lilac bushes."

"Notes here say Finnegan and Riley's shooting day canvass uncovered no other eyewitness. Time to let Marcie stew. See what breaks."

"What about lunch?" Luann asked.

"Well, sorta promised . . ." Caught off-guard, Adolph grappled for a response. "Promised myself a walk to the river. Need to stretch my legs and absorb a few minutes of the sun's Vitamin D." Gathering the file, Adolph allowed Luann to precede him into the hallway.

"I've an errand to run; see you at one."

Adolph wouldn't be surprised if her errand meant she'd birddog him. He blinked when sunlight struck his face as he escaped the station's shadow. Since hospitalized, he'd missed his regular walking exercise. It didn't pump the heart as much

Donan Berg

as soothe his nerves and sweep from his mind the vestiges of
sharp insults and useless anger. To be sure, he'd wave to
others and utter soon-to-be forgotten greetings, all positive
promotional PR. Yet, today he couldn't distract himself from
the Mulberry murder. He discarded his focus on whether or
not the triggering incident was a boy's gang recruitment or a
girl's defilement because either way a youth suffered. If either
had fired a fatal shot, a successful self-defense argument could
de-fang the legal system, but not erase the mind's violence-
effects scars that, once etched, psychologist's say, flourish and
never heal. Even from a lengthy time interval, Adolph's
mother's death validated his thoughts.

The walk's halfway point greeted the river, the ever
present, never-ending water, where the drop in Adolph's
vision could never be distinguished from the drop that tumbled
off an Itasca stream rock or that now rushed past the Gateway
Arch. He understood that and never cared to let it bother him.
Other drops, the red ones from youthful veins, did wreck
havoc on his psyche, coagulating into tentacles of terror that
squeezed his heart chambers and wouldn't let go.

Nevertheless, when he pinned on his gold shield, it'd be
proof he'd prevailed in one battle, but the wider war would
continue. That was life. His struggle. His journey. The extra
paycheck money earmarked for Mary's comfort. Without this,
or even any, goal he'd might as well jump into the mightiest of
all rivers and let it sweep him past the delta and dump him,
body and soul, into the unknown depths of warm, polluted salt
water.

He reeled his subconscious back to reality. He had to
admit two things he'd never tell anyone. One, he and Luann
had worked well together earlier this morning and, two, he'd
never tell her unless tortured. He still had to suspect Luann
sported a shoulder mark similar to Mrs. Connor and the still
unidentified woman in Ant's photograph.

"Excuse me," Adolph said. He sidestepped to avoid a
billowy pioneer skirt.

An arm reached out to grab him. "I need to speak with

you. Us alone."

"Not here?" Adolph gazed into Rebecca's fragile face. It's normal server gaiety missing.

Below crystal-clear, brilliant, and brittle eyes, her voice said, "Not at the station, either."

He remembered Officer Finnegan. "What about Patsy's party room?"

"Six o'clock tonight." Rebecca's skirt fluttered, resuming its journey to wherever.

Adolph hurried his stride to the station positive that Rebecca hadn't seen his nod nor heard his halting words into his cell phone to explain to Mary that, without a car, she shouldn't expect him until seven, perhaps eight. By Mary's reserved tone, he could tell she wasn't pleased with his "have-to-work" excuse devoid of detail. He dashed into The Corner Drugstore and purchased a single long-stemmed yellow rose smothered in baby's breath greenery.

He guessed the black-rimmed clock hands had rotated passed one when Luann glared at him. Laying the drugstore plastic bag on the Mulberry file Luann had obviously re-arranged on his desk, he offered, "What case of yours would be front 'n' center?"

Not wishing to resemble a whipped dog, he squared his shoulders and, with a forced, exaggerated spring in his step, didn't permit Luann to beat him to the parking lot to begin a round of doorbell ringing. No radio call diverted them. The criminals, he mused, must have gathered for an afternoon siesta. If his tag-a-long provided Adolph with any knowledge, it was that Luann had been assigned a disproportionate share of domestic disputes.

At four thirty, he requested Luann to drop him off at the station. He feigned an interest in running a computer criminal records check on a compiled Dragons' list. In reality, he would mark time until six. Bulldog surprised him by banging the squad room door at five thirty.

Bulldog grabbed a suit coat from his office chair. "Waiting for your car?"

"Tomorrow." Adolph shuffled folders as Bulldog hesitated close to Luann's desk. "Snitch heard rumor a new porn production company has invaded Bridgetown. You hear it?"

"Not a word. Will keep my ears open." Bulldog turned. "See you in the a.m."

Adolph, content Bulldog hadn't offered a ride, unlidded the shoe polish from his upper drawer and added a top-layer buff to his oxfords. The prosaic task adequately filled his void until he left for Patsy's. Past the cafe's front door, he didn't dilly-dally to count restaurant faces. Shoving open the curtained door into the unlit party room, he clicked a nearby wall switch. Despite an unlimited seat choice, he sat in the one he'd occupied when Finnegan had been there.

Rebecca entered, coffee carafe and two clear glass mugs in hand. "Thanks for coming." She poured without his objection and then slid a half-filled mug toward him. Hers already sported a golden liquid to which she added steaming coffee. "Couldn't talk without Irish coffee."

The mug warmed Adolph's fingers. He wondered why she'd not enlisted Finnegan's help. Perhaps he'd discover. "Your friendship's always been cherished."

Rebecca slumped into a chair across from Adolph. "If so, you're the last friend I have." He saw her eyes, when not obscured by her bowed head, had lost their sparkle. "And, after what I say, I'd not be surprised if you, too, abandoned me."

"Nonsense." His elongated coffee sip satisfied his hollowed anxiety more than words.

"I've been frantic these last two years." Her eyelids blinked, squashing untold secrets. "Randall's all-night gambling never ends. He's burdened Patsy's with untold credit markers he's tossed onto multiple poker table pots around town."

"Scuttlebutt's heavy that Ant has a large one."

Rebecca nodded and sighed until her shoulders collapsed. "He's ruthless." Her voice pinged like a released jack-in-the-box spring. "If it would help, I'd blow him away for sicing those Dragons on Bradford. And, it cost me more than my last saved penny to hire that lawyer to bring my son home."

"Sounds like you've done more than any parent or spouse should have to do."

Rebecca swirled the contents of her mug. "Then . . . early one morning, maybe three weeks ago, this note was slipped under the front door threatening to firebomb Patsy's unless Randall, now in jail, satisfies Ant's marker within thirty days. Then Randall blew up at me for selling my every possession to help Bradford. Christ, you were here. I can't siphon a dry diner bank account, and without Patsy's I'd be homeless without a mailbox for welfare checks."

"You sure it isn't a bluff?" He tapped the outside of his blazer to check for his notepad.

"Positive. Two day's after Randall's arrest a second note instructed me to drive that night to an abandoned farm at midnight, fasten a rolled handkerchief blindfold across my eyes, and stand under the yard light. I'm so ashamed." With one audible gulp, she swallowed her mug's contents. She stared at its glass foot and mumbled. "Had to offer up my body."

"Are you saying what I think you're saying?"

"Yep, spread my legs to the world." The mug banged against the tabletop and she covered her face with tightly closed fingers.

The timing and location didn't mesh with Adolph's peeping. He stretched forward to grab her right wrist and pull down her right hand. "Who?"

"Please, please you can't ask." Laced with trepidation, her fear radiated shivers from her wrist into his fingers. "If they discovered I even hinted this to you, they'd force my son to perform despicable acts without the mask that protected my last shred of dignity."

Adolph toyed with the idea of hinting at Lt. Hunter and/or Luann. However, his last shred of courage existing within him waned and he couldn't. "You want me to guess?" Rebecca's glazed eyes complemented a frozen facial expression. "If it's Ant, bob your head yes."

"Can't." She slipped her right hand from Adolph's grasp to unevenly press her ten fingertips into her pale cheekbone flesh. "I wish I'd the ability to hide."

Adolph's palms touched the tabletop in front of him. "You want me to do what?"

"Know that there's a letter in a bank deposit box naming names if something should happen to me. That's all I ask. Let the world know that in my heart I lived a decent life."

"I can do that. Can't I, perhaps, help you cast off your burden? What's the old saying? It's always darkest before the dawn."

Rebecca pulled a Jack Daniel's miniature from her server's apron pocket and emptied it into her mug. Adolph pursed his lips and watched Rebecca tilt the mug near her quivering lips. "Can't." She gulped the whiskey without the coffee dilution and her head twitched. "Just can't."

"No pressure, but I can be there for you." He stood to leave. "On a different subject, could you let your cook give me a quick ride home, drop me a block from my house?" Her perturbed gaze left him questioning his choice of words. "It's not that Mary would be upset."

Rebecca nodded and reached to thread her right forefinger through his mug handle.

Adolph exited Patsy's through the front door and walked to the riverfront. Two minutes later, a skinny Hispanic male with a sweating forehead dressed in baggy, striped cook's pants and driving a Mazda stopped to pick Adolph up and drop him off a block from his house.

Adolph, standing in his kitchen, forced himself to sound cheery when he shouted a welcome greeting. Mary, entering, said she hadn't heard a car or the garage door. Adolph explained a courteous citizen let him off at the corner. Mary rotated a stove dial left, opened the oven door, and pointed to a covered casserole dish. He hugged his wife, whispered he'd feed himself, and suggested she go and enjoy the TV program already on.

When his knife scraped the dish's bottom and a fork failed to find a noodle to stab, Adolph arose and wedged the casserole cover and upside down dish between dishwasher-racked plates and tossed his used silverware into the utensil basket. The televised banality of a Food Network cupcake contest allowed his unchallenged mind to whirl. Rebecca had to be at her wits end, or scared to death, to disclose sexual blackmail. In retrospect he praised himself for not divulging what his peeking observed for it most likely would have scared her off and severed all hope of his blockbuster arrest of Ant's boss. He smiled at Mary from his adjacent recliner and skipped his daily question about strange exterior noises.

"Luann called and said she'd pick you up tomorrow, same time as today."

"Thanks. Don't know why The Chief paired us. Can't wait until Yancey's back."

"I know, dear." She readjusted her hips to again be squared with the television screen.

Adolph gazed at the TV while his mind plumbed its mental depths without conjuring up one concrete idea. Tattoos circled his thoughts to Dragons. Rebecca's blackmail expose dashed the likelihood he'd witnessed a one-time playful frolic with a fake video camera. Bulldog didn't live on a farm—Rebecca's vital second point. Ant's fear causing him to dump the folder reinforced there existed a controlling master personality with tentacles in multiple illicit pies. While not a perfect plan, he decided he'd confront Ant, in Luann's presence, with the copulating-tattoo and tied-youth photographs he'd withheld from Finnegan.

He kissed Mary good night. He'd catch up on the local news by radio in the morning. Jumpy nerves delayed and refused to allow his mind an easy pass through the calming twilight that led to eventual absorbent creeping darkness and its numbing, if not energizing, sleep.

* * *

Adolph prepared a breakfast of toast and coffee and let Mary sleep in. She'd awaken him twice in the wee hours by coughing and he'd stumbled once to the bathroom for cough syrup. He swallowed the last toast point when Luann's car horn honked from his driveway. He hopped in and directed her to detour and cruise past the Sixth Street Bar. Adrenaline surged through his veins when an alley tour found a familiar Cadillac.

"Loop around and park next to Ant's Caddy."

"We'll be in trouble if we miss Bulldog's meeting," Luann grumbled.

"He'll get over it." Adolph clicked his seatbelt, swung its strap free.

"I don't think so." Luann didn't rotate her steering wheel to park.

"Then drop me off, sit in a damn meeting, and count the crooks around the table."

"You're insufferable." Braking to slow her Chrysler, she stared at Adolph before speaking. "Try to be nice and keep us out of trouble and all you do is dish out BS."

When the last alley gravel stone pinged against the undercarriage, Adolph seized the opportunity to alight from Luann's car, slamming the passenger door to complete the process. His right hand clutched a folder and he assumed she'd hightail it to the station to keep in good graces with Lt. Turner. Birds of a feather. When he knocked on the Sixth Street Bar's rear door, fingers squeezed his left shoulder. After a backward glance, he grunted an acknowledgement of Luann's presence. The door's window curtain fell straight before he could articulate any words.

Following a door creep slower than tapped January maple sap, Ant's hangdog face emerged. "Didn't do anything to violate my release. This is harassment. And, you know it."

"And a cheery good morning to you, too," Adolph replied.

"Crap. Come in before you ruin my reputation."

Adolph's Gold

Adolph, leaving Luann to follow, pinched his nostrils as the bar's back room reeked of industrial-strength cleaner. Above and beyond gleaming reddish-brown chair leather, he spied newly hung dark-green, light-darkening brocade curtains. Adolph equated the ambiance to a casino poker room. Ant, not bothering to offer either he or Luann a seat, retreated to the far wall and plopped into a high-backed chair, his left hand resting atop two plastic-wrapped card decks.

"You expecting a high stakes game?" Adolph asked as he signaled Luann to stand next to the room's door he'd left ajar. He tossed a folder, which landed flat, onto the poker table felt.

"What in the hell is this?" Ant whispered, making no gesture to acquire or disturb the folder that lay within his reach.

Adolph straightened his shoulders. "Oughta wait for your weaseling lies."

Ant's right hand utilized an unopened card deck to sweep the folder closer.

"If you look," Adolph began, "you'll recognize something you tried to frame me with. But don't get on your high horse, I've covered my butt." Adolph gazed at Luann's flattened eyebrows, tight lips, and intently focused eyes. He immediately realized that, if any of his exposed skin had interrupted her line of vision, the singed odor would've filled the room. Her right hand brushed aside her pantsuit jacket to rest her palm on the butt end of her 9mm service weapon. Adolph swung his concentrated attention to Ant.

Ant dumped the folder contents. "Never saw these two photographs before."

"Maybe not these particular ones, but you know where the studio is."

"Hell no." Ant's eyes spurted into glowing red fireballs.

Adolph unbuttoned his blazer to unsnap the holster restraint to his 9mm. "Maybe you didn't clearly hear the question? A long relationship should be honored by a second chance." Adolph fingered his weapon's grip. "If I remember right, the general, serious question asked a moment ago was if

169

you know where the studio is."

"Man, don't do this to me. We'll both be pushing up daisies."

"I've updated my will. Does yours still have wet ink?"

A clicking sound caused Adolph to glance Luann's way. She'd closed the room's door. "Why'd you do that?" He let his Walther's weight straighten his elbow and his right hand rubbed the barrel against his right pant leg. Ant didn't twitch a muscle.

"Well, if you're going to waste him, we don't need any shot alerting witnesses."

"Why? Is that because you're Ant's boss and you're protected if I plug him?"

"What? Go to hell, Adolph." Luann squared her feet under her shoulders and her pantsuit jacket again covered her 9mm. Adolph kept his service weapon pointed at the floor.

A smirk creased Ant's facial cheeks. "Wow. Better than TV. A totally screwed-up partnership. Priceless."

"You, weasel." Adolph glared at Ant. "You denying you tried to frame me."

"All I'll say is I favor faster horses, younger women, older whiskey, and more money."

"Yeah, and I ain't strumming an old country guitar." Adolph glanced at Luann. "Let's get out of here before this slime ball requires us to shower." He reached forward to gather in the folder and its original photographs.

"The police shower co-ed? Bet you two would enjoy bumping shoulders."

Adolph thumped his left fist on the poker table. "Sleaze ball." He peeked at Luann. She'd twisted the doorknob with her left hand to expose the employee-empty hallway. "We'll see ourselves out." Adolph motioned for Luann to precede him.

Ant, his lip corners upturned, fingered one of the card decks without uttering a word.

With half-strides sideways until the hallway, Adolph trailed Luann and, once outside, yanked the bar's exterior door shut. Without their gazes meeting, he asked, "If you would, drop me off at the body shop." He snapped his 9mm Walther P.38 securely into its holster.

"You sure. We might not've missed the lieutenant's meeting."

"No big deal." As he gazed at the passing cityscape, he knew he required time to think. The insulting generalized nature of Ant's denials and taunts hadn't worried him until the specific quip that both could be pushing up daises. The violence innuendo hadn't disturbed him, but the word "both" enthralled him. Adolph had never known Ant to outwardly express fear of anyone. But whom had Ant hocked his soul to? Had to be a player of substance. Such a person hadn't blipped on Adolph's radar. Luann's initial hateful stare and her retort, etched with personal bile, also troubling. "Drop me here. If need be, I'll let you fill me in when I return."

"What do I say if I'm asked about you?"

"Tell'em the truth. Had to get my wheels back." He deliberately left the folder on Luann's front car seat. If she noticed, she didn't remind him he'd left it. From the body shop's customer area he caught a glimpse of his gleaming yellow Monte Carlo's rear fender. The sight brightened his lackluster morning.

Brian, the shop's foreman, waved him into the detailing area. "She's a beauty."

"Always has been," Adolph said. "She ready to go?"

"If you can't find where we messed up."

Adolph's right palm grazed ever-larger concentric circles where the driver-door graffiti had been. Failing to detect a bump or grit, he stepped to the front fender and, standing, peered at the door before crouching to view an altered light contrast against the yellow paint. With three colored primer coats and a thick clear protective coat, he couldn't decipher a paint line separating old from new. Brian grinned at him.

"I'm ready to roll," Adolph announced. "Insurance cooperate?"

"You bet. Deductible's paid, too."

"What?" Adolph's instincts flashed a screaming alert. "Who?"

"Don't know. Receptionist got a call. Thought it was your insurance agent. The next day an envelope with cash and your typed name found after lunch, dropped through the door slot."

"Still got either the cash or the envelope?"

"Banked the five C-notes. Envelope trashed. Like I said, thought your insurance agent became involved and you'd have known."

"News to me." Adolph checked his vibrating cell phone. Office. He'd be there shortly.

Brian gazed at his boot tops. "Roscoe said you're investigating his home burglary?"

"Really can't comment on an open investigation."

"Heard a couple Jackson students had laptops pilfered. Thinking connection, maybe?"

"Not that I know of." Jackson High rang a bell. The Connor teens chiming Adolph's memory bank cells. He filed Brian's comment into the recess of his mind, although it didn't sound critically feasible or important. He released the Monte Carlo's driver door latch and viewed his keys in the ignition. "Thanks. Gotta be going."

The welcome breeze through the driver window buoyed Adolph until he spied two empty adjacent station parking lot spots where he could park straddling the separating white line. With lengthened strides taking him past Luann and Lt. Hunter's cars parked near the rear entrance door, he mentally braced himself for a confrontation with Bulldog.

Neither appeared as Adolph swiveled and then plunked himself into his desk chair. He eyeballed a confidential crime lab envelope laying in his inbox. He slit the seal on Len's updated Rose Garden B&B skeleton report and began to read:

"Examination found leather fragments. Size and length suggests they once had been sewn on a western-style shirt. Deteriorated blue cotton threads consistent with Wrangler brand jeans indicated by the inch-and-a-half-by-three-inch manufacturer label. A twisted black leather belt has a stained, discolored western-style metal buckle. The belt buckle exhibits generic cowboy qualities with a raised Texas longhorn symbol, a design widely purchasable in national retail stores, and a base alloy coated with low-grade silver.

"Small traces of burnt marijuana plant fiber and chemical 9-carboxy-THC residue present in the soil."

Digesting this newest information, Adolph's normal open case anxiety eased. If he spoke with Mrs. Hoskins again, she had to remember such an outfitted guest or visitor.

Adolph, in the detective squad room for nearly an hour with no Luann and no Bulldog, chose to again chance disobeying The Chief's partner directive. If the other two enjoyed a fling, his coast was clear and they wouldn't be in any position to squeal. Besides, he'd be helping The Chief's cousin, which presented a win/win. Sliding into his Monte Carlo, the pleasurable motoring world quickly returned with the invigorating pulse of a 303-hp V8. He lamented the end of an all-to-short ride across town to the Rose Garden B&B driveway. The new welcome sign, affixed next to the front door, greeted him as he rang the front porch visitor bell.

Mrs. Hoskins appeared in a flowered apron. "Detective, what a pleasant surprise."

"Thank you. Do you remember a past guest who wore western wear?"

Her shoulders jerked back without either foot shifting to an altered stance. "Perhaps if you came into the parlor and described this particular clothing that might help."

Adolph felt like he'd stepped into a refrigerator lettuce crisper. He folded his arms in an effort to warm his hands while describing for Mrs. Hoskins what Len's report had said. "Western-style shirt, maybe with a leather chest fringe, Wrangler brand blue jeans, and a black belt with a silver cowboy belt buckle."

"No." She lifted her apron's skirt to wipe her hands. "No one like that stayed here."

Adolph tried to rally his crushed expectations. Mrs. Hoskins didn't appear to have touched the sherry. "Well, maybe not necessarily checked in, could've maybe visited."

"Guests rarely had visitors, that is, except children. We aren't a romantic place."

"I can appreciate that." Adolph tried to grasp his next question. Mrs. Hoskins's answers thwarted the lab's most promising forensic lead to crack the case. He'd reviewed the updated report for DNA matches. None added to the previous zero total. He couldn't believe the bones buried in Mrs. Hoskins's garden hadn't been a B&B guest. Surely Mrs. Hoskins wanted to get back to normal; she couldn't be enjoying the notoriety. In his interviews with all six of her closest neighbors, none reported seeing anything suspicious except the two neighbors with a view of guests entering and leaving Mrs. Hoskins's front door. Both had snickered when mentioning the recent Mr. Lincoln look-a-like. Adolph's gut instinct gave credence to all neighbors except Dean Spenser Wainright, but then, even Adolph's suspicious nerve endings hadn't been connected with provable fact. Weirdness, he'd learned early in his career, didn't equate to guilt. Once or twice thinking that, and being burned, now eradicated his jumping to any unwarranted conclusion of Dean Wainright being the murderer.

Adolph shifted his body weight to his right foot. "What about a guest with heavy-duty moviemaking equipment?"

"One doesn't come to mind. Assume you mean more than a handheld tourist camera?"

Of course he did. Didn't he say heavy duty? "Yes."

"Still no."

"Rebecca from Patsy's ever visit? Say, within the past two years."

"Can't say she has. Her son raced through the backyard once."

He opted to chase what would surely be a dead end. "When?"

"Brain too cluttered to remember exactly." She scrunched her face. "Year ago, maybe."

"Thanks." He dismissed the information for it wasn't

uncommon for boys to hop fences or chase through yards. "If you remember a guest who wore western clothes, give me a call."

Adolph decided while ambling to his Monte Carlo that he'd return to the station. The lab findings had promised solid clues to secure meeting his self-imposed case-closing deadline. The failure of verification by Mrs. Hoskins built a wall for him to bang his head against. Convinced the critical clue wasn't the motor oil, he'd obviously missed a vital skeleton connect, but what?

When he entered the squad room, Bulldog and Luann cast him disapproving glances.

Chief Howard entered to accentuate the twosome's point. "About time."

Adolph arched his back. "Had to speak again with your cousin at the B&B."

The Chief stopped his advance at the word cousin. "She help?"

"Tried. Nothing substantial registered in Mrs. Hoskins's memory."

"Coulda figured that. Anyway, that satisfies her morning telephone call. Carry on."

When The Chief departed, Bulldog clapped for attention. "Luann tells me you called on Ant this morning."

"Yeah." Adolph stared at the back of Luann's head waiting for her rotated face to appear. It didn't. He dismissed all concern about her and his weight adjustment squeaked his chair's roller.

"You had photographs and asked about a studio?" Bulldog edged two steps closer.

"Sounds right." Adolph figured the less information he disclosed the better off he'd be.

"What'd Ant say? Luann claimed she didn't hear the entire conversation."

"Not much." Adolph stared at Bulldog. "Clamped his mouth shut fast."

Bulldog lowered both hands to his hips. "He tell you

where the studio was?"

"Too scared." Adolph knew that wasn't exactly true, but he'd let Bulldog squirm with misgivings about Ant as well. "At least, that's today. He'll come around."

Adolph observed Bulldog's carotid veins bulge as if the pulsating blood through his neck tripled in volume. "Keep me in the loop." Bulldog's soles creaked across the floor and the sound fused with the telltale floor scraping sounds of Luann's chair, swiveled by her to face Adolph.

"Got time?" Luann's voice tentative. "Time to join me on a retail theft complaint?"

"Right." Adolph figured he didn't have a choice with The Chief's partnership order.

And so, while Luann asked boring questions of the local department store manager, he jotted sketchy notes. Between scribbles he contemplated whether or not Bulldog's question about Ant's babbling twisted professional interest into personal survival. Ant could've been fearful Adolph's inquiries signaled that Bulldog had let something slip. Adolph contemplated he was being too meticulous and giving Ant credit for things the thug would've never dreamed. Adolph caught himself doodling notepad circles while the foppish store manager droned on. A fainthearted Rebecca had alluded to child perversion, probably worse than the naked beaten-boy photograph Adolph had squirreled away. His mind leapfrogged ahead to speculate about Luann and Bulldog. They had to have been up to no good when he couldn't find them in the squad room earlier, as he'd expected. He'd test his intuition with a late night basement surveillance encore.

Adolph let supper's heartwarming smell of Mary's meatloaf erase the do-nothing afternoon with Luann. When Kristen asked to be excused, he broached the subject of his need to leave the house after the ten o'clock news for maybe three hours. Mary's abrupt silence and contorted pressed lips provided ample evidence his absence notification wasn't well received, but she verbalized no objection.

The sportscaster's highlighting a losing Chicago Cubs

score jolted him from a recliner nap. He kissed Mary good night before changing into a blue long-sleeved sweatshirt and khakis.

On Bulldog's street, an unanswered owl's hoot pierced the silence and faded into oblivion. Adolph couldn't locate the bird even with the tree branches exposed. He strolled west for three blocks and found Luann's Chrysler parked a block from Bulldog's. An illegally parked Salvadore Pizza truck blocked a fire hydrant. He could ticket, but then he'd have to record his presence. Besides, he'd have to hike back to the Monte Carlo for a seldom-used ticket book.

With recon glances to convince no eyes observed, he dashed across the lawn he'd verified to be Bulldog's residence and dove past the juniper bush to position himself outside the basement window where he'd made his first observations. The slit of the parted inside window curtain narrower than on his first visit. With his right hand grasping a digital camera, his first peek observed a fully dressed Bulldog and a burgundy-robed woman with her back to him. Based on hairstyle and car presence, he guessed Luann. If consistent with his prior visit, it wouldn't surprise him if they waited for Mr. Lincoln, Rebecca, and/or Yvonne Whitenmire.

He focused his digital camera on the stage floor as the woman twirled and the robe dropped to confirm a lingerie-clad Luann. Before he could refocus on her shoulder, she retrieved a confederate soldier's cap from a stage left prop chair and pivoted. Her two hands crushed her hair tight within the cap and she shimmied into gray baggy sweatpants tied tight at the waist. She rotated to face him and button an-almost-too-small gray brass-buttoned military-styled jacket. She wiggled her toes, no boots. Adolph hadn't expected dress-up playacting. With a button push he cancelled the camera's automatic low-light flash, expecting it to both disclose his presence and bounce ineffective off the window glass. Adolph pressed the shutter button halfway to focus and then fully depressed it before releasing his finger. With two hands clutching the camera to his stomach to shield the screen display light from detection by others, the viewable image failed to show a recognizable figure in the blurred dark image he'd captured. Using his flash meant he'd have to watch and wait for one damning shot and be ready to run.

Bulldog untied and let drop from an overhead bar a backdrop of birch trees split by a winding road. Moving side to side, he switched on two floodlights before he angled the camera and its tripod to face the fake countryside. Adolph couldn't see what caused the large black shadow cast across a center-stage-standing Luann. He expected Bulldog to do something other than pace. But then, he couldn't hear any conversation.

A door slam startled Adolph. He held his breath. A car's engine revs startled birds across the street. Must be a neighbor. Adolph slowly exhaled. His rearward glance confirmed that neither of his shoes was exposed to the street. He returned his attention to Bulldog's basement. The shadow fell behind Luann who stood in front of the futon bed with her Reb jacket unbuttoned and her naked breasts propped up by lowered bra cups.

Adolph craned his neck. *Let me see your shoulder, Luann. Shed the jacket.*

When Bulldog sidled away, the figure of Abe Lincoln, stovepipe hat, long-tailed black coat, and beard revealed the shadow's creator. His oversized hands reached for the elasticized waist of the baggy sweats Luann wore. Bulldog strutted off the raised platform stage to twist the camera lens before he sidestepped left to obscure Adolph's observance of the other two.

Cursing his luck, Adolph's fingers fidgeted with his camera until he finally laid it on the grass. When Bulldog's movement unblocked Adolph's vision of Luann, she sat on the bed's edge nude except for the jacket. She reached her right arm up to unzip Honest Abe's fly to partially complete the presidential undressing. The black stovepipe hat presented a strong contrast to his tanned legs and white buttocks. Adolph anticipated Rebecca's walk-on, but she hadn't appeared. The historical figure struck Adolph as vaguely familiar in a way other than from his school's history books. Ah yes, Mrs. Hoskins's B&B guest. Had to be him. Adolph convinced himself he'd uncovered the rumored new studio location and needed to collaborate his eyewitness account with pictorial evidence.

He raised his left shoulder first and then his right to press his elbows into the grass and elevate his upper torso to create an opportunity to raise the camera above the windowsill. Confident the floodlighted stage provided sufficient natural light, and that he could escape before any basement participant would realize what happened, he struggled to narrow his camera's focus for his first shot. Seeing the military jacket cast aside, he activated the camera's telephoto feature and strained his right eyeball to catch a glimpse of Luann's naked shoulders. No matter how Adolph twisted the camera the viewfinder remained filled with the hairy flesh of a large naked male. Adolph waited and waited until his wrists ached. He cursed a pictureless camera and swallowed defeat when Bulldog switched the floodlights off.

Lying flat on his stomach, the noise of a second vehicle door caused Adolph to inhale and hold. The glow of switched on Klieg lights attracted his eyes to stare at the basement stage.

Honest Abe, redressed only in black pants, towered over, not Yvonne Whitenmire or Rebecca, but Sonja Maria Sanchez. Why her? Adolph had no clue. Rebecca's blackmail and Luann's promotion provided plausible motivations for them. Neither work nor social connection pieced the four women together in Adolph's puzzled mind.

Sonja Maria's bland expression was obscured when Honest Abe fastened the feathered mask in place by looping the rubber bands around her ears. Adolph's brief glimpse of Sonja Maria's face unremarkable in that she had absolutely fewer worry lines than Rebecca and Sonja Maria's skin and bones didn't shiver as Yvonne's upper torso had. With tonight's revelation, Adolph figuratively slapped himself on the back for having closed Sonja Maria's rape complaint by checking the box: Informant unreliable.

Clothed actors and switched off lights became his cue to vacate his post. Rather than retrace his steps, he circled the opposite way and a white Pomeranian, enclosed by a property line fence, barked and pumped its legs to match Adolph's elongated stride. A lit porch fixture dimly illuminated the dog-protected lawn, but no voice called out nor did any home resident appear bathed in light or marked by a silhouette.

Adolph, grateful he hadn't been required to falsify an excuse for his neighborhood presence, slinked his chilled and achy body into the Monte Carlo's driver seat. His right hand fingers delayed insertion of the ignition key. The pizza truck near Bulldog's stirred a beefy brain cell broth. While the driver could possibly live on the block, blocking a hydrant suggested not. Concerned about Mary's well being, he dismissed the idea of a rest-of-the-night pizza truck stakeout. Figuring he could waste thirty minutes, Adolph drove two intersections north of Bulldog's house and, from a cross street, waited with a clear view.

Ready to admit defeat for a harebrained idea, Adolph counted to five before he switched on his car's low beams after the pizza delivery truck drove through the intersection. Adolph cruised north, the truck's direction. At Bridgetown's junction of two major highways, the truck joined two cars heading west out of town. When his headlights bounced off the city limits sign, Adolph chose to be bullheaded and continue on even though he lost his official police authority to the Ore County Sheriff's Department.

The two cars ahead of him each slowed to turn off the highway onto separate county roads. Adolph let the truck's red-dot taillights guide him into the darkness. Unwilling to use more than his park lights, Adolph, as he equaled the posted fifty-five mph speed limit, strove to focus on the highway's white shoulder stripe. Four miles from Bridgetown, the truck proceeded north on an asphalt road for a mile, and then west on gravel. Adolph praised the night for being good for something—not showing his Monte Carlo's spiraling dust. He slowed from thirty to ten mph when he saw the truck's brake lights pump and its headlights arc north to enter a farmyard and disappear behind what Adolph assumed to be a wind-protecting grove. He cut his parking lights and coasted to a stop alongside a mailbox erected at a farmstead entrance. He'd remember the rural fire department number posted under the nameless mailbox for the "509" numeral represented Mary's birth month and date. Impetuously, he pressed his radio button to call in the Sheriff, and then released it, deciding to check out the farm's ownership and return in daylight.

* * *

Foregoing the unfurling of an umbrella, Adolph dashed from his Monte Carlo to the station's rear door hoping not to be drenched by the predicted morning downpour. His handkerchief wiped the last adhering raindrops from his chilled face as he opened his office computer to county land records. RFD 509 led him to a farm address and civil court records that identified owner George Bourdon as having filed for bankruptcy eleven months previous. The information erased the last of Adolph's skeptical doubt the pizza truck had left Castle Street to make deliveries. Whether or not the solidly built and cylindrical George and/or any family members remained in the house, Adolph couldn't decipher. He recalled the usually jovial farmer had been dreadfully sullen the last time Adolph saw him at Patsy's.

When Luann arrived at 7:45 a.m., he said they needed to check out the Bourdon farm. She resisted, arguing that the farm existed outside their jurisdiction. After Adolph detailed his trooping after her the prior afternoon, she reluctantly relented to giving him an hour. The rain, reduced to a drizzle, still threatened a downpour when Luann steered into the farmyard. No person stirred. When Adolph alighted from Luann's Chrysler, he stopped at its front bumper to allow a black cat to meow and meander on. Peering past the farmhouse's west side, he lost sight of the cat, while sparrows and wrens squawked and flew to the safety of a mixed hardwood and pine windbreak.

"Still don't know why we're out here." Luann's words, unlike the raindrops off her mini umbrella, dripped with censure. "This trip, even without the rain, seems to be a stupid waste of time." She lifted her soles high and free of the six-inch, unmowed grass leading to the house.

"Followed a suspicious truck to this farm last night. Came from Castle Street."

Luann ground the toe of her right pump into the soft turf. He deliberately withheld a mention of Salvatore Pizza. His reference to Lt. Turner's street enough for him to determine he'd struck a nerve. Luann's all-too-common stare mimicked the Alaskan tundra. As her expression morphed into a detached competence, Adolph had to give her thespian credit.

"How you going to cast tire treads? This farmyard's all gravel, with several puddles."

Adolph hadn't planned to. Experience taught him the morning rain would fill and severely degrade any eight-hour old tire depression. "Let's separate." He wanted to determine if the truck had been stored at the farm. "You check the house for anything suspicious. I'm headed over yonder to the machine shed and the barn." He marched off to find both structures unlocked and their interiors stripped to the bare walls, leaving no saleable metal scrap of any description. Ragged holes in the barn's concrete floor were a reminder of where the milking stanchions had stood. Within five minutes, he strode toward Luann and found her pacing the farmhouse's abbreviated flagstone path that pointed to its front door.

"Rear door won't budge," she reported.

Any teenager would've explored alternate ways to enter. "You try a window?"

Her clenched teeth should've been enough of an answer. "Why waste time?" The rumble of Luann's voice dropped a couple of Richter points. "Anyway, not procedure to proceed without local authorities . . . or backup."

"Follow me." Adolph's galoshes swished through wet

182

grass as he led the twosome around to the rear of the house. A twisted upper hinge barely kept an outer screen door from falling off. The six-panel wood exterior door, its white paint pealing, appeared wedged into its jamb. Adolph kicked. His right boot sole landed directly below the glass doorknob and the door banged against an interior wall. Emerging sunrays, originating behind Adolph, streamed into the kitchen to create light streaks across the black and white linoleum. Adolph's scan for appliances or furniture came up empty, except for a ripped brown-striped webbed lawn chair.

"Looks abandoned." Adolph's understated words spoken before his glance toward Luann.

"See. There's nothing here. We should end your wild goose hunt and get back to town where we can close cases to keep The Chief happy. I'll expect you at the car."

"Give me a minute." He heard no reply and, undeterred by whatever Luann thought, Adolph slid his wet soles across the linoleum until stopping at the kitchen's far side to open a cabinet. He coughed when the settled dust, his only find, swirled. The living room and dining room shades were drawn and tarnished brass rod brackets devoid of curtains hinted at previous decorating. That dust bunnies didn't overpopulate the wood floors of the first level surprised him. Stair treads to the second floor were likewise clean and shiny, at least in the creaky middle. Taking two stair steps at a time, Adolph paused at the upstairs landing to find four rooms to inspect. To his left, he surmised the two nine-by-ten-foot rooms to be bedrooms. Each contained dulled floor scrape marks partially covered by caked dust indicating beds, dressers, or chairs now gone. The third upstairs door opened into a bathroom with a yellow-stained toilet bowl next to a pedestal sink heavily stained by water drips long since evaporated.

Behind the fourth and last door existed a larger ten-by-fifteen-foot room. While the other rooms had been stripped bare, a rolled-up hemp-backed carpet lay stretched along the far wall beneath the room's two front yard-facing windows. On the opposite far wall, three brass clothes hooks, spaced three feet apart, had been fastened to the wall six inches from the ceiling. Adolph, standing just inside the room's door, scratched his forehead itch. An oak Windsor chair constituted the only furniture in a room that probably served as the master bedroom. Perhaps the Bourdon's hadn't enough moving truck space to pack the carpet and the chair. Logical. The three hooks? A former tapestry or quilt hung on the wall could've been the reason.

Adolph begrudgingly gave greater credence to Luann's wild goose comment. If last night's truck driver had become suspicious of a tail, pulling into a known abandoned farmstead ranked as a rational move. After verification that no one followed, the truck could've moved on. Adolph retraced his steps through the rear entrance and around the house to Luann's Chrysler.

Luann braced her body with her right palm; her four fingers splayed on her car's front fender. "Find anything?"

"Not a thing." The three words grated Adolph's pride. He hated to admit failure, especially to Luann.

"Thought so. Hop in." She slid into the driver's seat.

Adolph jerked the passenger door shut and didn't glance at Luann's expected smugness.

"I notified a case witness," she announced. "Said I'd meet him at ten."

Adolph reconciled himself to silently tagging along after Luann for the rest of the day with the exception of breaking free to cherish an uneventful noontime amble to the river. As he bid Luann good night in the station parking lot, Finnegan approached.

"Glad I caught you. Rebecca's said to be frantic."

"Why?" Adolph really desired to go home and shower off Luann's scent.

"Story is her son didn't come home last night. An early afternoon call from the school's truant officer alerted her to check his bedroom and she supposedly found its bed unslept in."

"Where's Rebecca now?"

"Don't know. Cook at Patsy's said she darted out to search for her son two hours ago."

Adolph telephoned Mary to advise he'd be delayed for supper. He directed Finnegan to the ritzy, gated residential communities and cul-de-sacs north of Main Street. "We'll keep in touch by radio." Finnegan nodded. "I'll start near the river and go up the bluffs staying to the south. If we don't find either in an hour, put out a general APB for Bradford."

Starting in a direction opposite to Finnegan's prowl car, Adolph's Monte Carlo crisscrossed downtown streets without success before cruising slowly along the river's Catfish Drive. Approaching a riverfront restaurant sharing a parking lot with a marina, he spotted Rebecca's parked blue Ranger and pulled up along side. Even from the angle of his Monte Carlo's front bumper, the setting sun's shadows obscured the driver's identity. He rapped his left knuckles on the Ranger's driver's window until a lowered window exposed Rebecca's red and swollen eyes.

"Don't move," Adolph ordered. "I'll get in." En route to the Ranger's passenger side, he tapped his right hand fingers on the hood to find the engine compartment cool. When he popped the door, his gaze found a brown bag filled with used tissue sitting on the seat.

"They took my son."

He would try to be reassuring. "You don't know that."

"I got this Polaroid." She reached into a tie-string purse and handed Adolph a picture.

He choked off a breath. Bradford, partially stripped, had been tied to a tree. A black-gloved hand rested on the teenager's mussed brown hair, obviously having twisted the boy's face toward the camera. Adolph, feeling his heartbreak, momentarily closed his own eyelids to lock out the rays of terror radiating from the boy's eyes. Summoning professional courage, he raised his eyelids and searched the photo for location clues. Bradford's bare feet glistened with wetness. This fact, Adolph calculated, meant the boy remained within driving distance based on the abduction's timing and yesterday's rain showers.

"They warned me." Rebecca sobbed. "I shoulda listened."

Adolph's left hand gently rested on her right shoulder. "We'll find him. Are these the same people you wouldn't identify for me the other day?"

"You can't file a police report. They'll kill Bradford. He's all I got."

"You've got to let me help." Between her sobs, Adolph fought off being overwhelmed by Rebecca's competing emotions of future trepidation and past guilt. "Who are they?"

"The ones Randall gambled with." She jammed a tissue into the bag, grabbed another.

"You mean Ant at the Sixth Street Bar?"

"Pleaded with him after the school called. He said he'd no control any more."

Adolph laid the picture face down on Rebecca's purse. "Your son's friends—"

"They said he's not hung out with them for two days. I promised to pay the money. Said I'd an infection. Had an OB appointment this morning."

"Have to ask." He paused. "You get a ransom demand?"

"No, no." Rebecca banged her forehead softly on the steering wheel. "Why this . . . why when I agreed to sacrifice my dignity to protect Bradford?"

Adolph recalled word of Ant holding Randall's gambling chits. The tie in with the son hadn't really registered. "Lemme see that picture again." He made sure his fingers touched only the edges. No doubt it was Rebecca's son. The longer he gazed at it the more his mind cells reverted to the photograph Ant gave him of an unidentified boy tied to a tree in what could only be a past Wainright home backyard. His jumbled thoughts raced. Bradford appeared to be shaken without visible blood or lacerations, but that didn't guarantee anything. He squinted, no distinctive landmark. Mumbling, his gaze flitted from a tree's ribbed bark to pine needles to the three-toed-patterned leaves indicative of maples. None brought greater clarity. Adolph keyed his focus on the sun direction indicated by the shadows. A faint darker green image on the tree trunk could be moss indicating the boy had been tied to the tree's east side. Low sunrays could indicate dawn. "Rebecca, would you take ride with me?"

She bobbed her head yes.

If his farm hunch proved correct, he'd have to swallow his pride and partner with the sheriff. He revved his Monte Carlo and they barreled out of the restaurant parking lot heading west on Bridgetown's main highway until zigzagging toward the Bourdon farm. He radioed Finnegan while Rebecca emptied one Kleenex packet and ripped into a second.

"Where we going?" She asked after he clicked the microphone into its holder.

"Just hold on. There's no guarantee." He swerved to miss half a dozen, but two western Ore County potholes filled to be bird swimming pools by a late afternoon downpour that had bypassed Bridgetown bounced his butt off the seat. He suppressed his own guilt pangs for not having walked through the Bourdon farm grove that protected the buildings from north and west winds. He parked his Monte Carlo in front of the machine shed.

Adolph pushed the trunk lid release button. "I need to check the grove." From the trunk he slipped on and zippered his black rubber winter boots. Rebecca, standing on the gravel, tensed and clutched the brown tissue bag. "Rebecca, stay here. Honk the horn if you see anyone or hear anything suspicious. This won't take but a couple of minutes."

Radiant reds and oranges of the setting sun streaked her moist cheeks. Suspicious he may have grown inured to the sufferings of others, Adolph, fearful of what he might find, refused to drag Rebecca through the grove. At the grove's southern edge, he counted maples, oaks, and pine in seven rows. He stuck close to the grove's center, committed to short sharp turns forged through knee-high wet brush while ducking low branches. He hopped a fallen log with the unwavering aid of a handy overhead branch. A broken red plastic squirt gun lay littered among pinecones and twigs. He imagined innocent children had played cops and robbers or hide-and-seek behind the one-to-two-foot tree trunks. At the northern edge, he ventured right to circle the barn. He delayed answering Rebecca's shout of his name.

He steadied his gaze on the ground, searching for telltale tracks or multiple footprints in the soft ground. Twenty paces after his trek east began, he noticed a discarded piece of rope at a silver maple's base, second row in. He lifted the four-to-five foot length with a stick. While wet, he estimated it hadn't been long exposed to the elements. He stepped out of the trees to a field's end row and stuck a three-foot stick six inches into the black muck. Responding to Rebecca, he scampered through the windbreak, emerged behind the machine shed he'd checked that morning, and followed its sidewall to his Monte Carlo.

"Don't tell me my son's dead." Rebecca collapsed against his Monte Carlo's hood.

Adolph grabbed Rebecca's shoulders to pull her erect. "He's not here."

Rebecca's sigh of relief didn't prevent her second collapse into Adolph's arms. He readjusted his stance wider and struggled against gravity to remain upright. "Can I let you go?"

Rebecca's flushed face nodded and, while her body trembled, she remained standing.

"I'm radioing dispatch to bring the sheriff here."

Rebecca's eyes widened. "You found something."

"Probably nothing. But I can't investigate without the sheriff." Adolph's hand lifted the Monte Carlo passenger door handle. "Have a seat. We'll be here for a while." With his cell he telephoned Mary and concluded with: "Yes, dear, I'll call when I'm headed home."

Adolph didn't enjoy explaining to Rebecca there wasn't much he could do, however, that was the truth. To relieve the tension of their growing silence, Adolph walked a circle around his car that kept him visible should the sheriff arrive and not cause Rebecca concern that he'd abandoned her. He

privately castigated himself for having traveled the easy road
the night before. Had Rebecca's boy been in the pizza truck?
He doubted it. He'd skirted two or three broken twigs on his
trip from the found rope to the machine shed. Unlikely one
person had snapped the widely dispersed twigs. Probably two
or more abductors marched, or carried, the boy to the tree. The
boy obviously selected to be a sacrificial pawn to torment an
uncooperative mother for the father's transgressions. Adolph
ranked The Dragons as his first choice to be the gang enforcer
carrying out the orders of a hidden higher power. He believed
this capsulation probably close enough to the truth to be
accurate. Yet, the boy's safety ranked a notch higher.

Heavy-duty tires crunched the farmyard gravel and
Adolph greeted Sheriff Edward Townsend with a cordial smile
that downplayed the disdain he felt toward the glory hound
who two years previous had called a news conference to claim
a meth drug bust Adolph had painstakingly investigated for
eighteen months to assemble the conviction's critical nuts and
bolts evidence. After the press snapped congratulatory photos,
the sheriff washed his hands of the case and its leads to drug
kingpins who ruled from chilling shadows. Hailed with the
proper credit then, Adolph would be wearing a gold shield, not
the nickel one he fastened daily to a black leather belt. Hiding
smoldering resentment behind brief snippets that divulged
minimal information, Adolph shepherded the sheriff to the
suspected crime scene tree and, after both had a cursory look,
returned to the farmyard. He offered the sheriff, with
Rebecca's help, a brief verbal physical description of
Bradford, holding back the Polaroid. The sheriff strolled to his
AWD SUV to contact his county dispatcher and broadcast a
statewide APB.

Adolph bagged the rope and tossed the evidence bag into
his Monte Carlo's trunk.

"Good news," Sheriff Townsend shouted and then
rejoined Adolph at the Monte Carlo. "Deputy found a boy
matching your description three hours ago. Transported him to
the Bridgetown Hospital."

Rebecca jumped out of the Monte Carlo's front seat with a frantic question: "How is he?"

Adolph pivoted to grasp Rebecca by her left elbow. "I'll get you to the hospital."

Squelching his desire to ask Sheriff Townsend additional questions, Adolph hoped for the best and maintained radio silence to shield Rebecca from the gut-wrenching news of whether or not Bradford was dead or dumped clinging to life. The hospital transport held out a reed of hope. He stretched emergency protocol by switching on the magnetic red light globe he stuck on the Monte Carlo's rooftop. He illegally parked next to the hospital's emergency room door, making sure not to block the ambulance entrance. Rebecca dashed in. He found her panting at the emergency room admit desk. The nurse twice asked Rebecca to speak slower.

Adolph interjected, "Julie, let me help."

Above pudgy cheeks, Julie's aflutter green eyes belatedly lifted toward Adolph. With Rebecca breaking into sobs at his side, he offered the defining crucial fact that a sheriff's deputy had transported Bradford to the hospital's emergency room.

Julie's stubby fingers punched letters on her computer keyboard. "Boy's in ICU."

Adolph seized the initiative and grasped Rebecca's right forearm. "Come. There's nothing more for us here." He led her outside and pointed to the hospital's front entrance portal. "This way's faster than the interior maze." The main desk receptionist, helping an elderly man, said it would be only a moment. Adolph rhythmically tapped his right foot while the receptionist photocopied Rebecca's driver's license and insurance card. Directed to a third floor nurse's station, they accepted a male nurse's request to have a seat in a small waiting area.

A pacing Adolph excused himself three times to step into the corridor to update Mary by cell phone on his whereabouts. He apologized profusely and promised he'd be home soon, but couldn't guarantee an exact time until a doctor showed.

Adolph hailed Dr. Tom Green, whom he knew from

Rotary. Dr. Green replied he wasn't the boy's attending physician and all he could assume was that Dr. Hopkins could be, considering the doctor's lounge page he'd heard. Adolph, trying to mask his knowledge that Dr. Hopkins consulted on cases other doctors abandoned, thanked Dr. Green. When Adolph re-entered the third floor waiting area, he paused, not anxious to engage a head-bowed Rebecca, traipsing the fifteen-foot distance between a plugged in coffee pot and her chair.

"Bradford's awake." Adolph sugarcoated his news. "Dr. Hopkins's been paged."

"Thanks." Rebecca ceased twisting her hands and plopped into the closest chair. Adolph poured himself a coffee, added extra sweetener. "This can't be good," Rebecca mumbled.

"Have faith." Adolph bent forward to a table and separated five magazines without finding one either current or of interest. "This hospital's earned a trusted care reputation."

"For heart surgery," she replied, lips twisted. "I don't want Bradford's chest cracked open." She grabbed a handful of tissues from a small plain gray Kleenex box.

Countless times, Adolph had waited long, boring hours in this hospital. Gunshot victims most often, or wounded suspects he'd slapped cuffs on once the doctors declared them out of death's grip. He'd never encountered gang violence in hospital corridors. Yet, news accounts recorded it happened six months ago when Dragons, swirling bike chains and clicked-open switchblades, chased a rival gang member into the hospital expecting to pummel him. Unfortunately, no safe haven materialized and the intended Dragons' victim banished a .38 revolver and a volley of his fired bullets wounded two Dragons. The melee initiated a two-hour standoff with the four initially dispatched patrol officers. All Dragons, except the two wounded, ran helter-skelter through the hospital maze, dived out windows, and vanished into the night.

"When are they going to let me know if Bradford's all right?" Rebecca blurted out.

"Let's let them do what's best." He balanced himself on

his chair's front edge.

She wiped her mouth with the back of her right hand. "You don't have to stay."

"It's okay." He couldn't duck out on a potential lie, nor stop his right toe tapping. Energy from his tingling nerves jumped from his eyes to bounce off the yellow walls he despised. After the umpteenth time, his gaze into the hospital corridor bumped into a white starched lab coat facing he and Rebecca.

"Mrs. Quimby?" She nodded. "Your son's sedated, but you can peek in for a moment," Dr. Hopkins said. He gazed at Adolph. "If it's official police business, you're also welcome."

"I'd like him to come," Rebecca whispered.

The two of them, Adolph with fingers crossed, followed Dr. Hopkins into the elevator and on a three-turn, third floor ICU wing corridor journey. Halting their advance, the doctor's right hand eased a portable curtain screen sideways to expose a boy lying on his stomach, covered by a tented sheet, head cocked to the side. Adolph recognized Rebecca's son.

She gasped. "Ohmigawd."

Bradford's uncovered shoulders exposed red welts and crisscrossing gashes.

"He's heavily sedated," Dr. Hopkins said. "Didn't expect him to nod off this quickly."

More like conked out from a horrific lashing. Adolph forced himself to breathe.

"We'll hydrate him slowly," Dr. Hopkins continued. "Several of his wounds have trapped dirt and we've tried to clean them all the best we could to forestall infection." He tapped an electronic chart. "Prognosis is guarded." Rebecca steadied herself with two hands clutching a bedrail. "Let's leave him be for now. He appears to be strong and will be well attended to. I'll instruct the nursing staff to telephone you when he's awake."

Rebecca mumbled undecipherable words as she bent forward to kiss her son's right cheek. Adolph tugged Rebecca's arm twice to coax her out of the ICU.

"Suggest I drive you to Patsy's. You need to eat to bolster your strength."

"I shouldn't leave. Bradford might awaken."

"Expect it'll be hours. You need to first take care of yourself."

"I guess."

Adolph acted as if Rebecca's words of resignation were an unqualified yes. He handed her the tissue box from the waiting room and punched the elevator button for the first floor.

When they entered the riverfront restaurant parking lot, Rebecca said she needed more tissue from her Ranger. Adolph noticed yellow paper flutter under the driver's windshield wiper. He doubted the vehicle would've been ticketed. When he rounded his Monte Carlo's hood, Rebecca shrieked. He grabbed her right wrist and pried the paper loose from her fingers.

In printed-by-hand black block letters, it said: "*avoir d'autres chats à fouetter*." Adolph pointed at the words. "You know what that means?"

In a quaking voice, Rebecca replied, "French. 'To have other cats to whip.'"

"Bastards!" Adolph exclaimed. "And this English doesn't make sense." He read out loud, "Don't cry me a river for unkept promises. Youthful screams float to the skyward nest."

Rebecca hugged herself and bent her forehead toward her Ranger's hood.

"Don't worry," Adolph said through his clenched teeth. "We'll find the one responsible." He scanned the truck's underside for booby-trap triggers not found. In the truck bed, he noticed a two-foot square cardboard box and shouted. "Is this yours?"

Rebecca approached him at the Ranger's rear bumper. "Never saw it before."

He unlatched the tailgate for a closer look. The box hadn't been sealed and the folded top flaps sprung open with his touch. Inside he noticed a blue-plaid shirt and blue jeans.

He asked the first question that came to mind. "What was Bradford wearing?"

"Blue plaid shirt, I think, and jeans. He always wore jeans, holes in the knees."

Adolph tipped the box. "These look like his?"

Rebecca wiped tears from her eyes. "Yes. Omigawd, yes."

"I'll take them for the lab. Maybe there's trace, a clue to who did this." Adolph punched his Monte Carlo key fob to spring its trunk lid. After putting in the box and the warning note, he slammed the trunk lid tight. "Now, let's get you fed at Patsy's."

A honk of his Monte Carlo's horn summoned the cook to open the alley door. As Rebecca exited with her head held high, he trusted her resilience. Belatedly, Adolph radioed Finnegan to tell him Rebecca was safe at Patsy's and that Bradford rested at the hospital in guarded condition. Adolph then had the Bridgetown Police dispatcher patch him to Sheriff Townsend to update the boy's identification. He refrained from mentioning he'd added the jeans and shirt left with Rebecca to his previously collected piece of rope and the Polaroid.

When his backdoor porch light came on, he surmised Mary must've heard the rising overhead garage door squeak. Comporting with his ritual, he hung up his blazer, left his 9mm on the vestibule closet shelf, and entered the kitchen. Rap music blaring from Kristen's room jarred his ears. Today wouldn't be a day for him to complain about a teenager's upturned radio.

Mary flipped the porch light off with the kitchen switch. "A plate's warmed in the oven."

After he kissed her, she guided her walker toward the living room.

Adolph, utilizing an oven mitt, set the hot dinner plate on the kitchen table next to four mail pieces Kristen had probably brought in from the boulevard mailbox. The roses on one envelope made him think of Francine Hoskins. If a thank you for the wine, he'd have to tell her he dropped it off for The Chief. He ripped the envelope to extract Yvonne Whitenmire's handwritten thank you for rescuing her son, Billy, from the river's current. She wrote she'd read somewhere that courage wasn't the mere overcoming of fear but the striving to do a greater good. In words he'd not often received, she praised his goodness.

He cradled the note in his hands. While he'd battled a personal submersion fear that day to plunge into the river, today's events—the brutal revulsion of a youth lashed—brought forth again the stark proof that he couldn't rescue every abused or tortured youngster. His soul resonated with the escalating dread he hadn't done enough. As his fork tine haphazardly speared green beans, he challenged his heartless copout that crime statistics fluctuated, never remained static. Had they really spiraled upward? Or, did he just uncover more?

From his blue blazer, he retrieved the Polaroid Rebecca had given him. Reseated and holding it at the edges above his half-eaten scalloped potatoes, he stared at it. Its obvious purpose was to terrorize. If so, why the windshield note? He felt a breath on the nape of his neck.

"Where'd you get that picture of Brad?" Kristen asked.

He jerked the photo toward his chest, having heard neither higher music decibels nor her footsteps enter the kitchen. "Police business."

"You always say that." Kristen pulled out a kitchen chair and sat. "Betcha I find out all about it tomorrow at school."

"Why? You know Bradford Quimby?" He'd never heard his name mentioned at home.

"Not really. I think it'll be like when you talked to Marcie."

"Wait a minute." Adolph squirmed sideways in his chair. "I didn't mention at home, or anywhere near you, that I spoke with Marcie Connor."

"Why?" Beneath Kristen's Goth eyes, a sly smirk etched her lips. "You denying it?"

Adolph cleared his throat. "Ain't . . . mean I'll not answer that question either way."

"Why?" Kristen's forehead furrowed. "Don't you trust me?"

He flexed an index finger towards Mary in the living room. "Please keep your voice down," he whispered. "It's not a matter of trust. It's a matter of safety."

"Ain't safety." Kristen scowled at him before her forehead muscles relaxed while her jaw remained tensed. "You can't follow me into the school restroom." She reached for the photograph, and Adolph's left hand palmed it against his chest.

"It's complicated." Adolph wouldn't explain even if he thought she could understand. "Better we stay with me not talking about work at home."

Kristen arose, and twirled, touching the small of her back to a cabinet counter. "Marcie told me you questioned her in the counselor's office. She didn't like it."

"What?" Adolph's right hand shoved his half-eaten food aside. He glanced for a dry table spot to lay the photograph face down, and then castigated himself for his excessive handling. He rotated his head and shoulders toward his daughter.

"Marcie and her lackey shoved me up against the restroom wall yesterday."

He clenched his right fist. "You should've told me."

"Why? Have you throw her in jail and cause me more problems?"

Adolph put an upraised right forefinger to his lips. "Ssshhh, she hurt you?"

"No." She cast her eyes upward.

He followed Kristen's gaze to the kitchen's ceiling light. "You being honest?"

"Yeah."

He gazed into the living room to see Mary still watching TV. "What did Marcie say?"

"Not much. With her one hand pushing my throat to the

wall, the other lifted my skirt like a pervert. She said to her smiling friend: 'See where the trickles of blood will run.' But she didn't touch me. Just said, 'You tell your dad to leave me alone.'"

"You report this to the principal?"

"Hell no—"

Adolph heard Mary stir. "Kristen." He expected his daughter to be defiant, not alarming. "Not in this house."

She glared at him. "Ain't no stool pigeon. Saw that Dragon standing in the hall waiting to see where I went after I left the bathroom."

His "little girl" surprised him. "You know who's a Dragon?"

"Yo. It's no secret. You see the tattoo. Watch the fake strut."

"I need you to be careful." He hoped his concern sunk in and Kristen didn't shrug off this advice as she did his fashion comments. "Don't go anywhere alone."

"I'm not afraid of Marcie."

"Trust me." How could he add strength to that? "It's not only her."

"So, you gonna tell me why you got a picture of Brad?"

"He's in the hospital. Someone tortured him. You'll probably hear about it as soon as he's released, sooner if Bradford has a cell phone."

Kristen bobbed her head. "Should I act like stupid?"

"Right."

Kristen straightened up. No waist chain jangled as she disappeared into her bedroom.

Adolph expected she was either on her cell phone or conducting a Google search for information about Bradford. Adolph realized he didn't command all the answers and Kristen's jolt about being scrutinized by a Dragon highlighted his woeful deficiency on what kids faced daily in the city's schools. He only hoped the turmoil in his gut hadn't been obvious to Kristen. Had his tactic to let Marcie sweat backfired into a threat against his own daughter? In a way it had, but had Marcie purposely gone halfway, that is, not drawn blood, to protect both her and Kristen? He doubted his swamped and jumbled brain could become productive by draining it of all fears and/or wayward crazy thoughts. It was another conundrum. He loved that word. Many who heard him speak it thought he did so to put on airs. Maybe so, but modern forensics had identified multiple physical characteristics of the Rose Garden skeleton, but the human, nonscientific brain of Mrs. Hoskins drew a blank to stop him cold. He'd uncovered an active porn studio in Bulldog's basement, but whom could he tell?

He scraped his plate into the disposal and called out to Mary, "You okay?" Receiving a yes, and not wanting to watch stupid animal videos, he told Mary he needed to take a short walk.

The neighborhood's swirling cool night air didn't accelerate his mental processes. Starting from the proposition that Bradford's torture wasn't random, Adolph had no substantial evidence as to who ordered the whipping. The why was ostensibly tied to the threats to Rebecca and the wiper verse. Randall's gambling debt obviously represented the underground taproot. From there, Adolph's thought progression ground to an unsatisfactory halt at Ant.

Adolph had to unravel something dramatic if he were to make a splash that earned him his gold shield. His second peeper excursion to Bulldog's basement found Luann, Bulldog, Sonja Maria, and the Honest Abe impersonator. No Rebecca, although she'd been there the first time with Yvonne Whitenmire. Was that the simple cause and effect? Did Rebecca's no show endanger Bradford with a jailed Randall unavailable? Why not put Rebecca to the lash? His gaze at the twinkling sky carved the emerging bumpy landscape of a red Mars onto Adolph's image of Rebecca's lush creamy flesh softly rounded into feminine curves.

He stepped off a curb to cross the street and head back. Both a photograph and a note seemed to be unnecessary overkill. What were the English words? "Don't cry me a river for unkept promises." Pretty straightforward. Pay the gambling debt. No excuses. The remaining words: "Youthful screams float to the skyward nest." baffled him. He didn't recognize them as a famous quote or unforgettable words lifted from literary prose or poetry, not that he read much. He guessed he could run a computer search. His only thought connected the words "youthful" and "screams." As related to Rebecca, that had to be Bradford.

As he greeted a jogging neighbor passing his driveway, he touched his nickel detective badge, resigned to the engulfing prospect Fate and hard work had abandoned him and his fingers would never tingle with the caress of a gold shield. That a voice in his head said he could protect Kristen and Mary and still retire as a second-class detective irritated him.

He punched in the garage door entry code. Upon seeing his Monte Carlo, he realized he'd forgotten to safeguard his digital camera, although his peeper pictures weren't expected to offer more that his strike out with the secret letters on the "two lovers" photo. He secured his camera and Bradford's Polaroid in his Monte Carlo's glove box.

Returning to the living room, he promised Mary that Kristen was in no danger. At the nine o'clock commercial break he forced a yawn to justify retiring early and, to fortify his decision, he explained to Mary he'd be leaving an hour earlier than usual the next morning.

* * *

In the early morning's cloud-filtering dawn, the drooping corn stalk leaves lining the county road to the Bourdon farm greeted Adolph with an ever-increasing gloomy familiarity. He angled his Monte Carlo onto the road's gravel shoulder, stopped, and popped his trunk, now empty of the rope fragment and Bradford's Polaroid dropped off at the forensic lab. He tugged on his rubber boots and struck out on foot through the windbreak. His stuck-in-the-ground branch identifier hadn't been disturbed although trampled vegetation ringed the tree Bradford had most likely been tied to and indicated the state crime scene team had come and gone.

Adolph stepped gingerly onto the crusted loam in the silage-harvested, first corn crop row to gain a broader scene perspective. To his left, the maple's fallen leaves exposed a black and yellow one-hole birdhouse suspended from a sturdy branch by thin black-coated wire.

If he'd not read Rebecca's note, he'd have dismissed the common birdhouse sight in a heartbeat. Adolph inhaled a deep breath; he hadn't climbed a tree in years. It appeared simple enough, he repeated to himself, as he laid his blazer jacket across a nearby tree branch.

Swinging his arms from a flexed-knee position, he counted "One, two, three" out loud and jumped up, extending his arms across the lowest six-inch diameter branch. Swiftly, he reached his right hand a half-foot upward to grasp the next branch while enduring gravity's weight-induced pain at the crook of his left elbow. He grunted, and with his boot soles on the trunk, raised his shoulders until his left hand could grab a second higher branch. Trying not to let either foot slip from a tenuous boot sole/bark friction, he contracted his abs to elevate his upper torso. He jerked his head left to prevent a twig from poking or scratching his right eye. His right knee bumped the tree trunk before his trailing foot eked out a steadying foothold on the lowest branch. His right hand grasp of a higher branch allowed him to lift his left foot onto a higher branch, his ankle pressing against the tree trunk.

Adolph peered at the birdhouse. A piece of yellow grade-school construction paper, blending in with the wood's painted hue, had been wedged into its hole. Only by climbing had he spotted the paper's existence. Testing the farthest lean from the tree's trunk that he dared, he tried and failed to twist the paper free. He lost his finger hold on his third gentle tug and the paper fluttered to the ground. *Damn.* With renewed determination, he twisted the wire loose from the closest screw head almost flush with the birdhouse's roof, unwrapped the freed wire end from the branch, and watched the birdhouse bounce on a carpet of pine needles and fallen leaves.

Adolph's Gold

Glad his Boy Scout adventure was history, he released one foot at a time and instinctively felt for a lower branch as he descended and finally dropped from the maple tree into a squat.

With no muscles strained or bones broken, he picked up the birdhouse paper to read the printed words stamped on by a child's old-fashioned printing set:

Black and white piano keys sing.
Strong swung whiplash cords sting.
By the banishment of a father's sin,
Only then does one's new life begin.

A motionless Adolph gawked and reread the four lines a third time. One crazy outlandish thought crept into his heightened confusion. These words weren't necessarily aimed at Bradford or Rebecca. Then why any note at all? Who was meant to find it? While a possibility, he believed the departed Bourbon family children to be unlikely suspects.

The birdhouse, filled with soiled, white spotted thatch, he left on the ground. Grabbing his blazer, he hiked to his Monte Carlo and radioed the police dispatcher to patch him through to Sheriff Townsend.

"You're up early," the sheriff said.

"At the Bourdon farm. Did the state crime team report a black and yellow birdhouse?"

After several seconds, the sheriff's voice broke through static. "Dismissed it as being unconnected to the incident. Why?"

"Found a strange poem inside it. I'll fax a copy later today. By the way, before I lose you again, any sighting of that Salvatore Pizza truck I described?"

"Dead end so far."

With the unreliable connection, Adolph clicked off without a formal good-bye. He expected he could be at the station before eight-thirty. En route he pressed his upper teeth into his lower lip when thinking about how photographs pervaded and expanded his current investigation. Finnegan hadn't yet reported on a successful evidence bag drop. Luann hoarded Ant's depleted folder that Adolph had left on her Chrysler's front seat. Yet, he mulled the irony of two photos, separated by decades. Both depicted a boy tied naked to a tree.

A visible inbox bottom represented good news to Adolph. He plopped into his squad room chair ready to power up his computer. A woman's heels clicked on the wooden floor.

"You left this in my car." Luann tossed Ant's folder into his inbox. "Disgusting."

"Anyone familiar?" Adolph used the tease to further gauge Luann's depth of knowledge.

She glanced toward Bulldog's empty office. "Thought you tried to run a bluff on Ant."

"Is that an apology?" Luann twisted the left corner of her mouth. "Guess not," Adolph said.

Dryly she asked, "You going to sit here all day?"

Adolph suggested a new routine of switching off cases. His tactic worked. Adolph's burglary witness interviews closed two of the four recent Chief-dumped files leaving the Carlson computer theft and Roscoe's tool heist still open. Sixth Street Bar patrons' faces registered blankness when he asked about tool sales, engendering doubt the sales ever happened. Adolph missed Ant, supposedly out of town at a supplier convention, and a received message from Roscoe said he'd found his edger in a neighbor's garage and he wouldn't be claiming it stolen. As for Luann's cases, Adolph acted gentlemanly, took copious notes and didn't once needle Luann for not being able to wrap up a single pending case.

She sat in her Chrysler, on her cell phone, as Adolph was ready to ring the Carlson house doorbell. He delayed and fumed until a panting Luann reached the front door. Aggravated by Luann's not informing him she knew Mrs. Carlson, Adolph cooled his annoyance upon learning Luann and Mrs. Carlson had children acting in the same school play. He explained he sought information on the stolen computer.

Mrs. Carlson displayed long wrinkles across her forehead. "Tom said, you know, he didn't report that. Wasn't worth the, you know, effort."

"He didn't. We recovered a computer that might be yours."

Luann cautiously edged from the entryway to perch on a living room sofa arm.

"We've purchased a replacement. That old one, you know, didn't work. Ask Luann."

Adolph gazed at Luann. "Well."

"My son and I," Luann began, "one day tried to help discover what was wrong. Wanda's son tore it apart downstairs. Don't think we ever got a balky Photoshop peripheral installed."

"Luann's right. Tom suspected a virus. You know, I couldn't begin to explain."

"How'd the thief get in?" Adolph asked.

A sheepish facial expression engulfed Mrs. Carlson. "Door left unlocked."

That matched what Roscoe had told him. "Did this computer have Internet access?"

"Dial-up," Mrs. Carlson replied.

If there had been an official open case, Adolph would've closed it. As for Luann's computer fingerprints, an innocent explanation with collaboration existed, that is, as far as it went. A third St. Mary's computer remained unaccounted for.

Adolph left Luann in the station parking lot and decided to brave the threatening clouds without an umbrella and walk the riverfront. Near the boat launch ramp, Adolph leaned into a squad car's lowered passenger window.

"Dumped that evidence bag outside the crime lab," Finnegan reported.

"Great." Adolph retracted his head. The black and white resumed its downtown creep.

Dangling black cloud whiffs, approaching from the west, hurried Adolph to his work desk. A new crime lab delivery filled his inbox. He broke its seal. "DNA Match" headlined the top form. Content to beam happiness without either Luann or Bulldog present to ask why he celebrated, Adolph read the particulars matching the St. Louis obtained toothbrush saliva to the Rose Garden B&B skeleton. He craned his neck to the ceiling and whispered, "Thank you." He telephoned Francine saying he'd visit in a few minutes with news. Once the handset clicked into its cradle, Adolph glided across the squad room floor and, in a euphoric daze, counted neither intersections crossed, minutes driven, nor how many energetic knocks he made until Francine answered the Rose Garden B&B's front door.

With her now familiar apron dotted with white flour stains, she led him to the kitchen's small table. "What's this news you wouldn't tell me?" Her floured fingers reached into a table-centered bowl of biscuit dough to add another miniature mound to a half-filled cookie sheet.

"DNA identified the man buried in your garden as Antoine Russell."

Francine gasped. Fresh biscuit dough splat on the linoleum. "Omigawd. He was such a nice man. His kids will blame me. They'll say they always wanted him to stay with them."

Adolph rose. His right foot kicked out a chair and, grabbing Francine by her shoulders, he guided her into a seated position. "Now don't go blaming yourself." He didn't believe Francine had been complicit, yet he suspected her memory harbored crucial case-solving details.

"I need a glass of sherry." Francine half-rose.

He maintained a strong pressure on her shoulders and refused to release his falcon-like grip. "Let me ask a couple of questions first." Adolph desired to ask narrow questions to elicit basic truths. "You said you never saw Mr. Russell wear western clothes, correct?"

"Think so."

His fingers relaxed without decreasing his palm pressure. "You think he did, or didn't?"

"Don't ever remember seeing him in jeans or stuff like that."

"I'll take that as approaching a no. When was the last time you saw him?"

Adolph's Gold

"Think maybe a year ago Labor Day."

His mind cringed at her pained befuddlement. "Monday? Day of the holiday?"

"No. Friday before . . . yeah, that's right. He'd only paid 'til Friday. I asked if he was staying with one of his kids. He looked a little pale as I recall."

He trusted she'd remember more than general details. "Anything else?"

"Hiccups. I guess I asked if he was all right. He said queasy . . . queasy in the stomach. Didn't ask more, but he volunteered he would drive the longer interstate route home."

Adolph thought it interesting she'd remember this conversation snippet. "He say why?"

"Don't think so. I needed to get his room linen changed."

"Had he vomited?" Adolph weighed this fact more important than highway routes.

Francine glanced at her interlaced fingers. "Maybe? One bathroom needed an air freshener. But the bathroom's shared. Coulda been him."

"You grow mushrooms in your garden?"

"What?" Her shoulders twisted against his pressure. "You think he was poisoned?"

"Not likely, but I gotta ask." Adolph knew the skeleton's vital organs and their tissue, even the eyeball fluid, no longer existed for examination. The time delay also made scavenger insect autopsies unavailable.

"Plant only flowers. Too many health regulations to harvest and serve vegetables."

Adolph eased his shoulder pressure and Francine rose to pour sherry into a glass. Adolph didn't recognize the bottle as the one given to him by The Chief. He excused himself. His expectation of not learning much largely fulfilled. Russell swallowing a lethal dose of either death cap or death angel mushrooms a long shot. Nausea a symptom, but he could've been nursing a hangover. Adolph had to assume Mr. Russell's driving home directly from the Rose Garden B&B to be a fabrication leaving many questions unanswered.

When he entered the squad room, a huffy Luann spit out a venom-laced greeting of "Where've you been? Sitting here an hour without a word." He ignored her and hotfooted it through the corridor to update The Chief on the skeleton's identification. To The Chief's one question, Adolph could only answer the crime lab hadn't isolated a cause of death.

Adolph realized five minutes wouldn't be long enough for Luann to self-milk her displayed fangs. He suggested, in response to her icy stare, she drop him off at the Bridgetown Community Hospital and he'd leave his portable radio on. When, without a word, she picked up her purse and her car keys, he tagged along. For him, the imposing BCH hospital tower couldn't break into the horizon soon enough, lest he lose his cool at her childishness. After clipped words that he'd radio the dispatcher before departing, he didn't twist his gaze rearward until the hospital's revolving entrance door swept him with a whoosh into the reception lobby.

Adolph warmed to the broad smile of the gray-haired volunteer greeter. From the receptionist, he learned Bradford had been transferred from ICU into Adolph's former head trauma room. With an air of official comportment, he nodded stiffly to bypassed staff and visitors to find the sought after third floor door ajar. He knocked twice and barged in without a response from within.

Bradford lay on his stomach, his shaved head cocked to one side.

To break the ice, Adolph asked, "You awake?"

"Yeah." The single word uttered without enthusiasm.

Adolph's abbreviated steps paralleled the bed until he lowered himself between thin mahogany armrests onto a red un-cushioned molded-plastic chair. When his legs bounced he and the chair close to the bed pillows, his left knee clinked the lowered bed railing. Three get-well cards propped up on the room's polished marble windowsill erased all doubt of Bradford's hospitalization having been kept a secret. Adolph skipped the how-are-you-feeling question. He could venture an accurate enough guess by the pallor surrounding Bradford's dull eyes.

"Can you tell me if you know anyone who did this to you?"

Bradford moved only his lips. "Day before, Marcie said Kristen wanted to see me."

Adolph gulped. "This Kristen have a last name?"

"Your Kristen."

Adolph nodded. He'd have to tread lightly or leave. Why would his Kristen be an accomplice? *Had it been that god-forsaken Goth influence?* Adolph breathed deeply to calm his activated nerves. So far, he'd heard only Bradford's hearsay. Yet, Adolph latched on to the fact Bradford had a personal connection to the mayor's youngest son. For a decade, the mayor had kept the proverbial hatchet sharpened and ready for Adolph's scalp whenever Adolph had been linked to even the slightest ethical or other misconduct. Wild conspiratorial fantasies flew and flashed like lightning bugs within Adolph's mind. The most plausible being that Adolph had rankled the mayor by factually scribbling into the margin of an official police report that the mayor's son, without a verifiable excuse, had been apprehended at three a.m. breaking curfew in the vicinity of a residential burglary. With a question of "Where did you go?" Adolph purposely tried to skip past Kristen's potential involvement.

"Searched for a lighted porch light at a house on West 15th Street. A bearded man looking like Abraham Lincoln opened the door." Bradford rotated his gaze into a pillow.

While Adolph had little doubt who the man was, he groped for an answer to the question of why would this man, if he lived in a house, stay at the Rose Garden B&B? "Go on."

Bradford wiggled his shoulders. The initiated movement rippled his torso before he spoke. "Walked in. Got grabbed from behind and pushed to the carpet. My hands tied."

"The Lincoln man?"

"No. When yanked to my feet, he stood in front of me. A black blindfold came from his front coat pocket. Got spun around and pushed outside. Heard a dog bark, tripped over a curb, and then forced to sit. Bumped along in a truck."

Adolph nonverbally guessed a pizza truck. "How long?"

"Guess maybe fifteen minutes. Had to have stopped at a farm. Cow manure smelled. Kicked small stones like gravel."

"Your captors ever take off that blindfold?" Adolph flipped his notepad pages.

"Next day when tied to a tree."

Adolph sensed he'd disrupted Bradford's timeline. "Go back. Any idea where this farm is?"

"Nah. Had to go up stairs." He coughed. "Heard voices."

Adolph didn't think water would help Bradford's hacking; regardless, the nightstand offered neither a pitcher nor a visible nurse call button. "Male, female?"

"Mostly men. One sounded high-pitched, maybe a woman."

"You recognize anybody's voice?"

"Nah." Bradford lifted his head and let its left side drop onto the pillow.

"You remember any specific words, perhaps, a mentioned name?"

"After my pants were pulled down—"

"Wait." Adolph hurriedly scribbled. "You were stripped?"

"Yeah. Upstairs. One guy swore 'Goddamn' when I kicked out at hands trying to take off my sneakers. I couldn't win. They tied me to a chair, naked."

"You keep fighting?" Adolph struggled to keep his voice matter-of-fact.

"Didn't want anyone touching me. Shook my head so hard and fast that what felt like a Halloween mask with rubber bands for the ears flew off. Stomped my tied feet. Twisted."

"Whoa. What mask?" Adolph's mind clashed between a youth swinging at a piñatas and Mardi Gras marchers. "Or did you mean the black blindfold?"

"Once on the chair, something like a plastic mask was pressed against my forehead and cheeks. Couldn't see so I assumed my blindfold hadn't been removed."

"Can you be sure there was a plastic mask?"

"Tongue licked it. Pushed it forward. Man yelled for me to stop. When I didn't, a low gruff voice says that, when he disobeyed his father, he tasted the whip's sting."

Adolph leaned closer to the Bradford's head. "In those exact words?"

"Ah, pretty close. His mouth so close to my ear I could feel the spit."

Adolph shook his head when a nurse appeared at the door. He expected her to return when Bradford's monitor on his near empty IV bag beeped. "This high-pitched woman you said you might have heard, did she speak more than once?"

"Don't remember. Nah, I'd say."

"How long were you in this room?"

"All night. Refused to drink anything, so afraid I'd be drugged. After a while, I'm thrown, chair and all, to the floor. This itchy carpet falls on my head, feel it across my legs too."

Adolph chafed at the sparse number of words recalled. "Remember anything else said?"

"One man, think the same one who talked about the whip, said that I'd behaved as ornery as my parents. Would have to take part of his punishment."

"Whose punishment?"

"My father's is the way I understood. He didn't repeat nothing."

"Anything else said?" Adolph watched Bradford's head shake no. "Then what?"

"Someone slaps my face. Hands yank me to my feet. Feel the ropes loosen. Fingernails dig into my shoulders. Soft fingers start at my chin. Rub my chest . . . across my stomach. A cold wet rag is forced between my legs. I scream 'leave me alone,' and . . ."

The nurse peeked in a second time. Adolph raised his right hand to display his parted index and second finger. The nurse nodded and departed. Adolph thought a minute. Bradford had confused him again by jumping time. "When again did you get tied to the tree?"

"Next morning. Had this itchy scratched skin. Fingers rub

209

chin, pinch chest, and linger lower . . . Closed my eyes tight. Didn't scream. When I screamed before sleeping, a fist punched my stomach twice. Had trouble breathing."

"Same men or woman talking as the night before?"

"Don't know. Remember a strange sweet smell. Can't describe it. A hand squeezes, jams my feet into shoes. Hear gravel again. Then branches hit me."

Adolph didn't expect a positive answer. "See anyone?"

"The Lincoln guy. My arms had been tied around a tree. He held a camera when someone pulled the blindfold off. Screamed for help 'til this wet rag's stuffed into my mouth."

"You don't have to tell me about the lashes, but how'd you escape?"

"Strange. Woke up shivering and cold in this ditch. That's all I remember." Bradford's shoulders and head jerked at the chair squeak caused by Adolph's thrust of his soles against the floor to shove the chair he was sitting in backwards.

"Sorry," Adolph apologized. "You rest."

Outside in the corridor, Adolph tucked his notepad into his blazer's inner pocket as his mind raced. The beating horror inflicted on Bradford made logical, if twisted, sense. The jailed father owed a debt. The nonpaying mother called upon first to submit to depravity, and, when she didn't show, the communicated threat executed. He understood the blindfold. The mask placed on Bradford could've made him blend into a scripted video scene motif. Why wasn't that enough? Adolph's memory returned to the black and white imagery of the boy in the Oxford photograph, obviously now grown. Had this bruised boy been tormented into a vengeful man? If so, why the Lincoln costume to stand out in a crowd?

Adolph, willing to endure Luann's sour face again, radioed dispatch as he stood at the hospital entrance with his foot resting on an early positioned bag of winter salt. After Bradford's tale, Luann's earlier attempt to torture him laughable. He requested she drive to Jackson High.

"Humor me, Adolph. Hospital, High School. Tell me the common investigative denominator is not that you find clues in places with the letter H?"

He bottled up his industrial-strength guffaw. "Should I say 'Heavens no.' or just ignore your ridiculous comment as being one from an overactive hilarious detective mind?"

Luann stared straight ahead until signaling a left turn into the high school parking lot. She exited her Chrysler first and waited at the school counselor's door while Adolph explained he desired to talk with Marcie Connor and his daughter, Kristen. He and Luann then sat in the guidance counselor conference room without bothering to engage in meaningless chitchat. Marcie appeared at the open door.

"Have a seat, Marcie," Adolph instructed, punctuating the command with a smile.

"I've nothing to say." Like a balking mule, stubbornness poured forth from Marcie's every pore challenging him to try and drag a worthwhile response past her lips.

"We understand," Luann said.

Adolph glared at Luann; happy she'd not said anything else. The major reason he'd sought Luann's presence, other than The Chief's order, was to have a disinterested witness to the question he'd pose to Kristen. Marcie's summons would mislead school authorities and build a smokescreen for his hidden agenda's true quest.

"You don't have to say a word." Adolph parted his lips and tried another smile. "If you don't want to talk, that's okay. You should know there's evidence that your mother didn't shoot dead the Dragon in your kitchen. The real killer face's prison, unless justification exists."

Marcie, still standing, clasped her hands in front of her. Her intensifying stare, Adolph estimated, would register a minus five degrees on an icy winter's morn. "Don't believe you."

"From my way of thinking, it's either you or your brother."

Marcie didn't hesitate. "Told you once; ain't saying nothing."

"We're not here to arrest you." At least, Adolph hadn't

expected to for he hadn't notified the grandmother to be present. "Only wanted to give you another chance to tell me the truth."

"The truth can't hurt you," Luann said, her palms flat against the table.

Marcie fidgeted and her right hand fingers, rising to hide her lips, didn't shield her eyes, which flitted between him and Luann and the door. He'd nothing concrete to pin Greene's shooting on Marcie and doubted she would rat out her brother. The seconds ticked in his head. The longer he gazed at Marcie, the higher his fatherly anxiety rose with regard to Kristen.

"You can return to class. Perhaps the next time I'll have my handcuffs out."

If Marcie's gaze could kill, he'd be bleeding right between the eyes. When he thought she was out of earshot, he rotated his head and shoulders toward Luann. "Don't you dare say a word. I'll do all the talking. After all, it's my daughter."

Kristen, her lips in a straight line, hesitated at the door. Adolph pointed to a chair, three feet from the table, which Marcie hadn't sat in. Kristen's hands pinched her belt. She walked stiff-legged to the chair and sat in it without disturbing its position on the floor.

"Kristen, please understand that I don't mean to embarrass you. However, the question I have is best not asked at home."

She gazed at the ceiling.

Adolph tapped his finger to gain Kristen's attention. "If you recall I've mentioned Bradford Quimby previously. Did you have words with him, maybe yesterday?"

"Why?" Kristen's upper lip rose. "We're not mad at each other."

"That's not my question. Did you have any conversation with him?"

"At school." She twisted in the chair. "No big deal."

"What was said?" Adolph's hands tensed, uncomfortable in whatever position he put them.

"Don't remember exactly." Kristen twirled a left hand

ring. "It wasn't any big deal."

Adolph flexed his right hand fingers. "You tell him to meet anybody."

"No."

The word's sharpness pinged his ears while the quickness wasn't always a harbinger of truth. He couldn't accent his next question by pressing his thumbs to her throat. "You sure?"

"Yeah." Snow wouldn't have melted on her facial features. "You going to ask if I have witnesses?"

"Hadn't planned to." He forced a lilt to his voice. "But now that you mention it, do you?"

"Katie and Dottie were there. I warned Brad to get out of my life."

Adolph skipped reminding Kristen that this response, partially, if not fully, contradicted her initial denial. "In what way was he bothering you?"

"He was gossiping about you and his mother seeing a lot of each other."

Luann gulped, loud enough to echo in Adolph's right ear.

Adolph fought to seal the crack in his composure. "Anything else?"

Kristen crossed her arms across her chest. "Nope."

Adolph, caught off guard that community gossip whisperers included his daughter in the speculative buzz of his activity, regretted Luann's presence. "Thanks. I'll see you at home."

When Kristen departed, Luann rose and shut the door. "Weird." She turned to face Adolph. "You acted just weird. Not so much with Marcie. I've heard what the crime lab said. But your own daughter. You treated her like a criminal."

"Had to." Adolph arose from his chair. "You believe she told us the truth?"

"Definitely. She didn't exhibit any signs of lying. Perhaps a skeptical teenager fearful of any adult inquiry into her world, but not a liar. What crime did Kristen commit?"

"Bradford Quimby accused her of being an accomplice to the men who beat him."

"Now that makes more sense." Luann's tongue moistened her lips. "You'd better take precautions that your detective personality doesn't erode your father's role."

Adolph refused to respond. He didn't want to know what made sense to Luann and he definitely didn't need parenting advice from Luann, porn star. He had tolerated her better when she impersonated an iceberg. The analogy struck an uneasy chord in him. Eighty per cent of an iceberg existed underwater. "Drop me off at the station."

* * *

Adolph, uncertain of continuing or going home, paced between the two oak trees. Halfway between intersections, the corner streetlights hadn't enough wattage to disclose his presence to Dean Wainright's neighbors. Being discovered didn't bother him, Kristen's not coming home from school did. The comfort of Mary telling him three hours ago that Kristen called near five o'clock and received permission to accept Katie's supper and studying invite was beginning to wear off. The insulated river-man's jacket kept him warm. The first student carrying a music satchel had arrived thirty minutes ago. The piano notes, at times halting and uneven, he assumed could be heard by the Rose Garden B&B guests through closed windows.

A Nissan Sentra pulled into Wainright's driveway. A sweatshirted girl in blue jeans emerged and walked straight to the front door. Clutching a dark-colored folder, she glanced toward the street. Adolph bent his head forward, gazing at the boulevard grass for that non-lost lost item. Her action of not pounding the door knocker puzzled him. Then, when the front door opened and the first male exited, he understood her admittance had to wait the first student's finishing. So far, his hunch that Wainright was engaged in illegal conduct didn't garner any prize.

The minutes, first one, then two, dragged on into twenty-eight, twenty-nine.

What sounded like a motorcycle muffler roared from faint

to loud to Adolph's left. From the corner of his left eye, he saw two parallel, spaced headlights, not one. A blue Camero with a red and yellow blazing-flame decal painted behind the front tire wheel well whizzed by, executed a wheel-squealing donut at the intersection to his right, sped back, and stopped on Adolph's side of the street, approximately twenty feet away. Adolph transformed a pacing step into a stroll and, at the block's end, turned right. Carefully staying in a sycamore's shadow, he gazed past the near house corner toward the Camero.

No person exited the newly arrived vehicle. The blue-jeaned female he'd seen enter Wainright's home bounded down the driveway to drive off in her Sentra. When the hanging frosted globe remained aglow, Adolph freed a small digital camera from his jacket pocket. Peering at the dimly lit entry through a telephoto lens, he watched Wainright reappear. A driver door slam extinguished the Camero's dome light and vibrated sound waves a block's distance to Adolph's ears. He swung his gaze to the bare-armed, tattooed male striding hurriedly toward Wainright. Adolph recognized Jack of the Dragons in the ripped muscle-T, dark-colored Levi's, and black engineer boots.

Who would've guessed? thought Adolph. Jack carried no piano music folder or displayed any other pretense of having arrived for piano instruction. Adolph snapped three long-distance photos when the two men met on the lighted stoop before going inside. Adolph cursed his bad luck the porch's wall-mounted semi-sphere globe didn't add additional light. Nevertheless, Adolph's hunch scored a jackpot connection between the Dragons and Dean Wainright. Whatever outreach program the music instructor had couldn't be worthy of mention in the college newspaper. An illegal drug delivery topped Adolph's mental list.

When Dean Wainright's door reopened five minutes later, Adolph retreated and stood motionless to have the corner two-story protect him from Jack's view. Unless Adolph clicked photo evidence of contraband he didn't visually observe, he lacked probable cause for a search warrant. A shorthaired terrier sniffed Adolph's right trouser cuff. He accepted the ball-capped older gentleman's apology before the stranger, grasping the dog's leash, continued straight across the intersection. While the single-A baseball season had ended, a South American film production company had arrived in Bridgetown to use the local stadium for on-location scenes. Adolph doubted a connection with underground porn films, although he speculated that a dedicated gold-shield detective would extend his lunch walk to the riverfront stadium and mosey on past the producer's production trailer to see what could be seen.

At the second hour's thirty-minute mark, a third male carrying a musical satchel arrived to be ushered in by Wainright. Adolph, worried he'd be recognized if he dilly-dallied much longer, surmised he'd seen enough and longed to know if Kristen had arrived home.

* * *

Adolph arrived an hour early the next morning to camp out in front of Chief Howard's office door. With a begrudging welcome, The Chief welcomed Adolph into his office. "Something new on my cousin's skeleton?"

Adolph stood, hands clamped to a visitor chair. "Trail's cold. Chatted with Yancey last night. He's willing to accelerate his active duty physical. Need you to release me from partnering with Luann."

The Chief unlocked his desk drawer. "You getting on each other's nerves?"

Adolph didn't wish to whine, well, not exactly. "You could say that."

"No dice. She's your partner. Buck up. Make the best of it."

"But Chief—"

"That's all. Good day."

Adolph promised himself he wouldn't accept defeat. He'd come up with a winning clandestine tactic. His drives past Lt.

Turner's home wouldn't be dry wells forever, even if, nowadays, Bulldog's wife's minivan had become a constant fixture in their driveway. If his peek could be repeated, he'd move to the closer basement window, activate the flash at the risk of exposing his surveillance, and erase the black squares his camera now held as photos.

Adolph decided to capitalize on the forty minutes until Luann's expected arrival. Into his squad room computer search bar he typed Luann's husband's name. The thirty thousand entries Adolph received deflated his self-serving intentions. He tried to narrow his results by utilizing the name and Stockbridge, Massachusetts, in a revised search. He began to click through the more manageable one thousand entries. The obit for a Herbert in Meadville, PA, listed a surviving wife named Luann, a son and a daughter. Promising. He leaned forward to peer at an infinitely more interesting linked probation website listing a prison sentence for a Herbert in Traverse City, Michigan.

"Adolph."

Instinctively, he clicked "Home." When his startled mind refreshed itself to register the presence of Officer Sean Finnegan, his latest best friend, Adolph said, "Slide up a chair."

Finnegan did. "Barge docked. Loaded with petroleum barrels. Fifty-five gallon."

"That's jurisdiction of Commerce or EPA. Not us."

The patrol officer smiled. "Not the cocaine."

Adolph decided to risk The Chief and Luann's ire. His forefinger pressed his computer's hibernate button and, following Finnegan outside, he declined a patrol car ride to drive his Monte Carlo. The Wainright Barge Company building rose but two blocks north of the docked paddlewheeler and the linked barge that together created the riverfront casino. Adolph parked inside the perimeter of two black-and-white units rerouting River Drive traffic.

He hurried to a knot of activity on the Wainright dock. "Sgt. McNamara, what's up?"

"Anonymous drug smuggling tip. We unclamped the top to this barrel and six inches beneath the rim is a welded-in compartment big enough for two kilos."

Adolph gazed at Finnegan who, bent forward, was reading a yellow label stuck onto an adjacent barrel. Adolph refocused on Sgt. McNamara. "Every drum like this one?"

"So far just these two with labels for Roscoe's shop on Fourth," McNamara replied.

Adolph ducked his head for a low-flying seagull twosome, one chasing the other. "Wouldn't it be risky to have drugs submerged in liquid oil?"

"Yes and no. The drug compartment is sealed with rubber gaskets, but these two barrels, labeled for used oil, didn't carry liquid. They were filled with a granular oil-drying-compound."

"Wainright Barge have invoices?"

"That's the quirk. This barge wasn't scheduled to stop here. Its tug developed mechanical problems. Blown head gasket someone said." Adolph nodded, uncertain where this all led. "Way I figure, this barge unloads upriver at Winona and these barrels are trucked to Roscoe."

"Empty? Doesn't make sense. Oil, most likely, travels north."

"Could." Sgt. McNamara tapped a lid tight. "Largest drug loads usually overland via I-35 to Des Moines, detouring east south of the Twin Cities. Likely barrels meet cocaine at Winona."

Finnegan interjected, "DEA doesn't scrutinize tagged used-oil barrels, either north or southbound. Someone should check Wainright's warehouse. See if they've stored barrels of used oil the EPA subsidizes for reclamation."

"You're saying what?" Adolph asked. "A barrel, like those found here, filled with fifty gallons of used oil or drying compound hides southern port arriving cocaine."

"Bingo."

Adolph called out to McNamara. "Finnegan and me have to make a call on Roscoe."

Adolph's Gold

As he parked his Monte Carlo in the station parking lot, Adolph's gander revealed Luann had yet to arrive. He hopped into Finnegan's squad car for the two-minute drive to Roscoe's.

"Where's Roscoe?" Adolph asked. An employee's pointed finger directed he and Finnegan to the shop's outside rear. Roscoe, his butt pointed at Adolph, was jackknifed forward under a raised hood, his grease-capped head bent into a pickup's engine compartment.

Finnegan angled his body to protect their rear and Adolph shouted, "Roscoe."

The shop owner popped up, both hands blackened with grease and engine soot. "Yeah."

"You expecting a drug shipment?" Adolph asked, his voice like the flick of a whip.

"What the hell, Adolph. Where'd you get that crazy talk?"

"You use oil drying compound I bet." Adolph didn't see any large drums.

"Yeah. So what?" Roscoe's tone edged with a cold fury. "Every shop does."

Adolph spoke lower to let the tension fizzle. "Show me yours."

Roscoe led the two law enforcement officers into his shop. Adjacent to a back wall stood a fifty-five-gallon drum, its lid propped against its side.

Adolph stretched his left hand into the barrel's grainy contents and inched it around the barrel's steel. Smooth. No welded-in compartment. "This the only barrel you have?"

Roscoe wiped his hands on a light blue paper towel. "Yeah."

Adolph's searching eyes gave Roscoe the benefit of doubt. "Thanks. We'll be going." In rapid succession, Adolph gave Finnegan a head flick and started toward the front exit.

"Aren't you going to give me an explanation?" Roscoe asked.

"No." Adolph's right knee brushed Finnegan's pant leg on their way out.

Finnegan didn't comment until both were inside the squad car. "You didn't ask much."

"Why tip our hand? We didn't catch him red-handed. If Roscoe's involved, do you think he'd confess? Drop me off at the station and then ask McNamara if he's going to let those empty barrels continue to Winona. He should; and then we can stand ready for those that follow."

"Smart."

Adolph waved good-bye to Finnegan. As he strode past Luann's car in the parking lot, he amused himself thinking how easy he would shrug off her chilly childish greeting. When he froze at the detective squad room door, he spied Luann, the room's only occupant, sitting at his desk, her two hands on his computer monitor. He stomped his left shoe heel on the wood floor.

A startled Luann rolled herself and his chair away from his desk. When he neared, she asked, "Find anything interesting?"

"Not much." Peering down, his gaze sliced her agonized expression. "How about you?"

"Partner thing would've been to ask. Not secretly pry like a common jerk."

The screen's confidential Traverse City prison logo meant his browsing history had been tracked. "So, is that it? You boot up my computer when I'm not here?"

"Bastard." She expelled the word with enough force to circle the room.

"Should really thank you." He embraced his growing sarcasm, ready to dual with the master. "I should be so lucky. You've displayed more than I'd been able to find."

She subdued her fury. "Here's not the place. Step outside." Luann reached her hand forward to log off Adolph's computer as he uttered a guttural good morning to an entering Bulldog leading a corporal to his office.

Adolph followed Luann to the parking lot. He calculated that open-ended questions would serve him best, sprinkled with pauses and silence to draw her out. It didn't quite work.

After five minutes of veiled accusations about invading personal privacy and ethical violations, their winless verbal fencing driveled to a stupid babble about who owned which computer.

Adolph rested his butt on Luann's rear car fender. "This is a waste. We need to ask The Chief, both of us together, to end this partnership thing."

"Suits me," Luann snarled, her palms tight to her hips. Her eyes bore into him.

"You musta slept well last night. No saggy eyelids."

"Knock off the faint praise."

"I'm trying to be nice, that's all." He lied. "When I figure out exactly, or you confide in me the true story behind who your husband is or was, maybe I'll understand better."

"For Christ's sake!" Luann's raised voice attracted the head turns of two citizens on the nearby sidewalk. Under her breath, she said, "You keep digging and it'll get him killed."

Adolph gazed toward the street and nodded to an arriving patrol officer. Adolph tried to smile at Luann and then deliberately pressed his lips together.

"Crap." Luann pivoted ninety degrees and then spun to face Adolph. "If I have to trust someone before I go insane, it might as well be you. Herbert's serving three to five in Michigan on a trumped up transporting stolen property charge."

Right. "Aren't all inmates innocent?"

Luann glared at him. "Be a cynical bastard." Her pump's toe kicked a stone that bounced and skidded opposite Adolph. "Herbert trusted a dirty cop who double-crossed him. When he arrived at the Lockport dock on the Hennepin Canal, he met undercover FBI agents, not the river drug smugglers he expected as sting targets."

"What about a reverse sting to nail the dirty cop?"

"Herbert pleaded for that. Prosecutor wouldn't buy it. Considered it a good bust."

Adolph's mind couldn't decipher how an Illinois crime equated to serving time in Michigan. Perhaps a Fed thing.

"Explain then how I'll get him killed."

"You're like a cattle prod electrifying the river, putting a charge into the canal."

Adolph didn't detect any hand wringing, twitching, or facial muscle tension that would've revealed her deceit, but then she'd received investigative training similar to what he went through. Her answer clarified nothing. He asked direct: "This involve Ant?"

"Don't know. Swear to the Almighty God, I don't know."

"You know." He rubbed his cheek. "Your fingerprints surfaced on the stolen computers."

"I thought I fully explained that at the Carlson home."

"Well, not completely. There's still one St. Mary's computer missing." Adolph shivered as his body absorbed the day's increasing chill. "You know anything about its whereabouts?"

Luann clasped her arms across her chest. "No."

He couldn't determine if Luann was as physically chilled as he or wished to shut him down. "Maybe someone's withholding it, threatening you to sabotage an investigation?"

"Never." Her nostrils flared. "I might sacrifice myself to protect Herbert, but I draw the line at engaging in criminal activity."

Adolph bypassed arguing her fuzzy rationalization to seize the opening. "You know where the man who looks like Abraham Lincoln is? He stayed at the Rose Garden B&B."

"Not exactly. He telephoned my house one day. Said he knew Herbert. I checked. He's the conniving cop who set up Herbert."

Adolph feigned with a nod that he knew at least the basic facts of which she spoke. "What's he doing here?" He hoped his silence would be his ally.

"Have no idea." She kicked a second stone and muttered, "He's a filthy pig."

"He ever expose . . . sorry, bad word choice." Adolph gazed away to break his eye contact with Luann. If this Mr. Lincoln had an opportunity to do in Antoine Russell, Adolph would have to pin him with motive. Used oil tied the B&B garden skeleton to drugs. With a cop executioner? Could explain why Luann's personal interest, not a command order, caused her to show and meddle in the skeleton excavation. "Can you contact this Lincoln fellow? I'd like to meet him."

"Guess so," Luann said softly.

"I'll not ask you how. You'll learn to trust me."

From the corner of his eye, Adolph caught a glimpse of Chief Howard exiting the station. Adolph swallowed hard and nodded. Luann's parted lips exposed two rows of teeth, clenched.

"Nice to see partners working together." The Chief didn't stop to chat.

Luann, with her eyes glued to The Chief striding toward the river, whispered, "I'll see if I can scout up that Lincoln son-of-a-bitch."

Adolph didn't wish to turn around. "If The Chief's outa sight, you want to meet later? I'll not tagalong on your cases." Luann nodded. "I've gotta speak with my good friend Ant."

Adolph, in his Monte Carlo, wheeled opposite to Luann's departure direction. He cruised past the Sixth Street Bar's front door and parked in the alley next to Ant's Cadillac. Ant, on Adolph's entrance into the back room, didn't mention remodeling before he slumped into his end-of-the-table leather chair. The smell of fresh green paint tickled Adolph's nostrils. The liquor boxes on the wall had been torn off and a full-length mirror disguised the storage room door and left Adolph wondering where the doorknob was. He gazed at a bored-looking Ant.

"Guests must adore this new mirror. Gives you a view of both sides of their cards."

Ant bristled. "Smart-ass. Suppose you're here to tell me you'll be my parole officer."

"Never." Adolph pressured his finger along the left side of the mirror to detect if it moved. "I'd then have to visit you more than I do now. Need to ask you about Jack."

"Don't know any Jack."

"Oh, did the Dragon leader go to court to change his name?" Adolph waited for Ant's exhaled low groan to fully escape. "Cut the crap and tell me if he's giving you piano lessons?"

Ant's jaw dropped without emitting a vocal cord sound. His front tooth gold glimmered.

"What's with Jack's visiting Dean Wainright?" Adolph gripped the back of a chair with both of his hands. "Pray tell, could it have anything to do with those college computers we found behind the mirror? Maybe, huh?" Ant's left hand fingers twiddled a white poker chip. "There's still one computer missing." Adolph decided to press. "And, also missing is that Green fellow who might be the one you're hiding after his buddy or you clobbered me in your alley."

"That's a hunk of stuff you're asking." The poker chip wobbled to a rest on the table felt. "Don't know nothin' about nothing."

Adolph rotated his eyes around the room. "Yeah, like Sergeant Schultz on Hogan's Heroes." His right index finger point reflected itself in the mirror. "Open the storeroom."

Ant didn't move a muscle. "Why?"

"Old trick." Adolph lowered his right hand to his side. "Hide stuff where the police have already searched." He waited while Ant used both hands to jerk himself erect, shuffle, and limp toward the storage room door. "You visit the hospital with that leg?"

"Minor trip. Don't ask." Ant's left hand fished a three-key ring from his pants pocket before his right hand slid the mirror a few inches to the right. He inserted a golden-colored key into the door-flush lock.

"Turn the key and stand back," Adolph advised. With Ant three steps clear of the door opening, Adolph reached past the doorjamb for the light's switch-plate. The incandescent glow bathed him in reflected light as he advanced inside. Nothing to his right. To his left, a desktop computer case. He called out to Ant, "What did I say?"

Adolph exited the storage room. Ant's contorted lips

expressed to Adolph all he needed to know. As he babysat a reseated Ant dealing a hand of solitaire, Adolph called in a lab crew.

Ant gazed up from his cards. "Don't you need a search warrant?"

"Why? You gave permission. Tell me about my new computer discovery."

Ant stared straight ahead. "I didn't put that thing in there." He rotated his moistened eyeballs toward Adolph's glare. "Swear on drawing to an inside straight."

"Who then?" Adolph squared his stance. "Not one of your bartenders?"

"Luann. That broad you brought here before. Your partner, isn't she?"

"C'mon." Ant didn't smirk. "You can think faster than that."

"If I had to come up with a lie, it would've taken me a helluva lot longer."

A rear door knock brought Len on the scene. Adolph uttered brief instructions, didn't mention Luann, and within minutes, after Len had gathered up the computer, flashed Ant a thumb's up. Adolph, in his own self-interest, would've liked to put the squeeze on Ant to learn if this ghostly Green fellow had also clobbered Ant. No one would've opened the bar's rear door without Ant's explicit approval. Adolph divined that survival for Ant's blackened soul had to be self-preservation trumping all other vices. However, wise experience had taught Adolph—if the breaks go your way—to forget psychoanalysis, i.e., the irrelevant couch stuff.

"If the computer's legit, it'll be back within the week." Adolph slammed the bar's alley door. He gazed at Len standing empty-handed next to his crime van. "No priority. Main interest is in identification of its handler's fingerprints. Pull the hard drive files, if there's one."

Adolph trailed Len's van to the lab and then continued to the station.

The telephone message light blinked across the squad

room until Adolph grabbed his handset. He listened to a familiar female voice and scribbled the address: 409 Tinley, Apt 3. Luann didn't leave her name. Tinley, named for a depression-era councilman, ran perpendicular to the river on Bridgetown's east side. Visiting there to listen to Sonja Marie had activated his old beat-day memories he'd like to forget, except at police reunions when head-knocking stories bolstered his standing with older graybeards. Constructed in the Roaring 20s, the three and four story brick buildings housed street-level flapper dress salons and haberdasheries filled daily by the city's political and social elite. Lifting store owners and the nouveau riche to fashionable upper floor apartments were jolting elevators decorated with art deco sculptured lights and designs. Fifty years later during the '80s, the infestation of drug dealers fighting turf wars in squalid partitioned apartments sent customers running for cover and store owners hightailing it with their wares to urban malls, resettling their families in subdivision-housing tracts. In the late '90s, gentrification attempts to revive Tinley Street failed.

From his Monte Carlo driver's window, Adolph gazed at the three peeling black-painted numbers that identified 409 Tinley. Rolling downstream industrial air pollution had dulled the original white square behind the numbers to fifty shades of gray. He began to count the withered dandelion stems, their fluff stuck between sidewalk cracks and brown un-mowed six-inch grass. "One, two . . . fifteen, sixteen, seventeen." Luann knocked twice on his passenger window. Adolph exited and clicked his key fob lock button as he joined her on the sidewalk.

"You think Honest Abe will be home?" he asked.

"Doubt it. We can double check with a ring to his cell."

Adolph would neither ask how she scoped out where he squatted nor how she obtained an unlisted number. "If he's home, let's surprise. I'll lead."

Outside the visitor foyer, the rusty wall-mounted eight-button intercom system didn't invite Adolph's finger to push any circular black button. Smeared white paint on the wall

226

documented failed attempts to eradicate gang graffiti. Whether
or not the unevenly varnished door was locked became
academic when, after a click, a Hispanic male pushed it
towards them.

"Buenos Diaz," Luann said to no response.

Adolph's left hand grabbed the door before it whacked his
extended calf. Beer cans, plastic water and pop bottles, and
empty clam-style Styrofoam food containers littered the
vestibule corners. Adolph, not touching a handrail, guessed
Apt. 3 would be up one flight. Luann's footsteps doubled his
wood stair tread creaks until they stepped into the second floor
corridor. A stained adult-sized dress lay crumpled on the
cracked linoleum hallway floor. Adolph kicked an uncapped,
dry, whiskey bottle to the side. Footfalls had worn a visible
traffic path down the hallway's center. As stench whiffs
engulfed his nostrils, Adolph estimated no cleaner had touched
the grime beneath his soles in two years. The odor,
disgustingly similar to what he had inhaled in the foyer, likely
came from decaying food amidst the debris. The malodorous
odors propelled him to find Apt 3 as quick as he could before
the smells infiltrated and lived forever in his blazer or became
an impregnable wall.

Luann had pinched her nose within the dozen steps they
quickstepped to a tarnished brass numeral three, dangling from
what had been its bottom nail. With a pick set from his inside
jacket pocket, Adolph mimicked the door's key and shouted:
"Housekeeping."

No answer. His gaze at Luann had expected a smile, not a
stoic pained expression with her pinched nose color imitating
Rudolph, the Yule-time reindeer. He kicked the door and the
stench almost gagged him.

He unsnapped his shoulder holster, jerked his 9mm free,
and peered over his right shoulder. "Stay here."

Luann, her erect stance squared, nodded. She likewise,
with her right wrist supported by her left forearm, pointed her
service weapon at the apartment's interior.

Newspapers lay scattered on the living room floor. From

the rear of a sofa flush against the wall, a line of black ants marched to and under a closed door into what Adolph presumed to be a bedroom. Adolph bumped his shoulder blades along a wall to peek sideways into an empty-appearing kitchen. His gaze returned to the endless single-file column of parading ants.

He yelled, "Anyone home?" No answer.

Adolph's left hand motioned Luann to retreat to the hallway door. Adolph tried not to dirty either sole by crushing a single ant as he repositioned his body, rotated the doorknob, shoved the door inward, and flattened his back against the living room wall to await what he couldn't imagine. With neither ants nor caution outlasting his curiosity, Adolph peeked past the doorjamb.

A tall figure loomed in front of him, barefoot toes dangling six inches above the floor. At the ceiling, a manila rope fashioned into a noose tight against the male's neck had been secured to, and probably bent, a steel brace designed for an overhead light receptacle box. A white T-shirt and black trousers, spotted with blood, clothed a body now puffy with a bluish skin tint. Ants swarmed the terminus of the blood trail on the floor. Adolph couldn't reach the elevated throat to perform the perfunctory fingertips-to-the-neck check to determine if life still pulsed. Nor did he desire to breathe in Abe's last exhaled molecules, if still suspended in the room's stale air. He backpedaled to Luann, screened her interior view with his body, and, with his palms raised in front of him, gently urged her out into the hallway.

"Abe's dead. Shot and hanged." He dialed 9-1-1 and requested the medical examiner.

"Can't understand how anyone could stay in their apartment or not report this gawd-awful smell," Luann said, again pinching her nose.

Fear would've been Adolph's first answer. "Let's meet the troops outside."

Luann didn't wait for him. She jogged through the clutter, kicked the discarded dress, and clamored down the stairs.

Adolph caught up to her standing on the sidewalk where she was bent forward, her hands on her knees, deep breaths exchanging inside for outside air.

"You okay?"

"Overreacted. I'll be fine in a sec."

Adolph strode to the corner and back. He expected to find a building cornerstone or nameplate, but didn't. Land records should tell him who the owner is. Three or four persons of various ages and descriptions gaped from the sidewalk across the street. Adolph eased his alert when none stood near his Monte Carlo. Above the group, a woman, her head wrapped with a scarf tied under her chin, poked her head out of a second-story window.

Len's crime scene van jerked to a stop in front of Luann.

"Rounding up more business are we?" Len asked of Adolph.

"You might tease me now, but not after your visit to Apt. 3. I'm staying here." Adolph tilted his head back and headed for the nearby crowd, now doubled in size. He flashed his silver badge. His questions could've obtained as much feedback from a river boulder. No individual, not even the window woman, admitted to having had even one Abraham Lincoln sighting.

He watched Luann, across the street beneath leafless small foundation trees, rock back and forth on the balls of her feet. The medical examiner's hearse banged hard against, and jumped, the curb. Its extended rear door faced the foyer and Adolph expected its gurney to be carried inside. He walked halfway across the empty street, now cordoned off by two black-and-whites at opposite intersections.

"Hey Adolph, you responsible?" Finnegan shouted. "Tell them to let me in."

Adolph waved to the crowd-control officer and watched Finnegan approach.

Finnegan glanced to all sides. "Any feedback on that favor I did you?"

"None. And that's good. What about the barge?"

"Sarge says we'll be ready for any barrel's return. I'll give you a shout."

"Thanks."

Finnegan ambled away toward the bystanders Adolph had questioned. At the ME hearse, Adolph waited for the gurney. He estimated it would've taken two strong men to lift Honest Abe's bulk to the noose and his gut told him the left wrist slashes were too superficial to indicate attempted suicide. The overturned kitchen chair a red herring prop placed in the bedroom.

He gazed at Luann. "Color's better."

"I'll be at the station." She pivoted before he could respond.

Adolph pressed his lips together. By protocol he should be up in the second floor apartment observing evidence collection. He trusted Len and it was far better to try to connect the multiple events when breathing fresh air. To date, events forged two or three diverse links without a unifying whole. Two Rose Garden B&B Labor Day guests murdered in successive years. Honest Abe linked to the porn films and Bradford's whipping. Rebecca's husband Randall linked to unpaid gambling debts, which, if he believed her, escalated to Bradford's flogging with her failure to participate in the porn filming. Luann's fingerprints lifted from a recovered stolen computer that Dean Wainright of St. Mary's College linked to nude photos and she'd also starred with both Rebecca and Honest Abe in Bulldog's basement video. Dean Wainright's connection to the Dragons and his familial barge company ties could possibly mesh with the river drug smuggling. Adolph sighed. Sandwiched in between were a pizza truck, his physical assault, Sonja Maria Sanchez, Nancy Whitenmire, and a Mulberry Street murder.

Adolph paced the sidewalk. Needing to ask Luann if she went back into the apartment, he dialed her station extension knowing that she'd had time to get back, and voice mail answered.

Len interrupted. "We've bagged several items. None the

suspected murder weapon. Needle punctures at the inside elbow joint suggests a drug injection. We'll run a full tox screen."

Both stepped aside to allow a sheet-covered gurney to be hoisted into the ME's hearse.

When the wheels' clickety-clack stopped, Adolph asked, "Drugs found?"

"Small plastic bag, white powder, in the bedroom, under the bed. Think it's cocaine. Four full condom boxes nearby suggests he was packaging."

"Doubt it," Adolph said. "Don't ask how I know, but consider the vic to be a porn stud."

Len twisted his lips into a sheepish half-smile. "If you say so. I'll have you a report who knows when but the bruising on the neck indicates strangulation as cause of death."

"From the rope?"

"No. Smaller diameter, like wire. Gunshot fired at close range, likely not fatal. Gotta run. All will be in my report. You're really piling up the statistics these days."

"Not closed cases—the stat The Chief wants."

Adolph hustled to the station. There he spotted Luann immediately upon her walking into the detective room carrying a file. Jumping up, he blocked her path to her desk. He gazed in every direction to guarantee they were alone. "How did you get hold of Honest Abe's location so fast? Not to mention a cell number."

"I . . . I had a snitch."

"Maybe, but odds are you couldn't have contacted one that quick without blowing a cover." He inhaled deeply. "Look, I've kept and will keep my cool. I don't care what you do in your spare time; but . . . when a Civil War fellow actor, who's fired more than a musket, turns up dead, I might have to air the sheets in public."

Her eyes flashed daggers. "You wouldn't—"

"Wanna test me?" Adolph spread his feet to shoulder width.

"Slander's not becoming."

He narrowed the space between them. "Shut up, Luann. How many more dead bodies?"

"I . . . I . . . Oh crap." Her upper body twisted left. Adolph used both of his hands to square her shoulders and stare deep into the recesses of her eyes. Luann didn't struggle. "All I know is I go to Roscoe's shop, put a written question in my car's glove box, walk outside, and wait at least ten minutes. If I'm lucky, there'll be an answer scribbled on the paper's reverse side. You want to see the notepaper?"

"No." He softened his tone. "I believe you."

"You can't mention that other thing. I can't have my child beaten like what happened to Rebecca. We're both scared out of our wits."

"How long you been involved?"

"Last year, little less." Adolph felt his eyebrows tighten. "Rebecca longer."

He reflexively asked, "How long?" His biceps relaxed and he dropped his hands.

"Fourteen, fifteen months. Some cowboy gave her VD before Labor Day last year. When a rash appeared with this new guy she got so scared she'd been infected she didn't show up one night. Next thing I heard was that her son's threatened, forced to participate in her place."

"You see cocaine passed at these so-called play rehearsals?"

"No. Why?"

Adolph cleared his throat. He had no reason to prematurely tip off Luann about the rumored drug shipments coming into town via the oil barrels. Sooner or later the cocaine under Honest Abe's bed would be in reports accessible to her. "Abraham Lincoln had cocaine in a baggie under his bed. That's why."

"You pushed me out so quick I didn't see it."

"Nor me. Len found it. I'll keep your other secret." She gazed at the floor. "Roscoe know about your message relays?"

"Don't know." He stared at her. "Honest."

Adolph couldn't picture Roscoe being involved in

anything illegal. Perhaps the burglary at his home wasn't to swipe tools for money, but to cover a search for something else. No computer or hard drive had been reported stolen from Roscoe, but the Carlsons lived close. "I'm going to Patsy's for a bagel to wash this morning's stench from my throat."

Adolph decided to forsake walking and drive home from Patsy's. The empty booths proved his hunch right that the supper crowd hadn't flocked in yet. A table with four eaters and two counter diners hardly paid the utility bill for the lights and the gas cooktop.

Rebecca, dressed in a traditional white blouse, black skirt server outfit, motioned for him to have a seat in the darkened party room. He switched on the light and slowly sank into what was becoming his well-used chair. Rebecca entered. Her outer room plastic server smile replaced by fatigue etched into her eyes. She carried a steaming coffee carafe and two mugs.

Adolph sat silent, unwilling to comment on her faded ingénue gaze.

Rebecca rested the carafe on the table and sat opposite Adolph. "Bradford mentioned you visited. Thanks." He nodded and she poured the black stench-quenching coffee he longed for. "His friends have shunned him. Afraid like they'd be contaminated with a deadly disease."

"It'll be temporary." His right thumb rubbed inner finger skin. "Kids are like that."

"So what's the reason you're here?"

He stopped his rubbing. "Gotta ask a few questions. Assume you've heard that Mr. Abraham Washington Lincoln, if that's his real name, was found dead today." He could've said he found the body, but inhibitions, his, to upset his psyche with vivid memories ruled.

"Saw on a TV newsbreak."

Adolph tried not to reveal all he knew. "Had he been in your acting group?"

Rebecca closed her eyes and bobbed her head in slow motion.

He forced a question to keep her alert. "When was the last

time he was there?"

"Time before last, I guess." Her eyes blinked open. "He didn't show last night."

Adolph gulped and hot coffee from the cup at his lips flooded his mouth until he pressed his lips together. He permitted a gurgle and gravity to begin the trickle of coffee down his throat. When he was no longer capable of spewing coffee, he asked, "What's this about last night?"

Body-wracking sobs streamed tears across Rebecca's cheeks. "I didn't want to go there. The pizza truck surprised me out back. Two guys grabbed me. One tied a cloth to my eyes. The brute pinning my arms lifted me and dropped me onto a mat. Threatening to kill me if I resisted, they ran their clammy hands under my skirt until one squeezed my head between his knees and bent forward, undid my blouse, and felt me up until his partner yelled to roll me over. Two or three palms roughly patted me. At my butt, one joked about digging deeper to find the police wire." Rebecca wiped her face with dispenser napkins. "One brute scratched me." She stood, lifted her skirt's hem, and the redness of a four-inch gash above the knee on the inside of her left leg showed through the nylon. She slumped into her chair.

"I'm sorry. Where didn't you want to go?"

She twirled her gaze 'round the room's white ceiling. "That farm."

Her mention of the word "farm" reactivated Adolph's recollection of his interview with Bradford. "You mean the Bourdon farm?"

She bobbed her head, its motion slowing with each up and down.

"Did you recognize either abductor?" His inquisitive voice adding: "Perhaps hear a name?"

"Don't know names." Her posture remained crumpled. "When one retied the blindfold, I caught a glimpse of an upper arm dragon tattoo although their faces were covered."

"Was Bradford's name mentioned at all?"

"No. One brute repeated this hideous laugh and said that I

could play Mrs. Robinson when he auditioned. The other giggled and told him to shut his mouth or he'd end up like Jonathan."

What had he stumbled into? "Did this Jonathan have a last name?"

"Wasn't said." She paused and rubbed both eyes. "Don't know why they kept me blindfolded. Cloth can't hide animal smells. Guessed I'd been to that farmhouse before."

"Maybe I've asked this before. You have a tattoo on your shoulder?"

Rebecca bristled in angry defiance. "No. And don't ask me to prove it now."

"While you were, let's say, acting, ever see a woman with one?"

"Didn't see, but heard a dark-skinned woman had one. She no longer comes."

"Can you describe her?"

"Don't need to. Name was Mrs. Connor. Same woman murdered on Mulberry Street."

Adolph gulped. The autopsy report listed the tattoo, not that Mrs. Connor had been playacting. This new wrinkle muddied why Jonathan Green had visited the Connor home. Adolph mentally listed four possibilities: 1. Sex with Marcie or her mother, 2. Recruit Leroy for drug running, 3. Threaten mother with harm to Leroy if the mother didn't act, or 4. Collect a payment for drugs. Mrs. Connor's unbuttoned blouse could've been, not a prelude to sex, but to show Jonathan her shoulder tattoo as proof she'd already paid with her body.

He couldn't jump into the thicket of Mrs. Connor's murder. He bypassed asking Rebecca if Luann sported a tattoo. "Ever been to the farm with an older gentleman, say within the last year-and-a-half, who dressed in Old West shirts and blue jeans."

"Yeah." Her voice volume spiked. "Pistol Pete was a repulsive, uncaring jerk."

Adolph's mind checked off the physical attributes she described as those of Mr. Antoine Russell, the man Adolph had identified as the one basted and/or lathered in used motor oil for a year while nestled between perennial and annual roots in the Rose Garden B&B flower bed.

Rebecca heaved her shoulders forward and rested both of her arms on the table. "This kinky guy only seemed to enjoy himself when talking about his kids. Never liked the cowboy clothes either. Carried them in a black bag. Came and left in dress slacks and a collared shirt."

"One important question: Ever see illegal drugs in his possession or in the bag?"

Her gaze flitted between blank and quizzical. "Never."

Adolph pressed. "Did he mention being allergic to any food or medication?"

"Don't remember." She sighed. "Are all these questions necessary? Jose can't cook and wait on supper rush diners by himself."

Adolph wanted to be compassionate, but if he didn't exploit the moment he didn't know when he'd have the opportunity to catch Rebecca this open. "At the farmhouse, who was there?"

"Turner, know his voice and his snide remarks about Viagra; Luann, she whispered she wouldn't let anyone hurt me; and, don't ask me who because my blindfold stayed on the entire time, but another male spoke muffled like he'd swallowed a handkerchief. Assumed the Dragons, after I heard their stomping down the stairs, mostly loitered outside in the pizza truck. They've never been allowed there for any filming."

Turner? Adolph would've liked to drive a hot, dull stake into his heart, but the other man's identity was definitely more important. "This unknown male voice. Ever hear it before?"

"Never."

The emphatic delivery and Rebecca's squirming in her seat couldn't dissuade him. "Could you decipher any words?"

"Days on something. Coulda been the river. Didn't make sense for me to listen."

Adolph switched gears. "This muffled voice sound young

or old?"

"Past puberty. That old?"

"Old enough." Since Luann had been identified as being there, he eliminated her son. That amounted to only one factor and it troubled Adolph that there were many unexplained factors. He couldn't be certain if Rebecca's farm presence matched or overlapped her son, Bradford, who also, before being lashed, heard an unidentified man speak. The substitution, but not the demise of Honest Abe, for a murdered Pistol Pete made gruesome logical sense, as did Adolph's supposition the reference to Jonathan had been to Jonathan Greene, killed at the Connor home.

He reluctantly concluded that, with Rebecca's heightened nervousness about Patsy's customers and her visible twitches, he'd drained her memory and had to dismiss her and digest what he'd unraveled. He couldn't let on to Rebecca that, as cruel and demeaning as she'd been treated, the Dragons kidnapping victims portended fiercer, darker, and more sinister violence, which escalation was contemporaneous with the duplicated mention of an unidentified man.

Chapter Eight

Adolph's headlights spooked an upright and motionless squirrel posed on a fading dirty-white Bridgetown street centerline. His strained eyes chased the brown blur until it darted into the darkness beneath a parked car. Adolph had been cruising aimlessly for an hour failing to spot his daughter, Kristen. At dinner she'd told he and Mary she would study with Katie. The TV news marked ten o'clock and his telephone calls to Katie's house had rung unanswered. Kristen's cell had forwarded Adolph to voice mail.

His first stop had encountered eerily dark windows at Katie's home. No one answered the lit doorbell button he'd pushed until his finger ached, nor responded to his storm-door-rattling fist pounding. He'd delayed relaying this unsettling news to Mary.

He drove past a desolate Jackson High. A late night dog walker struggling to control a wolfhound was the only human Adolph had chanced to come across as he randomly checked dark alleys, known lover's lanes, and quizzed casino parking lot security at an otherwise desolate riverfront. The Sixth Street Bar boomed Hank Williams country music to half a dozen highly polished chrome motorcycles parked at its front door curb. While he slowed his Monte Carlo, Adolph harbored no intention of stopping. His cell rang. Mary's choked words registered her heightened distress. In vague words encircling the core of a lie frosted with hope, he promised his wife that he'd be home with Kristen shortly.

Fifteen minutes later, waiting for a River Drive intersection green light, his cell rang again. Caller ID said Kristen. With fading euphoria, he listened to a halting voice speaking syllables that Adolph could barely piece together. He deciphered "school" and "cold grass."

Adolph, activating the portable magnetic red light he lifted through his open driver's door window, didn't hit the brakes until his car jumped a curb and its rear brake pads jerked his Monte Carlo to a stop in front of Jackson High's front traffic circle flagpole. His headlight beam outlined a dark-clothed figure, bathed in the dim light of one exterior roof-edge mounted security flood, lying on the school's grass. He ran the thirty feet to the figure and dropped to his knees.

"Kristen, Kristen say something." Adolph heaved his shoulders forward, his face next to hers. Her lips twitched and uttered unintelligible speech sounds. Her weak exhales caressed his cheeks with faint feather touches. Clad in black slacks with her shoes still tied, her raised knees modeled the fetal position. His hand touched the black fabric of a blouse buttoned to her chin.

Adolph's Gold

Kristen, to Adolph's hurried exam, exhibited all the physical symptoms highlighted in his last training refresher to conclude a person was drunk, except Adolph smelled no alcohol. He observed no physical bruises on his daughter's exposed skin. As a father, he longed to pick Kristen up and hug her close. He dared not and fumbled to extract his cell phone and dial 9-1-1.

"Kristen, open your eyes," he whispered. Her body beneath his cupped fingers trembled.

When Ralph, an EMT, dashed from the ambulance to be at his side, Adolph released Kristen's hands. He paced nearby until the scoop stretcher, with Kristen strapped on, was hoisted into the ambulance. Adolph told Ralph he'd pick up Mary and meet Kristen at the hospital.

Mary, alerted by his pre-arrival telephone call, withheld her questions as Adolph eased her into the Monte Carlo's front passenger seat and stowed his wife's collapsible walker in the rear seat. "Ready?" Adolph asked. Mary's nod and gaze said it was an understandable question, but his emotions, ripped raw by having seen an ambulance door close on his only child, weren't.

The hospital emergency room coordinator buoyed Adolph's spirits by stating that Kristen's vital signs were stable. Adolph suspected the doctor had ordered a full tox screen. After agonizing minutes, a nurse approached he and Mary as they sat in the waiting room's corner. She asked if they could explain what Kristen may have ingested in the last twenty-four hours. Adolph answered he didn't know. Mary, with deepening worry lines flaring from both eyes, haltingly detailed that day's breakfast of orange juice and cereal with milk and after school graham crackers. The nurse jotted notes on a clipboard and left.

"Did you see Katie?" Mary asked.

"No." In his myopic focus on his daughter, he'd forgotten Kristen's friend.

From an address book Mary carried in her purse, he dialed the seven digits. When Katie's dad answered on the tenth ring,

239

Adolph ignored the dad's mild protest to learn that Katie wasn't at home. In a second call, Adolph, playing the odds that Kristen and Katie had been in close proximity, alerted the police dispatcher to Katie's potential abduction and suggested the dispatcher issue an Amber alert and have uniformed officers sweep the grounds at Jackson High.

Adolph fidgeted and distracted his mind by having a business journal's latest river barge usage statistics float into and out of his mind until Katie's hair-tousled father, wearing a sweatshirt and jeans, peered into the waiting room. Adolph lurched forward out of his chair. The magazine on his lap, pages flapping on the descent, splattered onto the floor.

Hurt flashed in Katie's father's eyes as he clasped Adolph's shoulders and whispered that Katie, just wheeled into emergency, had been found unconscious behind a cemetery cross.

At five past one a.m., a white-coated young doctor asked Adolph and Mary to join him outside the waiting room. Adolph positioned Mary's walker in front of her, steadied it, and, with baby steps, followed her into the hallway, and then stepped forward to face the doctor.

"Your daughter had traces of morphine hydrochloride. She may experience terrific headaches for a day or two, but I believe she's past the danger point."

Adolph wrapped his right arm around Mary's shoulders. "You utilize an assault kit?"

"The nurse did, although your daughter presented no external signs."

"Can we talk to her?"

"Soon. But it's highly unlikely she'll be able to tell you much and I'd like to keep her overnight as a precaution. The drug detected, as you might know, causes amnesia."

The doctor guided Adolph and Mary to Kristen's ICU bedside. At the bed's head, the stoic doctor observed Kristen's eyeballs react to a penlight beam he swung from side to side. A summoned nurse spoke softly with Mary while Adolph trailed an orderly pushing Kristen, strapped to a gurney, to the elevator and into Room 204. Adolph suppressed a renewed hatred for the pale yellow rolled onto the patient room walls.

Alone with Kristen, he lowered his lips to kiss her clammy forehead. He hadn't done that since she'd been a little girl scared of the monsters under her bed. Only this time, her closed eyes in a partially turned face offered no reaction.

"Sleep well, Kristen. Your Mom and I will be back later this morning."

Adolph, with Mary buckled into the passenger seat, swept his Monte Carlo headlights across the high school lawn. That all emergency vehicles were gone didn't uplift him. Tied to thirty-inch wooden stakes, strung yellow tape warned all not to enter where Kristen had lain. Three blocks away, to the mausoleum's left, Adolph surmised the staked tape circle enclosing a stele indicated where Katie must've been found. Lowering his driver window, he breathed in the eerie cemetery quiet undisturbed by the piercing Monte Carlo high beams streaking elongated and narrowing light paths onto the grass blades of the dead marked by marble headstones. He removed his right hand from his Walther P.38; he couldn't kill imagined ghostly scumbags.

Mary's voice interrupted. "Let's go home, dear. It's chilly."

Adolph assisted an unsteady Mary into the kitchen. He helped her get seated, fetched her a glass of water, and then excused himself to close the garage door. Passing a garage shelf, he grabbed a flashlight. He stood beneath the retracted garage door, muscles tensed, scanning the street for unfamiliar vehicles and watching for any movement whatsoever. Only a far off dog bark disturbed the neighborhood's early morning cocoon of silence. His sixth sense excited him to check all window exteriors. Exposure had dulled the kitchen window marks he'd noticed days earlier so he traipsed to the backyard. His body shuddered. Three pry bar marks, freshly dug into Kristen's bedroom windowsill, left an ominous sign of danger.

* * *

With barely enough sleep to fill a thimble, Adolph, ten hours after Kristen's admission, closed his mind to the pale yellow cavern of depression created by Kristen's hospital room walls. Her open, if not fully alert, eyes and a half-consumed breakfast tray cheered him. Mary had brought Kristen clean clothes. Adolph, rather than wait in the hall while his daughter dressed, bounded up a flight of stairs to Bradford Quimby's room.

When he entered, the head of Bradford's bed had been raised forty-five degrees.

"How ya doing?" Adolph asked.

Bradford, lying on his left side, replied, "Okay."

Adolph approached to within four feet of Bradford's face and found it easier to remain standing. "The other day you said there had been a voice, a man's voice, who said something about what his father did, or would do to him. Can you remember anything else this voice said?"

"Nah. And, I don't care. My mom said we're getting out of this town next week."

Adolph's eyes checked for a person near the room's door. "Where you going?"

"Promised Mom I wouldn't tell." Bradford's steadfast and calm voice spoke as if running had happened before. "We don't want anybody following us."

"I can understand." And, Adolph really could. Rebecca's traumatic physical violation, plus Bradford's, made escaping a reasonable go-to reaction. Deep in his soul, a substratum of roiling anger, smoldering for revenge, yearned to erupt through the humanity of his practiced phlegmatic veneer. He had never fully bought into his pastor's preaching of forgiveness. Only his mother's words, active in his subconscious, restrained him. Adolph couldn't recall the number of youthful times he'd sat on his mother's knee with bandaged cuts and bruises and listened to her constantly repeat that, in the end, good triumphs evil. Adolph longed to jump start today's victory by firing hot lead bullets to sear, dismember, and rip apart every Dragon that dared roam his city's streets.

By the time a released Kristen was seated with Adolph and Mary at their home's kitchen table, he'd masked and subdued his reactionary passion without outward eruption.

"Tell me where you went last night," Adolph began.

"Katie's."

Kristen's scrubbed face without the smoky makeup, her blue robe without a dangling waist chain, and her feet in slippers and not clunky shoes struck him as the little girl the years had taken away. Mary rested both of her hands on the table. He tried not to stare at his daughter.

"After that. Where'd you get the drugs?"

"How many times." Her eyes squarely met his. "I don't do drugs. Katie said Gloria had new music and we should go to there. It was fine until three or four Dragons showed up."

"How'd you know they were Dragons?"

"D-a-d!"

He waited, refusing to acknowledge he lacked common sense. "Just you three girls?"

"Nah. Six, no, maybe seven. I was in the living room corner hanging out by myself, trying to go unnoticed, waiting for Katie when Gloria, across the room, mentioned my name."

"What then?" Adolph felt a forgotten pain twinge at the nape of his neck.

"These two Dragons squeezed me between them. One, think Jack's his name, ran two fingers across my chin and said we should party. Katie came over and said to leave me alone."

"Did they?"

"Sorta of. Jack backed off. Then the guy that had been on the other side of me grabbed my Coke. He wouldn't give it back. Put it behind his back and challenged me to press against him, wrap my arms around his chest to get it. I said, 'Go to hell.' He laughed. Jack came up behind the guy with my Coke still at his back. Katie stepped between me and the Dragon, not Jack. Finally, Jack almost shouted at this guy to find a prettier girl—one who liked to party."

"Did you drink the Coke?"

"Yeah. The guy handed it back to me when this Jack hurried off to the kitchen."

Mary's slight head nod told him to stop. He ignored her wish. "What about Katie?"

Kristen gazed at the kitchen's ceiling light fixture. "What about her?"

"Was she drinking?"

"Yeah. She had a purple metallic tumbler. A Dragon tilted a vodka bottle at it."

"You were drugged. Probably Katie, too."

"Damn."

Vertical line wrinkles deepened between Mary's eyebrows. "Kristen, watch your language. You should go lie down now."

Sitting there, not contesting Mary's directive, Adolph's uncapped internal rage flared. It commanded his senses and he almost didn't hear his pocketed cell phone. Luann rambled as he pressed the cell to his ear. He finally said yes when asked a third time to meet her on Tinley.

The midmorning fog he had driven through on his way home from the hospital no longer blanketed the river. In the soon to be forgotten mist, he spotted Luann outside 409 Tinley, parked behind her Chrysler, and ambled to the foyer entrance where she stood.

"Building owner's public identity hidden under a series of land trusts," Luann began.

Adolph had skipped his planned records search. "Doesn't surprise."

"Originally built by Wainright Barge." Adolph's forehead muscles tensed. "Had been a small hotel for tourists, especially those on river tours. Then later sold to Lem Lhur Realty before they went bankrupt."

"The barge company or the realty firm?"

"Guess both." Her right hand fleetingly shielded her lips. "Len said he didn't finish the apartment, but thought it should be given new eyes. I didn't care to do it without backup."

Adolph's Gold

Adolph, wary of a set up orchestrated by Lt. Hunter, temporarily squashed his disdain for Luann. Since he'd never known Len to shirk his duties, Adolph, on entry to the building, allowed Luann to pass through the foyer first and confront the stench of yesterday's second floor hallway trash. He heard country western music blare from Apt. 4 as he inspected the undisturbed yellow police tape that crisscrossed the Apt. 3 door. He and Luann donned vinyl gloves. With a right hand swipe, he ripped the tape and Luann's right hand shoved the previously damaged door inward. Choked by the intense putrid smell, he unlatched and flung up a kitchen window.

"I'll check here," Luann said. "Give you the bedroom."

Without uttering an answer, Adolph, making sure he avoided the blood-drop stains on the floor, stepped into the bedroom. Assuming Len had stripped the bed linens, Adolph ignored the mattress to exam a three-drawer mahogany dresser, the room's only other furniture piece. Its empty top drawer hung open and the half dozen articles of men's clothing in the middle drawer didn't spark his curiosity. A white dress shirt, wedged into the back of the lowest drawer, hindered the drawer's full outward extension. Adolph figured it was unusual for Len to have left it jammed like that. Perhaps the gagging assault of a gaseous corpse had hastened Len's exit?

Grasping the drawer's front, Adolph's double yank ripped the cotton cloth and the drawer free. He tossed the shirt and a floral sundress onto the already dark-stained mattress. Squatting, he flipped the drawer bottom side up to discover a brown eight-by-eleven inch envelope taped to the drawer's underside. He called out for Luann.

"You find something?" She stared down at him from the doorway.

He stood, laid the drawer on the bed, and his gloved right forefinger traced the envelope's two taped edges. "The kitchen have a knife?"

"Should have. I'll check." Luann pivoted and returned to

245

hand him a paring knife.

He freed the envelope from the drawer, poked a hole at the corner of the envelope's flap, and sliced it open. Onto the drawer's bottom tumbled three passports, one for a Hispanic woman; four driver's licenses in yellow sleeves, one with a feminine Hispanic name missing a picture; two library cards; and a faded Barnes and Noble receipt for Abraham Lincoln's life story by Carl Sandburg. Adolph appraised the full import of his discovery: an actor delving into history or, most likely, a con artist doing his necessary homework.

"Any letter or instructions?" Luann asked. Her right elbow bumped his left arm.

"Only a stuck-on sticker on the envelope's front giving the Rose Garden B&B address." Adolph poked through the identification documents and then asked, "You find anything?"

"Nothing."

Adolph sensed the increased shallow rhythm of Luann's breathing. "Guess this was the only item missed by the crime crew sweep. Unless, of course, there's something under the mattress." He expected her to frown, not dismiss him with a gaze out the window like a zombie. Until completely convinced that Luann was, or had been, a forced victim, he'd remain vigilant.

She recovered to angle her shoulders in front of him. Her gloved left hand reached for a passport, and she held it out in front of her. "Pasquale Peter, interesting name or . . . alias."

Adolph connected the dots. He gazed intently at the passport dated before 9/11/01. The face, with mustache shaven, matched his file photo of Mr. Antoine Russell, aka Rebecca's Pistol Pete. Adolph chuckled to himself, criminals now going green, recycling fake IDs. He said nothing as Luann helped him return the myriad items to the brown envelope. He guarded the restocked envelope until Luann retrieved an evidence bag from her Chrysler.

Adolph lifted the clothes he found. The small-sized white shirt wouldn't have fit this Abe Lincoln. The dress's hem contained a laundry mark: SM Sanchez. He dropped the dress on the bed and, when Luann returned, he acted with protocol and bagged the envelope and the dress in separate evidence bags. Stopping at the capped dress in the hallway, his exam found a similar Sanchez laundry mark. He added it to the evidence bag containing the prior dress.

"You going into the rag business?" Sarcasm dripped from Luann's question.

"Evidence." He quickened his step. "Maybe coincidental, but name's similar to that of a mother I interviewed about a suspicious assault." He didn't feel compelled to say more.

Luann, standing next to her Chrysler's raised trunk lid, didn't protest his suggestion to follow him to the Rose Garden B&B.

Adolph stepped up onto the B&B porch, careful not to bang his head on the two hanging baskets with their wilted flowers. While he knocked, Luann doubled the speed of her lagging pace up the driveway. When admitted, he followed Francine into the kitchen where the clock hands displayed 11:30 a.m. On the counter nearby sat a pinot noir bottle with a stopper shoved halfway into the bottle's neck. As they were three with Luann, Adolph suggested the back patio.

"You brought this nice woman." Francine extended her right hand. "It's such a pleasure. Have we met?"

"Labor Day weekend," Luann replied. She touched and released Francine's hand.

"Oh, so tragic. Adolph told me it was Mr. Russell buried like that." Francine gazed right of the apple tree, toward the flower garden. "Will my cousin, The Chief, be joining us?"

"Not today, Francine," Adolph said. He flopped into an armed lawn chair. If Francine gabbed, he could use a rest. "Chief Howard sends his apologies. Have you two spoken lately?"

"He's so busy. Never in when I call. Always with the mayor, somebody important."

Luann crossed her arms. Her lips parted without a sound.

"Would you remember what kind of suitcase or bag Mr.

Russell came with?" Adolph began.

Francine's son, Matt, craned his head from the B&B's rear door.

"Join us, son. I forgot to offer these nice people a drink. Bring the pitcher from the refrigerator. And I could use a . . . no, the pitcher and glasses will be all." Francine gazed at Adolph. "I hope you'll pardon me."

"Absolutely. Luann and I, we're really fine. Again, remember Mr. Russell's bags?"

Francine sat. "So hard to remember. Think he had a brown suitcase."

"What about a smaller black bag, cloth perhaps?" Adolph heard the rear door open.

"I'm afraid." Francine's eyes wandered. "Afraid I can't help you there."

"Mom," Matt interjected, placing a lemonade pitcher and tray of glasses on the patio's wrought iron table. "I saw Mr. Russell with a black beach bag. First thought it sorta strange and then figured that maybe he carried it for one of the kids he always talked about."

Adolph shifted his hips toward Matt. "Have any idea what he had in it?"

Matt rubbed his chin. "He dropped a handful of plastic bags one day."

Luann's rotating gaze settled on Matt. "How big?" she asked.

"Oh, not very. Like ones earrings come in. Could've had kids' trinkets in them."

"That's helpful," Adolph said. "Last year, say summertime, you ever see a fifty-five gallon drum in the neighborhood."

"Yeah." Matt's silver ring in his left ear glistened when he rotated his head.

Luann's eyelids stretched wide. Francine yawned. Adolph, his right hand extended, palm up, flexed it back and forth to encourage Matt to give him more details.

"Delivery van unloaded them in front of the Wainright

house when the street pavement cracks were being patched. Two men in the crew poured the contents into a hot tar cooker wagon. They were empty and gone in a day or so."

"How many did you say there were?"

Matt edged a step toward the house door. "Three or four."

"Remember any writing on the barrels?"

"Nah."

Clinking glasses interrupted Adolph before Francine filled them with lemonade. "Did you see Mr. Russell at any time after seeing those tar barrels?"

"Don't think so." Matt lowered his gaze. "Mom, did we?"

A startled Francine craned her head to the left. "Don't remember no barrels."

Adolph politely refused the offered lemonade. He rose to thank Francine and Matt and to signal Luann of their impending departure. Exiting through the B&B's sideyard gate, Adolph begged off staying with Luann as he told her he first had to check on Kristen at home and would rejoin her at the station's detective room in a couple of hours.

* * *

Adolph stood at Bulldog's open office door whispering his answer to Luann that Kristen seemed to be doing fine. As a seated Lt. Turner hoisted a football pool slip in his right hand, Adolph, to indicate no interest, shook his head side-to-side.

"I updated The Chief on closed case statistics today," Bulldog said. "He wasn't pleased."

Didn't surprise Adolph. Lately, The Chief rarely expressed enjoyment in the statistics and never mentioned the active detective roster was short two with a vacancy and Yancey on the shelf. The injustice of it all simmered in Adolph's mind. With his self-interest paramount, Adolph didn't speak up to add Honest Abe's unsolved murder. Nor did he highlight Kristen and Katie as he had convinced the dispatcher to list his call as a "found" missing person, not a criminal assault. "Guess you'll have to work harder," Adolph mumbled under his breath.

"What's that?" Bulldog asked, his upraised chin slanted toward Adolph.

"Oh, wondering if you ever worked construction."

"In college. Best paying job available." Bulldog's eyes slid from Adolph to Luann.

While she rubbed her left shoulder against the doorjamb, Adolph noticed Luann's mien much more subdued. Although her old self shined through occasionally, in general, she'd been less caustic to him since he spilled the beans on his knowledge of her late night porn star role.

Adolph let Luann take a separate route to her desk. From the corner of his eye, he watched Bulldog meander out to their desks. As Adolph's muscles tensed, Bulldog bumped his hip against Luann's desk corner. Her gaze at him stiffened.

"Chief asked me to update both of you that he'll be announcing a detective promotion next month. Six final candidates, four local. He didn't tell me who . . . so don't ask. You're best advised to run from the gossip. Perhaps new money in the football pool. Carry on."

Adolph recognized the last two words as Bulldog's pep talk and an indication he would be leaving them alone. Adolph spied the two crime lab envelopes in his inbox.

Luann, in her chair, swiveled toward him. "What do you figure is the oil or tar barrel connection to the skeleton?"

He leaned forward. "Don't know that I should explain. May jeopardize the collar."

"Hell, what's that to mean?" She mumbled additional words Adolph didn't decipher.

When he didn't respond, Luann reached for a folder on her desk. He fingered his top inbox envelope. His raised right index finger broke the seal. The top of the page summary stated the latest computer not identified with the original St. Mary's computer theft. A yellow post-it note had two words scribbled in pencil: "No Detective." That still left one St. Mary's computer tower unaccounted for. He exhaled slowly and waited for Luann to raise her gaze.

"I think you had, let's say contact, with the murdered Mr.

Russell, aka Pistol Pete. Two things I perceived today created this overwhelming inference that ties you to Mr. Russell."

"What? Tar barrels and jewelry plastic. C'mon." She stood and strode closer to brace her left thigh against the side of his desk.

Adolph shoved the crime lab envelope atop its report pages. "We don't know that all the barrels contained tar. I've a hunch one of the barrels contained used motor oil."

"Huh? A city street and sanitation employee part of a grand conspiracy to disguise used oil barrels as tar barrels. Ludicrous."

"Hang on. Not far-fetched. Cocaine coulda been delivered to the dean or the packages handed over his back fence to a B&B occupant or co-conspirator."

"What grand piece in all of this am I missing?"

"Beat cops found used oil barrels modified to smuggle cocaine or other drugs. If the barrel was full, the oil had to go someplace. My guess. Dragons poured it over the fence into the B&B garden. Probably unaware your playacting lover had been buried."

"Cut the crap. Dragons haven't been guests at the B&B. Doubt they take private piano lessons, either, and I leveled with you the predicament Herbert put me in."

"Oh. Maybe your church-certified lover trucked the oil in." Adolph recognized the quip as a cheap shot; however, getting even, although against his instincts, leavened his internal anger.

"That's B.S. . . . nothing more. Herbert was framed and I'm going to prove it."

Adolph, facing the squad room door, caught sight of Bulldog returning and whispered, "Ssshh." Placing a hand on his phone, Adolph blurted out, "We can verify with dispatch."

Bulldog cast a glance at Adolph, didn't stop, and, without a word, shut his office door.

Luann's right hand wiped a wry smile off her face. "Let's say you're right. How you going to prove that a barrel left on a city street, and removed a year ago, contained cocaine and that its used motor oil was poured over the B&B victim? That's whistling in the wind."

"Maybe not, but this Dean Wainright's up to his neck in suspicious activity." Adolph decided he needed to ask one more question, albeit indirectly. "Hear any street scuttlebutt about a new movie production after Honest Abe's last casting call?"

Luann glared, and twisted her lower lip above the upper. "Not a damn peep."

Adolph's telephone rang. He picked up and turned his face and the mouthpiece away from Luann. "Tell me more." A minute later he said, "I'll be there in half an hour."

As he replaced the handset, he double-checked to guarantee that Luann had taken his body-turn-hint to devote her attention elsewhere. He unsealed the second crime lab computer report. The lab had been able to raise a portion of the filed serial number. The computer tower, while similar, wasn't a St. Mary's computer. Adolph rose and offered Luann the opportunity to ride with him to the mall's used computer store. The telephone caller had bestowed a stroke of luck. Ron Darling, the store manager, greeted them at the front sales counter.

"Tell me again what was suspicious," Adolph said.

"We have a stack of cannibalized computers tossed outside the back door. Late yesterday, a salvage pickup count found a computer had been added. Checked our security footage this morning. A pizza truck about four a.m. stops near the stack. A computer gets tossed onto it."

"Any driver visible?" Luann asked.

"No. Tossed from the truck box." Darling tapped an e-cigarette twice on the counter.

Adolph stepped forward to resume command of the conversation. "You said a pizza truck. How'd you come to that conclusion?"

"Words 'Salvatore Pizza' visible in the video."

"Do you have any large plastic sheets or bags?"

Darling answered quickly. "Sure."

Luann, with a dumbfounded facial expression, stared at Adolph.

"We'll drive around," Adolph said. "Bring the plastic. We'll transport the computer to our crime lab." Earlier at his desk, he'd assumed Luann had somewhat told the truth after reading the lab's dusting report. Now, chagrined that he'd definitely tipped his hand to her, he feared he could get burned. If Len had griped before, Adolph harbored no doubt his lab buddy would go ballistic with what he was to do next to violate transport protocol. Adolph planned to argue he'd saved the crime lab time and expense and schemed he'd redeem himself on his next visit to Len's lab by donating five bucks to the staff's coffee fund.

The plastic-wrapped computer tower Adolph lifted into his Monte Carlo trunk remained as smug and silent as Luann riding on the front seat beside him, that is, until both reached the station parking lot. Her eyes bore into him as she spoke. "You must regard me as a slut."

He kept his gaze fixed straight ahead, lowered slightly to see his knuckles turn pale with his finger blood flow restricted by both hands compressing the steering wheel. He'd said too much already. Agreeing with Luann's self-categorization would dig a hole he couldn't climb out of.

"I . . . I love . . . love my husband . . ."

Without allowing his head to move, Adolph rotated his eyes to Luann. "If I understand why you've cheated on your husband and willingly became a porn criminal, should I forgive?"

"I ain't . . . ain't no criminal and Herbert knows I wouldn't cheat on him."

Adolph dropped his left hand past his driver door handle. "Huh?"

"Well, he does . . . sorta. I expected only to do revealing poses. St. Louis FBI calculated a dirty cop wouldn't think twice . . . or hesitate about confiding in another."

"FBI?" His right hand released the steering wheel. "I coordinate with the local FBI office and they don't at the

253

moment have any undercover sting going on in these parts."

"That's why the St. Louis office. They didn't want to use any Iowa office for fear someone like you might be too cozy."

Adolph cocked his head toward her. "Why should I believe you? Why not believe you're scheming to snatch your own skin from the fire?"

"Those photos you had. There's a box full of them at St. Mary's and, from conversation tidbits I've gathered, other similar photos are hid in the Rose Garden B&B basement."

"You've got to be kidding. Mrs. Hoskins a porn queen?"

"Probably not." Her voice volume plummeted. "Her son is the one I suspect."

"This is all too flabbergasting. Let's go inside."

"Trust me or not, but you've got to protect me. Act like you've never heard. My whole family's in jeopardy, especially Herbert, until . . . until he's released from prison."

Luann alighted from his Monte Carlo and marched into the station, not twisting once to look back. While Adolph wouldn't consider himself stunned, her revelations bobbed like freed channel markers on an unsettled river. A sting. He could verify Herbert's crime and imprisonment, but he didn't dare approach the local two-man FBI office. An undercover narc wasn't supposed to be a user, although it happened. Entirely plausible a woman drawn in to be a nude model could be forced to let a man enter her. Adolph switched mental gears. What about the depth of Lt. Hunter's involvement? Adolph definitely couldn't interrogate him.

If he gave credence to Luann, being a criminal rendezvous point overshadowed the B&B's importance as a crime scene. The college also a likely setting, given the stolen computers and the hard drive porn. What, or who, could he prove to be the common denominator? Dean Wainright? Honest Abe? The latter a dirty cop flipped by the FBI if he believed Luann. Sure, he knew it could be possible. However, the likelihood required that he accept that Honest Abe checked in to the B&B as merely a ruse to survey the premises and to follow the twisting trail of Antoine Russell—a bad guy, an undercover operative, or a man who just loved kids? While Abe hoarded Pistol Pete's ID, Adolph couldn't pinpoint whether or not Russell's killing represented a falling out among thieves or had been carried out at the hands of a kingpin or warring third party.

What did Adolph really know about Antoine Russell? Russell had visited the B&B numerous years and times. Abe only once, but that occurred twelve months subsequent to Russell's death. Abe obviously infiltrated the porn setup, but whether he gained entry into the cocaine distribution network wasn't clear to Adolph. It could take him months or years to figure it all out, especially with Rebecca leaving and his having to be circumspect around Luann and Bulldog. And then, if illegal drugs dominated, that would factor in an expanded Dragon's role.

What did the evidence suggest? The legitimate appearance of B&B in-and-out traffic created an explainable neighborhood facade. Matt had seen Russell with plastic jewelry bags suitable for cocaine. What other delivery methods employed? Pizza boxes? Would Dragon leader Jack, not content with drug profits, perhaps desire a sexual release with older white women rather than court young females? Adolph discounted that supposition as the evidence indicated no Dragon had been filmed playacting. So, what then? As observed by Adolph's own eyes, Jack had a verified connection to Dean Wainright who lived across the fence from the B&B. That educator/Jack relationship had to be extraordinary, but what was the motivation, if not drugs?

The dean, once a professor, had built his own positive community legacy via music. He could distance himself from the shambles of his family's barge enterprise. Or did the dean desire to reclaim past glory? Adolph needed his computer inside.

Luann didn't gaze up from her desk, either upon his entrance, or when he logged onto his computer. He bypassed the official files for newspaper accounts. The Wainright Barge bankruptcy had been front-page news in the early 1960s.

While Bridgetown tax authorities had scheduled a public property auction for unpaid levies, Adolph could find no record of the auction ever happening. He telephoned Millie at the county recorder's office requesting an immediate appointment. She agreed.

For two of the chilly three-block walk to the limestone county building, Adolph shivered in a silent rhythm with the goblins of unanswered questions. The recorder's office existed to the right of an interior second floor landing connected to a grand winding staircase. Millie, never elected recorder, had forty-five years of experience and would retire at year's end. Her accumulated wisdom earned her the privilege of the only gray-walled cubicle with a window. Adolph eased himself into Millie's one visitor chair.

"It sounded urgent," Millie said. Her chain-tethered reading glasses dropped from her nose to hang at her throat. "Haven't had a question about Wainright Barge since maybe 2003."

A robin, on Millie's outside windowsill, pecked at an oat morsel. Adolph spied a package of them propped against the wall, beneath the inside edge of the window frame.

"Why then?"

"Property sold by the city that year for unpaid taxes. City could never align itself with the county to redevelop the property into a waterfront park. Got close in maybe late '91 or '92, but then riverboat gambling chopped the architect's park property landscape plan in half."

"Who bought the Wainright property?"

"Investor group from St. Louis. They received a grant for a main dock rebuild. Renamed the site WR Barge, Inc., and hired seven or eight employees, about half local."

"Recall the name of the investor group?"

"No. But it likely won't help you much if I did. Two years ago, the limited partnership defaulted on a mortgage and filed papers to dissolve into a leveraged buyout, I think it was that. Anyway, two employees and an unknown backer assumed the title. They kept the name of WR Barge and dropped the incorporation reference. Tax notices get mailed to its local address."

"You remember any employee names?"

"Silas Maurer, an old river pilot, and Oscar, his son. I've seen Silas at church occasionally, but not recently. He shrunk into himself when his youngest son drowned last year in New Orleans. Xavier Downs, I'm told, became the boss. Don't recall seeing him at community events much. I know he doesn't RSVP to chamber of commerce luncheon invites because I'm on the committee. Taxes have been paid which indicates by a small measure the company seems to be making a go of it."

"What about Silas's other son?"

"Couldn't say." A self-conscious smile separated her lips. "Must be a senior moment, but if the names don't cross my mind every so often, I tend to lose track."

Adolph hadn't absorbed every spoken detail and, to fake contemplation, he gazed at a robin landing and taking off from the outside windowsill. Would be a no-brainer that an underworld owner didn't want to seek attention or make waves in the community.

"You know, don't you, Millie, the Wainright name is still painted on the main building?"

"Never thought to look. I'll have to jot that down for my to-do list."

"Hope yours is shorter than mine." Adolph laughed.

He thanked Millie and, on rising from his chair, watched her reach for the bag of cereal. As he left, another red-breasted bird landed to hop near a faithful friend offering food.

Adolph tugged his tie aside to fasten his shirt's top button. A freshening west wind underscored his foolishness to dart out not wearing a topcoat. A winter forecasted to be snowy wouldn't be his favorite time of year. He calculated the pros and cons of his next move. If Luann remained at the station, to avoid his Monte Carlo attracting attention, she could drive him to visit Silas again. Stepping into the station, he slapped the chill from his arms and thighs.

He spotted Luann sitting at her desk, chatting on the telephone and tapping a pen to a pad.

When her receiver clicked into its rest, Adolph asked, "Have time to drop me off in the old Wainright home district?"

"How long you need?" she whispered. "Chief glanced at me a few minutes ago. Sure he wanted to know why I was here alone, but didn't ask."

Adolph bent down to retie a tied shoelace so that his voice didn't carry across the room. "Maybe thirty minutes, forty tops."

"Parking lot in ten. I need to telephone a victim as promised."

Adolph reached into his desk drawer for an old notepad that had the scribbles of what he and Silas had spoken about. Adolph feared he might have been misled by the old man's bitterness. The short drive with Luann to Oxford Avenue refroze her temporary thaw and Adolph, refusing to be upset, focused his mind on the passing small tree branches waving like bony fingers in the wind. As Luann's car slowed, Adolph perceived the yellowish yachting cap and blue wool coat of the solitary figure huddled on the park bench would definitely be Silas.

"Drop me off here." Adolph pointed to the immediate curb.

"I can stop next to the bench."

"Better you let me out. Silas has an aversion to police. Give me half an hour."

Adolph buttoned his topcoat as Luann's car sped ahead. Silas's head jerked in Adolph's direction and then Silas's eyes reverted to starting at the concrete. Adolph sauntered past Silas without speaking, and then pivoted.

"Good afternoon, Silas. Didn't mean to be rude or scare you, but I didn't want any parked car or busybodies to spy on us talking."

Silas lifted his chin. "Don't I know you?"

"Yeah. Adolph's my name. You helped me understand

258

the Wainright family."

His eyes crossed. "You're police. You gonna arrest me for something I said?"

"Heavens no. I take care of my buddies. You remember that don't you?"

He shook his head. "Don't remember much sometimes."

Adolph's hand brushed twigs and dust off a section of bench before sitting. "I didn't know until I read an old paper. I'm sorry to learn of your son's death. You must've been proud of Oscar. Following in your footsteps like he was."

"Darn right." Silas's voice rose in strength. "He'd be on the river if safety had the priority every owner and boss says it does. Frayed lines and shifting cargo crashed him to a watery grave." Adolph listened to low throaty moan sounds exit Silas's unmoving parted lips. Stopping when he continued. "For me, the buoy bell clangs death."

"I recall you mentioned the Wainright family." He searched Silas's face for a nonexistent acknowledgment. "They couldn't have owned the barges you and Oscar piloted."

"Not exactly."

"Does that mean you don't remember?"

"Not exactly."

Adolph hated to try again for Silas appeared on the verge of a shutdown. "Help me."

"Well, with no pension. Oscar and me worked a little deal. You see, Oscar required experience to become a full-fledged pilot, but my license had expired. I'd be hired on as a tow deckhand, same as Oscar, only I'd man the pilothouse and teach Oscar things he could use like how the river surface changes hinted at hidden hazards lurking below."

"I don't mean to be cruel, but that doesn't make sense. The barge company had to have assigned a licensed pilot, right?"

"Not always. A pilot would hop on at an upstream lock-and-dam to sign paperwork, maybe ride to the next, and then hop onto another for a downstream ride."

"If I read between the lines, the employer participated in

this scam."

"Definitely."

"So, who was this barge company boss the last couple of years?"

Silas swiveled his head as far as he could in both directions. "Xavier Downs runs the dock. There's a bigger fish, I reckon. Downy always checked manifests with someone in St. Louis. And I didn't know that WR Barge had a dock or office in St. Louie."

"What? How?"

"Telephone. Had one of those cheap pocket phones. Kept it locked in a drawer. But I'll tell you this. Don't be like those TV cops who sneak around in the dark. You'll likely lose an arm or leg to one of the Dobermans they let lose to roam the warehouse."

Is his mind that easy to read? Adolph shuffled ahead to seek more important information. "What kind of cargo would be checked? Must've been expensive stuff."

"Confused me, yes siree it did."

Adolph needed facts, not the mush of a wavering mind. "In what way."

"Never saw anything but the usual corn, coal, scrap steel."

Adolph pulled his topcoat tighter. He wasn't getting anywhere. "Maybe asked this before. In the last year or so did Dean or Professor Wainright ever visit the dock when you there?"

"I never personally saw him. Downy, when he'd share a beer, complained a time or two he'd have to gas up the professor's small cabin cruiser."

Adolph used the back of his hand to press warmth into his lips. "It have a name?"

"Named Piano Chord. Stupid. That's all I'll say." Silas clamped his lips tight.

"Piano Chord, you say?" Adolph desired the confirmation to pursue another lead. Sooner or later Adolph would weave the strands into an inescapable net.

Silas nodded.

"Appreciate your speaking with me. Won't be many days to sit out and enjoy."

"You got that right."

Adolph began walking towards 415 Oxford. Lately, the weight of human misery weighed heavy on his shoulders and he couldn't shine even the feeblest of light on individuals in the shadows pulling strings and being enriched by shady business operations. He neither complained when Luann showed five minutes late to pick him up, nor when he uncovered new crime lab reports in his office inbox beneath The Chief's memo soliciting United Way donations.

The first lab report on the third St. Mary's computer began with an admonition to read it cover-to-cover before jumping to conclusions. His front-to-back, line-by-line scrutiny authenticated that Luann's fingerprints were nowhere to be found on the computer store pickup, however, traces of cleaning solution in three screw holes indicated it had been doused and wiped. The report's unstated conclusion required that, if he were to trust Luann, it rested on blind faith. Congealing in his brain was the report's missing hard drive notation with an offbeat reference to peripherals—an Ethernet card, two in fact, and a wireless card. Having one Ethernet card made sense for a college campus hardwired with an Ethernet network.

In the every day workings of St. Mary's music department, as he understood it, Adolph could fathom no earthly reason for a stationary desktop wireless connection. Even if a police rookie, he'd determine it unlikely the desktop would be carried to the college library where a wireless hotspot radiated upward through four stories. He wiped his eyes and tried to quit worrying about technical stuff. Exasperation gnawed at his innards for he'd hit another stonewall. Without a miracle, he expected the hard drive digital files to be lost forever.

Under the crime lab envelope, he lifted a reply from Newscom in response to his inquiry about whether or not Dean Wainright's home had Internet service. He'd bristled when the local manager wouldn't give him a simple verbal reply. Instead, citing legal privacy restrictions, the manager ended his written reply with a final refusal to answer, suggesting an official letter signed by Chief Howard, approved by a judge. That initially struck Adolph as overly formalistic since he sought only knowledge of connection, not content.

Adolph, like many, could live without being connected, and Mary shied away from all computer keyboards as her arthritic finger joints had become increasingly painful and inflexible. The counterweight dragging Adolph to the Internet sign up desk had been Kristen's argument she needed to have a high-speed computer connection for schoolwork.

Adolph double-checked the city directory for the one person who'd respond to his verbal information request and tossed the Newscom letter into the file. He punched in the seven numbers for Griffin Moriey, Streets and Sanitation Commissioner. American Legion members, they'd worked on several patriotic projects. A 'Nam vet ready to retire, Griffin took pride in gym workouts to maintain his ability to outlast younger workers.

"Yeah," Griffin said. "We had a patch project on Lilac Lane last fiscal year."

"Can you tell me who worked on it?"

"Let me check my work order database." Adolph drummed his fingers. "Regular crew, Stan, Joseph, Ryan, and a summer temporary. Which person you interested in?"

"Depends. Who was the temporary?"

"Relative of your chief, Matt Hoskins."

"You don't say. Never heard it mentioned around here."

"Well, you didn't hear nothing from me, although, it wasn't a secret on the street."

"What employment dates? Did he return this year?"

"June 1 to August 28. Didn't work streets and san this past summer."

"Understand you cook tar for patching. Any unusual incidents with Matt?"

"Don't recall. If summer employees show up as scheduled

and don't goof off, they get an excellent recommendation, if one's requested of me. Don't recall even the slightest complaint."

Adolph, after dodging Griffin's request to join him for a beer, pocketed his note listing Matt Hoskins's work dates and scribbled a second note, which he placed on Luann's vacant desk, that she should telephone him, if he was needed.

His left hand fingertips grazed across the newly mounted Rose Garden B&B sign. When Francine, displaying a surprised look, opened the B&B door, he apologized for bothering her twice in a day, asked to speak with Matt, and descended the basement steps after her.

Off to his left, twin stacks of haphazardly piled linen covered a table wedged between humming washers. To his right, a door, propped ajar by a six-inch brick, freed light rays to streak the gray concrete basement floor. Adolph, distracted by Francine's clomps up the stairs, didn't even think to show his badge.

"Come on in, detective."

Adolph gawked at Matt's mountain of electronic equipment that flowed like lava from side-by-side salvaged pedestal desks across all available floor space. The room's unkempt twin bed rose as a machineless atoll in a sea of circuitry with no gap large enough to permit a broom to touch the floor. Adolph, hesitant to disrupt or step into what he perceived to be chaos, employed his two hands to brace his torso between the room's doorjambs. He counted three monitors in front of the room's double-armed office chair on rollers.

"You weren't exactly free with information earlier in response to my street repair questions. Why didn't you tell me you worked for the city a summer ago?"

Matt angled his upper body toward Adolph and pressed his lips together. Matt's right forefinger picked at a chin pimple. "Mom's deathly scared of me contracting skin cancer. Her uncle attributes his to his days as a beach lifeguard. She thinks I get my suntan from a bottle and two summers ago I told her I worked in the city maintenance garage. Even wore long sleeves home to hide the best tan I've ever sported. Hope you understand that, when you were here, I couldn't let her learn I lied to her last summer."

"Girls go gaga for tans I'm told." Matt's stoic reaction convinced Adolph his attempt at young adult informality missed its mark.

"Didn't play the field." He flipped two toggle switches. "Had a steady that summer."

"Anyway, forget I mentioned girls. I'm interested in all you can recall happening when patching the street in front of the Wainright home?" Adolph blinked when sequential luminescence bathed Matt's face in ghastly green. "Are those Internet websites flashing across each monitor?" He didn't wish to enter or alter his stance for a better view.

"Yeah. I build interactive sites and have ten domain names where I'm the Webmaster."

Adolph tempered his eagerness to be diverted. "Let's go back." He waited for the washer hum behind him to subside. "Anything out of the ordinary when patching?"

"Don't really remember. That boring job required a strong back, no mind."

"Think harder. Specifically, any mix-up with the tar barrels?"

"Got one addressed to a Fourth Street garage. Ryan at the cooker said it wasn't tar. He banged the lid on and rolled it to the side. Didn't seem to be any big deal."

Now Adolph knew he was getting somewhere. "What happened to it?"

"Gone the next day. Where, don't know." Adolph interpreted Matt's comment as sincere.

"Need to ask again. Was Mr. Antoine Russell around the B&B after that?"

"No idea." Matt kept his attention focused on the monitors. "You must understand I didn't spend time here except to sleep."

"Let's take a walk out back?"

"Sure. Give me a couple of moments to switch this one program to hibernate."

Adolph didn't have a specific reason to stroll the backyard. A practiced glance showed not much had changed except the abundance of wilted flowers and fallen leaves. Summer rains hadn't eradicated the wooden fence's oil-darkened eight-to-twelve inch streaks as detailed in Len's final lab report. He pivoted from the garden's edge and halted his steps at the patio pavers.

Matt joined him. Through a kitchen windowpane, Francine's shadowy image emerged, partially obscured by the sun's reflective rays.

"Guests still serenaded with piano music from across the fence?"

Matt awkwardly leaned to his right side. "Guess so."

Adolph paced, criss-crossing the patio. "When, a year ago, did you last see Mr. Russell?"

"Week or two before Labor Day, I guess. Distinctly remember it was a Friday night. I'd arrived home late from a downtown bar, fortunate enough to recognize the correct house."

Adolph decided to dive right in. "You experiment with drugs?"

The whites of Matt's eyes showed above the iris. "What gave you that idea?"

"Oh nothing. Drugs and youth seem to partner in life. I'm not interested in an arrest."

"I'm sober. That's why Lucy's no longer my steady. She charmed me into her college crowd. I could talk computer stuff, but the initial thrill of partying every night wore off."

"She still around?" His question masked his unsteady gaze past the backyard fence.

"Graduated in May and headed for New York. Packed her music degree and her belongings into an old van." Adolph let Matt ramble. "Mailed a congratulatory graduation message to her parents' address. No response. None expected."

Adolph's mind didn't retain Matt's words, distracted as he

265

was by the image of a figure moving across the Wainright family room window. Could've been the housekeeper. He thanked Matt for his cooperation and requested that he give his regards to his mother, half expecting to have Francine, after Adolph departed through the side gate, meet him at his car. She didn't.

Making nice to Luann at the office, Adolph helped her answer a stolen vehicle property question. The routine bored him. When Lt. Hunter left, Adolph checked out for home.

Mary shooed him out of the kitchen and he knocked on Kristen's bedroom door. After she said come in, he, with his right arm tight to his side, braced his body against the doorjamb.

"How you feeling?"

Kristen, lifting her face resplendent in fresh Goth makeup, answered, "Fine. I'm going back to school tomorrow."

He noted a tinge of hesitancy in her voice. "You prepared for questions?"

"Katie e-mailed me. We're not going to say anything."

Adolph meandered back to the kitchen where Mary sat at the table.

Without sitting, he asked, "Did you get a telephone update from the doctor?"

"Nurse called after lunch." She glanced up at the door leading to the bedrooms and lowered her voice. "We're supposed to telephone or bring Kristen in if we notice strange behavior. Exam kit showed no sexual assault."

"Thank God. Should I set the table?" He didn't expect Kristen's life's troubles to go away or that she'd barricade herself into her room. With Mary's lack of mobility, he'd reinvestigate installing a home protection system. Leaving his job was not an option . . . anyway, not yet.

After dinner he answered the back door and invited Katie in. With an uneasy queasy stomach feeling gnawing, and knowing the grocery store would be open until ten p.m., he offered to pick up eggs for Mary and clinched the deal with a promise it wouldn't take all night.

Adolph's Gold

He detoured to Castle Street to find no sought after pizza truck. On a second pass, he caught Bulldog's wife parking her minivan in the Hunter driveway and easily concluded there'd be no acting activity this night. Across town, he drove slowly in the sun-generated dusky haze past Roscoe's shop. With an outside security light reflecting off lowered and shadowed overhead doors, it appeared closed for business. With two strikes against him and daylight fleeting, he clocked his steering wheel in the direction of the Bourdon farm and his right foot punched the accelerator. Entering the farmyard, he braked his Monte Carlo in response to a pebble's ping against its underside.

When, from near the barn, a white box truck's metallic grill reflected his headlights, Adolph clicked them off. With no descriptive lettering visible, he assumed the parked truck to be Salvatore Pizza and directed his gaze upward. Light rays from two second-story farmhouse windows streaked the front lawn. A blue Buick had been run up on the grass. He surmised that, if his Monte Carlo's lights hadn't alerted the house occupants, its crunching tire treads had. He switched his headlights to low beam and mouthed the numbers 763 255 on the Buick's Illinois license plate while he forced his power steering to initiate a pebble-throwing one-eighty exit from the farmyard utilizing the way he'd entered.

No headlights followed. He dismissed a Rambo-style scheme to park along the road and traipse in the dark across freshly plowed fields. Once there he'd be out-manned and out-gunned and lacking the legal jurisdiction to make an arrest. He'd put family first, stop at the store as originally promised, and warm his recliner next to Mary before retiring early for a restful sleep.

* * *

Adolph chose to drive Kristen to school, picking up Katie on the way. The student stares flitted after his Monte Carlo, not his daughter. Feeling in a better mood, he still declined Luann's squad room invitation to interview the parties to a domestic. He desired time to rearrange the pieces of last evening's drive. His slam-dunk for the gold badge not as guaranteed if Luann could twist her claimed sexual slavery into information for a headline-screaming bust.

In his notepad, he'd written the scrambled letter riddle, as raised from Ant's photograph. Random attempts to solve the knotty letter sequence had been unsuccessful. With a clean sheet of white bond paper, he printed out the alphabet from a-to-z beneath the centered "wuqsvnw" letters. He tried to recall all the seven letter words he knew. No luck. A dim thought migrated from the back of his brain. The repetition of the "w" indicated it represented the same letter or, perhaps, a number. He printed out numerals zero to nine. An answer evaded him.

He flipped the paper facedown on his desk and hit the john to relieve himself of the two cups of coffee he'd already drunk. A return trip detour to the coffee pot provided him with a full steaming cup to reinvigorate his brain. A town's name, "Anamosa," fit with the first and last letters the same. The possibility intrigued him until he realized the interior "a" didn't mesh. He tried the Tinley Street house numerals "409" to get "suhoues," which, even repeated, didn't make any sense to him at all.

He tinkered with the transposition of the "es" to be "se" for the word "house," but the combinations led nowhere. Repeated, the four hundred street address number for the Wainright Oxford house changed three letters into "stlouis." That had to be it, but what more? There was the City of St. Louis, or a Louis surname with the initials S and T, or a church or school named after a religious saint. Considering his fact knowledge that tied the Wainright name to the Mississippi River gateway city downstream, he bet on the city reference.

He tried the 415-number combination on the second series of letters. The words "piano chord" represented one possible combination. He could fathom a Wainright using the four words. The mother had moved to St. Louis, Dean Wainright had played music there, and now taught piano. If the writing had existed from when the boy was a teenager, he could dismiss the latter construction. Several other hypotheses were equally valid. He rubbed his neck. Even if he'd correctly solved the puzzle, he hadn't identified the boy tied to the Wainright backyard tree.

Grabbing his blue blazer, Adolph drove to the park on the Oxford Drive corner. The old barge pilot had lifted anchor. Adolph's door knocks at the home address Silas had given him went unanswered. Adolph would have to try later or on a different day to find Silas.

Adolph's Monte Carlo circled through the neighborhood, past the still empty park bench before his uninterrupted drive to the station. Luann leaned back in her chair with a telephone receiver glued to her ear. He flashed her a perfunctory right-hand wave and chastised himself for not locking away the overturned paper with his crazy letters solution. While his desktop appeared to be undisturbed, a sealed, non-departmental eight-by-twelve inch manila envelope lay in his inbox. He suspected Len had dropped off an unofficial heads up.

Adolph ripped the shorter length and slid out an untrimmed five-by-seven inch photographic headshot of Kristen with a dazed disorientated blank stare. *What the hell!* His shoulders shuddered as what he saw left him hollow and numb. From the way her nostrils stood out, it scared him that she'd been prone when the shutter snapped. This was no Halloween prank. Able to steady his trembling fingers, he shoved the photo into the envelope.

What he anticipated was a worse scourge than his never-ending fear of drowning. He peered across his desk to a head-lowered Luann who was writing something. If he swiveled his chair, the squeak would invite her attention. He couldn't have that. He swallowed his breath's exhale as he peeked inside the envelope to find two additional items: a smaller sealed envelope and a sheet of white bond paper. Careful to touch the paper by the edges, he read the typed words:

"Look hard and you might see

"What fun her body could be.

"She may not be fancy free

"Or, yet be tied to the tree.

"Think then what goal you seek

"One misstep gives world a peek."

With his fingers jiggling like chilled un-molded Jell-O, Adolph allowed the paper to flutter onto his desk. When his right knee banged against his desk, he felt no pain radiate up to his clenched fists as his squared fingernails dug into palm flesh. He heard a chair squeak.

"Adolph, you all right?" Luann asked.

Allowing his right forearm to lay flat across the sheet of paper, he jerked his gaze to Luann and marshaled his wits to quell radiating even the tiniest hint of disquiet. "Fine," he lied. "Too much coffee." His suspicion flickered that Luann, with a twist of her lips, would ask to see the envelope contents. The tinge of fear in the corners of her eyes sprouted an inkling within him that his appearance had somehow stirred the alarm creeping into Luann's reaction.

Adolph did feel lightheaded. He stretched his right hand fingers to inch the lab envelope sideways to conceal from view the photograph and the threatening poem.

"You look pale." Luann arched her shoulders forward. "It's as if you saw a ghost."

"Indigestion, that's all." A second lie and more than that morning's greasy breakfast bacon pressed on his throat from below. "I'll be right back." Adolph reached into his desk drawer for antacid tablets and willed his legs to be steady, at least until he reached the bathroom. In a stall, he bent forward at the waist and vomited into the porcelain bowl. With his softly uttered "amen," he understood it wasn't a virus that propelled his body's reaction. He'd been targeted before. Graffiti on his Monte Carlo. Prior physical attack bumps and bruises, one newly healed. Yet, the threats never extended to his family. He dreaded what the yet to be opened interior envelope contained. He could avoid it; refuse to slit the edge. It wasn't an Iraq War battlefield where he'd been ordered to attack an enemy machine gun bunker—single-handed.

Adolph's Gold

Then, like today with his exploding dry heaves, his options were few. He hesitated to trust Luann. Everything with Luann parlayed into an everlasting continuum of gray's fifty shades. With no Yancey, he'd need to count on Len. Since the crime lab eventually would inspect the envelope, relying on Len wouldn't expand the circle of those with knowledge.

Outside the metallic stall, Adolph splashed cold water on his face and prayed the mint-flavored antacids would disguise the stomach's backwash and freshen his breath. The mirror's reflected image seemed to deepen his forehead furrows and open-fanned crow's feet.

"Is this your new office?" Officer Finnegan's grin spread across his face, a strong contrast next to Adolph's perceived pallor.

"Could be." Adolph heard his voice fail to carry the strength of good-natured banter.

"Word on the street is of a new shipment." Finnegan braced his forearm against the door.

Adolph's detective instincts took command. "Any particulars?"

"If there are, lips higher than mine are tight on the who, when, and where. Word's buzzing in street shadows that the residue discovered at that apartment building where you found that hanging president was cocaine."

Adolph's mind went blank. "What found quantity?"

"Not enough to get a midget high." Finnegan chuckled as his right hand scratched his chin stubble. "According to the super, that apartment had been un-rented for the last three months."

Drying his face with a brown paper towel, Adolph asked, "That building had a super?"

"Well, in name. Guy says he watched out for six buildings. Had skipped this one for months claiming he'd not been paid."

"Who's the owner?" Adolph splashed his face a second time. "Did the guy say?"

"He said he didn't exactly know. Seems he was hired by

271

telephone two years ago and he'd pick up monthly money orders from the barge boss."

"Sounds fishy." Adolph backed his butt against the sink.

"You bet. However, I found the guy's name and a telephone number scratched out on a sheet posted inside each floor's trash collection closet."

"Interesting." Adolph hadn't desired to spend more time in 409 Tinley than necessary.

"Scuttlebutt surfaced from a lady across the street that she sees Dragons enter frequently. A guy sporting cowboy boots said they gather in the large apartment on the top floor. Didn't check that out because I decided against going knocking for trouble."

"Get hold of me when the special barrels arrive. The office is yours."

Finnegan smiled.

* * *

That Len's lab office resembled the aftermath of a tornado didn't faze Adolph as he politely rapped on the door's glass and turned the doorknob, anticipating Len's wave to enter.

With upraised eyelids, Len said, "I don't have it done." Len bowed his head, closed one eye, and his tweezers squeezed a sliver of an object Adolph didn't recognize.

"What?"

"Whatever it is you're visiting for."

Adolph didn't comment on the exasperation that underlined Len's words. "Ain't interested in any results, although there's two things on my mind."

Len dropped the examined specimen into a pint mason jar, screwed a lid on. "Shoot."

"Several of those ugly Ant photographs have gone missing. Evidence room claims they didn't misplace them. Anyway, city attorney called to put my appearance on hold as this unnecessary diversion, probably orchestrated by Ant, has delayed Ant's trial."

Len gazed to his left and then sat on a stool. "And, the

second?"

"Got a touchy subject. I'd ask you not complete a receipt for a day or two." Adolph's right hand held out the latest manila envelope received. "Inside here is a photograph of my daughter Kristen, a piece of paper I've touched by the edges, and a sealed envelope."

The raised gaze of Len struck Adolph square in the eyes. "You being blackmailed?"

"Boy, you're sharp." Len's comment eased Adolph's mind. Unburdened to the extent he'd chosen the correct course of action, Adolph laid the envelope on Len's office table.

"Comes with the territory. Police brought in a morphine sample for a Katie somebody or other and Kristen's name showed up in the comment section."

"Crap." Now Adolph knew how the mayor reacted when he'd listed the mayor's son on a report. "You'd think the officer would've had the guts to contact me before smearing family names on official paperwork." Adolph swallowed hard. "Who?"

"Reginald Burkhart. He's a new rookie."

Adolph had heard the name. "What else did the report say?"

Len stood. Opened a table drawer. "Here's a copy. I'll deny I ever gave it to ya."

Adolph, without reading, folded the two pages and stuffed it into his blazer's inside pocket.

Len's right hand grasped Adolph's envelope. "Now, what do ya want me to do?"

"First, can you open it? Say in the clean room?"

"Follow me."

Adolph stepped aside as Len exited his office and executed a sharp military-like left. Striding past two doors, Len opened a door on his right and exited the hallway with Adolph close on his heels. The spotless glass exam table was a marked contrast to Len's office. Len began a ritual Adolph had witnessed often. Donning a pair of vinyl gloves, Len laid out a piece of white butcher paper, poured the outer envelope contents onto the paper, and reached for what had to be a surgical scalpel. Adolph edged sideways, avoiding any bump to Len's extended right elbow.

After the scalpel completed a long slit, Len's fingers extracted from the interior envelope four photographs nominally-sized about four-by-six inches, all snapshot images face down.

Adolph's shoulders flexed backward and slumped, accompanied by his elongated sigh.

Len bent forward and lifted the nearest photograph by the edge and peeked. "Don't know that you'll want to see these photos if they're all like this one."

"I don't understand." Len was just, well, calm. Adolph's compressed abs elevated his shoulders into a stiff marionette posture. "Kristen's been home, safe."

"Wanted to forewarn you, that's all." Len's left wrist twist displayed the image side.

Adolph gasped. His right hand reached forward to grab the exam table edge. Len stayed calm. A more personal than professional calm that steadied Adolph. The photograph depicted Kristen, partially nude, tied upside down on what had to be ten-by-ten foot deck posts crafted into the shape of a saltire cross. She wore only clunky shoes and black panties. Her ankles had been wrapped in white cloth and lashed to the X's top prongs.

Adolph inhaled. His abs squashed his stomach to his spine. "Show me the other three."

The three photographs depicted Kristen in different poses. In the first, Kristen spread-eagled with white cloth strips binding ankles to the wooden X, the junction of her legs hidden by a stretched, black-clothed arm with a yellow rubber-gloved hand. The second, hand gone, exposed her totally naked. In the third, her toes touched the floor with each ankle clasped by a rubber-gloved hand, the left one larger than the right. White cloth strips still lashed her outstretched arms and naked body to the crude St. Andrew's Cross.

"I'll kill the sons-of-bitches," Adolph muttered through a

274

tightened jaw. His clenched left fist pressure whitened his knuckles. Seething with anger, he pointed his right index finger at the envelope. "Anything else in there?"

Len lifted the envelope, puffed the middle, and peered in. "Nothing."

Adolph's stomach refluxes surged against his throat. He belched, which didn't clear his mind of envisioning being stranded on a sandbar in the dark of night with strong river currents an invisible force field denying his lifesaving plunge to shore. Two of his fingertips rubbed the nerve sensation beneath the skin above his jawbone near the earlobe to generate little physical or emotional relief.

"What can I do?" Len asked.

"Find any gawddamn speck that will hang whoever did this. I'll also be eternally grateful if you also give me a twenty-four hour head start after identification."

Len nodded. Adolph didn't press for a verbal commitment that Len would have to commit perjury to deny. When Adolph exited the lab, the street's increased vehicular traffic signaled the approaching noon hour. His unsettled stomach craved no food and Adolph strode toward the riverfront with his unbuttoned topcoat flapping behind him. His mind grappled with the scant information he commanded on Officer Burkhart. Trying to visualize a crew cut and aviator sunglasses above a starched blue uniform didn't isolate Burkhart from the current rookie contingent. After years of affirmative action diversity, the latest graduates reminded Adolph of three identical Ken dolls, each popped out of the same plastic mold.

Small whitecaps on the river cast an ominous weather forecast. He strayed from the river ramp and the casino to avoid the wind gusts, preferring the windbreak effect of downtown business district buildings. When Patsy's front door opened as he passed, the mixed pitches of loud lunchtime voices swarmed both of his ears. He adjusted his shoulder-holstered Walther P.38 and buttoned his topcoat before offering a weak hello to a couple exiting Patsy's. The recurring image of Bradford's lashed shoulders increased his stride's length, their speed, and elevated his body temp. He undid his topcoat buttons.

Traversing three blocks brought him to WR Barge. The warehouse building with the painted word "Wainright" beneath the roof edge blocked his view of the dock. He tried the door with the lettering "Office." Locked. He pounded on the wood next to its paned window. His chagrin morphed into shrugged off banker-hour amusement. Adolph reversed course.

When he strode into the police station parking lot, Luann, resting her butt on his Monte Carlo trunk, gazed off into the opposite direction, attracted by what he didn't know.

Adolph withheld his disdain until he got close. "Shining my beauty?"

He expected a startled Luann could've recovered with a smile. She didn't. Instead, the furrows etched across her brow when she turned heightened Adolph's apprehension.

"Chief questioned me when he caught me inside without you." A snarl underscored her words and Adolph couldn't help but cringe a little at the escaping built-in hatred. "I lied you took an early lunch and that we planned to hook up at your car."

"Thank you." The crispness of his words matched the slacks that had lost their vertical crease beneath Luann's yeoman's jacket. From beneath a multi-colored knit cap, her loose hair strands, like the sharpness in her voice, poked out every which way. Adolph sought refuge in his Monte Carlo, not an argument, and urged Luann to hop in.

After Luann slammed the passenger door, he asked her where to. He toyed with the brazen idea to confide in her about the latest pictures, but then tightened his jaw fearful that if Luann had been there she'd feed him lies, and if she hadn't, she'd be of no help. Opening a small notepad cradled in her hand, she suggested a drive to a fashionable subdivision on the city's edge where three citizens had reported home burglaries. In response to Adolph's questions, Luann said the patrol officer's report listed the thief's target as jewelry, not power tools. Each victim's two-story home had been protected by electronic alarms installed by different contractors. Two alarms had summoned security personnel while the third homeowners found an interior garage door propped open and their alarm unarmed. The wife insisted she'd heard the two activating beeps after punching in the keypad code. A female neighbor recalled a strange Buick drive by; and, minutes later, she didn't think twice about hearing a garage door go up, and then down.

On a day with Yancey, Adolph wouldn't have milled around while a crime scene technician photographed, whirled fingerprint dust, and bagged potential evidence. His meandering around each home's outside perimeter didn't disclose any clue, but did allow him to release his pent up, reoccurring intestinal tension without embarrassment. The victims' home alarm's wireless technology generated the kernel of an idea. When visiting Dean Wainright's home, he'd glossed over a black dome semi-sphere mounted above the front door. That evening he hadn't made the connection that behind the black orb a camera could've been recording.

Luann joined him on the subdivision sidewalk. "Had to be polite. Forget about closing these cases. You'd never guess how hard it is hire a good maid these days."

"Spare me." To Adolph's left, the crime scene tech snapped his crime kit closed. "Ready to be dropped off?" Adolph opened his Monte Carlo passenger door and waited to close it.

"Yeah." Luann buckled herself in. "Without a miracle, add three to The Chief's open-case statistics. Anything suspicious outside?"

"Zip." He eased his Monte Carlo into the street. "Any computer missing?"

Luann hesitated, gazed at the passing scenery. "None reported."

"Did you view any surveillance video?"

"At two homes. Nothing. Third has signal sent to All Safe via a TV cable. The manager promised to save the last two days from being erased by re-recording."

"You're right on. Open: three; closed: zero."

A red traffic light halted Adolph's progress. A slow-clearing intersection and filled turning lanes signaled five o'clock and a workday's end. At the station parking lot, he paused until Luann's backup lights went on and then telephoned Mary he'd be home after one brief stop.

The wind stacked billowy gray clouds to threaten rain or sleet. The front porch light shined bright at the Spencer Wainright residence. Adolph's left hand fingers buttoned his topcoat and his free right hand let the brass lion-headed doorknocker drop twice.

A heavy-waisted Latino woman greeted him. After stating he wished to see Dean Wainright, she responded, "Uno momento pro favor." Upon returning, she motioned for Adolph to follow her. He kept his topcoat folded across his left arm. Dean Wainright, a half-filled old-fashioned glass in hand, pushed himself up out of a winged-back chair upon Adolph's family room entry.

"Detective, it's after five, care for a stinger. Helena mixed a pitcher. More than I can drink." His hand with the glass swung left. A tray with three glasses rested on the piano bench.

"No thanks. Still on duty."

"Please, please have a seat." The dean sank back into the chair he'd arisen from.

Adolph spied the chair he'd sat in last time. His butt squished the air from its cushion and he felt the warmth rise in his facial cheeks. "Thanks for seeing me."

"Have a further question about the computers?"

"Not a question, but information." Adolph stroked his left eyebrow hair. "Found the third computer stripped of its hard drive." The dean didn't flinch. "And, I guess I do have a question. Does your porch camera create tapes or send them to a security company?"

The dean's expression remained placid. "Sorry. Can't help you there. If you wish, I can show you the gizmo on the cabinet shelf that's supposed to record a tape, but I could never get the hang of it. Hasn't held a cassette tape in six months. A music colleague told me to leave the outside globe in place. Deterrent, she said."

"Appreciate your courtesy, but it won't be necessary for me to see."

"Haven't seen you in my neighbor's backyard. You must have solved the case."

"Partially. Identified the victim. A Mr. Russell. Perhaps you recall him. Wore blue jeans and western-style clothes."

"Can't say that I do." He sipped from his glass. "There's always a parade of people."

The evasive answer hoisted a red flag to Adolph. "You don't recall the clothes, or you don't recall seeing a person known to you as Mr. Russell?"

"Neither. You still don't wish a cocktail?"

Adolph shook his head no. "You visit St. Louis lately?"

"Sad memories there." Adolph caught a slight twitch in the dean's left eye.

"That's right. Your late mother lived there."

"She was . . . is a saint. I'll adore her forever."

Adolph remembered the mother's picture as the only family photograph he'd seen hung. A mother's memory could account for the dean's quick, elevated emotional response.

"Your father buried in St. Louis as well?"

The dean's eyes deepened to remind Adolph of a black well hole. "No." His Adam's apple bobbed as he gulped the last ounce of his stinger.

Adolph expected the dean would rise for a refill, but he didn't. To fill the awkward void Adolph changed the subject. "You spend much time sailing on the river this past summer?"

"Fair amount. Find it relaxing."

The clipped answer created a definite pattern—polite, vague, and little information. The muffled unexpected sound of a neighborhood lawn mower highlighted a conversational lull until the dean's slightly louder voice asked: "Any more questions?"

"One, the university music dean that drowned. You know him well."

"Of course."

"I read about his drowning. Did he have his own boat?"

"No." The dean rose, grabbed a clean glass, and poured from the pitcher.

"Do you know whose?"

The dean remained standing. Ice cubes sloshed on the pitcher's return to the tray. He swirled the alcohol with a piston motion of his left arm. His downcast eyes fixated upon, almost lost, in the liquid's center. "I'd loaned him mine."

"Were you there?"

"No." The sharp inflection the only hint of emotion. "Said I'd loaned him the boat." His voice volume sank. "Perhaps if I hadn't . . ." The dean swallowed hard. "If you've no more questions. I must really eat the supper that's been prepared before my first student arrives."

"Right." When Adolph arose, he spied the Latino housekeeper ready to enter the family room. He surmised she'd want to collect the drink tray. "I'll show myself out."

Adolph tossed his topcoat on his Monte Carlo's passenger seat and, settling into the driver's seat, he telephoned the Rose Garden B&B. Francine answered and Adolph asked to speak with Matt. No, he replied to Francine, Matt wasn't in trouble with the police. He heard her muffled shout for Matt. When Matt picked up, Adolph asked if he could speak with him in the morning. They agreed on nine-thirty.

Adolph pressed the end call button and Mary's "Charge of the Light Brigade" ring tone filled his car's interior. She said Katie's father had called for him, didn't say why, but claimed it was urgent. She explained she'd hold off starting supper until he showed his face at home.

* * *

Adolph's oxfords stepped into the diamond patterns sprayed onto the front walk by the porch light at the Marichiori home. Glenn Marichiori had to have been on the alert for him as the door opened before Adolph elevated his soles onto the porch. After Adolph perched himself on the edge of a cushioned living room chair, a solemn Glenn joined his wife, Marjorie, on the sofa. A clutched balled handkerchief and red puffy eyes presented dead giveaways that Mrs. Marichiori had been sobbing.

"Mary said it was urgent. Perhaps you should've called 9-1-1."

"We need your advice, not cops swarming." Glenn grabbed and stroked his wife's left hand. "We don't know what to do."

"You talk like someone's been kidnapped. Not Katie?"

"No. No. Worse. Remember that night at the hospital?"

Adolph nodded slowly. He should've smelled supper aromas, didn't.

"Hour ago we found a plain envelope on the porch." Glenn's jaw froze. His tight lips barred even guttural sounds from escaping.

Adolph patiently waited so as not to interrupt Glenn's grasping for the words he needed. "I'm listening." He braced himself to learn that Katie had been victimized the same as Kristen.

"We got these terrible . . . terrible, horrible pictures."

"Don't say more." Adolph heaved his shoulders forward. "Have you kept them?"

"Ripped one to pieces before I corralled my rage. Dropped the pieces into the envelope with the other two disgusting pictures. I can get them from the kitchen."

"Don't. Not now. Were the photographs of a naked Katie?"

Mrs. Marichiori broke out into loud wailing sobs.

"Be strong, dear." Glenn rotated his gaze to Adolph. "Yes. And a poem saying not to call the police or the pictures would become public."

"Do you have a sleeping bag?" Adolph ignored the couple's puzzled expressions. "Someone may be watching your house and know I'm a detective. I'll not stay long. But the ones who took those photos of Katie took similar ones of Kristen. Wrap some white tissue paper around the envelope and I'll take it with me along with the sleeping bag. If anyone asks, say Kristen forgot it at a sleepover and I came by to pick it up."

Glenn rose stiffly. "Is that believable?"

"It'll do. Now, let's get me outa here. We'll have coffee next couple of days at Patsy's."

Adolph kept to himself all similar details of Kristen's photographs like the manila envelope, no postmark, hand-delivered, sized five-by-seven inches, and his poem receipt. He draped the sleeping bag over his right arm to both hide the tissue-wrapped envelope and make it abundantly obvious he carried a plaid unrolled sleeping bag. On the walk to his car, his eyes observed no other parked car and neither vehicle nor person passed by as he deposited the envelope and sleeping bag into his Monte Carlo's trunk. A quiet digestible supper and adoring glances at Mary would hopefully pacify and calm his frazzled nerves. He throttled the urge to phone Mary and ask if Kristen was home safe.

* * *

He dashed to the roofed B&B porch for shelter as a renegade cloud lightened its watery load on the four blocks directly below its drooping wispy tentacles. Matt answered the door and Adolph suggested the privacy of Matt's basement quarters.

"What's this about?" Matt asked, swiveling in his bedroom's sole chair.

"I needed to consult with an electronics wizard and you came to mind." Adolph squared his back against the doorjamb, a sideways glance showed the basement laundry tables empty.

"Doesn't the police have their own experts? Or, the FBI?"

Adolph couldn't let his real reason be known. "Don't even know if what I need is possible and they take forever requiring horrendous paperwork. So let's assume it's between us."

"Yeah. Cloak and dagger." Matt's face brightened. "Green Hornet. Mighty Mouse."

Adolph, amused at the light tone, said, "Forget those guys, and James Bond. If I had a wireless house security system, could a neighbor intercept the signal even if I wasn't recording?"

"Depends. Distance, password encryption, wireless frequency."

"With all the thingamajigs in this room, could you possibly demonstrate and snoop on one of your neighbors. Maybe that'll help me understand the difficulties."

Matt reached to the floor for a black box and a tie-twisted length of black cable with colored plugs. He plugged a power cord into the box and attached separate red, white, and yellow plugs between the box and a computer. Interference snow filled one of his three computer screens. Matt jiggled a plug and pointed at the screen's gray box with distinctive stacked icons. "Six homes within a quarter mile show wireless security. Five have passwords."

Adolph shuffled forward to peer over Matt's shoulder. "Let's try the closest."

"That's the top data line stating 'SWIII.' It's password protected."

Adolph recognized the initials. "Try Saint Louis with the word 'saint' abbreviated."

"No luck. Blocked."

Adolph didn't wish to give up so easily. "Maybe the words 'piano chord' will work."

"Separated they don't." Matt readjusted his keyboard. "I'll eliminate the space between."

The screen flashed black and then showcased a pocked concrete sidewalk next to grass.

"Terrific." Adolph's pulse quickened. "Is that live?"

"Absolutely." Matt pointed to the lower right screen corner. "See those two robins peck."

Adolph needed more, much more. "Can you record what the screen shows?"

"Yeah, but it won't be in anybody's top 10. It's not peeking into a bedroom window."

Impulsively, Adolph asked, "You do that?"

"No. Just kidding. I'd have to install my own camera for that. This merely captures what the installed security camera sees." Matt ran his right hand fingers through his hair. "If the home system has an interior camera we could see inside."

Matt clicked on a second icon associated with "SWIII." His monitor screen split into four equal-sized pictures: family room, kitchen, front walk, and garage.

Adolph, impressed by the technology and an eerie recollection of the family room, didn't ask if that depicted the Wainright home lest he'd expose his true desires. "Do me a favor. Go back to that first sidewalk picture. Is it possible for you to start recording at 6:30 p.m. each night, say until 9:30? That would satisfy my curiosity of how valuable a system would be."

"Give me a minute." Matt searched through a stack of DVD discs. "Got a blank." He then filled with dates and times a series of data input lines appearing on screen. "Request done."

"Fantastic. I'll give you a call. See what's there."

"You'll love watching grass brown I reckon." Matt chortled a small laugh.

"Long story, but I've a hankering to add a security system myself. This'll help me decide if it'll be worth it. Didn't realize so many homes have it."

Adolph let himself out. Now he'd wait for Jack, or perhaps another character of interest, to visit the dean. Unfortunate that Francine hadn't had Matt rig up surveillance of her garden two Labor Days ago.

He pondered his next step with the photographs of Katie secured in his trunk. Assuming them to be undated and mimic the vile saltire cross-posed photographs of Kristen, his brain failed to offer a satisfying resolution that didn't include the discharge of a gun. Rather than simply connecting existing dots, recent events added more dots. Yet, he'd made someone nervous. The latest threatening crude poem made that clear. Had the poet expected him to find the one in the birdhouse? If so, why? Bradford had been lashed in the country, not the city. Dragons? Probably.

He endured Luann all day and closed one shooting where a neighbor had tackled the perp. Alone at day's end, he detoured to cruise Castle Street. No pizza truck. No vehicles parked near Bulldog's house. He dismissed his paranoia-created impression that a car that had followed him for two blocks had been a tail. He slowed when he noticed Katie's older-model Camry parked in front of his house. Maintaining his normal routine, he entered his kitchen from the garage.

"Hello, dear. Kristen have friends over?"

"Just Katie." Mary had the dinner table set for four. "Please don't ask about the night in the hospital. They should enjoy life."

"Left my badge in my topcoat. You've got family guy."

Mary's smile wasn't complete. "We'll see."

Kristen and Katie joined them for supper. True to his word, Adolph asked about the school football team only to receive two scornful teenage looks. Kristen brought up that the principal had exonerated her and her classmates for Angelica's missing bracelet.

"Did he tell you that?" Adolph asked.

"Sorta," Kristen said.

"Please be more specific." Adolph glanced at the lines deepening on Mary's forehead and held off on his further question as Kristen swallowed a forkful of mashed potatoes.

"She claimed to have found it in a shoe at the bottom of her locker."

"That sounds fishy."

"Adolph—" Mary clamped her lips together.

He shifted his gaze from Mary to Kristen. "What have you two planned?"

"Hanging out," Kristen replied. "Maybe homework, if we get bored."

Katie hurriedly nodded in agreement, although Adolph

thought her eyes flashed astonishment at his daughter's words. He hadn't exposed his photographic receipt to Kristen, and he half-expected Katie's father hadn't done so to Katie either. When supper ended, he stacked the dishwasher, pleased that Kristen helped. At the table, Mary struggled to flex her knees. By her accentuated eye dullness, he suspected she'd swallowed an extra dose of pain medication.

An hour after Adolph had kicked up his recliner's footrest, Mary's eyelids drooped along with her head. Music, without human voices, filled the background. If the girls were doing homework, he'd never know with Kristen's bedroom door closed. He wanted his thoughts to be only of Mary, but selfishness crept in. A decade ago she'd have been enthused to hear about his day. And, while he withheld confidential facts like the names of informers, he could trust her intuition to reveal, or her recounting chats with town friends to provide, insights unavailable to him alone. Her arthritis sapped both her and him. His insensitive lapses, more so lately than before, had caused Mary to initially chide and then forgive him. His life's joy welcomed him home daily and, growing within him, the realization that expressions of pity didn't become him.

When the telephone ring interrupted, Adolph rushed to the kitchen.

Finnegan spoke first. "Barrels arriving tomorrow afternoon."

Adolph tried not to let his voice carry. "Is a dock raid planned?"

"No. DEA wants to allow a trace farther down the food chain."

"What time?"

"Three."

Adolph hung up the receiver.

"Who was that?" Mary asked, leaning on her walker at the kitchen door.

"Officer Finnegan. I'm reminded of a fraternal meeting tomorrow. Let's finish our program." His left hand fingers grabbed her right forearm and her facial wince made him release his grip. "Sorry. You lead."

An hour later, Kristen and Katie sat cross-legged on the living room floor to watch a television awards broadcast. His mind wandered. Perhaps it had been a blessing that the drug had blocked each girl's memory. His rationalization knifed terror into his being. Whoever planned the violation, a fiendish tribute to evil, had been devilish in its construct. Any sting attempt limited to Katie, assuming her parents would play along, foreclosed by the threatened blackmail release of both Katie's and Kristen's photographs.

When Kristen cheered or groaned with the award announcements, he nodded or smiled. Mary, when jarred to consciousness a third time, pushed herself up from the recliner and excused herself for bed. Adolph said good night to Katie when the late local news came on and a moment thereafter to Kristen. When the TV weather forecast promised sunny skies, he ushered himself to bed and stared at the ceiling's green fire detector light. Adolph forced his eyelids closed lest he be sluggish for an expected next day's extended drug surveillance.

* * *

With clouds obscuring the afternoon sun beyond the station's bathroom window, Adolph switched on the overhead light and splashed sink tap water on his face. He expected Finnegan to ring his cell at any moment. The tip had been for three o'clock, but he wasn't surprised the downstream barge would dock a few minutes late. He'd purposely kept Luann in the dark, encouraging her to use the afternoon for telephone calls on her cases.

Across from her, Adolph sank into his desk chair seconds before his office landline rang. Surprised that Sheriff Townsend was on the line, Adolph listened, interpreting the sheriff's comments more by what wasn't said than what was. Adolph had no idea why a fed mail cover to the abandoned Bourdon farm could be justified as critical? Sheriff Townsend, without Adolph asking, detailed the interception of a cryptic letter, postmarked St. Louis, that said Bourdon's non-itemized order had been shipped to arrive today.

"That's strange," Adolph agreed. "Didn't Bourdon skip months ago?"

"What I thought." The sheriff coughed. "You see Bourdon at the farm lately?"

Adolph recounted his last visit, including the upstairs farmhouse lights and the Buick, emphasizing that he hadn't exited his vehicle.

"Sounds like squatters to me," the Sheriff said. "Keep me informed if you run across Bourdon. Bankruptcy judge has issued an order I'm supposed to serve on him."

Adolph hung up to piece together a new possibility that any shipped oil barrel was slated for delivery to the farm. He wouldn't have anticipated that. Fearing that his Monte Carlo could easily be an undesired tip off, he didn't wait for Luann to get off the phone, and briskly strode toward the river and WR Barge.

Finnegan intercepted him two storefronts past Patsy's.

"What's up, Adolph? I didn't call."

An east wind gust jangled the jeweler's screen door next to Adolph. "Antsy, I guess."

"Word came down this morning the DEA plans to run the operation without us locals."

Adolph wasn't astounded. "Swoop in and hog the whole glory?"

Finnegan nervously glanced to his rear. "You got it."

"Bet we could horn in." To Adolph's amazement, Finnegan's expression remained stoic. Adolph briefly explained the suspicious notice of an order destined for the Bourdon farm. Not even Adolph's offer to let Finnegan pass on the Bourbon farm message and take sole credit for the tip unfroze Finnegan's facial features.

"Wouldn't be taken as worth a damn," Finnegan lamented. "DEA's determined to surround Roscoe's Fourth Street garage." He shrugged his shoulders. "They're not going to rush the dock and we're told to stay far, far away. Not spook anyone."

Adolph's gut told him disaster loomed. But, he wasn't prepared to stick around or gloat. He hustled to the detective squad room. Luann, at her desk, welcomed him with a frown. Without an explanation until they were on their way, he convinced her to drive to the Bourdon farm and, once there, he pointed to a weedy spot on the barn's north side that would shield Luann's car from anyone peering out a farmhouse window. However, while it gave him a visual of any vehicle entering the farmyard, observant visitors could glimpse his presence.

Satisfied he'd made the right call, Adolph leaned back against the passenger seat.

"Still don't think your mail cover poppycock is worth a plug nickel," Luann complained.

While he felt like he was talking to a wall, what did he have to lose, stuck as he was at a stakeout? "If Roscoe's involved, we'd have scared him with our used oil visit." He considered Luann's not objecting granted him this point. "You've convinced me Honest Abe's somehow involved." Luann continued to stare straight ahead. "And, I suspect that Antoine Russell preceded him. With both dead, it wouldn't be a stretch to conclude the Buick I saw here represents the latest go-between." On this point Adolph wasn't as confident and he tried to expand his supposition. "The Buick driver could've been here for a shot to star in the movies."

Luann's features instantaneously bristled and her rotated eyes flashed angry darts. She slowly exhaled. "What'll we do now? I didn't bring a deck of cards."

Adolph didn't challenge Luann's sarcastic tone. "We're going to check out the house." His memory of being struck from behind caused him to add: "Hide if we hear noises."

"Searching for what?" Luann sounded reluctant.

"Anything that might lead to who's the wizard behind the curtain." His neck muscle twist propelled his face toward Luann and he tried to smile. With his verbal effort having fallen flat, Adolph seized the initiative and, with Luann lagging behind, he easily forced the damaged rear farmhouse door, unconcerned if any of the Sheriff's claimed squatters were home. Past the deserted kitchen, Adolph squeaked two stair treads while bounding to the second floor. A superficial glance into the master bedroom didn't slow his advance to a second bedroom where he spotted two large wooden posts and strips of white cotton bed sheet along the outside wall. He kicked, and one post tumbled off the other. He choked off a four-letter expletive when he glanced down at his scuffed spit-shined shoe toe and spotted black balled-up cloth. Adolph squatted for a closer look—same black-colored feminine panties as those in Kristen's photo.

"Find anything?" Luann called out from the hallway.

Adolph wasn't about to let Luann in on the blackmail pics. "Nothing. Checking a closet. Be out in a sec." Glancing left and right, Adolph picked up a Chinese restaurant's plastic takeout sack and, worried Luann would enter, dismissed all officially sanctioned ways to gather evidence. Turning the sack inside out as if to collect dog excrement off park grass, he squeezed the plastic over the panties and stuffed both plastic and panties into his topcoat's outside pocket.

"Adolph, come check out the bathroom," Luann shouted.

As he hustled to meet the urgency of her summons, his shoulder brushed the bedroom door without slowing him down. He slid to a stop behind Luann at the upstairs bathroom door.

Luann's right hand, raised above her shoulder, pointed to an opened medicine cabinet. "Look. Man's razor, shaving cream, Old Spice. This stuff's new."

Adolph, after a step sideways, agreed. Yet, how would Luann know, unless she'd been here in recent days? Stupid. The pizza truck. Rebecca's admitted abduction. Could be Luann knew Honest Abe's replacement? Stooping to complete honesty with Luann always represented for Adolph a crucial decision. His thoughts were still congealing when Luann spoke.

"These weren't here a few nights ago."

Adolph stared at the back of her head. His silence caused her to pivot.

"Ain't embarrassed at what you're thinking. I do what I have to do, nothing more. Ask Rebecca if you don't believe me. I'm as scared as she."

Adolph withheld expressing judgment to concentrate on uncovering the identity of Kristen's captors. "Can you identify or isolate the man who might have left this stuff?"

"Unfortunately not." The sadness in her eyes bespoke truth. "I was a bound slave, tied like a rodeo calf, and blindfolded. Remember Rebecca saying she couldn't find anything in an empty medicine cabinet. That's all I'll say for you or the world to know."

That didn't jibe with Rebecca's story of being blindfolded and he wouldn't let Luann off the hook that easy. "You had to have seen or heard someone."

Luann alternately rubbed the backs of both her hands. "Rebecca was lying half-hidden under a blanket in the box of the pizza truck, when they picked me up at the river boat launch. By the tats one displayed, he had to be a Dragon."

One name flashed in Adolph's mind. "Jack?"

"If he's the leader, then I'd say yes."

"What about other male voices here at the farmhouse?"

Her finger tapped the cabinet door closed. "Heard two whisper."

A start. *C'mon, Luann.* "Can you identify?"

Luann slumped forward, and her two hands rested on the white porcelain sink. "Don't think so. Plugs stuffed into both my ears muffled sounds and the other things done to me distracted."

Adolph, afraid she'd collapse, grabbed her by the waist.

Luann's rigid body relaxed in his hands. "I'm okay."

Adolph released his grip. "Wasn't worried you'd faint." He felt the bile of his condescension scratch his throat before he swallowed hard. "Perhaps there's fingerprints or other trace evidence here we must protect. I'll telephone Sheriff Townsend."

Luann twirled. "Please don't. I don't want anyone else to know." Dread outlined Luann's eyes. "My prints are here."

"We don't have to lie about your presence. We're partnered. Remember? Fingerprints aren't dated and it was my idea to drive out here. I'll vouch that you and I investigated. No big deal. You touched the sink before we found the stuff in the cabinet and called in the crime lab." Adolph unfastened his topcoat buttons to disguise the bulge in his outer pocket. "We'll just go outside. Wait in your car."

He allowed Luann to lead. When the crime lab scheduler said no investigator was available and wouldn't be for the rest of the day, Adolph took the news as a godsend. He paced behind Luann's car and watched her walk into the grove, scare a pair of squawking blackbirds into flight, and then settle behind the steering wheel and turn the ignition without comment.

Adolph made an attempt to brighten Luann's spirits as she slowed for a county road stop sign. "That husband of yours must be something special for you to endure all that you have." With no immediate response, he gazed at her. "We'll crack this soon, trust me."

"Wish I was that confident." Wisps of her hair, which she ignored, fell and fluttered across her forehead.

"We must be close. The threats and all."

Luann's response was quick. "How'd you know about the threats? Rebecca?"

"Seemed a logical guess." Adolph's thoughts meandered into vivid visions of Kristen's photographs, not Bradford's beating or Rebecca's rough handling by the Dragons.

"That last night I was threatened with a fate worse than hell."

"Huh?" He lurched forward as her foot stomp on the accelerator jerked them across the intersection. "C'mon. Two minds have to be better than one."

She flicked her gaze at him. "Rebecca told me she was shown it."

"Have no idea what you're talking about." And, he didn't.

"Old farms had underground passageways from the house to the barn to cope with the harsh winter weather. There's a room under the barn, dug out at the end of the tunnel. Those three steel pipes along the milk house wall near the stall area door provide ventilation."

"That shouldn't scare anyone."

"Should." She picked a piece of lint from her shoulder. "Ask Rebecca. She shook with fear when she told me. Said the room had all sorts of chains, leather straps, and iron ring restraints. And, a cage, only no bunny rabbits, lions, or tigers. Let's do a uey and we'll search the basement for the entrance."

"It can wait." He was satisfied he'd found Kristen's place of captivity and she was safe.

Luann tapped the brake twice as road dust swirled beyond the windshield. She angled right and Adolph heard gravel crunch and dried ditch grass rustle beneath her Chrysler as she continued forward. A pizza truck passed, going the way they had come.

"Slow down. That pizza truck, or another like it, was at the farm the other night."

"Yeah. I told you Rebecca and I were picked up in one."

"That was night. This is day. Feds told earlier today the farm was a possible drop-off for the river drugs. Could be why we didn't find the lab guys in."

Luann locked her elbows, squeezed both hands on the steering wheel, and flicked a glance past her left shoulder. "News to me."

He ignored the subliminal accusation. "See any truck tail?" He didn't. "Pull over." Adolph alighted from Luann's car. While steadying himself on the ditch's slope, he spied no evidence of a vehicle, except the pizza truck's dissipating dust trail. Through the windshield, he noticed Luann hadn't unfastened her seatbelt. Neither the whine of a small plane engine nor the rumble of whirling helicopter blades perforated the settling road dust.

"We going to the farm?" Luann asked as Adolph resettled himself into her Chrysler.

"No. We don't have backup nor jurisdiction. And I'll be damned if I'm going to pull the DEA's or the FBI's bacon out of the fire if they want to do everything themselves."

Luann snapped, "The guys in St. Louis aren't jerks."

Adolph observed her for a moment with astonishment, not sure if she was serious or her normal sarcastic self. "How can you say that after what they've let you go through?"

"Have to be positive. They're my only hope to prove Herbert innocent."

He opted to test Luann. "You don't suppose you could persuade them to pass on to you, and then you to me, an information tidbit that should exist in St. Louis?"

"What?" Luann accelerated onto the main highway heading into Bridgetown.

"WR Barge has private investor owners. This drug shipment has an obvious connection to river traffic. The top boss, and, I suspect, an investor in WR Barge, hails from St. Louis. You think your FBI contacts could have access to who that might be?"

"I dunno."

Adolph didn't sense any determination in Luann to help, but he wanted to keep the door open. "Think about it. Wouldn't be the first time porn kings and drug dealers had a working partnership. And, with Honest Abe dead, who knows where Bulldog's usefulness lies."

"You've lost me."

Adolph's vague rambling was confusing enough in his own mind. Luann didn't afford him a gaze at her expression. "Well, you ain't playacting in his basement lately."

"Doesn't mean anything. He could've been the hidden-from-sight male at the farm."

"Doubt it." Adolph shifted his torso on the seat. "Why wouldn't he have shown himself? His participation's no secret." He glanced at Luann. She was fixated on oncoming traffic and the flashing yellow lights indicated they'd have to stop at the next semaphore. "Jack scare him away?" Luann remained silent, even with the red light. "He didn't get all religious, did he?"

"How the hell should I know?"

Her flash of anger wasn't unsettling to Adolph. The excursion to the farm had begun frosty and hadn't thawed to any measurable degree. When she half accusingly asked: "You gone crazy?" Adolph fluctuated between considering her question really serious or merely rhetorical exasperation. As he pondered it, they passed the Welcome to Bridgetown sign and he decided he didn't need to respond for he would soon be out of her car. And he was. Leaving Luann three steps behind in an unusually empty station parking lot, he abruptly halted when Chief Howard stood in the hallway near the detective room door.

"Where you guys been?" The Chief's question wasn't polite banter.

"Following a burglary tip," Adolph offered. "Trail led out of town."

The Chief's furrowed brow didn't relax. "DEA was all over me for manpower. They lost a drug bust this afternoon."

Luann, her right hand half raised, interrupted, "What? There wasn't any briefing."

The Chief continued his gaze at Adolph. "DEA expected cocaine to be smuggled south on the river, stopping here. They staked out the barge dock and Roscoe's garage. Listening to the secure radio channel, chatter indicated three identical pizza trucks pulled up at the dock. In quick succession, one went to Roscoe's and an agent stopped another outside the city limits headed north to Elbow Lake. The third escaped the dragnet and disappeared."

Adolph watched the sly smile on Luann's lips disappear behind her right hand. Adolph didn't call attention to it while thinking the smugglers were obviously tipped or extra smart to have executed the plan described by The Chief.

"Chief, have the sheriff, or whomever, check the Bourdon farm. RFD 509. A pizza truck passed us on County Road 12 traveling fast in the farm's direction."

Backing her butt to the corridor wall, Luann added,

"That's correct."

The Chief, heels clomping on the hallway floor, bolted past Luann without a parting word to either he or Luann. Her exposed lower lip dropped as if she planned to speak. Expecting that the escalating footstep noise meant The Chief's return, Adolph delayed his entrance into the detective squad room. Bulldog appeared; his short, choppy steps closed the gap between them.

"Chief's searching for you two."

"We know," Adolph said. "We've passed on our tip and he just hightailed it for, I would assume, either his office or that of the dispatcher's."

Bulldog rocked to and fro, not gazing at Luann still against the wall. "What tip?"

"Pizza truck heading for the Bourdon farm."

Bulldog's response delayed and measured. "Where's that?"

"It's currently the biggest male hangout in the county."

Luann smirked and ducked into the squad room.

"That doesn't help," Bulldog said. "And today's no day to pull my leg or play silly games."

"Few miles outside Bridgetown, County Road 12, RFD 509."

"Thanks." Bulldog departed in the direction of The Chief's office.

Adolph lagged behind Bulldog until he reached the men's room door. Entering, Adolph stopped to avoid being hit by the opening of a stall door. Sean Finnegan stepped into his vision.

"You hiding out?" Adolph asked.

"Wish I could," Finnegan replied, turning on a sink's hot water. "DEA blew the drug raid. Scuttlebutt is they're blaming us locals. And that puts me directly in the crosshairs."

"Why you? It was all their muck-adée-muck. That's what you told me."

"Yeah, but you've been around long enough to know memories change based on results." The officer flung water droplets from his rinsed hands before he reached for the brown paper towel hanging from its dispenser. "The tip you told me about?"

Adolph stayed mum.

"Boy, my not passing that on will smear glue onto me coffin lid."

"Hold on." Adolph flushed the urinal. "No one knows you and I talked. Here's our story. If I get pressed, I'll say I told that rookie, what's his name, Burkhart, and the jerk told me to cram my tip where the sun don't shine. You've helped me. Only fair I return your favor."

Finnegan flipped the towel he'd soiled into the trash. "You sure?"

"Damn right." Adolph's emphatic reply hastened Finnegan out the door.

When Adolph saw Luann in the squad room with her ear adorned by the telephone handset, he speculated that she had by this time prejudiced the ranks with her spin of their latest jaunt. He hated brown-nosing, even more so when it was necessary for his legitimate promotion. Adolph slumped into his chair. Not only should Finnegan be upset, Adolph lost by not following channels and going through The Chief. If his prior observations were accurate, the farm had to be but an intermediate transfer point for he'd never noticed a cutting or bagging operation there.

A breathless Chief called out to Adolph from the squad room door. "Sheriff's deputy and a DEA agent got to the farm too late. No pizza truck. Gravel, let alone multiple criss-crossed farmyard tracks, doesn't present much hope for incriminating tire tread impressions."

Adolph tried to sound sincere. "Sorry, Chief." He noticed Luann keep her head down.

"Don't be. Truck we're after maybe never even stopped at the farm."

"What if the drug barrels never left the barge warehouse?" Adolph grabbed at straws. "All trucks with bogus loads to draw the Feds from the dock with a later pickup."

The Chief's eyes bugged out. "Point well made. I'll

suggest DEA search the entire warehouse." He departed, his heel stomp echo crescendos farther apart this time.

Adolph gazed at a seated Luann. "Let's go."

She moved nary a muscle, except her lips. "Where to?"

Without conscious deliberation, he delivered his one word answer: "Farm."

A perplexing facial look tightened her features. "You sent The Chief to search the warehouse. If that's bogus, he'll burn you, maybe me if I can't convince him I didn't know."

Adolph's shove cleared his knees from his desk's kneewell. "He's a big boy."

Lt. Turner's office door squeaked and the door's window blinds rattled. He jutted his chin into the squad room, his right hand on the exposed doorjamb. "I thought I heard The Chief."

"He's gone," Luann replied as Adolph ducked his head. "Nothing to worry about."

"I'll go to his office just in case." Lt. Turner turned right at the squad room door.

Rising quickly to his feet, Adolph grabbed Luann's right forearm. "Lets go. Now, before we gotta face questions."

Luann's right hand, set in motion by Adolph's arm grab, swirled in an arc and knocked a notepad from her desk to the floor. Adolph ignored it as he shifted his right hand to physically push an upright Luann between the shoulder blades and exert an unrelenting forward pressure to force her to the parking lot.

Luann barked at him: "I can get my own car door."

Adolph relented and hastened to buckle his Monte Carlo's driver's side seatbelt. Stopping at the first intersection, his rearview mirror glance caught a dark-colored sedan pass the cyclone fence into the station parking lot. Had to be the Feds. Exalted that he and Luann had escaped in the nick of time, he lowered his dispatcher radio volume, intent on ignoring all calls.

"You lose a screw?" Luann asked. "Chief said no pizza truck at the farm."

Adolph kept his used motor oil hunch to himself. "Just

wait," he muttered to Luann.

"Hell." Luann folded her arms and stared out the passenger door window.

Adolph drove in silence until the familiar gravel crunch of his tire treads welcomed him into the Bourdon farmyard. He braked his front wheels on the grass in front of the farmhouse.

"This place is deserted," Luann grumbled. "I ain't going in that house."

"What about the secret room? An hour ago we were to turn back."

She directed her gaze to the windbreak, away from him. "Don't care."

"Then follow me. We'll start behind the barn. If no luck, we'll check the woods."

She remained as if glued into the passenger seat. "What am I to look for?"

Adolph sprung the driver door latch. "Large, black spots or stains."

He'd got her thinking, but only her lips moved. "Like oil?"

"You got it." Adolph didn't glance back as he strode for the barn. A welded metal hood with a rusted-closed padlock protected the well pump motor and foreclosed the well's use as the perfect dump for any liquid. Behind the barn, a skinny cottontail startled Adolph as it scurried from a brush pile into the harvested cornfield that Adolph skirted to traipse along a compacted earthen path past waist-high wilted and sagging weeds. None showed any black tinge.

His gut tightened as he passed the site of Bradford's lashing. Trooping to the western windbreak, Adolph's soles crushed dull brown grass. Amongst the trees, he willed his heavy legs and cautious footfalls forward and occasionally allowed his skyward gaze to linger.

"To the right," Luann shouted, from where Adolph didn't know. "See that dark spot."

Luann, passing Adolph's left shoulder, darted forward in a clumsy zigzag to where she pointed. A black spot, roughly twice as large as the splatter in Francine's garden, spread out in a ragged-edged circle. Adolph squatted. His forefinger lightly swiped a half-inch smear across a fallen oak leaf and he raised his fingertip to his nostrils.

"Motor oil," he said aloud. "Not new."

"Now what?" Adolph measured Luann's words as expressing a burden fringed with self-righteous arrogance, if not the petulance of a child. "Let's notify the sheriff so we can leave."

"No. My hunch is the drugs are long gone. Let's return to my car."

"Look at this." Luann held up a torn three-by-five foot plastic decal with the words: Wiese Boys Pizza. "What you want me to do with this?"

"I'll roll it after I get gloves from my trunk. That magnetized decal could've disguised almost any lettering. Best we forget a pizza truck. Let's see if we can find a glass jar."

Adolph's luck found a small crudely emptied baby food glass jar in the barn that he could rinse clean in the farmhouse kitchen. With a task at hand, he didn't keep track of where Luann wandered off to since she wasn't at the Monte Carlo when, without fanfare, he grabbed a pair of vinyl gloves from its trunk and, at the oil spill site, repeatedly dipped a three-inch smooth twig into a miniature oil puddle and let the liquid drip into the jar. With a one-quarter inch sample, he twisted the jar lid tight and rolled up the decal. He locked both into his car's trunk.

He surveyed the farmyard twice for Luann and couldn't lay his eyeballs on her. He called out her name. No response. The dispatcher's voice cracked over the radio. Adolph cast bravado aside and answered. The message was short and sweet: where was he? He replied truthfully. The dispatcher requested he standby for The Chief.

"Why in the blazes are you at the Bourdon farm? Where's Sheriff Townsend?"

"Not here," Adolph replied. "His office said he was out."

"We've a meeting here with the DEA in thirty minutes.

300

Move your butt."

Adolph counted to ten and decided insubordination wasn't an option. "Yes, sir."

He left the radio mike on the driver's seat, repeated his shout of Luann's name, and began pacing behind his Monte Carlo. A robin's flight distracted his eyes toward the barn as his fingers fished out the ignition key from his front pants pocket.

"You ready to leave?" Luann called out, striding from the farmhouse's rear corner.

Adolph paused at his Monte Carlo's front bumper. "Where've you been?"

"Verifying Rebecca's story. She had it right."

"What right?" His vehicle's hood separated them.

"Real masochist dungeon. Never thought cobwebs could be a calming sight."

"Huh?" He twisted his shoulders away to indicate the conversation's end.

"Cobweb presence indicates the dungeon hasn't been used lately. You can look."

He glanced backward after opening the driver's door. "Can't. Chief ordered us to the station." Her seatbelt latch echoed his. "DEA called for a meeting. I suspect blood-letting."

En route from the farm, Adolph raced through two intersection flashing yellow semaphores so as not to delay his filling the front row corner seat at the station's conference room table. He didn't recognize by name the two suits huddled together near the room's blackboard. Their long hippie hair and beards contradicted the tailored single-stitch tailoring. Had to be Feds.

Chief Howard's sullen and collapsed facial expression contrasted sharply with his crisp uniform. He called the room to order. "Ladies and Gentlemen, Agent Shanisky has an update on today's adventures."

A snicker rolled halfway around the room until hammered by The Chief's stare.

Donan Berg

"Thanks." Agent Shanisky squared his stance at the table's end, opposite The Chief. "We had good intel on today's drug shipment. Sad to say support failed. My partner and I doubt that, in the long term, we've deterred the smugglers. We're instituting a diversion by spreading street word to make it appear us Feds have left. If you hear it, don't deny."

Adolph gazed across the table. Luann appeared ready to say something. He deliberately stared at her and twitched his head left to right.

"And, keep your eyes and ears open," Shanisky continued. "Coordinate through Chief Howard. That's all. Any questions?"

Luann raised her right hand.

"Yes." Shanisky gestured toward her.

Adolph glared at Luann. She sheepishly lowered her hand. "Sorry, nothing."

He grasped that Chief Howard's taciturn demeanor and curt responses to attendees as registering The Chief being upset with what the Feds had probably said to him privately. Adolph lingered in the conference room until Luann preceded him to the squad room.

Luann, in her desk chair, rotated towards him. "What were you afraid of in there?"

"Not afraid of anything." Deep down, maybe a little. "If you mean what we found at the farm, that information would've only buried The Chief deeper."

"Run that logic by me again."

"Feds blame us . . . local police for a blown drug raid. Not fair, but that's how it is. If you said anything about the oil without telling The Chief first you'd have shown him to be out of the loop and lacking our support. I'll not do that."

"How do you know the Feds blame us?"

Adolph didn't wish to explain his conversation with Finnegan. "Fact this meeting was called, and what was said. That's all." He crashed into his chair. "Been there. Trust me."

"You going to tell The Chief?"

"Not yet. I'll get the crime lab to give me report on the sample in my trunk first."

Luann's head wobbled side to side. "You still don't trust anyone, do you?"

"That's being a detective." Adolph excused himself. Using his cell phone, he called Len. Lucky to catch him, he had the oil sample and decal on Len's crime lab desk in five minutes.

"This another below the radar request?" Len asked.

"Add it to the Rose Garden B&B file. We need your precise, clinical opinion if this sample matches the used motor oil found there. Decal might have a stray fingerprint. It's a long shot. Don't miss your child's christening to get an answer."

"You still chasing computers?"

"Not so much. Only missing a hard drive and, who knows, it could've been tossed off a bridge, rusting at the bottom of the river. You get that second set of nasty photos Luann said existed at the college and the B&B?"

"Wait here a minute." Len left his office to return two minutes later with a sealed evidence bag. "Here. Best if you use the clean exam table down the hall."

Adolph's right hand grabbed the bag's top and strode down the hall. A female technician cleared a spot at the table's end. Adolph reached for two vinyl gloves from a popup box dispenser. Self-conscious, he peeked at each photograph individually rather than spread them across the examination table. Each photo set off his subliminal horror. He gazed extra seconds at a young girl's face partially obscured by dark, possibly brown hair. He'd swear the girl was a dead ringer— he choked on his bad choice of words—for the picture in his desk of Nancy Whitenmire, older sister of the toddler he'd saved from the river. He tucked the photograph into the evidence bag, resealed the top, and duly initialed the tag to note his inspection.

Outside the lab, he reached for his cell phone and dialed the dispatcher to look up a telephone number for Sonja Maria

Sanchez. The found Tinley dresses reactivated his interest in her. When he punched the numbers in, Spanish words filled his ear.

"No hablo espanol," Adolph mumbled. He tried, "Ms. Sanchez, please."

Sonja Sanchez identified herself and, in English, agreed to meet Adolph the next day.

* * *

Five minutes before the ten a.m. appointment time, Adolph and Luann arrived at a grand old brick home in a historic district residents often referred to as the Gold Coast. That Ms. Sanchez now lived there caused Adolph to raise his eyebrows. As they stood on the expansive veranda, Ms. Sanchez exited the front door to greet them. The white apron and the rubber gloves she held tight in her left hand announced she wasn't the mistress of the house.

"I'd like to introduce Detective Luann Nettleton. Thank you for meeting with us." Taking a clue from the fact that Sonja didn't suggest they go inside, Adolph nudged Luann along the veranda to four white-painted Adirondack chairs positioned into a semicircle around a low table. Adolph sat on a chair's front edge opposite Sonja Maria. "We've found the computers stolen from St. Mary's. They tell us you weren't attacked. You had sex with Jonathan Green, who, like you, lived at 409 Tinley, and, maybe, just maybe, Dean Wainright watched."

A mask of thespian horror descended across Sonja's face. Adolph couldn't hear Luann breathe. While he tried not to slip off his chair, his outstretched hands mimicked Italian gestures.

"No. No." Sonja's shoulders slumped and the rubber gloves fell to the concrete. Each of her reddened hands grabbed her opposite wrist.

"If that's not true, then tell me why your dress was found in Jonathan Green's Bridgetown apartment, downstairs from where you lived."

She bowed her head and began sobbing. "Wish stay in

this country."

"Sonja Maria, I'm not trying to deport you, but to save women and children from harm. No employer should do to you what Dean Wainright did."

She didn't lift her head or utter any response.

"Tell me where I'm wrong. You put that Jonathan Green ID into the music building janitor closet. Your fingerprints were on it. Then you went to his Tinley apartment to get your new passport and he wanted more than money and made you change your dress for a costume. Speak to me, please." Adolph detected neither her agreement nor a nod of disapproval. "You escaped him. Then one night, Dragons in a pizza truck kidnapped you, took you to a farm to do unspeakable things with Jonathan Green. Dean Wainright, watching, threatened that, if you didn't have your music department job, you'd be deported."

"I no fight no more."

Adolph couldn't pin down what part of what he said struck Sonja as truth. However, he understood he'd breached a dam of lies and silence. "You have to help me."

"I'm scared."

"We all are sometimes," Luann interjected.

Adolph shook his head at Luann. "You need to help us, Sonja. You'll go to Dean Wainright and tell him you need $10,000 to get rid of your baby."

Her lifted eyelids allowed her deep inner plea to accompany her words. "I'm scared."

"I'll be nearby, and Luann will help fix the wire." Sonja's eyes widen and he absorbed her escaping fear. "That's a recorder so we can later tell what was said. You'll do fine."

* * *

Outside the shadows, the afternoon sun erased the air's chill. Adolph and Luann sat in her Chrysler with a clear vision of Dean Spencer Wainright's front porch. Officer Finnegan, stationed at the college campus, radioed at three p.m. the subject had departed. When a BMW entered the Lilac Lane

garage, Adolph activated the wireless receiver and heard Sonja
Maria's footfalls on the dean's concrete walkway. Adolph cut
short a breath as Sonja's hand reached for the door's brass
knocker.

"Ms. Sanchez, what are you doing here? You having
problems at that job I got for you?"

"No, no. Do what you say for Senor Green. Need $10,000
to get rid of your baby."

"That's crazy."

Adolph crossed his fingers the dean would let his guard
down. He hadn't told Luann about Matt's electronic
interceptions and his trusting Luann with this new recording
would also be his test for her. He pushed his shoulders against
the seatback listening to Sonja continue.

"You touch me in office where Senor Green give me
drugs."

"Please come inside? Need to call my bank."

Adolph had prepped Sonja Maria not to enter the house.

"No, no. Philippe wait for me. He be angry if baby not let
me work."

"You'll get money. Give me a few days and I can help
you."

Luann gazed at Adolph. "What'll we do now? That
wasn't much of an admission."

"Maybe not. But perhaps enough to crack his self-
confidence or perceived invincibility."

Luann shifted gears and backed her Chrysler around the
corner. Adolph sipped coffee until Sonja approached and
Luann exited to open the rear passenger door. "Good job,"
Luann whispered as she patted Sonja's shoulder. Adolph tried
to smile through the somber mood engulfing the car's interior,
even after they dropped Sonja off at her Gold Coast employer.

Adolph asked Luann to hold on a moment as he
telephoned Yvonne Whitenmire. Fortune smiled. With Luann
in tow, he knocked on Yvonne's condo door. She ushered
them into her modest living room. Adolph left one of two
straight-backed chairs for Luann as he sat, beneath two framed

landscape posters, on Yvonne's futon, adjusted to its sofa position.

Yvonne, dressed in gray sweats, hair in a bun, dropped lazily onto the vacant chair.

"Late yesterday I looked at a picture police have that resembles Nancy," Adolph began.

Wispy curls couldn't soften the growing tautness of Yvonne's cheeks, the tension ebbing from the corners of her eyes. Through clenched teeth, she asked, "Is . . . is she dead?"

"Wasn't that kind of photograph." The words he spoke failed to lighten Yvonne's expression. "She, she appeared to be restrained, but very much alive."

"Tell me . . . tell me where she is." Yvonne stood, and then collapsed onto her chair.

"We can't, not yet. The photograph was a close-up. Has someone asked for money?"

"No." Her shoulders slumped. "Why?" Yvonne's taut facial muscles shattered like delicate crystal. Tears streamed down her cheeks. Luann rose, knelt on one knee by Yvonne's chair, and placed an arm about Yvonne's shoulders as Yvonne's head drooped. Adolph saw the corners of Yvonne's lips move, but he didn't hear any words spoken. Yvonne lifted her head, squared her shoulders. "I haven't been truthful."

Adolph allowed his legs to push himself erect. He instinctively rocked forward, and then forced himself to stop. He didn't comprehend where Yvonne was headed. "About what?"

"My grandfather said enemies had promised revenge."
Adolph expected a dead end. "Who's your grandfather?"
"Cornelius Johnson."

"The grain merchant?" Adolph swallowed hard. While Yvonne may have appeared to be an unemployed caregiver, she was an heir to a distinguished Bridgetown family. Cornelius Johnson lived as a noted eccentric recluse with an open wallet to the arts. He'd written the check to sponsor, behind the scenes, a historically relevant purchase of native West Caribbean art on local permanent display at the city's historical and fine arts museum.

"My mother, God rest her soul, was his youngest daughter. Three weeks ago two photographs of Nancy were left inside his screen door with a note asking for twenty-five thousand dollars."

"Did he pay it?" Adolph asked.

"Yes. But Nancy never come home." Yvonne's tears flowed anew. "I go to the river many times hoping to see a special boat. That true the day Billy fell into the river."

Adolph leaned forward. "What boat?"

"The scary photograph of Nancy, collared like a dog, showed her scrubbing what my father said was a deck, a millionaire's deck. I hadn't noticed. Only saw my daughter as a slave."

"Do you still have that photograph?"

"I wanted to tear it up and spit on the vile men that do this. Grandfather said we could never prove blackmail unless I keep it."

Adolph wished he had a handkerchief to offer Yvonne. "Could I see it?"

"He locked it up, so scared I'd change my mind and destroy it."

"You or he must give me a call." His words said as a signal to Luann that their visit was concluded. "I'll stop by." Luann took his hint and preceded him to the condo's outside curb.

Adolph waited until Luann rounded her car's hood. "Drop me off a block from the station in case The Chief's lurking. I'm assuming you can busy yourself with your cases without me."

"I knew you saved that little boy," Luann said en route. "You never said anything about the girl or a missing older sister."

He chafed at the implied criticism. "Why should I? It wasn't a case we were working on. Lots of people come up to me and say this or that crime was committed. If I tried to investigate every single one, I'd go bonkers. So would you."

He sucked in his breath. Softer he said, "If you haven't learned that by now, I can't teach you."

"That's not the point and you know it."

He recoiled at the stronger accusation of deceit; yet, his exhausted mind couldn't lift the mythical lance for a lengthy jousting contest with Luann. "What point?"

"Modern crime work."

Adolph laughed.

"Damn you. How do effective police forces solve crimes? They have a war room with large boards for assembling details, or touch technology screens if they're really into high tech. What do we have? Desks and drawers that you like to lock."

"When you become chief, you can lobby the city council to install those fancy screens with pushbutton instant database access to DEA, Interpol, and the kitchen drawer with Aunt Suzie's secret apple cake recipe that's a code to deflating the Goodyear Blimp with the hidden bomb before it spirals or plunges into the stadium halftime show at next year's Super Bowl."

"Be sarcastic. If that's how you want to live, go for it."

"I respect the truth. It's not determined by gathering around for a majority vote." Adolph readied his right hand to open the passenger door when and if Luann applied the brakes.

"Didn't say that and you know it. If you want to be a lone avenger, more power to you, but it'll likely eat you up inside."

"Who gave you a license to practice psychology?"

"Shove everyone away. So, forget me, don't need your blessing to sanction my actions. What photograph did you have of the missing girl?"

"Had two. Yvonne Whitenmire gave me one the day her son was pulled from the river and pulled one from those boxes you collected from St. Mary's or the B&B without telling me."

Luann glared at him. "I told you and I didn't have to inspect or personally deliver."

Adolph, not enjoying this conversation in the least, gazed

ahead for the station's facade. He should've shutdown after Luann first spoke. Trouble was, and he knew it, her comments were laced with undeniable truth. The only point she didn't jab him with was the reputation superiority of his father's public service as a police officer.

"Unlike you," Adolph snarled, "I'm upset with seeing abused children, even if only in photographs."

Luann fisted her right hand. "You've a short memory. I'm concerned about my own kids." She slowly released her fisted fingers before they lost all color. "I've transferred them to an out-of-state boarding school for a reason."

"How?" He felt envy, not fear, double his pulse rate. "I can't afford that."

"Part of the FBI deal, and I'm trusting you with their life."

"Why should I believe you?" Kristen's cross image flashed onto the back of his eyelids.

"Don't. I'm sure you heard about the CIA giving money to killers like that suspected killer in Peru. FBI giving at home is U.S. government stealth economics."

Adolph barely noticed her truncated snort beneath her left palm plastered to her mouth. He had no time for politics on a day shattered by the knowledge of an abused child ransomed. Horrific statistics suggested that a child seldom lived after the money's delivery. Upon exiting Luann's Chrysler, he purposely left Sonja's audio recording tape on its rear seat.

* * *

Ambling along the police parking lot fence, he scanned all directions until safe to make a beeline past Luann's parked car. He didn't gun his Monte Carlo's engine until ready to kill it a dozen blocks later.

The imposing stone mansion behind the wrought iron gate caused Adolph to pause. He'd once visited Cornelius Johnson's home for a United Way fund-raiser reception hosted by the man himself. The dull black iron points pierced the sky three homes from where Sonja Sanchez worked. A young lady, dressed in a drab olive-brown peasant dress, who answered Adolph's knock left him alone to glance at three walls awash in floor-to-ceiling books. The only interruption, a floor-to-ceiling fieldstone fireplace, basted him in unaccustomed warmth. Crackling log sparks glinted off the brass nail heads of a green leather chair. The spacious parlor dwarfed a circular highly polished walnut table at its center. Craning his head left to right, Adolph couldn't remember when he'd seen so many gilded literary book spines.

"My good man." The frail voice disrupted Adolph's reverie.

Adolph shuffled his body toward the walnut double-door to be surprised by the man's splotchy facial skin and wobbly stature. "Sorry, didn't hear you. I'm Detective Anderson."

"These damn slippers scare everyone," Cornelius mumbled. "Can't wear my Dockers for another two weeks the doctor says."

"Need your help. Your granddaughter says you took the ransom photo."

To Adolph, Cornelius Johnson's instant flicker of paler translucent skin impersonated a Charles Dickens ghost. "To your left, third shelf, grab the red book spine."

As soon as he lifted it, Adolph felt the lightness of the volume he cradled in both hands. He lifted the cover and the hollow center contained a photo, undeveloped side up. Adolph dumped the photo onto the seat of a nearby leather club chair. A young girl on all fours pushed a scrub brush with her right hand. Her uplifted forehead barely tilted to the camera lens. A yellow rubber-gloved hand behind the girl's crown grasped a lease tether clipped to a steel ring fastened to a dark collar. Yvonne hadn't lied. Adolph could visualize the extended laminated wood swimming platform at the boat's stern. "Someone should've notified the police." Adolph didn't intend to rub salt in an open wound, but citizenry silence rarely added a happy homecoming to any abduction.

Cornelius braced himself with his right hand on the edge of the room's center table. "Let's not . . . shall we say, cry over spilt milk."

Adolph accepted the rebuke. "I'm going to assume that this boat is probably long gone."

Cornelius hobbled to a club chair, the identical twin of the one next to Adolph. The leather didn't squeak when Cornelius plopped backward onto it. "Maybe the pirates, but not that mini-yacht. Reminded me of a Mangusta once seen in the Mediterranean. Oh, not in size, but a replica of the one I saw that stretched maybe twenty to twenty-five meters."

Adolph bit his lower lip. "How's that fit in now?"

"There's a small yacht, named the Piano Chord, that docks at Wainright Barge."

Adolph could almost see the light bulb that went off in his head. "See anyone on it?"

"No. I assumed that since I let a day pass, the hijacked boat had kept Nancy hidden from a house search while the pirates awaited delivery of the ransom. Then they vanished."

Adolph swallowed hard, getting the gist of what was said even if it wasn't perfect English. He didn't wish to think how the pirates satisfied their pedophile fantasies defiling Nancy. He repressed the crossed beams he'd seen in Kristen's photos, happy to have Kristen home. To drag a girl like Nancy along on their escape or to let her go free weren't the most likely options. Given Cornelius's long life, with its assumed understanding of human nature, Adolph didn't need to elaborate on his ever-present distress. "That boat still on the river or at Wainright's?"

"Assume so." The patriarch's words barely bounced off the carpet.

Adolph twisted his torso, right side forward. Why did old men, whether Cornelius or Silas, hide their faces from the world? Perhaps it was because they'd seen too much or didn't like what reality had shown them. "Do me a small favor and give me a call if there's further contact or anything else that occurs?"

Cornelius tilted his chin up. "You mean about Nancy?"

"Exactly." Adolph didn't wish to expand upon the boat name connection to Dean Wainright, nor the photos in Ant's file or Len's lab. "You gotta believe we police can be helpful."

Cornelius bowed his head. Adolph let himself out. He circled his Monte Carlo to River Drive, parked next to Wainright Barge, and stayed in his driver's seat long enough to verify with the dispatcher he wasn't being tracked by The Chief. Down the street, past the late afternoon sun glistening off the river's ripples, a nondescript panel van with two workers not seemingly engaged in any worthwhile activity presented the only noticeable movement. Undercover DEA, thought Adolph. While he could care less if he ruffled Fed feathers, not catching a glimpse of Dean Wainright's yacht bobbing in or racing the river current disappointed him.

The scent of fertilizer polluting the river and the dust swirling off sand piles seeped into his Monte Carlo's interior and rode with him to Oxford Avenue. Adolph blinked first as he swerved to the right curb to avoid the approaching jacked-up red pickup truck hogging the roadway and threatening a game of chicken. He'd seen it before, near the corner park. *Damn Dragons.*

Thirty seconds later, he sat on the park bench with Silas. "Those Dragons bother you?"

"Learned to live with them. Stay out of their way and they don't harm an old fellow like me." Silas tugged at his left hand glove where a flash of gold about his wrist glimmered until he tucked the black-leather driving glove under his coat's sleeve.

Adolph raised his gaze to Silas's craggy face. "You ever find any old picture of Spencer Wainright?" As he waited for the blank expression on Silas's face to wane, Adolph counted the six round black buttons, each inserted into a buttonhole on Silas's coat.

"Any boxes way too high in the cold attic. Maybe when summer comes."

Facing the prospect of further conversation being a waste of time, Adolph bade farewell.

* * *

Adolph tried unsuccessfully to slip into his squad room desk

chair without causing Luann to shout out a greeting. He
trusted that by whispering into the pad on his desk his sound
wouldn't carry father than across the two desks. "The Chief
been around?"

"Not in the last few minutes," Luann replied. "Bulldog's
been bugging me. Tried to draw me out if I would favor
including a teenage girl in our next play rehearsal."

He jerked his head upward. "What?"

"Keep your voice down. Don't know specifics."

Adolph reverted to keeping his head lowered. He
whispered, "When?"

Luann glanced to Bulldog's partially closed office door
and shielded her mouth with her left hand. "Tonight, but not at
his house. Wife's home. Said new location."

Hearing Bulldog's office door creak, Adolph delved into
the nearest file. He didn't gaze up as footfalls exited the squad
room. He assumed Bulldog left and Luann confirmed so with
her question. "Sonja get her money from Wainright?"

"Too early." Luann hadn't caught on he'd ignored Sonja
to waste his time at Wainright Barge and with Silas. "Your
snitches say anything about Nancy Whitenmire?"

"Nothing. I'm assuming she's dead."

"Cover for me. I'll be back in an hour." Adolph didn't
wait for Luann's answer. His mental circuitry instantaneously
flashed the well-trodden path to the Rose Garden B&B that, it
seemed, the Monte Carlo's onboard computer had memorized.
The engrained arrival rituals enacted in a numbing sequence:
greet Francine, say nothing new, ask to speak with Matt, and
finally state he knew the way to find him in the basement
bedroom.

From Matt's bedroom door, Adolph asked, "You get
anything from neighbor Wainright?"

Matt scrambled to set aside a box with blinking lights and
a handful of multi-colored cables. It sunk in to Adolph that the
room's first encountered disorder hadn't changed. "Not much.
Want to view the disk?" Matt's right hand fingers scrambled
to press an orange-lit button to have a monitor screen flicker.

Adolph's Gold

Adolph, opting to stand amidst the clutter, dismissed the first images of Boy Scouts at the front door selling wreaths and didn't peer closer until Sonja appeared. Relieved to see that Sonja, able to shield her hands from his on-site surveillance, hadn't given the dean any apparent signal, Adolph was ready to sign off his video watching. "Can you freeze that?"

Matt complied. "You know that old man?"

On the screen was the image of a man in an overcoat wearing a yachting cap. "Name's Silas. Met him a time or two at a park on Oxford Avenue. You ever see him here?"

Matt wiggled his computer's mouse. "You mean onscreen?"

"That, but really interested in if he ever visited your mom's B&B."

"Don't think so. Saw him one day on the street next to Mr. Russell when working with the city crew on Lilac Lane."

"You close? Were they talking?"

"Hard to tell. Coulda been passing by at the same time. People often stopped and gawked. After a while it became second nature to ignore it."

Adolph stared at the screen watching Silas raise his left hand for a third time before it dawned on him that Silas reached for the doorknocker. The surveillance footage counter raced ahead, Silas departed, and the picture reverted to its uninspiring framing of concrete and grass. Adolph quizzed himself: "What business did Silas have with Dean Wainright?" The harder he tried to pluck an answer from his brain, the more strenuously it resisted. Chagrined at his failure, he abandoned the self-induced strain and let the cells drift to the cerebral surface in their own sweet time. Adolph excused himself and, halfway up the stairs, called out: "Francine."

"In the kitchen."

Adolph rested his left hand on the kitchen table chair and gazed at Francine's now familiar floral apron. "You recall an older gentleman, likely wearing a yellowed yachting cap, ever visiting Mr. Russell?"

"Couple of times. Don't exactly remember when, except it was hot."

"What kind of vehicle did he drive?"

Francine's answer prompt and definite. "Didn't."

"Huh?" He'd heard right, but maybe Francine had misinterpreted. "You mean he walked?"

"No. No. Young lady was with him. She drove."

Adolph knew of Russell and older women like Rebecca and Luann. "Can you describe her?"

"Thin, extremely thin. Poor girl, thought bulimic. She only left the car the first time. Would say she was no spring chicken although she could've been the older man's daughter." Francine gazed at the ceiling. "Second thought, not dressed like daughter. You won't quote me, will you?"

Adolph shook his head, his definition of young not necessarily the same as Francine's.

"Would say Mexican or Hispanic. Don't recall much else."

Adolph mumbled Francine's remembrances until he added them as cryptic notes into his notepad he'd pulled from his inside blazer pocket before he sat in his Monte Carlo. As one minute became two, his anxiety rose. His brain froze trying to interlock the mounting number of puzzle pieces. And, he couldn't dump his memory on a table for a trusted confident to rearrange the information and its multiple graduations. He had no choice but to drive back to the squad room and wait to see if Dean Wainright carried through with the promise to pay Sonja's blackmail. If worse came to absolute worse, he'd ride with Luann to beguile his mind with her domestic interviews. Adolph would grit it out to make The Chief happy. The desired reward being that the latter would fill out and sign Adolph's gold shield nomination form.

He parked in an aisle adjacent to Luann's Chrysler, straddling the line dividing two spots. He hurried his pace to the squad room.

"About time," Luann chided.

Adolph knelt next to Luann's desk to tie a shoelace.

"Where's this play rehearsal tonight? I'll get there early."

"Some farm outa town. That's all I know. After what was delivered to my house yesterday, I don't know that I want to find out exactly. Now, sit down and wait a minute."

Adolph obliged and, seated at his desk, held up half a dozen folders, fanned as if by a Geisha. He observed Luann amble halfway to Bulldog's office and then return to her desk. Bulldog, visible through a door crack, remained gazing at his office wall, telephone receiver plastered to his ear. Adolph dropped his folders as Luann handed Adolph an evidence bag, which he opened without a flourish. He stared in disbelief. There on a sheet of plastic-like material was a Dragons' tattoo. Printed instructions said it could be affixed to the skin and then washed off when no longer desired. He thought of grade school, Cracker Jack, and bubble gum prizes. While smaller, these kids' temporary tattoos were no different than this two-by-three inch tattoo resting flat in his palm. He thrust it into the evidence bag.

"Who's this for?" Adolph tossed the bag in Luann's direction.

"Last time we had one," Luann whispered, "the Dragons initiated Dorothy Connor."

"The Mulberry murder victim?"

"The same. Only time I knew that any Dragon came to Bulldog's house. They herded Rebecca, Pistol Pete, and me upstairs. Could only imagine what was happening to Mrs. Connor in the basement, although the whoops and shouts of 'I'm next' gave one a pretty good idea. Saw Mrs. Connor leave. She didn't appear to be bloody or bruised, but she could hardly stand."

"Bulldog, that bastard."

"He told Rebecca he didn't join in. But who knows."

Adolph felt conflicted. Even though Luann wouldn't meet his definition of a friend, he wouldn't stand aside to allow even his worst enemy suffer the trauma he assumed Dorothy Connor had had inflicted upon her. The temporary tattoo blunted Adolph's quest to see Luann's naked shoulder. If she were indeed the woman in Ant's photo collection, a strong scrubbing would've destroyed the proof he'd sought. *Damn.*

Adolph doodled the names of six officers, headed by Finnegan, to be recruited into an unofficial task force. Acting on the ten-to-one odds the Bourdon farm was the chosen location, he confided in Luann he was leaving early to set a trap and relied upon her to protect his butt by telling The Chief he had a follow-up medical appointment to make sure there'd been no lingering effects from his Sixth Street Bar head trauma.

Luann snorted. "I'll tell him you needed to check if your head's screwed on right?"

* * *

Officer Finnegan unlatched the transfer crate in the paddy wagon's cargo area and displayed to Adolph upon their arrival at the Bourdon farm the four shotguns and two tear gas launchers he'd signed out. Adolph deployed Finnegan and the five other officers throughout the farm's windbreak, sent the paddy wagon on its way, and ended his walkie-talkie communication check with the instruction of no more transmissions until he gave the "go" signal.

Adolph, to ward off a stakeout's dreaded anticipation anxiety, busied his mind to fine-tune his calculation that the last bluish rays of twilight would slip into blackness within ten minutes. After un-holstering his 9mm Walther, he refitted the Kelvar bulletproof vest Velcro and marched in place on the east side of a tall spruce to drive blood to his toes and to allow the branch needles to absorb the sting of the intermittent westerly breeze. Warmer than his blue blazer, the insulated jacket he wore didn't prevent his left hand grasping the bullhorn from becoming chilled. His right hand he could slide into a pocket, but not the outer right thigh pocket of his black cargo jeans filled with three extra eight-round clips or his left thigh pocket with the walkie-talkie.

"C'mon, dirtbags, we're ready for ya," Adolph muttered to no one in particular. He endured the itch his black stocking cap created. The freshening breeze carried the arid smell of burnt field stubble into his nostrils. He'd made Kristen promise, before he left the house, not to leave Mary's side and had personally verified that all exterior home door locks were engaged. He heard two owl hoots and edged forward, using a mature cottonwood tree trunk for cover.

Two pairs of headlights entered the courtyard with the first pair those of a small van. If Luann's prediction came true, she'd be in it with Rebecca. A Buick sedan's headlights illuminated the words "Salvatore Pizza" on the panel van's visible side. Adolph's eyes strained, his vision partially blocked, to count two women, five males, and an unidentified smaller person before the doused headlights returned the farmyard to a murky darkness. Luann had been truthful. *Damn.* Small person could be the teenage girl. Adolph hated the complication.

The visitors paraded single file into the backlit farmhouse front door. Interior shadows quivered across the first floor living room windows. Shortly thereafter, second story bedroom lights illuminated perimeter cracks in the pulled-shades. He thanked his lucky stars no vehicle guard patrolled and that the numerical odds were even, better than even if he could count on Luann's inside help. He fumbled for his walkie-talkie, not regretting he hadn't invited the SWAT team with its audio headsets. He pressed the walkie-talkie channel button and spoke one word: "Go." The human-officer noose spread out and tightened around the farmhouse.

Anxiety diluted Adolph's adrenaline to slow his steps. His right shoulder brushed against the Salvatore Pizza decal before he ducked behind the van's hood. Finnegan would take longer to get in position at the rear farmhouse door. An owl hoot pierced the rustle of trees. Adolph raised his left palm holding the megaphone's pistol grip. He peeked across the van's hood. Lights remained on on both farmhouse levels. To his thinking that wasn't a good sign. If the impromptu studio existed in the master bedroom, all inside should be upstairs.

A black form passed in front of what had to be a lamp and

behind a living room window curtain. A basement light flashed on and off skittering beam fragments through a dirty window and across the curled, dying leaves scattered on the brownish lawn.

Adolph calmed his fears. He expected someone inside to be checking the entrances and exits. Patience. Keep cool. He lowered his left arm.

Two irregularly spaced owl hoots signaled Finnegan in position. Adolph waved to the shadowy figure on his left and exposed his body from the protective cover of the van. Until he reached the solid surface of the front walkway, he tried hard not to kick the pebbles in the gravel underfoot. The stillness of the night slithered at the heels of the tightening police approach.

To his right, a third figure, slowed to muffle the crunch of fallen leaves, matched Adolph's advance across the lawn. The three men joined forces on the front porch. The flanking officers, shotguns vertical, fingers on their respective triggers, nodded to Adolph and flattened their backs against the house clapboard on opposite sides of the front door.

Adolph gulped two breaths and pressed the megaphone to his lips.

"Police. Come out now. Hands up." He angled his body to the door to protect against bullets shredding the wood and striking him. Thousand one . . . thousand ten.

He tapped his 9mm barrel against the megaphone's bell end. His companion officers stepped out and pointed their loaded shotguns at the front door.

Adolph called out again. "Police. Come out with hands up. Now."

No answer from inside. The silence irritated, but didn't surprise, Adolph. The Dragons had to be calculating their escape. *Or, eliminating hostages!*

Adolph shouted, "Finnegan." His bellow wasn't the planned signal, and Adolph's shoe sole slamming into the rickety front door below the door handle elevated Plan C to Action Plan A.

Adolph's Gold

Leading the vortex of officers past the vibrating door, Adolph burst into the living room. Empty. He heard the back door squeak and sharpened his gaze to the kitchen. A shotgun barrel preceded Finnegan's emergence. Adolph tossed his megaphone to the carpet and pointed his left forefinger at the ascending stairs. He ordered one of the officers behind him to retreat and stand guard outside at the two vehicles. "Don't shoot wild. Expect hostages or innocents fleeing."

With Finnegan's butt tight to his, Adolph tiptoed up the stairs. He stopped two treads from the landing. An eerie silence. *C'mon, Luann, knock something over.* Give me a hint as to which room you're all in. He braced his left hand against the peeling wallpaper. The 9mm weighed down his right hand. Moisture gathering on his palm streaked the gun's black plastic grips. Adolph endured an intensified scalp cap-itch. Brain cells warned his timing had to be perfect or someone would get hurt.

He rotated his head toward Finnegan. Their eyeballs met. Finnegan's gaze mirrored Adolph's thoughts of: *What now?*

Adolph leaned forward, placed his left knee on the higher tread, and slid his left hand lower on the wall. Without exposing his head, he listened ever more intently for the slightest of noises. His ear canal might as well have been an empty laboratory vacuum chamber. He straightened up. His butt bump alerted Finnegan to his next move—a bolt ahead and a pivot into the upstairs hallway before flattening himself against the wall.

All upstairs inhabitants might as well have been possums playing dead for the amount of sound Adolph's ears detected. When Finnegan's grim face appeared, Adolph motioned toward the master bedroom door, his choice for the room most likely occupied. He swallowed a premonition that he wouldn't like what he was about to find.

Adolph called out: "Come out. Hands up. Play's over."

Only the scratch of Finnegan's boots as he sidled up to Adolph drifted to the ceiling. Adolph lifted his right foot and feigned a kick. Finnegan nodded and braced himself against the opposite hallway wall, shotgun shouldered, and aimed.

The cracked bedroom door, propelled by Adolph's kick, rammed its inside door handle three times against the wall and gouged a crescent into the plaster.

"Damn." Adolph's expletive echoed among the disturbed dust particles floating beneath the lit ceiling light fixture. "Damn. Damn."

"What the hell!" Finnegan exclaimed.

Finnegan's surprise wasn't lost on Adolph. He pulled back the window curtain and waved to the officer standing next to both suspect vehicles, still parked where first seen. Adolph's worsening nightmare verified when he raced through the two adjoining bedrooms opening closet doors and finding not one breathing soul. Even the upstairs bathroom was empty.

He met Finnegan in the hallway. "What'd we miss, Sean?"

"Thought you'd know . . . Sorry." He pointed his shotgun at the floor.

Adolph closed the hallway's bathroom door. "No one came out the front."

"Definitely not the rear."

Adolph slumped against the wall. Think, stupid. He recalled house lights on both the first and second stories. He'd seen a figure last moving on the first floor, and then the basement light. "Let's check the basement. Only chance left."

Adolph led the twosome's clomp down the stairs. "Nothing upstairs," he reported to the officer in the living room who relaxed his trigger finger at the sight of Adolph. "Hand me your flashlight and stay here. We're headed to the basement."

Finnegan unclipped his own flashlight and the two beams preceded Adolph and Finnegan's descent into the dark and dank basement they found devoid of human life. Arachnoids skittered fast and far from the web heaven they'd created. Adolph swiped at a cobweb before he noticed a cleared path above his head and scattered dust on the concrete floor.

"Was told a torture chamber existed with an entrance here

in the basement," he told Finnegan. Adolph purposely left Luann's name unmentioned. Where was it? She hadn't explained that. "Check behind those shelves moved out from that wall to your left."

"There's a door."

"Let's go."

Adolph ducked his head. The four-foot wide passageway he entered had to have been built in the 1920s era of Prohibition, although common later for farmers to connect homes with barns and avoid trudging through winter snow in subzero temperatures. The light from the hanging twisted-wire string of forty-watt bulbs advancing in front of him did little to assuage his fear he wouldn't be accosted. While confident Finnegan would safeguard his rear, Adolph feared he couldn't escape if rushed from the tunnel's not yet visible far end. Any assailant firing a gun wouldn't need to aim, other than straight ahead.

Stooped to allow forward steps, he tilted his head left to avoid an overhead light bulb. One bulb's radiating warmth, in stark contrast to the chill trudging up and down his spine, illuminated what his daughter would refer to as yucky grottiness. At irregular intervals, his shoulders brushed against the vertical cinder block walls, crossed overhead by rough-hewn wooden beams, to be stained by the gray-streaked lime residue evidencing past moisture invasion. He counted ten bulbs, including a burnt out one, to estimate he'd traversed sixty feet before the outline of a door appeared. His neck began to throb. Halting his steps on the packed-earth floor, his jerked head hit the ceiling. The impact scraped off his stocking cap and Finnegan's shotgun barrel struck him between the shoulder blades.

"Sorry," Finnegan whispered.

Adolph let the black knitted wool lay, camouflaged by the dirt; his ears pricked and he froze to await the cry of his being discovered. Raising his left hand, with words designed to bounce off the palm and to ricochet to Finnegan off the passageway's sidewall, Adolph cupped his mouth. "At the door, we'll stop. Listen. If quiet, I'll push through."

He accepted Finnegan's grunt as assent.

Slinking forward, Adolph again stopped when his extended left hand absorbed the chill of the metal door. Looking for a doorknob, he found none. Feeling the doorjamb's vertical stop indicated the door was restricted to a one-way push movement. A muffled cry from the other side of the door raced the pulse in his veins. The voice sounded gagged. He rotated his head right for his left ear to have direct reception. No distinctive syllables. No mingled voices. The unrepeated sound swallowed by the same darkness capturing the tunnel's pale stray light.

Adolph faced a decision. Now or never. It wasn't a unique predicament in humankind, nor, over the years, in fulfilling his own sworn duty. He squeezed the flashlight tight in his left fingers, squared his feet, and shoved the door with his left forearm, ready to duck and roll.

The door swung in. Adolph twirled, his back solidly against the door, and he presumed the wall. His and Finnegan's flashlights provided the only illumination. Luann had been right. He'd entered a torture chamber. Chain links, secured by eyebolts to the ceiling, hung to his left. Two concrete blocks on the earthen floor beneath them had looped rebar imbedded in their centers. On the far wall a steel ladder rose to what appeared to be a trapdoor. Not until Finnegan's flashlight stopped on the tattered and filthy Indian blanket in the corner, diagonal to his right, did Adolph separate possible human form from object shadows.

Adolph could stand upright; he doubted an NBA player could. Twisting his pistol sideways and resting his right wrist on his left fist holding a flashlight, Adolph aimed both at the blanket. A glimpse to his right confirmed Finnegan's combat readiness.

"Stand up, whoever you are," Adolph called out.

The white of one eye popped hauntingly visible, surrounded by the darkness.

"What's your name?" Adolph asked. He slid his soles

three steps closer. Finnegan crisscrossed behind him in the space Adolph had vacated to better protect he and Adolph from both perceived entrances into what Adolph estimated to be no more than a small nine-by-ten-foot bedroom, but it was far more than that. Assorted mallets, a hammer, pliers of multiple description, and wires connected to anodes of a vehicle battery decorated two upended wood crates to the right of the door he had pushed. The white of the seen eye closed. Adolph laterally rotated his wrists to spread the light of his flashlight beam across the cone-shaped blanket form trying to detect any miniscule movement beneath the coarse multi-colored fabric.

"What's your name?" Adolph repeated.

The white of the eye reappeared. Garbled sounds reminded Adolph to look for a gag. He lifted the flashlight beam. The black rag wedged between puffy lips was barely discernible against her skin.

Adolph gasped. "Connor, Marcie Connor?"

The response, to Adolph, sounded to be between a grunt and the word, "Uh-uh."

Dispensing with police protocol, Adolph holstered his Walther, quickstepped to the girl, and genuflected to lower his body, touching his right knee to the hard-packed ground. As he extended his freed right hand to undo the gag knot behind her head, he noted Marcie's left eye swollen shut, bruises on her cheeks and chin, and a dried rivulet of blood on her neck. "Don't move, Marcie. Other than your face, what else hurts?"

"Stomach. I'm tied."

Adolph laid the flashlight on the ground and reached both hands forward to pull the blanket up and away from Marcie. Exposed, her wrists and ankles were bound with black cloth strips similar to that which he'd removed from her mouth.

"Don't move. We'll get you help." Adolph quashed his mind's fermenting questions. He twisted his head and shoulders rearward. "Finnegan, play it safe. Double back. Call for EMTs and detail two officers to secure the barn. I'll be here."

"Ten-four." Finnegan's shotgun butt thudded against the doorjamb and he was gone.

"Suspect you're cold." Adolph replaced the blanket, draping it across Marcie's shoulders.

To stretch a tightened thigh muscle before a spasm and to be prepared should any Dragon return, Adolph elevated his torso with a jerky push of his legs.

"I didn't tell. You can't tell my brother." Marcie's teeth, a brief band of white, diverted Adolph's vision from the grotesque spectacle of the one eye.

"Don't understand. Is your brother here?"

"No." Her gaze wandered off.

The pain in her words morphed Adolph's thoughts to Rebecca and Luann. If they're not in the house, and not here, where? The question dangled unanswered as the trapdoor above Adolph's head creaked. He instinctively unholstered his Walther P.38, kicked the flashlight into the corner, and shielded Marcie with his body.

"Adolph, don't shoot. It's Finnegan."

Adolph relaxed as an emergency medical technician descended, via the metal ladder, into what Adolph characterized as a dungeon. The EMT assessed Marcie fit enough, with supporting help, to climb the ladder. Adolph followed Marcie and the EMT into the barn's milk house. He ambled, in the wake of the gurney, through the crisscrossed fire truck and ambulance headlight beams toward the house. Two human forms huddled beneath dark-green Army blankets on the farmhouse porch. One head was wrapped tight in a towel.

Adolph couldn't explain who he recognized first, Rebecca or Luann. Both gazed at their shoes. He hesitated to interrupt. "You both all right?"

Luann tilted her head back and untwisted the towel. A two-inch swath of scalp parted her hair. "Other then a new do, I'm fine. They didn't have time to get to Rebecca."

"Who?"

Luann gazed at the departing ambulance lights. "Dragons.

One, called Jack, more interested in what Marcie knew, or would admit."

"Huh?" Luann didn't make sense. Was she giving him a false lead? "Say what?"

"Seems Jonathan Greene was his best buddy and he didn't believe Dorothy Connor killed him. Vacillated between Marcie shooting him and the brother, what's his name?"

"Leroy." But Marcie had said Leroy wasn't there. "What'd Marcie say?"

"Nothing, as far as I know. I heard one female scream from downstairs while I faced a hair-cutting shaver with Rebecca restrained next to me in an upstairs bedroom. Didn't see Marcie or any other girl as we were shoved through the tunnel and finally into the grove."

Rebecca, except for the one shudder Adolph perceived, hadn't moved until the second ambulance arrived. She waved off his offer to help steady her walk to the open ambulance doors. Luann climbed in after Rebecca. Adolph declined to be examined when an EMT shined a penlight into his eyes. After commanding his lungs to take in and exhale half a dozen breaths, he, with an athlete's ardent stride, stretched his leg muscles across the farmyard to engage Finnegan inside the milk house.

"Luann says they were taken to the grove when we encircled the farmhouse. Anybody find any trail leading from the barn?"

"Nah, escape likely through the corn," Finnegan replied. "Reckon we'll need daylight."

* * *

Adolph drove Kristen to school and idled his Monte Carlo in the bus lane until she entered the school's front door. At the station parking lot, Lt. Turner's empty spot suggested he hadn't arrived. Adolph doubted Bulldog was at the Bourdon farm helping the crime scene technicians scour the farmhouse, barn, and surrounding fields after the prior night's activities.

While Adolph expected Marcie to have been admitted to

Community General, he delayed going to interview her until he could re-examine the Mulberry murder file. Thirty minutes of review documented only one gap. Leroy Connor's hands hadn't been tested for gunshot residue. If Leroy had fired the fatal shot into Greene, Adolph hadn't suspected the possibility then.

Clicking heels on the wooden floor interrupted his thoughts.

"You're not at the farm?" Luann's question laced with more surprise than inquisitiveness. She settled into her desk chair without a glance at Bulldog's closed office door.

"Nice hat," Adolph began, and then felt a pang of conscience not spurred by Luann's blank reaction. He salved his conscience with an honest and sensitive: "You okay?"

"Need work's distraction. Home's too quiet."

"Willing to go to the hospital with me? Need to talk to Marcie. But, considering you're a victim too, it might not be such a grand idea."

"Forget legalities. That girl needs friends." Luann gazed away. "Proper friends."

* * *

A square two-inch gauze patch taped to Marcie's left eye permitted the swelling to creep out from below the bandage's edges. Adolph stood on her bed's good-eye side, Luann at its foot. Marcie tilted her head and nodded once to him when he asked if she was feeling better.

"You wanted to tell me something last night. What was it?"

Marcie closed her right eye. Adolph didn't wish to disturb the room's silence. Upon hearing the repeated click of a ballpoint pen, he gazed at Luann and shook his head. An impulse deep within wanted to chortle Marcie, not for her faltering willingness to come clean, but for her threat to Kristen. The old adage of live by the sword, die by the sword, tailored itself to Marcie.

He choked off his personal animosity to let

professionalism pour forth. "Marcie, there's no one here to hurt you. We can help only if we're told everything." Meant to comfort, his words invoked no immediate response.

The right eye re-opened. "You can't. You couldn't save my mother."

"But we can do our best to make whoever did it pay."

Marcie shivered.

Adolph didn't require subtle perceptions to gather he'd said the wrong thing. "Help me." He glanced at Luann to find no lifeline tossed his way. "You were home from, not at, school that day, right?" He trusted she'd know he spoke of the day her mother was shot.

"Yeah."

"And, Leroy?" Adolph placed his left hand on the bed rail.

"Not at first."

He steadied his hand. Marcie was at least talking. "Why was Jonathan Greene there?"

"Don't know."

Adolph presumed Marcie's statement to be a dodge. He had to keep her talking. "You had to have heard something. What did you hear Jonathan say?"

"He left Jack and me in my bedroom."

Adolph's abdominal muscles tightened. He couldn't fathom whether or not getting new information of Jack's presence helped or hindered. "Jack your boyfriend?"

"Never. He'd been to the house with Leroy. Mother told me in the past to treat him nice. I didn't know what that meant. I'd just leave the kitchen or the living room when he came."

"And, that day in your bedroom?"

"He said I could be a man's woman and he'd show me. I first wiggled away. Then screamed. Mother beat on my door until he finally unlocked it. She said she'd done everything the old man wanted and that he, Jack, should leave me alone. Jack just stared at Mother and pushed her away to run downstairs when Jonathan screamed."

"What am I missing? Why would Jonathan scream if he

were by himself?"

"He wasn't. Leroy had come home."

"Did you see Leroy? Did he come upstairs?"

"No. No. Mother ran downstairs after Jack. I stayed to fix my clothes. Heard Leroy shout 'hell no.' Mother then yelled louder she had a tattoo and to get out."

"Who's to get out?"

"Don't know. Heard something like a chair hit the wall. Then two shots."

Adolph tried to assimilate Marcie's words without slowing her down. He calculated that if she stopped she might not continue. "Who all had guns?"

"Jack had one."

"Did you see it?" Luann's dropping her notepad caused Adolph to pause.

Marcie didn't seem to notice. "In his belt when he lifted his sweatshirt in my room. Don't know if it was the same one I saw Leroy with when I got to the kitchen."

"What'd he do with it?"

Marcie gazed as high up the room's wall as her head position allowed. "Leroy took it."

Luann asked softly, "Where was Jack?"

Marcie's gaze remained fixed. "Thought that Leroy chased after him."

This statement, which assumed Jack would run scared, didn't make sense to Adolph. Marcie's entire story could be bogus. He'd dampen his skepticism, but it was often commented on that the best lies contained interlaced truth. "You touch anything or anybody in the kitchen?"

"Too scared. Ran to school and hid in the bathroom until class let out. Leroy found me by my locker. He said we had to help Mother. We agreed I'd go first and he'd come home later."

Marcie's version defied logic. She'd have had to have seen her mother lying on the kitchen floor before racing off to school. "Then, you found me at the house?"

The rippling top sheet indicated her chest heaved. "Yeah."

Adolph's Gold

Adolph didn't wish to rehash the kitchen scene. He gazed at Luann. She still wore the Borsalino felt hat that he'd said, in the car during the drive over, paled in style to a baseball cap.

"Get out." The yell preceded Leroy's burst into the hospital room.

Adolph twisted to his right. "Hold your horses, son."

With his neck veins bulging, Leroy's eyes glared at Adolph. Luann blocked Leroy's ability to retreat without a collision. Adolph couldn't decipher if Leroy's facial redness and veins popped because of bubbling anger or physical exertion.

Leroy tapped his clenched fists in front of his chest. "Don't say anything, Marcie."

"She hasn't," Adolph lied. "She didn't know how that gun residue got on your hands the day your Mother was shot."

"It was self-defense."

Marcie shrieked, "Leroy, I didn't say that."

Adolph, ready to unsnap the handcuffs from his belt, held off. "Quiet, Marcie." He stared at Leroy. "Where were you last night, say, between eight and ten p.m.?"

"At the library."

Adolph kept his hands free and in front of his waist. "Anyone with you?"

"Three others. We were doing a science project."

Adolph trusted Henrietta would remember Leroy amongst the three other youths in the library if he inquired or invited her to a lineup. He twisted his gaze to Luann. "Let's go."

* * *

Adolph purposely gave up his regular seat in Patsy's party room to Luann. Rebecca, again in her elongated Annie Oakley costume, sat across from them, a steaming glass coffee carafe and four mugs on the table separating the threesome.

"Rebecca," Adolph began, "need to have you recall everything that happened last night."

Rebecca folded her arms across her chest. "Luann knows."

"It's important. People see and hear different things."

Between glances to Luann for help, Rebecca recounted how the pizza truck picked her up outside Patsy's rear entrance, then Luann. A young teenage girl Rebecca didn't recognize already on board plus three Dragons in the truck box and at least a driver upfront. After they were herded into the farmhouse living room, two Dragons surrounded the girl and kept her there while two Dragons shoved her and Luann upstairs. The girl musta done something for Rebecca recalled hearing a scream, if not two or three.

"What did either of the Dragons with you say?" Adolph asked.

"Nothing much. One, who'd been humming during the ride, came upstairs, sent one Dragon downstairs, and then said something to the one remaining about the old man will be upset if they didn't get their job done. Isn't that right, Luann?"

"Didn't hear no mention of any old man," Luann replied.

"Was the Dragon who spoke named Jack?"

Rebecca gazed intently at Luann. "He had a small scar, chin, left side."

Luann interjected, "That's Jack."

"Who's this old man?"

"Don't know," Rebecca said. "Thought it may have been the voice I heard an earlier time, but I never saw a face. Everything got tenser when Jack was there or his name mentioned."

Adolph left his notepad closed. He'd trust his recorder. "What was said?"

"Do you want the demeaning crud to give you a high?"

"Hell no." Adolph was taken aback by Rebecca's outburst. He didn't understand what or if he'd precipitated this or if Rebecca's mind had been drugged haywire. He hoped reason would prevail. "Need to determine if we can decipher a recent trigger to this escalated abuse involving the Dragons or if we're dealing with a long, slow-burning fuse."

"Whatever," Rebecca said. "Nothing there for me."

Adolph had a hunch—Dean Wainright. "Did you at any

332

time hear a similar male voice?"

"Hardly. After we got inside, it was such frantic chaos. Right, Luann?" Luann, with closed lips, nodded slightly. Rebecca continued, "One of those young jerks purposely kicked my side when I fell onto the dirt in that tunnel. I prayed not to die in that cornfield when a gun barrel pressed skin under my nose. All I could think of to keep me scrambling forward were the scars on Bradford's back."

Adolph shuddered. He'd seen one too many kids whipped, in person and in pictures. "How'd you escape?"

"Give Luann credit."

"What?" Adolph felt a twinge in his neck as he cast an awkward glance at Luann. At the mention of her name, she shielded her eyes from his direct view with a duck of her head.

"She fell in the field's corn stubble. Deliberate, I think. Ask her. So I did, too. I'm sure Luann was kicked. The boot toe aimed for my chin missed. We lay there, possums in the dirt. The Dragons got nervous. The smallest was sent to steal one of their vehicles. The others circled us and whispered about seeing flashes of light between the trees and crunching sounds coming from the farmyard. Murmurs between them feared jail and their being abandoned and not getting their share from the big guy."

"Maybe Jack?" Adolph suggested.

"Bigger." Rebecca rubbed her hands. "Jack's a puppet. Carries out orders; doesn't think."

The sincerity and forcefulness of Rebecca's answer added credence. An undertone troubled Adolph. Should he be skeptical of Luann's actions? Had she executed a pre-arranged signal to save herself irrespective of Rebecca? He dismissed his jaded perspective.

Adolph wrapped up the conversation with a long sip of undesired coffee. Luann's companionable silence on the stroll to the station helped his mood, but didn't solve how the myriad puzzle pieces fit together. Whenever he followed the drugs, his thoughts circled back to Wainright Barge often and lately to the Dragons. Whenever he followed the porn trail, with its side cutoffs and paths, up popped stolen computers, x-rated videos, and nude photo subjects. Whether winding or expanding, the trails crossed the Sixth Street Bar's threshold and Ant's poker gambling. Adolph doubted Ant was the lynchpin. With the latest activities, the Dragons were involved deeper than he first thought, and Jack possessed direct ties to Dean Wainright.

Luann's right hand shoved the squad room door open for them. "Whatcha thinking we should do next?" She squirmed into her desk chair, fussing to keep her hat tight to her scalp.

Adolph gazed at his refilled inbox.

"You got a suggestion?" she asked again, not having lifted the telephone receiver.

He ignored his two new files, not Luann. "Find Sonja Maria, collect the bounty, and squeeze that dean hard." Front 'n' center in Adolph's mind, a gold shield shone bright.

* * *

Adolph adjusted his binocular focus. Sonja Maria's profile image at Dean Wainright's front door sharpened. Luann, seated behind the wheel of her Chrysler, coughed.

"Bless you," Adolph said. "The dean's opening the door."

He and Luann heard the dean offer to have Sonja Maria come inside through the receiver of the wireless mike fitted inside Sonja Maria's bra. If she remembered to again act pursuant to his instructions, Sonja Maria wouldn't go inside.

"No, senor. I take gift and leave."

Adolph assumed the plastic grocery bag the dean produced contained the $10,000 dollars. Sonja Maria crushed the plastic between her two palms and his hand let go. She scurried from the stoop. Adolph drummed his fingers on the dash until she turned left at the intersection behind him. When convinced she wasn't being followed, he requested Luann to drive around the block and meet up with Sonja Maria.

"We now should have enough to run the dean in," Luann said.

Adolph gazed at her. "Not until I feast my eyes on that

money in the bag."

Luann parked her Chrysler in front of the Rose Garden B&B. Adolph hopped out to meet Sonja Maria waiting on the sidewalk. He peeked into the offered bag and confirmed banded stacks topped by U.S. currency. Without removing a wad, he fanned its edges.

"The cheat," Adolph exclaimed.

"What?" Luann rounded her vehicle's front bumper. "No money?"

"Top and bottom are twenties, cut paper in between." *Damn.* "Probably not enough here to reach a felony's statutory dollar minimum."

"Won't a misdemeanor charge, obstruction or some sort, do?"

"You're right. We'll squeeze his guts like grapes in a wine press." He pivoted. "Sonja Maria, you did good."

They dropped a still shaking Sonja Maria off at 409 Tinley and drove straight back to Lilac Lane. Adolph banged the dean's door with his right fist. No one answered.

"Stay here," Adolph said to Luann. He walked to the backyard. An upward glance and he thought he saw Francine at a second story B&B window. Not even the housekeeper was visible through any Wainright home window. He rendezvoused with Luann.

"No luck?" Luann asked, stopping her pacing next to her Chrysler.

"None." He rubbed his eyes. "We should go to the B&B." Adolph was ready for a question why, but Luann didn't ask. This newly exposed docility in her conduct he couldn't explain. Perhaps the nighttime brush with the Dragons injected a horror Lt. Hunter never had. The thought awakened a sleeping question: If videotaping was on the agenda at the farmhouse, why wasn't the lieutenant or another video stud in attendance?

While he could of walked, he let Luann drive. Francine answered the B & B's front door.

"We need to see Matt," Adolph said.

"He's downstairs. Think you know where."

Adolph nodded to Francine and led Luann into the basement. "Matt," he called out.

"In here." The words came from the bedroom opposite the laundry area. Adolph stopped at the door. "Matt, this here's Luann." They both stepped into Matt's cluttered bedroom.

Matt tilted his head away from a bank of monitors. After Matt's eyes took in Luann's entire frame from hat-to-toe, a twinkle shone at the edge of Matt's eyes. "Madame LaFlame." His voice choked off the next syllable.

As if backlit by a Christmas tree bulb, Luann's pink cheeks blushed cherry apple red.

Adolph, sensing a connection between the two, gazed at Luann. "You know Matt?"

Matt interrupted, "She doesn't." He rose from his chair and shoved aside a stack of discs. "I've seen her videos. Or, at least, behind the mask, I think I have. Perhaps I can find one."

"Not necessary." Luann's voice squeaky.

"More important." Adolph, foreseeing his parlay of this latest knowledge into denying Luann's snatch of the one up-for-grabs gold badge, squelched his lustful groin warmth. He turned to Matt. "What video of the interior of the dean's house do you have for today?"

Luann punched his side. "Illegal surveillance?"

"Hush, Luann. Or is it Madame LaFlame?" Adolph dropped his gaze to the disc Matt offered and shook his head. "Pop it in."

The video ran and ran. Adolph shifted his weight, first to his left foot, and then to his right one, increasingly bored with watching the housekeeper, day after day, dust and vacuum. The dean's lips drained two martinis a sitting and his fingers danced across ivory piano keys, punctuated by raised taps on the black. When the counter indicated three hours ago, Adolph noticed that the darkened interior broke the normal day-night light cycle. Hadn't the housekeeper opened the backyard-viewing drapes? Adolph saw no visual proof the flicker of light seen emanated from the dean's rear door or a lamp.

Adolph's Gold

When a shadowy human image scurried across the room, Adolph surmised that, coordinated with the monitor's time counter, it was the dean answering the front door in response to Sonja Maria's ringing.

Without requesting a switch to the exterior camera, the switched on lamp confirmed the dean's return to the family room after the amount of time equating to Sonja Maria's visit. The dean didn't sit at the piano. Adolph craned his neck. "Backup, give me those last five minutes again." The replay showed Adolph had missed a shadowy movement, which appeared to be the arm of a person, his or her body hidden by the winged chair's style. In the black-and-white video image, a dark-colored coat would've blended into the chair's fabric. When the dean's backside filled the camera view for three minutes, Adolph cursed under his breath. After Wainright moved and the chair's arm returned into view, its uncompressed fabric was ample evidence that, if there had indeed been any human arm, its owner had departed.

"Is that all?" Adolph asked.

"To the minute," Matt replied.

Frustrated, Adolph requested Matt replay the front door disc. There, digitally, was Sonja Maria and the plastic bag. Adolph pounded his right fist into his left palm. Discovering no new information increased his discouragement. The family room visitor, if he'd left, had wisely not used the front door. With the visitor unidentified, Adolph tallied being in the hole with two strikes. He rotated his gaze to Luann. "We need to get back to the station."

Luann, without an announcement, resumed her silent tour guide role, homing in on the station parking lot. The squad room was empty when Adolph swiveled his desk chair prior to inserting his oxfords into the kneehole. Lt. Hunter had left him a terse written message. Cornelius called. Rumor. The Piano Chord seen heading upstream at Lock and Dam No. 17. Adolph easily calculated that Dean Wainright couldn't have been piloting, or even on, the yacht when observed, but perhaps the dean planned to meet it and/or its cargo at the barge dock.

Across from him, Luann sat scribbling notes, appearing absolutely ridiculous in her hat. Adolph tried to reach Finnegan. The dispatcher said he'd called off, taking a personal day. Adolph stared at Luann briefly before clearing his throat. "Got time for a stakeout tonight?"

"Where?" The flatness in her eyes said he shouldn't have asked.

"Wainright Barge. Bulldog says the yacht connected with Nancy Whitenmire's abduction is cruising up river," Adolph lied, exaggerating Bulldog's information conduit role. If Luann hemmed and hawed, Adolph expected she'd be of no help whatsoever.

Unenthusiastically she asked, "What time?"

"Nine. I'll get unmarked."

* * *

Adolph couldn't judge what was more uncomfortable: surreptitiously peeking at Luann stripping or trying to think up inane chitchat sitting next to her on a dark Bridgetown street listening to river waves lap against the shore and staring at a hulking, unmoving warehouse building silhouette. To his right, the light beam scraping the water surface gave the all clear to the upstream tug advancing to Lock and Dam No. 15.

"We gonna sit here all night?" Luann moaned.

Adolph tried to placate her. "An hour, two tops, would be my guess. That is unless we get word the yacht will still proceed after being delayed."

Luann's fingers crinkled a mint's wrapping before she eased the candy past red lipstick.

Adolph ignored Luann's airborne spearmint assault. If the moon had been up, he could've counted craters or amused himself with fanciful rhyme images of cows jumping from horizon to horizon. Adolph folded his forearms across the steering wheel and squinted both eyes to the right, past Luann to the tug's stern. A smaller boat rocked at the far reaches of the tug's wake. He heard an engine rev. A yacht angled for the

Wainright dock.

"Let's go," Adolph whispered. "Stay close."

He fought to restrain his charging steps and tugged at Luann's right elbow to do the same. A padlocked steel fence gate denied them easy access to the dock. Adolph pointed ahead to the last fence's last post, secured by screwed-in brackets to the warehouse's corner. Three yards past the post, Adolph bent forward, expecting the little-used side door to be locked.

Adolph gave Luann an upward sideways gaze. "Watch for visitors."

When she'd complied and his gaze met non-existent street traffic, Adolph wiggled his lock pick tools until he heard the third tumbler click. "I'm going in." He released his left hand from the doorknob, expecting Luann to remain on guard. After one step, he paused to collect the sense of where the muffled voices came from. They were either on the warehouse's far side or walled off inside another room. He opted to believe the latter and faced a narrow industrial shelving aisle with barrels above his head and a passageway that required he snake past boxes and pallets randomly stacked on the floor. To avoid detection, he paused a half step before the aisle's end. Beyond, fluorescent light crept right-to-left across the concrete floor's black forklift skid marks. He heard the muffed bang of Luann closing the warehouse door ten to twelve feet behind him.

Adolph's head extension focused his eyes toward the light's source, listened for Luann's approaching footfalls, slowly pumped his fisted right hand one time, and, in an upright position, strode forward, expecting, at the least, that Luann would have his back.

A snarl, followed by an animal's growl, punctuated the louder muffled human voices. When Adolph gazed down, bared white teeth, inches above the floor's skid marks, sprang at him.

In self-defense, Adolph crossed his right forearm in front of his chest and instantly felt the pressure and pain of sharp German shepherd canines as he fell backward. *Don't let them feel your fear. Be in command.* He violently twisted his arm, unable to toss the dog away or hit the back of its skull against an upright steel shelf post.

Coming from behind his head, a beam of light sparkled in the vitreous dog eyes, within inches of his face, until the beam journeyed upward. A bullet whistled past, deafened Adolph's left ear. His right ear caught the agonized, piercing yelp of a second dog.

"Stay still," Luann shouted.

Her lowered flashlight beam, again glistening off the dog's frenzied eyes, sparkled the leather collar stainless steel beads of the dog, its mouth clamped onto Adolph's arm. Blood spurted across Adolph's face. The German shepherd's haunches lay motionless on his stomach. Luann's second shot had been perfect. Adolph pried apart the dog's jaw and, when his arm had flopped free, Adolph himself gasped for breath.

"Ranger, Daisy," a voice called out from the other side of the aisle.

"You in pain, bleeding?" Luann asked, bending to Adolph's side.

"I'll make it." Mollycoddling wasn't in his nature. "Where's that other dog?"

"Limped away." Luann tugged at his right sleeve to separate fabric clinging to skin.

"Thank goodness." Adolph, still lying on the floor, raised his left forearm and pressed it hard to his perspiring forehead and closed both eyes. When he blinked them wide to reality, his left hand fingers lightly traced the saliva-edged punctures in the blazer's right forearm cloth. He guessed that, at most, considering the blood radius, the dog had punctured his skin in two places. Shoving the dog carcass right and off his stomach, he clumsily scrambled to his feet. "Let's see if that other damn mutt left a trail."

Next to a standard interior door, its top half a clear glass window, Adolph located paw-smeared blood drops concentrated on the floor. The lit room lights illuminated two upturned chairs along a sidewall in front of a floor-to-ceiling cabinet. Without opening the closed door, Adolph judged the room to be unoccupied and he couldn't spot blood drops on the interior floor or furniture. Upon hearing approaching footfalls, he jerked his body left in an aborted pivot.

"We're safe," Luann announced. "I'll call for medical and backup."

"Wait." Adolph's muscles tensed. In the room's far corner, the end of a blanket mostly hidden by the angled cabinet fluttered without Adolph's gaze noticing a ceiling air vent. "That blanket moved." Pain stung his right hand as he twisted the door's knob. His left awkwardly pointed his 9mm Walther straight ahead. "Duck and cover me."

Adolph kicked aside a chair. He stared at the blue blanket. "Police. Show yourself."

A left edge of the blanket twitched and then lifted. Two sneakers emerged, bound at the ankle. Adolph switched his weapon to his right hand, crouched, and grabbed the blanket edge with his left hand nearest the bound sneakers and yanked.

"Who's the girl," Luann cried out, as she hurried to Adolph's side.

He holstered his 9mm before he tumbled forward onto his knees, crawled, and again sat on his haunches. He loosened the dishtowel gag from the young girl's mouth and let it hang loose at her scarred neck. "You're safe now. We're police. What's your name, dear?"

"Nancy." The girl's eyes flitted nervously from side to side.

Adolph ventured a guess. "Whitenmire?"

The girl stiffly nodded.

"Don't move. We'll get you to the hospital and call your mother."

Adolph waited until the EMTs attended to Nancy Whitenmire before he let them remove his blazer. "I've had my shots." He winced twice in response to the removal of his shirtsleeve and the antiseptic swab. His slow exhale ended as the EMT taped a sterile gauze bandage into place. Adolph stuffed two pain capsules into his shirt pocket as he watched the ambulance depart.

Luann approached him at the stakeout car. "The girl couldn't identify anyone. Said Black males, more than one, maybe three, and one old guy."

Adolph rested his butt on the unmarked squad car's front fender. "All Black?"

"No. Old guy was white. She didn't see face, just hands. Said old."

He needed more than that. "Rough or smooth?"

"Didn't get that far. Why?"

Adolph hung back. "Just trying to be thorough. Connect all the dots possible." There'd been an unidentified man's voice mentioned, especially by Rebecca's son, Bradford. While hindsight said he should've had the dean as his number one pervert suspect ever since Sonja Maria's initial assault interview, he couldn't dispute the paperwork he'd signed and filed. Recent and tonight's information, plus the dean's unanswered front door, would let Adolph craft a new self-serving scenario. It was his luck Luann hadn't reported what Nancy knew of the old man's hands.

Luann's head and eyes, hesitating at times, pulsed like a rotating lawn sprinkler. "It's not Bulldog, if that's what you're thinking."

"You know where he is? I don't."

"Late meeting with The Chief is my scuttlebutt."

"Oh." Adolph thought of the expected upcoming promotion announcement. If Bulldog was with The Chief, he could verify. That is, if he gathered enough brass to ask the awkward questions. The many unanswered questions of "if this or if that" piling up behind Adolph's eyeballs required that he visit Matt again at the Rose Garden B&B.

Allowing Luann to drive, they, after a B&B knock, followed Matt to his basement bedroom and its multiple computer screens.

"Sorry it's late. Need to see videos made this evening across the back fence."

Matt, reaching for a disc, said, "Can do." He punched a

monitor's keyboard.

Adolph didn't need to request Matt to rerun any footage. The dean's time-dated image, often with a student, convincingly substantiated for Adolph that Dean Wainright earlier that evening hadn't been river boating or sic-ing dogs on WR Barge trespassers. Adolph's eyes led his body rotation toward Matt's bedroom's door. Luann's wide-eyed bedroom gaze remained animated and frozen, even after Adolph pulled close the unmarked squad car's passenger door.

"What other video you got?" Luann's voice barely audible as it ricocheted off the interior windshield glass in front of the driver's seat.

Adolph continued to stare straight ahead. "Lots."

"Oh." Luann gunned the engine, the car's gearshift locked in neutral.

He rotated his head left. "Drop me off at home. Car's checked out 'til tomorrow."

"Don't you need to go to the hospital?" Her question voiced matter-of-factly.

"Can see a doc in the morning." Adolph braced himself for a rebuttal that didn't come. The growing itch on his right forearm told him the skin punctured by the dog bite would mend. Physically he'd always been a quick healer, not so fast this night with the cerebral cracks expanding within his mind. He needed to identify and tie all the loose ends from multiple cases into a new knot. While the B&B bones were identified, the perpetrator wasn't and the peril for the youth of both sexes and Bridgetown women continued unabated. "Turn off the headlights."

"What?" Luann's stair-stepped volume rose. "We're almost at your house."

"Do it. Don't argue, damn it." Adolph reached for his seatbelt. "Do it now."

With the exertion, Adolph's muscles tightened. Stings in his right arm shot dizziness into his brain. His head drooped forward. Then darkness crowded out the light of reality.

"This is crazy." Luann again gripped the steering wheel to

fight the car's sideways lurch and guide it to the curb.
"Adolph, you all right?"

"Fine. Fine" He lifted his head and wobbled a stare
straight ahead. A hazy image of a silhouetted figure stood
motionless in front of the porch light Mary must have left on
for him. "There's someone outside my kitchen window."

Adolph felt the car frame tremor as Luann slammed the
driver door.

"Wait," Adolph called out through the space between the
opened passenger door and the windshield. "You'll scare him .
. ."

Adolph shrugged. The hooded figure darted across his
home's lawn. Each elongated stride extended the lead between
him or her and Luann. Within in a minute, a defeated, outraced Luann staggered his way, breathing heavy. Adolph had
watched the suspect be swallowed up by the shadows past the
far intersection streetlight.

"Sorry, no energy left." Luann spit out the words between
pants.

"Would you be able to identify?"

Her hands rested briefly on her knees. "'Fraid not. Too
dark."

Adolph squelched his suspicion Luann acted, not for his
benefit, but for hers. In the morning light he'd check for new
screwdriver marks on the kitchen windowsill. Tonight's figure
appeared heftier than the previously surprised hooded figure
who left a softball and was built more like Bulldog. No, not
possible. Bulldog wasn't that speedy. He doubled down on his
suspicion of Luann without reaching a conclusion. Adolph
clenched his teeth and waited for his right arm pain to subside.
Perhaps, he could think clearer in a few hours, if his arm throb
waned.

"Go home, Luann."

"I can wait. See if everything's all right inside."

A switched on light visible in the kitchen window
indicated to Adolph he had nothing to fear. Kristen's quizzical
shout of "Dad" through the partially opened house door

confirmed.

"See you at the station tomorrow. Good night." Adolph angled his blood-spotted oxfords toward the rear stoop where Kristen stood bathed in dim yellowish light.

* * *

Adolph left the rays of an early sunrise outside to grab coffee at Patsy's. Rebecca acknowledged his seated presence with a smiling nod and her raised right hand forefinger before she scurried away to serve four other patrons.

"Top of the morning."

The cheery baritone greeting interrupted Adolph's daydreaming. He swiveled on his counter stool. Finnegan plopped his wide-brimmed hat on the counter. "Strange to find you here. Word circulating is that the EMTs wrote you a hospital ticket."

"Just a scratch. Shouldn't be a big deal."

Finnegan waved his right hand to catch Rebecca's attention. "But it's one reason given in support of Luann getting the gold shield."

"What?" Adolph's backward lean nearly toppled him off his stool.

"Wait a sec, Adolph." Finnegan turned toward Rebecca, on the server side of the counter, who stood directly opposite him. "Two coffees, cream. One Danish."

"Coming up."

"Say, Rebecca, you got play rehearsal tonight?" Adolph asked.

"On hold."

Rebecca hastened away before Adolph could ask why. Gazing after her, he vowed to privately corner her later to ask her what "on hold" signified. Perhaps Lt. Hunter needed to find a suitable stud replacement for Honest Abe. Regardless, with a new camera battery he'd get the evidence to derail Luann's wearing a shiny new gold badge.

"Hey Adolph, you're married," Finnegan whispered. "Although I must say Rebecca's swaying hips are a tempting

345

advertisement."

"Huh, oh yeah."

"You hear what I said about Luann?"

"Yeah. She's been brown-nosing the lieutenant for months."

"I'd take it pretty hard to lose out if I was you. All that you've done."

"Nothing's ever enough." He paused, inwardly acknowledging his self-interest. Rebecca clinked two mugs and a plate with the Danish on the counter and quickly departed. He watched Finnegan powder his upper lip with a bite into the Danish. "Nothing's ever enough. You oughta know that." Adolph tried to smile and had no idea if he'd broadcast a smirk instead. "Had a prime suspect for burying them garden bones, and then a video makes it go poof."

"So, get a new suspect."

"Easy to say and you'll learn, if ever a detective, and, I'm not saying you don't have my support, but clues don't necessarily grow on trees." Adolph introspectively recalled the birdhouse poem and Bradford's physical humiliation earning a hospital stay.

"Could, if you believe the movies. Nevertheless, I suspect you'll probably stumble onto the case solver using your exceptional common sense."

"Don't I wish?" Adolph sipped his lukewarm coffee. He cast a stealthy unacknowledged disconcerting glance at Finnegan. With his entire being, Adolph fought the invading negativism of failure. He had to get back to Wainright Barge, dogs or no dogs.

Declining a coffee refill, he left Rebecca and Finnegan and flashed his silver badge to gain entrance into WR Barge's warehouse. Smeared blood traces on the concrete floor and whiffs of a strong lingering disinfectant were proof enough of his previous night's dog encounter.

He eyeballed Xavier Downs, his escort. "Where's the used oil barrel storage?"

"We don't have those."

"C'mon." Adolph flashed an upraised brow.

Downs kept his gaze strong and straight. "Believe me."

Adolph laid his right hand on a shelf rack. "If not now, did you ever store them?"

"Of course." The warehouse manager wasn't adept at hiding his facial lines of irritation.

Adolph paused at an aisle end. "Then, who knew about them?"

"Anybody connected with WR Barge."

"Oh." Neither the vague answer nor its clipped delivery surprised Adolph. The unanswered question was: who were these people? "Can you give me a list?"

"I guess." A cautious facade dropped from Downs's forehead to his chin.

Adolph chafed at having to drag out every little detail. "When?"

"Give me a couple of days."

"Don't have the time. You know Dean Wainright?"

"I guess." Adolph, gingerly patting his right forearm, stared at Downs until the manager rescinded his equivocation. "Yeah, sure."

"Does he know about these oil barrels?"

"Could." He glanced at empty space beyond his left shoulder. "Doubt it, though."

"Why?" Adolph thought the question simple enough. The thought Downs gave it meant that he was afraid to answer, didn't know, or couldn't come up with a fast lie.

"What difference does what goes on here make to him? Bankruptcy courts took this business from his father. There's no family legacy."

"But wouldn't that make him more desperate to create former wealth?"

"I'd suspect not, if it doesn't advance his passion for music."

"Point made." Adolph was now ready enough to drop similar lines of inquiry.

Downs gazed toward the glass door's room. "Although

it's a complicated world."

"Hold on," Adolph said. "You're switching gears on me." The dogs hadn't zapped his ability to discern inconsistencies. "When last did you see the yacht that was here yesterday?"

Downs squared his scuffed Red Wing boots beneath his swept-back shoulders. "Best guess, two weeks ago."

"Did that include the dogs?"

Downs's frown furrows deepened. "Dogs?"

"Yeah, the dogs. Aren't you in charge of everything?"

"I guess."

Adolph let his exasperation surface. "What's this 'I guess?' Aren't you in charge?"

"Just because I'm in charge of the warehouse," Downs snapped back, "doesn't mean I know about any dogs."

"Didn't this blood on the floor pique your interest?"

"You can't hang any OSHA rap on me." Downs's eyes blazed. "Cops last night said one of their own was taken to the hospital. And besides, workers get accidentally cut and bleed and don't want no damned injury report to restrict their ability to keep getting paid."

Adolph understood illegals didn't want to be noticed. If they didn't care, he wouldn't either. If Downs honestly didn't know about the dogs, then how did Silas, the old riverboat pilot? "Has Silas been seen around the warehouse lately?"

"That old geezer, nothing but gripes. Coulda been here on the pier yesterday or the day before. Guys tolerate him more than me. One or two hung out years ago with his son. You maybe heard he died on the river. Creates a kinship, you know."

"Yeah. Know when this yacht may becoming back?"

"Guess, couple of weeks."

Expecting a similar answer, Adolph asked anyway. "What about a used oil barge?"

"Same, I'd guess."

Adolph had his fill of Downs's guesses and barrel knowledge contradictions. "Call me if either are scheduled to dock." Adolph showed himself out.

Adolph's Gold

Steering his Monte Carlo into the Community Hospital parking lot, he parked to check his gauze bandage for dripping blood. He buttoned his sleeve cuff before flashing his silver badge to dissuade the nurse who sought to block his entry to Nancy Whitenmire's hospital room. Yvonne Whitenmire sat next to her daughter, the latter propped up by pillows behind a breakfast tray.

"Sorry to interrupt. Two, maybe three, brief questions." Nancy's eyes narrowed, but held their gaze at him. "On that yacht, were there dogs?"

Yvonne Whitenmire glared at him. "How would she know if blindfolded?"

"Smell, sounds," Adolph replied.

"Don't remember no dog," Nancy said.

"What about oil smells?"

The mother glared at him. "This is crazy. It was a yacht with a motor."

"Let Nancy answer and I'll go."

"Only sound I remember was paper, like wrapping Christmas presents."

"Thanks, Nancy." He glanced at Yvonne. "Best of luck to you both."

En route to the office, Adolph detoured to Oxford Avenue and the corner park. It would've been a lucky long shot to find Silas and Adolph wasn't surprised that Silas probably slept in.

Luann and Bulldog's cars were both parked in the police parking lot. Expecting to confront both in the squad room, he marched in, letting the banged door announce him.

"You look whiter than a ghost," Luann said, after glancing up from her desk. "Why don't you go to the hospital?"

"Can't get rid of me that easy." Adolph plopped into his desk chair. "Bulldog give his morning briefing yet?"

"Done. Same old, same old."

"We need to stake out Dean Wainright's house this evening."

"Can't. Scheduled to visit my kids."

349

"Guess I'll have to do it myself." Adolph shrugged. Downs's use of the "guess" word musta been contagious. He telephoned the college music department pretending to be a student named Jack to inquire if Dean Wainright had any lesson openings before tomorrow. When told the dean wasn't giving any lessons this evening, Adolph said thank you and hung up.

* * *

He sipped hot coffee from a thermos prepared by Mary for his three-hour surveillance of Dean Wainright's front door. Adolph knew his yellow Monte Carlo would stand out, but he didn't care if someone reported his presence, even to the dean himself. Adolph's information from the music department receptionist had been that the dean would be out of town.

By nine p.m. with the dean's front door approached by no one, Adolph rang the Rose Garden B&B's doorbell. Matt appeared.

"Need to have you show me the latest four hours on your backyard neighbor."

"Sure. Follow me downstairs. Mom's out, in case you needed to speak to her."

"No. Let's see the video." Adolph tapped his right toe waiting in Matt's bedroom for Matt to rewind a blur of video images. When the blur reversed itself at normal speed, Adolph saw Dean Wainright sitting on his piano bench with a male student dressed in a red shirt.

"This can't be right, Matt. You sure this is earlier tonight?"

"Positive."

Adolph squelched his suspicions. He thought, possible, if unlikely, maybe the student arrived before his surveillance started and stayed the entire time. If so, why wasn't there a car or bike parked in front of the dean's home? "What's the time stamp?"

Matt pressed a pause button. "Seven-thirty tonight."

"Keep it going." Adolph shifted his full weight to his left

foot. He wanted in the worst way to rub the itch beneath his arm bandage, but his intellect warned him it would do more harm than create relief. The red-shirted male arose, left the room with the dean, and the dean returned, leading a female to his piano bench. "Stop," Adolph commanded. "Show me the front door feed for the ten minutes before and after that red shirt and the dean left the piano bench."

A blur across the monitor followed Matt's punching keyboard keys. When the blur disappeared, an empty porch and green grass filled the screen for twenty minutes.

"This exterior the same time as tonight's inside shot?"

Matt ejected one disc, read the label, and re-inserted. "Absolutely."

"How come we don't see the male leaving or the female arriving?"

"Gawd, you're right. That shouldn't be. Give me a sec."

Adolph didn't understand why Matt's tensed torso leaned intently forward and his eyes swiveled from one monitor to another. Images appeared and disappeared on more than one monitor, oftentimes leaving one blank, but then two screens showed the same image.

Matt's shoulders slumped into his chair. "We're being shown a loop."

"A what?" Adolph asked.

"Prior day, stripped of its date/time stamp, later rebroadcast."

"Then the time before when I supposedly verified the dean being at home, it could of meant he wasn't, and you and I viewed a rerun."

Matt's fingers were idle as the female student played for the dean. "Yep."

"Damn." Before he left, Adolph asked Matt to dub a recording showing both the original surveillance footage and its rebroadcast with a new date/time stamp.

Leaving the Rose Garden B&B behind, Adolph, waiting for his home garage door to rise, gunned his Monte Carlo for no reason other than frustration. Mary, meeting him at their kitchen table, said she couldn't understand why he had to go out again after the ten o'clock news. When he reluctantly repeated the words "police business," Mary, leaving the coffee maker refilling another carafe, pushed her walker into the living room.

Adolph, sitting in his recliner alongside Mary until Jay Leno finished his monologue, arose and kissed Mary good night. He refilled his silver thermos, set it on the kitchen counter, and tiptoed down the basement stairs. After retrieving Ant's folder, he stared at the picture of the naked boy tied to the Oxford Avenue backyard tree. Back to square one, Dean Wainright resurfaced as Adolph's prime suspect. How the code words on the back of the photograph fit in with Silas, if they did, still loose and unexplained in Adolph's mind. And, the poem that fell from the farm birdhouse had to be important. The unanswered questions plagued Adolph.

He tried to mentally re-examine the pieces that came to mind. Downs had to have had an inkling of the warehouse dogs' presence for Silas had warned Adolph. Only a slight logical jump allowed him to connect the canine protection to the yacht travels, and/or, its human or its drug cargo traveling up or down river in used oil barges. Who or what link connected the yacht's docking and the too coincidental used oil barrels arriving. He stashed Ant's photo folder into his basement-hiding place, grabbed his coffee, and headed out toward Oxford Avenue.

As he expected, Silas's house cast off no light, nestled as it was in darkness. Adolph couldn't justify knocking. What he could rationalize was disregarding Rebecca's vague answers and checking out the Bourdon farm. If a shipment of illegal drugs had arrived, imminent distribution loomed more likely than not. While a spacious warehouse would've been most logical, his barging in (He chuckled at his unrehearsed pun.) and the resultant splattered canine blood and crime scene tape likely dissuaded criminals to use it as a staging point. The right turn into the Bourdon farm unsettled him. No vehicles. No house lights. He made a crowd of one.

Adolph's Gold

Under the lackluster three-quarters moon, the barn, unadorned by artificial lights, and the surrounding grove were hazily encased in non-distinct fuzzy-on-the-edge shadows. Adolph's soles crunching gravel echoed into the nearby rows of harvested corn stalks. He fished his cell phone from a trouser pocket to speed-dial the dispatcher. Officer Finnegan wasn't on duty and Adolph wouldn't trust any other officer or detective.

Watching vehicle lights pass the farmyard entrance, Adolph hustled to tail one sedan to a Bridgetown Catholic church where two youths carried a cardboard box into a side basement hall entrance and departed within five minutes.

Disappointed, Adolph detoured to River Drive. Other than music and the occasional shout, Adolph gleaned nothing unusual pouring out of the bars onto the streets. He thumbed Finnegan's number into his cell phone and persuaded the officer to join him at the boat launch. While he waited, Adolph's slow pacing wasn't fast enough to raise a sweat, yet, his armpits wet his shirt.

"Where's the Guinness? Doesn't look like a party to me."

Adolph turned to greet Sean Finnegan. "Wish there were more."

Finnegan unzipped his brown jacket. "You honed in on the missing pizza truck?"

"Dead end." Adolph's glances caught a trio of downtown drinkers staggering in the distance. "More interested in a yacht named "Piano Chord" and its owner." The crack of a muffler from the drinkers' direction distracted him. A red pickup crawled slowly toward WR Barge.

Finnegan whispered, "Looks like the Dragons are checking you out."

"More likely my car." Adolph strode toward the curb, purposely patting his right hand twice on the Monte Carlo's rear fender. When he peered back at Finnegan the lights on the river cruising in the same direction as the red pickup wouldn't have sparked his curiosity if not for the combination and a touch of paranoia.

"We gonna follow them?"

"Let's watch those river lights first. If they stop anywhere near the barge dock, we'll mosey on toward them."

"Why?" The inquiry rested lazily in Finnegan's voice.

"Maybe I delayed the drugs delivery and panic forced them to get rid of the girl."

Finnegan shook his head. "Doesn't make sense. Girl coulda been dumped overboard."

"Then." Adolph paused. "Then that would of brought the yacht into the limelight."

"You think the kingpin was on the boat, waiting for the dingy and a payoff?"

"Yes." Adolph jogged to the river's edge. He shouted at Finnegan. "Let's go."

Finnegan, hand on his Monte Carlo's passenger door handle when Adolph rounded the car's front fender, rested his strapped-in butt on the seat when Adolph pulled away from the curb. Finnegan radioed for backup.

Adolph swerved in behind Luann's Chrysler parked a block from WR Barge. Finnegan bet him it was Luann who emerged from a passageway next to an antique store.

Finnegan proved right and Adolph asked her: "What you doing here?"

"Heard the radio call. Could say backup." Luann smiled and nodded to Finnegan. "But then you'd figure I lied. You tip the Feds about the back-to-back drug shipments?"

"What I suspected." Adolph allowed the vague response to wash him with more credit than he deserved. The red pickup idled within in a dash of the warehouse fence entry he'd used two nights previous. "That yacht dock?" He presumed Luann had seen it.

"Fed spotter said no. Four tied up barges clogged all the dock space. Some water depth or navigational problem down river, near St. Louis, slowed traffic."

"What we gonna do?" Finnegan asked. "Didn't come prepared with vest."

"There's an extra one in my trunk," Luann said. "Tac 3

will tie you in with Feds."

Adolph tapped his right toe to the concrete. He didn't like sharing; and, he definitely hated following. As he popped his Monte Carlo trunk for riot gear, he calculated that cleaning the streets of two or three Dragons would send a message, be a good thing.

"Follow me," a vested Luann urged.

Adolph fell into march-step. When he reached the fence, all hell broke loose. A helicopter swooped in from the north, two boats with sharpshooters raced to cut off the yacht maneuvering to do a 180-degree exit. Gunshots rang out from inside the warehouse and then silence dropped like an opera house stage curtain.

Adolph abandoned all caution and dashed into the river towards the yacht having trouble maneuvering to return to the main channel. Likely hit a sandbar, thought Adolph. He splashed into chest-high water, fighting the current until he clambered up the yacht's diving platform. A blow from behind knocked his Walther from his right hand. Bolts of pain shot up his right arm. He clenched his teeth and twirled. His left jab connected squarely with Jack's jaw.

An aggressive street fighter, no doubt, but considering the way the yacht pitched and yawed, Jack was neither a sailor nor a river pilot. Adolph flexed his left hand fingers. Jack wouldn't stay collapsed on his right knee for long.

The yacht's stern deck tilted left. First Adolph hit the railing and then Jack collided with Adolph and the railing. Pinned against the railing, Adolph couldn't launch a punch, even if his right arm could function at full strength. His hands grabbed Jack's shoulders. They wrestled with neither gaining a measurable advantage. Adolph struggled, determined to stay on board.

Both men crashed to the deck. Adolph absorbed the landing with his left shoulder. Jack bounced on his right side. Together they rolled, their arms clinging to each other and their legs flailing without one of their four shoes making solid contact.

Jack stood and dragged Adolph up with him. He tried to slam Adolph against the railing.

The first try loosened a groan from Adolph's lips. Jack's second attempt, aided by his lift, smacked Adolph's thighs into the railing's top bar and a top-heavy, ungrounded Adolph began to tumble off the yacht. As he fell, Adolph's left hand grabbed the front fabric of Jack's jacket.

They hit the river's surface with a resounding thud. Adolph's submerged eyes couldn't see how far the water splashed. He couldn't measure the distance needed for his shoes to touch silt.

Finally, Adolph's soles slipped on riverbed muck and, against the current's force, he couldn't stand. Algae, decayed after a summer's growth, forced him to close his eyes. His conscious thought beginning to be overpowered by his fear of submersion and drowning. The pressure of a hand pushed at the back of his skull. When he rotated his head left, the pressure never subsided. It swung close behind when his head spun right. The cold water elevated the constant sting radiating from his right forearm wound.

When his feet secured a mud foothold, he lowered his butt, and used his knees as springs. His head popped through the water's surface. The hand previously on his scalp now joined by another pressing hard from behind on both his shoulders.

Before being submerged, he had heard a splash. *Backup.* He only needed to stay alive.

Fighting to stay above the surface, Adolph glimpsed a second figure free-stroking his way. Adolph gasped for breath and the new arrival dived for his ankle. A second Dragon. Jack now had help; Adolph didn't. He scissor kicked. His legs stayed free, but Adolph's re-submerged head and burning lungs would soon require oxygen. He harbored no expectation that his forty-year-old lungs could outlast Jack's, twenty years younger and gym trained, as Jack pulled on Adolph's waist much like a tethered anchor.

He doubted Luann would bail him out and Finnegan

couldn't be expected to hear his cry.

Adolph grappled with the fear paralyzing his body. His legs had stopped thrashing. When a hand encircled his left ankle, he couldn't be certain from which side the attacker came. The second attacker's head had to be within a three-foot radius. Adolph kicked out his right foot. It recoiled, a lucky strike.

Adolph's freed left leg kicked, a second strike. Only the pressure on his waist prevented his re-supplying his dwindling oxygen. How could an infant boy survive the river, if Adolph couldn't? The infant had no fear.

Adolph tried to somersault. His first attempt failed; a second didn't. His eyes wouldn't voluntarily open. When he forced them, the swirling grit compelled him to clamp his eyelids shut. He imagined Jack had surfaced behind him.

Adolph had never ever flipped backward in the water. He'd done it on land years ago. What could he lose? His lungs ached. His pressed lips struggled to open. He couldn't let them.

One, two, three. He rammed his shoulders backward and raised his knees to his chest. Jack pushed in the opposite direction and thwarted Adolph's effort.

Unwilling to lose, Adolph tightened his abs, and then, after feigning a left pivot, lifted both knees and simultaneously thrust his shoulders to the rear.

It worked. The toes of his shoes slammed into Jack's back. Jack's hands released their hold.

Adolph spun left and his head broke the water's surface. His mouth gulped air and he blinked his left eye. His hands reached for Jack's throat and he pressed his thumbs to Jack's Adam's apple. Jack's struggling to free himself couldn't overcome Adolph's determination.

He dragged Jack to shore. An FBI agent ordering Adolph to the ground failed to duck when Jack slugged him and ran off. An arriving, breathless Finnegan helped the agent to his feet and persuaded the agent that Adolph was a good guy.

A dripping Adolph entered the warehouse through the

side door. Once he cleared the warehouse aisle, he found a knot of federal agents circling three males forced to their knees—two Dragons and an old man in a yellowed yachting cap.

"You arresting Silas?" Adolph asked the nearest agent.

"That old codger, he's the ringleader," the agent replied.

"Don't believe it."

* * *

Chief Howard commanded the attention of all in the conference room as he entered in full dress uniform. Adolph's ears could've been jammed with cotton for all he heard.

Luann smiled when The Chief pinned the gold detective shield on her chest. Her son and daughter crowded in when Josh Myles of *The Examiner* requested The Chief redo the pinning for his camera.

"Doesn't that beat all," Yancey whispered to Adolph as both stood in the room's corner. "Came in special and I gotta watch a broad getting your gold badge. Ain't right."

"Cool it. Grab a piece of cake, make nice, and join me in the squad room."

Bulldog's office was empty as Adolph swiveled in his desk chair. Despite the downer of the day, he felt overjoyed by Yancey's return to duty.

"You didn't polish my chair while I was resting up?"

"Hell no." Adolph lowered his volume. "Ain't no maid."

Yancey broke out into a grin. "Glad to see you haven't changed. Thought you might've gone all prissy on me, new partner and all."

"You should know better than that. Chest-thumping Feds are all bragging they cracked a major drug ring. But, mark my word; it's only a hiccup. That old pilot, Silas, no matter what the Feds say, isn't a cartel honcho. Even with a full deck, no Dragons would listen to him."

"Maybe not, but there's no doubt in my mind the Dragons raked in big bucks street-selling rock cocaine and meth."

"Which ones are in jail? Not Jack."

"Don't think so. Bulldog last night hinted the Fed dragnet couldn't locate Jack."

Adolph pressed the loose surgical tape required to keep his right arm gauze in place. River water had infected the dog punctures. "He should fry for trying to drown me."

"While you were in the hospital last week getting checked out, Luann cleared two murders."

Heels clicked on the wooden squad room floor. "That's right," The Chief said. "Luann had Jack on tape admitting to killing the cowboy dumped at my cousin's and he and two other Dragons hung that big guy, I forget his name, the guy dressed as Abraham Lincoln."

"She didn't tell me." Adolph kept his skeptic gene tuned in.

"Feds told her not to is what she's told me. She said both were couriers for that old pilot. Rotten shame Francine's reputation got smeared in the same breath with drug trafficking. You can be sure I won't be digging into any dirt at the next Labor Day party." The Chief flashed the plastic grin that adorned his face during his press conference Q&As when he wished to avoid a question's direct answer or other perceived controversy.

Adolph tossed a glance at Yancey and then gazed at The Chief. "Now that Yancey's on duty, you tearing up that order partnering me and Luann?"

"Consider it done."

"Thanks." Adolph kept silent as The Chief gazed at Bulldog's office and then departed.

"What'll we do now, partner?" Yancey smiled broadly. "Say, donuts at Patsy's?"

Heel-click sounds floated off the wood floor and Adolph wondered what The Chief had forgot. His first glimpse of a patrolman's uniform sleeve told him it wasn't The Chief.

"This lady says she wants to talk to you," Corporal Riley said.

Adolph rose. Sonja Maria sagged against the corporal's arm. She sported a bandage above her left collarbone, a split lip, and a black eye. Adolph circled the squad room desks and wheeled out Luann's chair. "Please sit her down here." His extended right hand helped the corporal guide Sonja Maria into it.

Seeing a battered Sonja Maria, Adolph felt emotionally deflated, mentally lost. Not unlike many other times on the job when he'd actually be, or just feel, scared, sick, or nearly insane. He wasn't perfect and, when the job gnawed at his soul, like right then with chills racing up his arms from cold hands, he forgot about the gold luster missing from his detective shield and longed to do the right thing.

"Who did this to you?"

"The man I told you about," Sonja Maria said softly.

Adolph retreated and leaned close to Yancey's ear. "We'll get a statement and then mosey on over to Patsy's. There's a dean at St. Mary's I need to fill you in on."

* * *

Bradford served Adolph and Yancey coffee before Rebecca approached and asked Adolph to join her in Patsy's party room. Without formally asking Rebecca, he invited Yancey and shooed his partner away from the chair Adolph unofficially claimed as his own.

Rebecca didn't sit. "You should know Jack's back."

"Where?" Adolph asked. "And, while I trust you, what proof can I use?"

"Saw him two nights ago." With her eyes darting hither and yon, Rebecca whispered, "Luann got her tattoo. She said a hooded white male started . . . let Jack and another in, and then the white guy finished, if you know what I mean."

Adolph held up his right forefinger and pointed it at Yancey and shifted his gaze to Rebecca. "Where? What white guy?"

"Wasn't Bulldog; wasn't young. Don't know who all, except Jack, was at the farm."

"The same male voice you heard at earlier times?"

Rebecca flattened the cowgirl frills on her blouse front.

"Seemed like it, but different. Sorta creaked or was muffled. Only heard it once before I was pushed into a room without Luann. Figured he was purposefully trying to disguise it. Scared more of Jack than the white guy with a whip before I was blindfolded. I'd heard Jack blamed me for ratting him out."

Adolph supposed the Feds never connected Luann with, nor gave local law enforcement credit for the tape of Jack, and probably tore up Adolph's report of Jack trying to drown him.

Never bashful, Yancey jumped in and gazed directly at Rebecca. "Why? In my experience Jack talks big, but backs off when confronting a backbone."

Rebecca glared at Yancey. "Does he have to be here?"

Adolph nodded. "What did Jack say to scare you?"

"He promised the hooded guy he'd get him another teen. And the hooded guy mumbled something that sounded like back or black." She glared at Yancey. "Don't ask. I thought of the whip and Bradford. That's why he's helping here, so I can keep an eye on him."

Adolph dismissed the mental picture of another boy, not Bradford, from days long ago. Adolph rated Marcie, who had once spurned Jack and whom Adolph had found trussed up in the farm's dungeon, as Jack's likely offering. Adolph considered uncompleted revenge to be a powerful motive.

Chapter Nine

With Yancey at his side and an itchy white beard on his chin, Adolph opted to forego staking out the dean's house and chose East Mulberry Street. He stood two blocks away from Marcie's house talking with Finnegan on his cell phone. "You hear any more word on Jack's whereabouts, give me a call.

Say: 'my buddy's' in town and give a location." He glanced at Yancey. "Let's go, partner." He enjoyed the familiar echo of his long-awaited summons.

Adolph ambled a block closer to Marcie's and sat on a steel bench's bird droppings. The ragged clothes, too ratty for donation to Goodwill, suited him fine, as did the straggly beard. He mused he shoulda traded the whiskers in for the Abe Lincoln version. He watched Yancey stroll past the house-for-sale sign at 735 E. Mulberry and wasn't surprised when he returned to report no activity seen. He didn't expect Jack to prowl until the sun dived beyond the horizon and that wouldn't be for an hour or so.

"You coulda brought cards," Yancey teased.

"Wanted you to keep your money. Pay those doctors you said you've visited so often." Adolph laughed. His cell phone blared out the "Charge of the Light Brigade." He answered Mary's ring tone. "Hi, dear."

"Kristen's bedroom door is closed, she's not answering, and the music's off. I wanted you on the phone when I unlock." Adolph kept the phone to his ear. "Adolph, she's gone. My darling's gone. The window screen's been cut. I'm going to be sick."

"Keep calm, dear. I'll call her cell and I've still got Katie's number. Boil some water for chamomile tea. I'll get back to you or come home."

Adolph's stomach began to churn, squeezing his abs didn't help. He didn't require thinking about how he'd act to get a gold shield. This was his family and, besides, Luann had it. He rang Katie's house. Kristen's friend said she last saw Kristen in the school hallway when Kristen mentioned finding a strange tattoo in her locker. Adolph shoved his cell into his pants pocket and cautioned himself not to act foolishly. "Yancey, still get the Internet on your iPhone?"

Yancey nodded.

"Search for Kristen." Adolph refrained from crowding too close to Yancey.

"Yikes. Someone's playing serious games. You don't

need to see this."

"Show me." Adolph immediately recognized the St. Andrew's Cross and the naked Kristen. He hadn't given the photos to anyone but Len, and he trusted his lab buddy. His only cerebral flash was that he was being blamed for the Feds' dock raid. He recalled Rebecca's words and reasoned "Black" didn't necessarily mean skin color. It could be a reference to Goth clothing.

"Yancey, I need to get home. All the tea in China tells me Jack's a no-show here."

Adolph pulled himself up into Yancey's beat-up Ford pickup and waited for his partner to drive. With a shake and a rattle, the pickup cruised into Adolph's peaceful neighborhood. He bounded up the driveway, punched in the garage door code, and shouted "Mary" as he braced his left hand on the kitchen table.

Mary's voice came from her recliner. "Living room. Kristen home?"

"Still looking." He stood beside Mary. "Katie's mother offered to come over."

Mary's sunken red eyes pleaded. "I don't need a babysitter."

"Not that. She said she needed someone to talk to. I volunteered you."

Adolph was pleased when Mary smiled. "You'll be careful? Your arm's infected."

"Yancey's outside. I'll be in good hands." He bent forward and kissed her. Mary's soft lips nevertheless transmitted her inner tension and escalating fear.

* * *

Yancey, per Adolph's request, shut off his pickup's headlights after a Salvatore Pizza truck, headed in the direction of Bridgetown, passed them. Yancey's pickup coasted to the Bourdon farmyard entrance. Less than five minutes away from being draped with darkness, two vehicles, three, if he counted the pizza truck, had beaten Adolph to the farm. He recognized the two remaining. Luann's Chrysler was easy and the blue Buick with Illinois plates he remembered from a former visit, although the names of its owner and/or driver eluded him.

Adolph confided to Yancey that they were probably outnumbered. The only help they could rely on would be Finnegan.

"This'll help." Yancey handed Adolph a 12-guage Remington shotgun he'd retrieved from behind the pickup's front seat. Yancey toted an identical shotgun. "Sorry, no vests."

"We'll shoot first."

Yancey grinned and nodded vigorously while stuffing extra shells into his pants pocket.

Adolph needed no advance knowledge of the farmhouse. His devised plan was simple. Yancey would station himself behind Luann's Chrysler with a clear view of the front porch and sightlines to anyone charging across the lawn to the vehicles. Adolph jogged to the milk house. If luck prevailed, he'd surprise the house occupants with entry through the tunnel's basement portal. If all were in the second floor master bedroom, as he suspected, he'd pepper the stairwell with birdshot pellets. The only wild card was Kristen and his daughter's safety. His trump card had to be surprise.

He clamored down the metal ladder into the dungeon and, with a three-foot plank, blocked the tunnel entrance door to keep it from closing. He refused to amuse himself with the knack of his head dodging the dangling light bulbs. He paused at the foot of the basement stairs to check for human-made noises. The eerie silence offered vibes of encouragement until, during his stealth creep to the kitchen; a tread creak from the second floor stairs fueled his apprehension.

Standing on the kitchen linoleum, he began to sense it was too quiet when he couldn't hear any overhead floorboards creak. No human taunts, commands, or cries pierced the air. From all accounts, the prior Dragon tattoo ceremonies had been rambunctious, vocal contests for all participants except the chosen woman. He wanted to feel good that he could spare

Kristen at least a portion of the trauma that would haunt her all the days of her life.

He executed, without one tiny board squeak, his spread-leg ascent to the bedrooms.

Moaning came from behind the closed master bedroom door. It wasn't joyful and he strained to decipher who, man or woman, adult or child. He couldn't.

He shouted, "Stay back, men. You in the bedroom, come out with your hands high in the air. There's no escape."

Adolph mentally counted to ten and kicked the master bedroom door. It crashed into an inside wall. Through the opening, he saw no one except two trouser-encased legs and bare feet with black painted toenails. He dashed forward; three choppy steps into the farmhouse bedroom exposed everything to him.

Luann lay supine. Her slacks the only item of clothing worn. Dried blood coated her neck while fresher drops pooled on the nearby floor. Strips of white cloth, some bloody, lay scattered about. The posts of the St. Andrew's Cross, flat on the floor, still lashed into an X. Adolph gasped. Luann's gold shield had been pinned to the fabric of her crotch.

He stood motionless. *Where's Kristen?* A low moan caused him to whirl towards it. He faced the closed door of the room's closet.

"Come out, hands up," Adolph shouted. Out loud he counted to ten. Tensed and irritable, he never would accept getting no respect. His finger itched to blast the closet door. "I'll shoot."

The moan rose in volume.

Adolph abandoned caution to grab the doorknob, yanking it as he stepped backwards. A black male in his teens, bound and gagged, filled the closet floor. A bloody knife lay next to him. He recognized Leroy and untied the gag, but not the other bindings. "Who did this to you?"

"Jack and another."

Adolph stepped closer with his shotgun poised and ready to fire. "Was Kristen here?"

"Old man said to take her to the boat."

"What boat?"

"Don't know." Adolph glared at Leroy. "Honest, don't know. That lady cop dead?"

"Think so. You stab her and now feel guilty?"

"No! No!" Leroy cried out and then really started to sob. "She tried to help me. Jack mad because I shot his friend Jonathan. He wouldn't believe his friend attacked my mother."

"Don't move." Adolph scurried to check that neither Kristen nor anyone else remained upstairs, including the end-of-the-hallway bathroom. He returned to the master bedroom, unlatched a window, and shouted to Yancey to radio for a fire department ambulance. Sheriff Townsend could wait. Leroy hadn't budged. Luann's arm flopped to the floor after he performed the perfunctory effort to locate a pulse in her wrist. He unpinned her gold shield.

Finnegan appeared in the bedroom doorway. "Luann?"

"Dead." Adolph didn't desire to book Leroy or wait for a fire truck. "Wait here, Sean. A fire department ambulance is on its way. You'll find me and Yancey at WR Barge."

Finnegan stepped aside as Adolph dashed past him to race out of the farmhouse. He coughed into his left sleeve as dust filled Yancey's pickup truck cab. Yancey's accelerator stomp never let up during the entire trip into Bridgetown. After streaking through three yellow traffic lights along River Drive, Adolph yelled for Yancey to stop at the river's boat launch. The lights of a yacht off shore bobbed in the distance. While Adolph couldn't identify it as the "Piano Chord" he sought. What choice did he have?

Yancey's eyes radiated the enlightened glow of an all-knowing Buddha for Adolph had brought him up to speed between passing other vehicles. In silence, Yancey reached under the seat and dumped shotgun shells out of a Ziploc bag large enough to hold Adolph's Walther. Adolph grabbed the bag and jumped out of the pickup. He stripped off his shoes and socks, jacket, and holster. His Walther P.38 he sealed inside the Ziploc and tucked both into his belt.

Adolph's Gold

The river current was swift and chilly when first grasping Adolph's bare feet and bringing back dreadful memories of fighting Jack and trying to find Billy Whitenmire lost beneath the surface ripples. He'd test if Jack had really cured his fear of water submersion. He estimated he could easily swim to the boat lights, especially since they hadn't move. He swallowed hard when a patrol car cruised past the boat ramp. *Don't stop.* It didn't.

He ended his never-submerge-your-head swim when his right palm touched the side of the yacht. A surface reflection of the aboard lights were bright enough for him to make out the black words painted on white: "Piano Chord." He prayed the sound of the river waves lapping against the starboard hull would be sufficiently loud to disguise his presence. Adolph listened for and heard no voices on deck, and then floated aft, planning to board at the stern.

With his biceps straining and his right arm stinging, he grasped and hung to the railing until his toes inched upward to extend his butt. One, two, three. He pulled and propelled himself onto the yacht's deck. He inhaled and slowly exhaled while gazing left and right.

The closed translucent curtain inside the window of the door leading to the below-deck cabin diffused a brilliant white light. Leaving water drips on the wood deck, he sidled up to the door and heard two obviously male voices from the cabin. Was Kristen dead, or gagged? Other than Leroy's earlier word and his prior knowledge, through the enslaved photograph of Nancy Whitenmire, he had only circumstantial evidence that Kristen might have been taken aboard.

"You can't stay here all night." Adolph identified these words as spoken by Dean Wainright. He and Jack? That made sense.

Adolph dropped the plastic bag from around his Walther. Tightening his painful right hand grip, he twisted the unlocked cabin door with his left hand. "Police. Hands up." He ducked his head, descended the six steps, and swiveled his eyes every which way to find Kristen. He didn't.

Dean Wainright and Silas Maurer gazed up from seated positions at a small table.

"You're both under arrest," Adolph declared.

"Bilge water," Silas said. "Feds tried a couple of days ago and had to release me."

"Don't reach for that cap," Adolph replied. He had to be cautious that Silas's faded cap didn't hide a pistol. "Where's Kristen?"

"Don't know who you're talking about." A bare-chested Dean Wainright didn't raise his hands above the tabletop.

Adolph slid a step to the left. "Both of you stand, real easy like, hands where I can see them, and we'll go up top. Silas here should be skilled enough to return this boat to the barge dock."

While hesitant, both followed his instructions. Adolph planted his Walther barrel beneath the dean's scarred back as Silas piloted the yacht into a portside semicircle before adjusting and straightening the yacht to be on a course to the barge dock. When the yacht banged against the dock bumper, Silas jumped off with a line and secured it to the nearest cleat.

"Don't move," Adolph shouted to Silas.

Under a floodlight, the healed scars on the dean's shoulder blades really stood out. "Don't turn around, but where'd you get those scars?"

"Father."

"Yeah," chimed in Silas. "He owes my father for having saved his hide. If I'd known then, you can bet I'd have told my pa to leave him be."

"Backyard tree?" Adolph asked.

Dean Wainright's head twitched to the right. "How'd you guess?"

"Just lucky," Adolph lied. He felt a shove from behind slam his stomach against the deck's railing before his body splashed in the water. Hands on his legs tried to keep his head submerged. Adolph kicked and his mind fought the demons of being a youth held underwater by bullies who jeered and laughed when he choked and spit out water and algae.

Adolph's Gold

He tried to execute a diver's half gainer and kick with his legs while his hands flailed wildly. His right clutched his Walther that, if he could get close enough, would be useful as a club. He dared not open his mouth, lest the slime choke him before the water filled his soon-to-be oxygen-depleted lungs. Giving it his all, his right leg broke free and the pain of his big toe striking a solid object, he knew not what, blunted his desire to continue his frantic kicks. The buoyancy of his body ebbed to the weight of a steel anchor. His left hand oozed itself into the riverbed muck before Adolph yanked it free.

Without an explanation of how, the hands on his ankles rotated to be under his armpits. Adolph's face broke through the river's surface. The yacht loomed yards away. The warehouse's dock stark floodlights were mixed with the swirling, rotating reds and blues from a launched rescue run-a-bout. Additional hands lifted him up onto the dock and wrapped him in a blanket.

"You're an ornery cus." Adolph recognized Yancey's voice, broad smile, and the whites of his eyes before his partner's complete face emerged from the night's background.

"Kristen? Didn't find Kristen."

"Quiet," Yancey said. "She's on the way to the hospital. Ralph said she's shook, but will be okay. We'll get you adjoining beds. From what I hear, you need constant supervision if you're to follow a doctor's orders to stay put in a hospital bed."

Adolph had to laugh. Yancey knew him better than most, except Mary. Adolph hugged the blanket around his shoulders. "What about Silas? The dean?"

"We've given them free room and board at the station. Jack, too."

Shivers, from the water or old memories, engulfed Adolph. "I didn't see Jack."

"Should've. He had you underwater and I assumed it wasn't because you were dirty."

"I mean I didn't see him on the yacht."

"Kristen said he had her in a cabin closet. A threatening

369

knife kept her quiet."

Adolph chastised himself for not hearing his assailant approach from his rear. "Then he musta been the one who jumped me when I had the dean on deck after Silas tied up?"

"You got it. Now, be a brave hero and take a ride in the city's chariot to Community General. And, don't worry, I'll pick up Mary."

* * *

Adolph awoke before Kristen, who slept in the hospital bed next to him. Of course, Mary was already awake with her walker parked in front of a reddish-brown recliner. "Hate these yellow walls." He said no more as Mary waved a disapproving right forefinger.

"You accepting visitors?" Finnegan asked, his head visible inside the door left ajar.

"Sure. Anyway, Kristen should be up," Adolph replied, using an extra loud baritone.

Finnegan tiptoed to the foot of Adolph's bed. "Evidence mounting that the ring leader was that old river pilot."

"Hard to believe," Adolph said. "Guessed Dean Wainright, abused as a boy, would look the other way while spurred on to reclaim his father's wealth or community standing any way he could. The Dragon drug dealing probably summarized pretty much by classic gang motivation. Yet, I can't figure out what drove Silas."

"He blames all Wainrights for his son's death and the Dragons became his muscle to recoup the pension he believe was stolen from him, although I don't doubt that Jack skimmed off the top." Adolph nodded. "I guess we should thank Luann for exposing that Honest Abe impersonator as a drug intermediary, but mostly a crooked cop who lusted after the good life."

"Like that cowboy, Pistol Pete?"

"Yeah." Finnegan glanced at his wristwatch. "The Chief left the briefing this morning saying he was going to stop by and see you. I'd better run or I'll be late for my sergeant's badge presentation."

Adolph sprang his upper torso upright and slid his buttocks and legs rearward. "That's great. We'll celebrate. And, that's a promise."

"Gotta run. I'll smuggle in the Guinness tomorrow." On his exit, Finnegan pulled the hospital room door until the latch almost secured it.

Adolph stretched his legs and laid back, head again centered in the pillow. Yancey had telephoned near eleven p.m. that Leroy Connor and Nancy Whitenmire had IDed Silas from a photo and voice lineup as present when they were molested. Leroy promised to testify that Silas was with Jack in the Bourdon Farm bedroom before Luann had her throat sliced. Sonja Maria Sanchez wouldn't sign a statement against Dean Wainright. Adolph's gut told him the dean was in deep, but unless Silas gave him up, and that wasn't likely as long as Silas yearned for personal hands-on retribution or, in the alternative, a huge monetary sum equal to his lost pension.

"Who was that, Dad?" Kristen asked.

Adolph gazed at her fresh-scrubbed cheeks and sleep-encrusted eyes. "Sean Finnegan." Adolph amazed himself by remembering Officer Finnegan's first name. "He gave up his free time to try to save you."

"Your father was there." Mary interjected with pride.

"I know. I know," Kristen said, her words interrupted by a knock on the door.

"Come in," Adolph said.

Hat in hand, Chief Howard stood in the exposed space between the doorjambs. "Meeting the entire Anderson family like this is, I'm happy to say, a joyful occasion. For you, Adolph, there's a small hesitation." Adolph didn't have the foggiest. "I've been invited to Cousin Francine's next Labor Day party, but only if you'll chaperone."

"If that's an order," Adolph replied.

The Chief smiled. "Before then, however, she might bring a sherry toast to the police station when you're awarded a gold detective shield complete with a medal of valor."

Donan Berg

Adolph shifted his gaze to the ceiling. "I don't mean to say I'm not happy, but, with what happened to Luann, it's bittersweet." He hesitated. There were things he wanted to say about Luann, both negative and positive. Yet, he couldn't. She, for a short time, had been his partner. Partners keep confidences. The press had given her a hero's treatment. He wouldn't tarnish her reputation or image in death. Not so with Lt. Turner, but he couldn't prove anything with an imageless camera. He gazed at The Chief.

"I can understand that," The Chief said. "Yet, we must move on."

Adolph had heard those exact words or similar sentiments numerous times. He'd taken one step to equal his father's stature. He envisioned he'd complete the additional ones and one day write his final report tidying up all the Wainright Barge and Rose Garden B&B loose ends. Yancey had pledged his all out support.

"Yes, Chief, we'll move on. There's more to do and Bridgetown needs us."

If you've enjoyed reading *Adolph's Gold,*

please consider writing a review.

You may also wish to read Author Donan Berg's

debut murder/mystery. An excerpt follows on the next page.

Donan Berg's First Skeleton Series Mystery

A Body To Bones

Excerpt from *A Body To Bones*

"So it's a brick. What's the big deal?"

Myron turns the brick. "Look at this side. See the letters?"

"Wow! Why would these three letters be important? What if . . . what if the brick was only a brick later reused in the well?"

"Tunnel," corrects Myron.

"Well, cistern, tunnel, whatever. Those letters could have meant anything. Was there anything on other bricks?" asks Wanda.

"No, nothing that I could see. Yeah, they were blank." Myron hands the brick to Wanda.

"So, we have three letters that don't make sense. Could be lover's initials. Who it was, heaven only knows, but could be. You tell me." Wanda gives back the brick.

"I can't. I only found it week ago Saturday. I think there are important. You talk about lovers and initials, but what about my father?"

"How does your father fit in? That's weird, really weird." Wanda bites her lower lip.

"No. It's not. See, fill in this third letter to form an O, and you have the beginning of my family's last name. I reckon the person trapped in there, rest her soul, had begun to scratch out the killer's name before dying. Like in the movies or on TV."

"Sure, and Gary Cooper is going to ride in at high noon." Wanda mimics a rider on a horse. "That's a tall story, and the bit about your father's name is even weirder."

"Not so. Remember, my father was the last person to see Father Murphy before the priest disappeared. Maybe my father has information about this body. The name Goostree is in large letters across my father's storefront. Everyone knows him; even a tramp passing through could easily learn my last name." Myron pushes his hair back, off his forehead.

"You're incredible. Hanging your own father. I think your dream of reaching high altitudes in this here glider has marooned your mind at 20,000 feet. Right?" asks Wanda.

"I don't know, but who can I tell? They'll all think I'm crazy, trying to pin it on my father, and, heaven knows, I don't want to do that. He's my Dad; I can't change that." Myron says forlornly.

"I know that, but what'll you do? You got to tell someone. Maybe my Dad can help?" Wanda stretches her arms.

"No, no. I don't think so. Your parents just don't understand me, and besides, I think they, or maybe it's only your mother who doesn't like me." Myron glances under the fuselage next to him.

"You're wrong, Myron," says Wanda. "They may want to protect me against life, but they don't hate or dislike you. You must understand." Myron walks three steps to where Wanda is sitting.

"Kiss me," Myron says as he leans over. "Enough of our babbling. I haven't talked this long since Aunt Helen promised me a sucker if I'd read a story and not make her cry." Wanda stands.

"Oh, Myron," says Wanda as she puts her arms around his neck.

Their bodies cling longingly in the tenderness of their embrace. The hot, searing first brush of the slightly parted lips is enough to smear, crumble, or crust the best of Wanda's fashionable lipsticks. Telltale signs of Wanda's lips brand Myron's face.

The brick, with its secret, sits on top of a gunnysack, ignored for the time being.

To order the novel visit http://www.abodytobones.com, your favorite neighborhood bookstore, or go online to a major book retailer and ask for Author Donan Berg's novel, *A Body To Bones, First Skeleton Series Mystery*.

www.ingramcontent.com/pod-product-compliance
Lightning Source LLC
Chambersburg PA
CBHW071205250626
47159CB00001B/212